Brownfields

Brownfields

By Elizabeth Goudy

Brownfields

www.revelizabethgoudy.com
egoudy@rocketmail.com

ISBN-13: 978-0-9970804-0-7
ISBN-10: 099708040X

Edited by Stephanie J. Beavers Communications
www.StephanieJBeavers.com / 610-247-9494

DEDICATION

This book is dedicated to clergy and church members restoring brownfields

ACKNOWLEDGEMENTS

I'm so grateful for the congregation of Metropolitan Community Church of the Lehigh Valley for the provision of a sabbatical in 2015. Without the "holy time" of an extended (two-month) Sabbath, this book would not have been written.

I'm so grateful for the generosity of my parents, Willis and Jean Goudy. They housed me for a month while I wrote the first draft and have fostered my writing for over four decades.

I'm so grateful for the Greater Lehigh Valley Writer's Group and their monthly Writer's Café. The feedback given was always thoughtful and helpful.

I'm so grateful for the editing gifts of Stephanie Beavers, who took the final draft of *Brownfields* and made it a better book.

I'm so grateful for the design gifts of Flavius Petrisor, who created a book cover that speaks so clearly to the themes of *Brownfields*.

I'm so grateful for friends Parker Holmes and Shannah Eitter. Parker graciously read the rough first draft of *Brownfields* and offered invaluable advice. Shannah is a friend since kindergarten and a constant supporter of the project.

I'm so grateful for Goudy-Stevens-Silver-Stewart-Haht-Myers-Javorski-Kutz family members who expressed affirmation throughout the writing process. Special thanks to Becca Stevens for her excellent and speedy editing assistance.

I'm so grateful for my spouse, Carol, who dances with me in the kitchen and loves me abundantly. Carol enthusiastically encouraged me throughout the multiple drafts of *Brownfields*.

If I have left out any names, it is unintentional and I ask forgiveness.

Brownfield sites have always fascinated me: polluted and repelling, yet still possessing potential. In some instances around the United States, communities and governments have come together to effect a resurrection of brownfield sites. This transformative work uplifts neighborhoods and also provides spiritual hope.

I continue to enjoy viewing abandoned factories and thinking about how they could be transformed. I have also been honored to journey with people who are on a path to spiritual redevelopment.

This book is actually also a redevelopment project, as it was originally a work of nonfiction theology. One reader of that initial work, Jennifer DeWeerth, pointed out that the brownfields metaphor was worth pursuing.

From 2008-2015 the church where I serve was located in a sewing factory building called "The Silkwerks." I loved working in the Silkwerks building and I loved the feisty north Allentown neighborhood around it. During long days at the office, I would often take a walking break and was inspired by the sights and sounds of the neighborhood. *Brownfields* is written out of respect and admiration for the people and places of north Allentown.

The thirteen major characters in *Brownfields* are not based on family members, friends, or church members. Some situations in the story do, however, resemble things I have directly experienced as a pastor, such as leading an event-planning meeting or facilitating Bible study. Additionally, I have described several incidents that occurred in the Allentown area, or elsewhere, but re-imagined them with fictitious characters.

Some of the characters in the book are identified as Christian, others are "spiritual, not religious," one is agnostic, and there is a married couple whose actions border on antireligious. Unlike most works of mainstream Christian fiction, there is no conversion for the non-Christian characters. I do not hold the theological viewpoint that "Christ is the *only* way." While the life, death, and resurrection of Jesus guide my spiritual walk, I recognize that one need not be Christian to be whole and do good things in the world. One of the main points of *Brownfields* is to show the power of a community coming together across religious boundaries.

Several of the characters in the book work in the public sector (a police officer, postal service worker, county home administrator, and a teacher). These characters were inspired, in part, by a line in Garret Keizer's book *Privacy*: "A world managed by mail carriers, park rangers and public librarians has never looked like an ugly world to me."

Brownfields started at the Lehigh Carbon Community College Rothrock Library in Schnecksville, Pennsylvania. The book continued to take shape at the Ocean County Library in Lacey, New Jersey. The bulk of the book was written in the Iowa State University Parks Library in Ames, Iowa. Libraries continue to provide essential public space for inquirers, writers, and dreamers. Consider supporting your local public library!

For readers concerned about profanity, there are no curse words used in *Brownfields*. However, the profanity of corporate arrogance makes an appearance in various parts the book.

In my experience, overcoming sinful systems and oppressive structures does not come solely through out-fundraising the oppressors or out-maneuvering them politically. Instead, an alert, active, and spiritually centered community is the most effective means of battling the greed and overreach of corrupt institutions, organizations, corporations, or governments.

Alert and active communities need alert and active individuals. Unfortunately, brownfields sometimes get in the way of people's full participation in their communities. Thankfully, literal or metaphorical brownfields are not eternal. In the church business we put it this way: there is nothing too far gone for God to heal!

Thank you for your interest in *Brownfields*.

MAIN CHARACTERS
ALPHABETICAL BY FIRST NAME

ABIGAIL BARRETT-THOMPSON - Pastor of Faith United Church of Christ. Wife of Ted Thompson.

ALAN PECK - Vice President, Department of Research & Analysis, Vigor Health Insurance Company. Married to real estate agent Amy Peck.

ANNA RAMIREZ - Works for the U.S. Postal Service. Mother of Willie and Genny. Ex-spouse of Eddie Ramirez.

CONSUELA GONZALEZ - Mother of Gina and Anna. Grandmother of Willie and Genny.

EDUARDO "EDDIE" RAMIREZ - Police Sergeant. Husband of Isabella and ex-husband of Anna. Father of Willie, Genny, and Sofia.

EVAN LEMMON MOORE - Works in customer service for BlackBox Video Game Company. Next-door neighbor to Sergeant Eddie Ramirez.

GENESIS "GENNY" RAMIREZ - Is in the fourth grade. Lives with her grandmother Consuela, mother Anna, brother Willie, and aunt Gina.

GINA GONZALEZ - Lives with her mother Consuela, sister Anna, nephew Willie, and niece Genny. Works as the Assistant Director of Social Services/Admissions at Elm Pond County Nursing Home.

ISABELLA RAMIREZ - Runs Christian Moms Group at Church of the Living Water. Second wife of Eddie Ramirez, mother of Sofia. Daughter of Johnny Ramos.

JOHN "JOHNNY" RAMOS - Pastor of Church of the Living Water. Husband of Anita, father of Isabella, father-in-law of Eddie.

RICHARD MOYER - Retired Army veteran. Next-door neighbor to Consuela, Anna, Gina, Willie, and Genny.

TED THOMPSON - Art teacher for Allentown Consolidated School District. Husband of Abigail Barrett-Thompson.

WILLIAM "WILLIE" RAMIREZ - Middle school student. Lives with his grandmother Consuela, mother Anna, sister Genny, and aunt Gina.

*With certain legal exclusions and additions, the term "brownfield site"
means real property, the expansion, redevelopment, or reuse of which
may be complicated by the presence or potential presence of a
hazardous substance, pollutant, or contaminant.*

(U.S. Environmental Protection Agency)

*But I wrought for my name's sake, that it should not be polluted
before the heathen, in whose sight I brought them out.*

(Ezekiel 20:14, KJV)

WINTER 2013

Richard Moyer walked his beloved mutt, General Ridgway, on the usual route from his Cedar Street home, walking first down to Greenleaf Street and continuing past the Austrian Hungarian Vets hall until reaching Meadow Street. They turned left on Meadow, and Richard glanced at the abandoned battery factory to his right. As they toddled by the site, he recalled talk of some millionaire developers having completed the cleanup and that construction would start on the property sometime this year. *They'll make more millions to add to their millions, with a few crumbs for the little guys.*

Richard and General Ridgway continued their stately pace down to Jordan Park. It was just after sunrise, so they had the park mostly to themselves, except for a stray jogger by the creek. They'd circle around and return home via Fourth Street, as it had the gentlest rise.

At Fourth and Whitehall Richard paused in front of Faith Church, skimming the grounds for stray plastic bottles and candy wrappers. Though no items captured his attention, he would return later in the day, retrieve the bucket and grabber from the sexton's closet, and comb the property carefully.

Continuing down the next block, Richard came upon a large, three-story brick factory building that occupied most of the street. An endless array of garbage speckled the front and side lots, and Richard did not hide a look of disgust. Twice a month Richard phoned the city to complain, and the building owners would eventually send someone out with a large garbage bag to gather up the biggest pieces of refuse. Within a week, however, the property reverted to a trash-strewn state and Richard would growl when he viewed it.

His agitation receded as he walked by a section of neatly kept row homes, the porches swept, appropriate seating in place, and the front doors all in good repair. Their holiday decorations had been removed promptly and their walks were always shoveled. He nodded approvingly. It was almost as nice as his block.

Richard was not obsessive-compulsive or particularly fastidious. He simply liked things to be in order and reasonably well kept. His clothes were old and worn, but clean. He shaved every day with a razor he had purchased in 1973 and went to the barber once a month to get his remaining hairs trimmed. A Pennsylvania Dutchman, Richard looked like any other elderly German working-class man in Allentown or Pittsburgh or Milwaukee. Slightly bent from decades of standing and cutting sheet metal, he was not often noticed by others, but took note of most people and things through watery, pale blue eyes.

#####

TED THOMPSON cut the spinach in narrow strips and the olives into small slivers. They were placed on the counter next to the quarter cup of feta cheese. The four eggs had started to bubble, so Ted quickly dumped the ingredients in the pan and cranked in some pepper. He hesitated with the black truffle salt because of the saltiness of the feta and olives, but decided a few crystals wouldn't do everlasting harm. He plated the omelet next to a small cranberry muffin and wiped his hands on the front of his apron, satisfied once again with his artistry in the kitchen.

"Thank you. Sweet and savory—my favorite," Abigail said.

"For my sweet and savory wife," Ted responded.

Satisfied with the first bite of his creation, Ted mentioned the Allentown Art Museum gala exhibit opening featuring a massive collection of early twentieth-century dresses. "I'm thinking it'll be pretty packed tonight at the show."

"Can't wait for the flappers!" Abigail exclaimed.

"I've never seen you so excited for an art opening. What is it about these flappers that has caused you to become unhinged?"

Abigail laughed. "Hey, buddy, do you know how many pencil-and-ink drawing exhibits I've endured? All those collections of artist preparations—which I still don't understand why a museum would display them."

"For a person who constantly talks about healthy processes in making congregational decisions, why wouldn't you want to see the process an artist used?"

"I like finality in my art. I don't need to see what led up to it."

Ted rested his elbow on the arm of the chair, and with his chin atop his chubby hand, he teased, "Is anything really finished or final?"

Abigail smiled and asked, "Is this my cue to talk about the eternal joy of the heavenly banquet table?"

"Nice try, but let's detour back to the flappers. Why the giddiness over those dresses?"

"They'll be pretty and flashy and make me think about feisty women dancing around Allentown in the 1920s."

"Ah, empowerment from textiles."

"Sure. I'll see them and it will be a good reminder to me to amp up the feistiness."

After a long pause, Ted replied, "We have become a little lackluster of late."

Ted's love for Abigail would never wane, of that he was sure. They were a sturdy couple physically as well as emotionally, and it would take something apocalyptic to topple their solid bond. It wasn't the marriage that was boring him, but rather the daily grind of teaching children and interacting with broken-down adults. An affable man, he was high energy in the classroom, but in recent years avoided spending time with most of his colleagues, as he found their interactions deflating. The dull feelings about life affected his creativity and he had not completed a canvas or any piece of art in over five years. He was restless and listless at the same time and knew he had to escape his rut or risk total surrender to the gods of tedium.

#####

ANNA RAMIREZ pulled on her uniform shirt and applied makeup in front of her bedroom mirror. Momentarily, she'd see the kids off to school, say goodbye to her mother and her sister

Gina, then drive the mile to her workplace, the Allentown Post Office.

She was quick and expert with the daily makeup application. To her, it was not quite a mask, but more of a subtle barrier from the unrelenting public gaze. They would never see all the way to her soul—she made sure of that.

Enhancing what she believed to be her strong facial features, Anna concentrated on her high cheekbones, thick eyelashes, and full lips. She minimized her nose and made sure her hair covered the tops of her ears and forehead.

As she walked out the front door to her car, she saw her neighbor from the adjoining rowhome—Richard Moyer, with his adored dog. Even on the coldest days, he wore his old Phillies cap. Anna had never seen him in a wool hat. And while she was bundled up in her heaviest coat for the winter, Richard wore the same thin jacket in every season except when he wore only shirtsleeves in the summer.

"Good morning, Mr. Moyer." Anna gave a wave.

"Hiya," he said.

In minutes, Anna had completed her commute. She turned off her car and wondered why in the world anyone would drive deep into New Jersey or even to New York every day for work. *I want a little bit of give in my day, some stretch and some space so I can think.*

Anna had no need to be in possession of the deepest or most righteous thoughts in Allentown. She was content to think mostly about the people in her life, reflecting on their impact on her and her influence on them. She smiled when thinking about the talents and frustrations of her son Willie or her daughter Genny, knowing that they were making their way in the world as unique creations. She often reviewed recent conversations with her mother, mining them for bits of wisdom and direction. Sometimes she thought about her sister Gina's escapades or her ex-husband's choices. In the moments before entering her workplace, Anna often thought about her interactions with her coworkers as well as how she would best assist customers, granting them dignity even if she received none in return.

Anna's warmth was abundant, and postal service customers always wanted to land at her window to soak up some of her sincere courtesy. Other postal clerks were polite, but only because they had received voluminous training on the mechanics of customer service. Anna was a natural. One look in her dark brown eyes and most people experienced a kind of understanding unavailable from ninety-nine percent of humanity. The average person was too self-focused to extend consideration to anyone except close family members and perhaps a few friends. But Anna's generosity of care extended far and wide. If not quite queen of the post office, Anna definitely reigned, gracious and compassionate every day. She gave deeply and refused to receive anything back from her customers beyond a "thank you" or a smile. The point of her service was to provide for others and mutuality was unnecessary.

#####

GINA GONZALEZ parked and walked to the main entrance of Elm Pond County Nursing Home, a large, ten-story brick building on the western edge of Allentown. Resident Barbara Petty was in her usual morning location—in her wheelchair right outside the front door, smoking a cigarette and keeping an eye on all of the comings and goings.

Gina chirped, "Good morning, Mrs. Petty."

With a smoker's croak, Barbara replied with her customary, "Good morning, sunshine."

"So cold out here. How can you stand it?" Gina asked.

"Wakes me up, and I make sure to bundle up on days like this."

"Any news to report on the parking lot?"

"There's one of the aides, Duncan might be his name?"

"There's a young man named Dustin that recently started working here," Gina said.

"Dustin. That's it. Well, this Dustin tears in and out of the parking lot like it's some sort of racetrack. I told him he better watch it, but he pretends like he doesn't hear me."

"That's not good. We'll make sure a supervisor is alerted."

"It's not safe, drag racing around here."

"I'm sure I'll see you later. Have a good day, Mrs. Petty." Gina continued inside, greeting the young receptionist as well as those who were seated near the entrance. A covey of residents gathered daily on the comfortable entryway chairs where they could look out the large windows and keep abreast of visitors and employees entering and exiting the building. Gina recognized it as their particular form of social media.

As she checked her mail behind the receptionist desk, Gina overheard a conversation between two female residents. "She's such a pretty girl, that Gina. So slim and trim."

"Yes, I've never seen a hair out of place, and her clothes so nicely tailored, like how we used to make them at the factory. I wonder why that girl's not married."

The woman replied, "Well, everyone's not the marrying kind, you know?"

"None of our business, probably."

Nodding, the resident agreed, "So much of it is none of our business."

Gina smiled to herself. They never knew how loud they were when they talked. The entryway picked up every sound.

Buoyed by the compliment, Gina entered the Social Services/Admissions department and flipped on the computer in her office with more flair than usual.

Gina was gifted with an athlete's body that did not require much maintenance. Unlike Anna, her chubbier sister, she ate just about anything and never worried about gaining an ounce. Her concerns were more about self-presentation, and she took time each morning to put forth her best look. She checked her mirror at home at every opportunity, and looked again in the rearview mirror of her car. Gina kept on top of makeup throughout the day with a small mirror in her desk—ensuring no one could speak negatively about her appearance. A polished exterior would keep people from poking at the interior. It wasn't the lesbianism she was afraid of people seeing—Gina was comfortable with her orientation and her family had known since she was in her teens. Her sensitivity lay in her feelings of unsteadiness and doubt, even though she was now thirty-two and had navigated the dramas of her twenties with no major scarring. Externally, she radiated confidence and assurance, even to the point of becoming abrasive in some settings. Only her sister and mother knew her vulnerability—that soft spot of uncertainty about whether or not she could be loved wholly and unconditionally, just as she was.

#####

ALAN PECK pushed through his fifth meeting of the day at the Allentown offices of Vigor Health Insurance Company. The main topic on the agenda was Obamacare, and while Alan appeared to pay attention, he was daydreaming about the upcoming weekend trip he was going to be taking with his wife to Atlantic City.

"Alan?"

"Huh? Excuse me?" Alan realized he was being directly addressed.

"Again, Alan," fellow vice president Connie Kozak prodded, "what are the most current numbers?"

"Oh, yes, apologies. I've got them right here." Alan passed around handouts listing best and worst-case scenarios for Vigor. "I've outlined the pros and cons of merging with each of five different regional companies, which I still think is our best option."

"We've been around since 1952, and you think we should just cave in and give up our name and all that we've done and accomplished?" Connie asked.

Alan adjusted his glasses and patted his thick gray hair. "I don't think it's about giving up. I think it's about Vigor being smart and preparing for the long term. Things are changing rapidly. A merger might lessen volatility and ease anxiety."

Connie crossed her arms as a sign she was ready for combat. "Or heighten anxiety and result in much greater volatility for the four hundred employees here at Vigor."

Five other managers in the meeting continued the discussion while Alan's mind wandered to the whirlpool at the hotel and the restaurant he and Amy would dine at Saturday night. They were frequent visitors to the local casino in Bethlehem but enjoyed the occasional getaway from the Lehigh Valley in exchange for Atlantic City ambience. And of course the food would be better than in Bethlehem, not to mention the people-watching.

Alan's demeanor aligned with the name of his company. He was vigorous and healthy, mindful of keeping in shape and on top of every aspect of his life. A wrestler in high school, he still had a thick neck. Shorter than average, he made up for his lack of height with a booming bass voice. He had little patience with overweight people, people who complained, or even people who walked slowly. He'd shake his head in disgust when he saw a wide-bottomed woman seated at a slot machine. Anyone who worked for him quickly learned that Alan did not tolerate whining, and he charged a dollar anytime an underling voiced a complaint. He understood himself to be self-made, and saw his success as a direct result of his efforts to produce a valuable product and provide a service that enhanced people's lives. Alan's father had focused on life insurance, but he had branched out into the health insurance business, not wanting to follow in his father's footsteps too closely. Alan had been well compensated in his thirty years with Vigor, and was looking forward to an amply funded retirement.

#####

GENNY RAMIREZ waved goodbye to her fellow fourth graders about the same time Willie Ramirez checked his phone in front of Trexler Middle School. The siblings met at the public library on Hamilton Avenue. They said "hey" to one another, and

Genny headed directly to the nature photography books while Willie continued toward the computers. After an hour they would walk to the post office to catch a ride home with their mother.

Genny was the bolder child in terms of adopting edgy trends, with multiple strands of pink hair and a bright blue paisley scarf around her neck. Willie took on a more conformist style, wearing high tops and a plain navy blue jacket.

The librarians never had to discipline or shush Genny or Willie. The siblings knew that if word got back to either of their parents about any type of misbehavior, their library privileges would be instantly revoked and it would be a long time before they would get them back.

#####

EVAN LEMMON MOORE strolled out his front door, flopped on the couch on his porch, and stretched out his long legs. He would not spend much time outside—it was too cold—just some brief fresh air before starting dinner. It was a little after six and he had just finished his ten-hour shift. He loved his bedroom-to-home-office commute.

Evan's next-door neighbor, police officer Eduardo "Eddie" Ramirez, appeared on his adjoining porch moments after Evan had submerged into the ancient cushions. In contrast to Evan's hoodie and jeans, Eddie wore a neatly pressed collared shirt and zippered jacket like the kind Evan's grandfather used to wear. For a thirty-something, Evan thought Eddie was oddly old-school.

Like many kids growing up in his Midwestern town, Evan had seen every episode of the television show *Home Improvement*, and was loyal to the show's quirky neighbor greeting the main character with his friendly "hi ho" from behind a fence. Evan carried the tradition into adulthood. "Hi ho, neighbor," he said.

"How's it going?" Eddie asked.

"My customer service work for the day is officially done. All is well and taken care of in gaming land."

"I need you to check out our game system sometime this weekend, okay?"

"Sure. What's the problem?" Evan asked.

"It's soooo freakin' slow."

Evan said, "I'll try to work my wizardry. How about tomorrow night? I could come over around eight."

"Thanks, man."

"No problem. Anytime." He meant those words because he felt indebted to Eddie. Evan and the neighbors on their Jordan Street block had endured a slug named Paulie who lived three doors down. Paulie seemed to do a bit of dealing, though mostly relied on his girlfriend for money. After seeing her in scrubs on numerous occasions, Evan guessed she worked some kind of nursing job.

Paulie was not a particularly gifted caregiver for the four young children in the home, and often sat on his front steps on the phone or with his buddies, cussing up a storm. One afternoon, all three men were on their respective porches, Evan nesting on his couch, Eddie weatherproofing his front window, and Paulie spewing his typical string of curses. In an almost balletic scene, Eddie moved swiftly to Paulie's stoop and quite effortlessly had him in a sort of chokehold.

"We're not going to be a block like that, oh no, no, no, no, no. You are never going to use those words again in front of your children or my children and anyone's children on this street, got it? Understand? We're on the same page, yes?"

Paulie, almost out of breath, gasped "yeah," and a little bit of ugliness immediately disappeared from their street.

Out of the corner of his eye, Evan noticed Eddie stood a little straighter as the sparkling red sports car—a Chevy Corvette—pulled near. Evan witnessed these exchanges every other week, and knew they took place across the city at countless other homes at around the same time.

Eddie's ex-sister-in-law Gina was at the wheel and his ex-wife Anna in the front passenger seat. As the kids, Willie and Genny, clambered out of the car with backpacks and bags, Eddie said to Anna, "Couldn't walk the five blocks?"

Gina rolled her eyes, leaned across her sister and said, "You've always got something to say, always got an opinion on *everything*."

Anna shushed her sister and reminded her children they'd be together again soon. "See you on Sunday, my beautifuls."

In unison, Willie and Genny said, "Bye, Mom. Bye, Aunt Gina."

Evan grinned and waved at the kids. He also smiled at Anna. He had never had a long conversation with her, just brief words during the drop-offs and also at the post office when she was on the front desk. He found something akin to magic in her exchanges with customers.

Gina pulled the car away and the kids went inside with their father. Evan closed his eyes for a moment of rest and reflection. He'd soon go back inside to catch up on some movies via his Netflix subscription, but he needed the brief brush with real human beings. After being online all day with disgruntled, frustrated gamers, he often set aside time for decompression. A house in the woods would have been more his style, but Allentown was fine for now. He had landed in the city due to a romantic relationship that had since fizzled and was without the resources to reestablish himself in a more remote location. As a younger man, he was determined to never have a life that was overly concerned with money or maximizing profits or keeping ahead of his peers with the stuff of life. So Evan settled into the neighborhood and focused most of his energy on being as environmentally conscious as possible in his urban surroundings. He walked most places, maintained a sizable garden, and followed national and local political efforts on climate change. He also kept up with current environmental scholarship and his latest research interest was "net positive buildings," buildings that created more energy than they used. Evan had a simple and thoughtful approach to life—one that suited him well most of the time.

#####

ANNA RAMIREZ glimpsed at her beautifuls on the porch in the passenger side mirror as Gina pulled the car away. She noticed Eddie's neighbor Evan was saying something to the kids from his couch.

As they motored down Jordan Street, Anna leaned her head back, "I wonder about him—that neighbor guy Evan."

"Why?" Gina asked.

"I don't know. I just want to know more about him."

"There may be nothing there, 'cause he could just be an empty, shallow guy. Or maybe he's just like Eddie—a control *freak*."

"You know Eddie wasn't always like that. Iraq messed him up. Anyway, there's something about Evan that I like, and he's so polite when he comes into the post office. Maybe he's deep and sweet."

"Deep? Who needs deep? Deep doesn't make good money. What does he do, anyway?"

"Some sort of customer service from home."

Gina elbowed her sister. "Sounds kinda' creepy. Maybe he's a stalker type. Watch out."

"I don't think he's a jerk, just quiet."

"Yawn. Now he sounds *boring*. Oh, and remember that sweet always turns sour eventually."

"Speaking from experience?"

"No, Anna. Just talking about you and Eddie." Gina continued to make her way south through rush hour traffic toward Rubies Bar & Restaurant.

"Well, you're in quite a mood tonight!"

"And, what is *up* with his wife? What's with the skirt or dress *every* day?"

"All the women in their church wear skirts or dresses. It's some sort of religious teaching. You have to admit, though, that she's gorgeous—a size two even after having her kid. She could be a model."

Gina was nearing peak intensity. "But does she *ever* talk? It's like she's some sort of psycho doll that just stands there and looks pretty, but has no voice."

"I think, when it comes to our interactions, Isabella lets Eddie do most of the talking."

"Don't you think she must have some skeletons in her closet?" Gina asked.

"I don't think so. She's pretty pure."

"C'mon, everyone has something. Maybe she was a slut or had an abortion or snorted some coke."

Anna had decades of experience defusing her sister's tirades and knew how to settle her down. In an even voice, she said, "Nah, I really don't think so. She was raised in that strict family, and it looks like she wants things strict for her children. That's why she and Eddie are a great match. Eddie's not at all that pure, so he's hoping some of her religious mojo will rub off on him."

"Ugh. I need a drink," Gina said.

Tonight was Sister's Night Out and they would do some serious people-watching at Rubies, a bar that catered to the local lesbian, gay, bisexual, and transgender community. Gina was not seeing anyone presently, so Anna was quick to take advantage of the opportunity for some quality sister time. Anna also kept in mind that Gina knew how to work it, and once Gina had a girlfriend, everyone else in her life would cease to exist for period of time.

"Thanks for inviting me along," Anna said. "I'll be your wingwoman."

SATURDAY, JANUARY 26, 2013

EDDIE RAMIREZ poured the pancake batter on the hot, buttered griddle, attempting another Mickey Mouse head, his specialty. Standing alongside him, Isabella expertly fried bacon while at the same time talking on the phone with her mother. Genny played dolls with three-year-old Sofia and Eddie directed Willie to set the table.

As they sat down to eat, Eddie said, "Okay, phones on silence now." After Isabella, Willie, and Genny pushed the appropriate button and set down their phones, he offered a brief prayer. "Thank You, Lord, for this food and this family. Amen."

Willie grabbed for the plate of bacon and lifted three slices onto his plate. He took a big bite, practically devouring an entire slice. Eddie asked, "What shot you working on today?"

After swallowing, Willie answered, "Three pointers."

"Excellent. What's Kobe Bryant's goal when he practices?"

"Eight hundred made shots, Dad."

"Eight hundred made shots, *then* he scrimmages, then he goes to the weight room. Practice, practice, practice, it will bring you far, young man."

"I know, I know," Willie replied.

Eddie turned to his oldest daughter, "And, Genny?"

"I'm looking for more bags."

"Baggy Genny!" Willie said. He pointed at his sister and laughed.

"Shut up." Genny crossed her arms.

Eddie quickly intervened and was firm with Willie. "Hey, your sister believes in something. Let her be, and you'd better defend her if anyone calls her that in front of you."

Willie scoffed. "It's just embarrassing that she goes around picking up all those nasty bags."

"It's better I pick them up than they get swallowed by some poor animal," Genny declared.

Eddie raised his arms, signaling an end to their sparring, "Okay, okay. Enough, you two. Now go out and enjoy the park. Run around a lot, because you know what I want?"

"No fat Latino kids and no diabetes," Willie and Genny said in unison.

"And what's the procedure?"

"Keep the phone on at all times," Willie replied.

"Text you when we get to the park and when we get back home for lunch and the same for the afternoon," Genny recited.

Eddie smiled. His children understood. They got it. He wanted independent kids who could make good decisions in all sorts of situations, kids who knew their way around town. None of those clingy, whiny, chubby kids who sat inside in front of a computer all day and had no idea how to talk to people or handle themselves.

Willie ran out the door with his basketball and Genny followed soon after with her postal bag around her shoulders. They headed to Jordan Park. Eddie left the cleanup to Isabella and departed for the police station to catch up on paperwork.

Eddie kept moving as much as possible between home, work, church, and neighbors. Even so, he rarely appeared rushed, and when on the move, he was always taking in information. He knew the city of Allentown well, both its streets and inhabitants. He was not a busybody or gossip, but was aware of the activities and pursuits of anyone within eyeshot. He was frequently amused at how easy it was to keep tabs on both law-abiding citizens and criminals, because both lived much more openly than they believed. He kept a running log of blocks where drug arrests were high or domestic calls common. Social media was also a great help in monitoring the community, as public posts and tweets provided a wealth of information. Unlike those he observed, Eddie was skilled at making himself unobservable and carefully cultivated his privacy, keeping strict boundaries around a number of personal activities. He lifted weights in his basement rather than spend time at a gym. His military bearing made him appear six feet tall, but he was actually only five foot eight. He was well respected by coworkers and fellow church-goers, though no one knew him particularly well.

#####

ISABELLA RAMIREZ settled Sofia down for a short nap and then phoned her mother in hope of some motivation.

"Mama, help me!"

"What? You okay?"

"Yes. Sofia's napping and I need to get going on the presentation."

"Well, get going."

"How does Dad do this all the time?"

"He's had a lot more practice than you," her mother replied.

"I don't even know where to start."

"Have you done an outline?"

"No."

"Try an outline. Your father always starts with an outline. Maybe it will help you."

"This is a lot of pressure. I'm feeling like maybe someone else would be better."

"They chose you because word has gotten around that God is doing some important things through you. Now, stop calling me and focus on your work. I'll pray for you. I love you."

In a resigned tone, Isabella said, "Bye, Mama."

She thought about the different ways she could start her speech to the National Christian Moms Conference. *I could talk about growing up in the church. Being in church every night—Youth Group and Bible Study and Wednesday Service and Friday Healing Services. How everything was fine until me and my brothers were in middle school and then everyone started making fun of us as preacher's kids. But not everyone in the audience is going be a preacher's kid, so maybe it would be better if I started with how I met Eddie. Falling in love with my handsome man and making the husband the head of the household. Or maybe something about raising faith-filled kids. Or maybe something about staying fit. Wives staying attractive for their husbands and husbands keeping fit for their wives. Or maybe I could say something about how sex within a marriage covenant is completely freeing because there is complete trust.* Isabella smiled at the thought of the lovemaking session she and Eddie had had the previous weekend, and how much they had enjoyed it, and how they talked about it as one of God's great gifts. Isabella remembered reading something online about how faithful couples actually have more sex and are more satisfied with their sex lives than unmarried couples living together. *That would get all the moms whooping, but talking about sex is also a little dangerous. Might want to save that for smaller groups.*

Isabella slapped her palm to her forehead. "Of course! First talk about God. How could I forget that? Always talk about Him first." She rapidly tapped notes into her cell phone.

A young wife and mother, Isabella was a dynamic woman, smiling frequently and laughing easily in the company of her family or church friends. She loved connecting with the other moms at her church and was popular with her peers and the teenage girls who emulated her. Her circle probably seemed small to an outsider because she spent most of her time with only like-minded people. After all, her spaces were her home, her parent's home, and her church. But for a woman in her early twenties, her connections were solid and extensive. A pastor's daughter, she was fluent in social skills, and enjoyed meeting new people, participating in groups, and keeping conversations lively. She was equally fluent in texting and social media, and used them regularly to keep in touch with her church community. Isabella was not a spoiled pastor's kid or a pampered princess. While she was not aware of it, many in her circle viewed her as a bit of a woman warrior, ready to defend and propagate the faith.

#####

ANNA RAMIREZ looked out at the packed post office lobby teeming with customers of varying ages, sizes, and shapes. The wait was not excruciating but Anna sensed the hordes were getting restless. She made note of several adults standing in line with their heads tilted to the side, a sure sign of impending exasperation. Some constantly scanned the front desk as if it would make the clerks go faster and others played games on cell phones. A toddler walked up and down the line singing "wheels on da' bus go round round round, round round round."

"Next in line, please," she announced in a loud, clear voice just in case the person was hard of hearing, but also so the rest of the line saw she was doing her part to keep things moving along as efficiently as possible.

An older woman made her way to Anna's counter area. She used a cane, which made her movements slow and deliberate. Anna recognized her as one of her regulars and spoke to her in Spanish, "*Buenos días, Señora Torres,* how may I help you today?"

Mrs. Torres carefully placed a small box on the counter. "I have to mail this to my sister in San Juan."

"I have cousins in San Juan. Let's get your box weighed. Insurance or confirmation?"

EVAN LEMMON MOORE guzzled some chai as he waited for his next call. He looked around his home office. He had decided to place his work station in the second-floor room with the most windows and natural light. He kept his bedroom in a darker and narrower room, figuring it was only a place to sleep at night, so who cared about windows? He had restored the hardwood floors throughout, and decorated in his own way with five wall hangings—framed maps of the nature trails he helped tend on the weekends.

Soon enough the next caller intruded on his headphones. "My bill is messed up and it's messing up my games."

"Okay, let's get it figured out. What seems to be the problem?" Evan asked.

"It's saying that they won't accept my card."

"Let's see what's on file. Could I get your name?"

"Rasheed Jefferson."

Eight Rasheed Jeffersons popped up on Evan's fifty-inch television screen.

"And your address to verify."

"2030 Eighteenth Street, Tallahassee."

There was only one Rasheed Jefferson listed for Tallahassee. Evan clicked on the name.

"Okay, Rasheed, I'm pulling it up now. Let's see, your payment plan seems to be tied to a Visa card. Would that be right?"

"Naw, I had that one closed. My cousin got a hold of it."

"That happens sometimes. Sorry to hear about it. Okay, do you have a new one?"

"Yep. It's a MasterCard."

Evan entered the new number and said, "Looks like you are all set. Give it a try now and call us back if there are any other problems."

Evan hoped the next customer had a technical issue, as those were his favorite calls to resolve. Unfortunately, most of the problems were related to billing. The next call beeped in and Evan scratched his beard, ran his hand through his close-cropped blond hair, and said, "You've reached BlackBox customer support, how may we help you today?"

#####

CONSUELA GONZALEZ sat in her tidy front room with her neighbor and fellow widow, Marta Colon. The two women were drinking tea and chatting in Spanish.

Consuela mentioned, "We're starting to look alike."

Marta gave a dismissive wave. "All old people look alike. Maybe we could start seeing different hairstylists."

"Or maybe I could grow six inches."

Marta laughed. "Wouldn't that be something? But you'd still probably be short enough to wear petite sizes."

"Okay, how about I grow one foot? Then we would look less alike."

Marta pretended to look hurt. "You don't want to look like me? You don't think I'm *guapa?*" she asked, and fluttered her eyelashes.

"You've still got it."

With chagrin Marta replied, "Yeah, I got it. But who cares anymore?"

"Clara Sanchez died last week. The funeral Mass was this morning," Consuela announced.

Marta replied, "Then there was Raul Rivera who died yesterday. His Mass will be early next week."

Consuela reminded Marta, "Plus, Miguel Cordero dying earlier this month."

"And Miranda Hernandez died Christmas Eve, so hard for the family. Now every year for Christmas they'll be thinking of her."

Consuela offered a truncated Hail Mary, "*Santa María*, mother of God, pray for us sinners now and at the hour of our death!"

"*Amén!*"

Consuela and her late husband had resided in a number of rental apartments in the early years of their marriage until, in 1983, they moved into the three-story rowhome with their toddlers, Anna and Gina. For over thirty years, Consuela's world had centered around that home on Cedar Street. Her husband frequently worked overtime in the meat department of a local grocery store chain while Consuela took care of all the cooking, cleaning, and making sure her daughters completed their schoolwork, even though she never spoke English. To supplement her husband's income, Consuela offered childcare for several neighborhood families. When her grandchildren arrived, she closed her childcare business and devoted her time to helping raise Willie and Genny. She continued to speak mostly Spanish. The transition from Puerto Rico to Pennsylvania had been bumpy at first and the homesickness debilitating at times. Not wanting to upset her loved ones with any displays of sadness, Consuela had timed her grieving precisely, usually giving in to tears while doing the laundry. She'd think of the laundry line in Ponce on the southern coast of the island and the clothes flapping in the warm breeze. In time, she had made peace with the Lehigh Valley. Attending Mass helped her heart heal, as did occasional visits back to the island, but mostly it was her daughters who kept her attention in the present moment. Gina had always lived with her, and Anna and the kids had moved back in after the divorce. The full house was a source of joy for Consuela and she took seriously her role as matriarch of the family.

#####

RICHARD MOYER drank coffee with Robert Schultz in the fast food restaurant at the intersection of Fifteenth and Tilghman Streets. For seven decades Richard maintained a friendship with his fellow Allen High School graduate and Korean War veteran.

"You're looking pretty thin there, Richie," Robert commented as he rested a hand on his own substantial gut.

"Had to pound another hole into my belt so my pants don't fall down."

"You've got to eat."

"Who has an appetite anymore?" Richard asked.

"Well, I do!"

Richard asked, "Schultzie, you hear that Bob Kuhn bit the dust last week?"

"We're dropping like flies, Ritchie. Mitzi Martin passed away too."

"Oh, too bad. I liked that Mitzi. She was in the home the same time my Ellie was there."

Robert looked out the window. "Then there was John Holloway, right on New Year's Day. Happy New Year's."

"And Jane Heinrich a few days later."

Robert turned back and squinted at his friend, "Not much longer for us, fella."

"Ah, I'm ready anytime," Richard declared.

#####

GENNY RAMIREZ continued on a second bag hunt through Jordan Park after lunch. She spied a plastic bag flapping in the wind up a large tree. She wanted a long picker to get the bags that were out of reach but her Dad had said no.

She heard laughter in the distance and saw a pack of kids from her school coming toward her. *Uh oh. Here we go.*

"Baggy Genny! Baggy Genny! Baggy Genny!" they shouted.

In her most upbeat voice, Genny asked, "Hey, guys, want to help out?"

"Baggy Genny! Baggy Genny! Baggy Genny!"

"I'll take that as a no." Genny walked away from her classmates and took off northwest through the park. Her plan was to do a circle around the businesses on MacArthur Road—always a good source for bags.

Earlier in the school year, Genny and her fourth-grade class had viewed an environmental video about the effects of pollution on wildlife. Genny could not get out of her head the images of the birds and otters who had choked on plastic bags. That night she told her mom that they needed to save the animals. Her grandmother, mother, and aunt now all had reusable shopping bags, and only Willie continued to bring plastic bags into the home, mostly just to torment his sister. Her mom had given her an old postal delivery bag, and on Saturdays Genny walked around the park and neighborhood picking up bags that littered the area.

Genny wore work gloves over her winter gloves, because sometimes the bags she picked up contained leftover food or garbage. Most of the time they just had weird stuff, like the bag full of napkins from different restaurants, or the bag with the watch and chef's hat, or the bag full of cell phones which she gave to her dad. Genny learned early on which bags had dog poop or dirty diapers, and she avoided them as much as possible.

She watched the older men who were regulars on the handball court before continuing on past the dormant pool and through the parking lot of the grocery store. In the lot she saw her classmate Marcus getting out of a car.

"Hey, Marcus!"

On the other side of the car a woman said, "You two talk a bit while I go in the store. Marcus, meet me in there, okay?"

"Okay, Mom." Marcus turned to Genny and asked, "You getting more bags?"

"Yes. Look." Genny opened up the postal bag and showed Marcus her morning's collection.

Marcus put his hand on top of his afro, "That's a lot! What're you going to do with them?"

"Mr. Thompson said he would help me put something together in the art room."

Marcus looked confused. "Hmm..."

"Mr. Thompson said it's 'Found Art,' like things made out of garbage or recycled things or things people put on the side of the street for trash pickup."

Marcus said, "I better go help my mom."

Genny crossed MacArthur Road to circle the donut shop and the Vietnamese take-out place.

WILLIE RAMIREZ made what may have been his 350th shot while his best friend Alex Gomez provided commentary.

"Willie Ramirez makes the shot over Kevin Durant and the crowd goes wild!"

Willie pumped his fists in the air and howled at his friend who was holding the ball as he checked his phone. "C'mon, Alex. Pass it to me, yo." Alex was always too engaged in his cell phone to pass the ball back as promptly as Willie liked.

Alex finally put his phone away and returned to calling the game. "His team is down forty points. It's all on Willie Ramirez now."

Willie made the next shot, too, and then stopped counting because he kept losing track. He apparently needed both a statistician as well as a ball boy because it was difficult to keep a precise count of baskets amid distractions.

Willie asked, "Hey, could we watch some games over at your place?"

"Yeah, cable is back on. The bill got paid."

"Cool."

The two walked up North Penn Street to the top of the hill where Alex lived in a third-floor apartment with his mother and sisters. Along the way, Alex texted and Willie occasionally bounced his basketball, thinking of the games that were scheduled for the afternoon.

At the apartment, Alex wiggled the key in the lock. Upon opening the door, he said, "We're home, ladies! Time for Best Sports Network, yes!"

Alex's sister Daniela was not happy that her brother had come to take over the TV. "Always sports. Boys are *obsessed* with sports," she said.

"C'mon, Daniela, you had the television most of the day so far."

Daniela put a hand on her hip and said, "You know, when Mom comes home, it's her programs."

"Yeah, yeah."

Willie laughed and said to Daniela, "Bring us some snacks."

Daniela contorted her face as though she had just smelled something bad. "Are you kidding? No way."

Alex rummaged around in the kitchen. He found a bag of cheese puffs in the cupboard and sports drinks in the refrigerator.

Daniela dismissed them. "You think you're men, but you have only five mustache hairs between you. You're still boys."

Alex playfully poked his sister in the ribs, and she then went with her sisters into another room to make braided bracelets.

The Best Sports Network was showing an ACC men's basketball matchup. Willie and Alex stretched out on opposite ends of the couch. Alex continued multiple text conversations while Willie was mesmerized by the athleticism of the players.

SUNDAY, JANUARY 27, 2013

JOHN "JOHNNY" RAMOS awoke energized at four forty-five. He leaned over and kissed his wife Anita. She mumbled back, "Breakfast in fridge." Johnny loved the way she looked all the time, but especially in the morning when she was chasing down her last bits of sleep. Before leaving the bedroom, he paused and looked at her a moment longer. *She has definitely aged well, with a good shape, and her hair still thick and dark.* Anita had made him egg salad with pimento the night before. He toasted some white bread and had a protein-packed sandwich.

For Johnny, it was going to be another great Sunday, with close to four hundred in service and fifty adults in the Bible study. And he knew there would be over a hundred kids in the Sunday School.

He walked next door to Church of the Living Water at the intersection of Jordan and Cedar Streets. "The Lord has been good," he said. The original red-brick building had been built by Lutherans and sold to Church of the Living Water twenty years previously. They would need to build an addition soon to accommodate the growth.

After turning on the utilities, running through his Bible study, and making last edits to his sermon outline, it was eight o'clock. The earlier risers were already trickling into the church building.

Sunday School was at nine, and service was supposed to begin at ten, though sometimes it did not get going until half-past ten. Worship started with an hour of praise music from the Praise Him Wholly Band, which was followed by a deacon sharing announcements and prayer, a church member's testimony about God's healing of a broken life, and then the deacons would take the offering. By noon, Johnny was in the pulpit. He started things quietly, but soon enough built to a crescendo. By the time he'd conclude with prayer, it would be one o'clock. Another offering would be taken, there would more singing, and by one thirty, things would wind down at Church of the Living Water.

Johnny looked out over the congregants. "Church, I want to tell you today that we are in a battle!" It was a little after noon and the volume in Johnny's voice was on the rise. The spotlight reflected off his black, slicked-back hair.

A worshiper called out, "Preach it, Pastor."

"Evil is around us—demons and forces that just want to mess with our heads." Johnny looked to the right. In the pulpit, he kept his motions slight, not wanting to distract from the words.

"Yes!" More responses from the congregation were heard here and there throughout the church.

"And mess with other things." He jabbed a thick finger in the air.

"Yes!"

Johnny looked to the left. "We're not going to let any of that mess come near us!"

"Amen!"

He was shouting now. "Here's the deal. You are a *chosen* generation, a *holy* nation!"

Half the congregation, spellbound, responded, "Alleluia!"

"You belong to God. You are His. You are *called out* of darkness into His *marvelous light*."

"Yes, Lord."

"Here's what we have to do, Church. This is where you start taking notes: 'Three Ways Out of Evil.'" Johnny switched from a preacher's cadence to a more measured teacher's rhythm as the words appeared on the screen at the front of the sanctuary.

"Okay, number one: 'If we see evil, we will call on the Lord and ask that it be removed in the name of Jesus.' Number two: 'Something cannot claim us if we are not open to it, so we are going to close ourselves off to evil.' And number three: 'We seek the opposite of evil, which is the goodness of the Lord.' What are the evils today? There are so many. There is a long list, all the things of the world, anything that pulls us away from the things of the Lord. Evil even comes from the so-called Biblical scholars, oh, yes. They tear apart the Bible with their historical-critical approach. They start questioning things. Well, God is not a question!"

"Amen!" The entirety of the congregation was riveted.

"God is the answer."

"Yes!"

"Who is the way?"

"Jesus!" the congregation bellowed.

"Who is the truth?"

"Jesus!"

"Who is the life?"

"Jesus!"

Outgoing and extroverted in and out of the pulpit, Johnny was fiercely loved by his congregation. Everyone in the church knew his personal story about receiving a word from God to leave the life of drugs and drama that had embroiled him. His honesty and humor about his past was endearing, and his life was an inspiration to congregants who had struggled with addictions and the remains of ruined relationships. Having been saved and restored to a relationship with Christ, he couldn't help but want that for everyone. Even nonreligious people, while disliking his constant evangelistic orientation, recognized Johnny as a persistent purveyor of hope.

#####

ABIGAIL BARRETT-THOMPSON hit the snooze button at four forty-five but roused herself with the next buzz at 4:54 a.m. She leaned over and kissed her husband. His groggy response was simply, "Fridge." After retrieving Ted's fruit salad creation from the refrigerator, she glanced at the headlines on her e-reader, checking the local news first and then independent news sites for national news, as she was no longer able to stomach corporate media.

Abigail typically arrived at Faith United Church of Christ at six o'clock. Church sexton Richard Moyer had already turned on the utilities. Although it would not be toasty in the sanctuary, people would not need to keep their jackets on. Built by German immigrants, the solid stone building and parking lot were well maintained. Richard always kept the line of bushes that encircled the building neatly trimmed.

Abigail took a moment to sit in a pew in the middle of the sanctuary. *My favorite day. I hope I never get tired of entering into God's gates with thanksgiving in my heart.*

She lifted up a prayer for more people to attend the worship service. *God, if we could just hit seventy-five people here today, that would be such a relief. And bring the four regulars to Children's Sunday School, too. Help Your people hear You through the sermon, not because of all the time it took to prepare it, but because You're in it. You know, God, that the media gets their say, the politicians get their word in, Hollywood gets its time, technology has its way, Wall Street gets its demands met, yet You get lost in it all again and again. The powers and principalities laugh uproariously. They have millions of people receiving their constant communication, while we might have seventy-five this morning, if that, and some with better hearing than others. Help me be steadfast, and thank You for Your steadfast love that endures forever. Amen.*

The service started promptly at ten. The small choir made a valiant effort on the opening hymn, "How Great Thou Art."

After prayer and scripture, Abigail preached. "We heard in the news this past week the governor announcing more cuts to education. The powers that be keep wanting to cut rather than fund, because it is always easier to live in scarcity than abundance. It's always easier to exclude rather than include. Our reading today from the second chapter of Peter's First Letter reminds us of our strength as a community. Peter's first and second letters were written to Christians just when the church was beginning to take hold at the end of the first century."

The sanctuary was quiet except for the clanking of the heating system. When she started her pastorate at Faith over a decade ago, the hushed worship services had unnerved her, but she had since grown used to the stillness.

"Many Biblical scholars argue that the letters were not actually written by the apostle Peter, but rather by someone in the *name* of Peter. This was common in ancient times—for someone to write under someone else's name. It meant the writing was more likely to get published."

Abigail glanced toward the back pew where the ushers were seated. She continued, "Our main focus today is on the idea of what it means to be God's people. We sometimes feel as though we are not a people, but then God reminds us that we are indeed God's own. Here at Faith United Church of Christ, one of our core values is inclusion, and we know that *all* people are God's people."

A few congregants turned their heads as a loud car rumbled by, the noise from its muffler permeating the church's antiquated windows.

"Cutting funding to schools is not debatable. Our kids—all kids—need the best education possible. Once the politicians start deciding who *is* 'a people' and who is *not* 'a people,' we're in trouble. We are all God's people. This scripture passage is very clear that we are God's own people."

Smart and organized, Abigail was a capable spiritual leader. Most importantly, she was viewed as a woman of discretion. Even her childhood friends acknowledged her as an accomplished keeper of secrets. At the church, she listened to confessions of garden-variety sins or more intractable spiritual rebellions, and the stories all went to the same place—a deep well of mercy within her that had been dug and formed by God when she was a young adult and first exploring her calling. As she grew into her pastoral role, she came to understand that not everyone and not every pastor had her gift. It didn't make her better than anyone, just different and able to offer something unique to the world. Quiet and shy when not in the lead, Abigail loved books. The best winter days with her husband Ted were spent sitting next to each other on the couch under her grandmother's afghan, enjoying a non-fiction find or magazine article offering a well-argued analysis of current events.

#####

EVAN LEMMON MOORE arose well-rested at six. He made himself an omelet with three eggs, mozzarella cheese, spinach, and tomatoes. He would be clearing brush most of the day on a hiking trail north of the Lehigh Valley, and he needed a good start. He kept additional fuel foods like granola, fruit, and an organic energy bar in his hydration backpack.

He walked two miles up to St. Elizabeth's Catholic Church at Fullerton and Highway 22, not for early Mass, but to catch a ride with his friend Bill Daly at seven. The two had met at one of Evan's previous jobs selling mobile phones. Except on holiday weekends, Bill and Evan volunteered every Sunday morning as "Trail Tenders." They worked on a variety of trails—the Appalachian, the Delaware & Lehigh Trail, and occasionally some of the waterfall parks in the Poconos. They made the trails walkable, removed poisonous plants, built picnic tables, extracted logs, and did the things that needed to be done to keep hikers safe and the trails clear. Today, because there was no snow on the ground, they would be able to clear a lot of brush.

Evan and Bill were part of an elite group of five men, all of whom had achieved Eagle Scout status, and they met weekly to care for the area's pathways. Other trail tender groups were oriented to young families who wanted a group activity or catered to college groups looking for volunteer hours. The five-man group didn't want to be slowed down by little kids or clueless students.

The trail tenders all bore a physical resemblance with their beards or goatees and looked like they could be members of a folk rock band, at home on a scuffed stage strumming guitars. And their clothing, while functional, was also similar—wool caps, jeans, hiking boots—with multiple layers on top, a layer to wick away sweat, a layer for warmth, and a layer to keep out wind and rain.

Bill was timely, and the two started down Highway 22 West toward the Delaware & Lehigh Trail near the town of Jim Thorpe.

Bill sipped on coffee from a travel mug. With one hand on the wheel, he said, "I love Sunday mornings on 22. Look at this. What a breeze!"

"All the lovers of carbon are at home right now, asleep until tomorrow when they'll spew it generously."

"How's your carbon footprint these days?" Bill asked.

"Not as impeccable as I'd like," Evan admitted.

"You've got no car. When was the last time you flew on a plane?"

"I can't remember. It's been a really long time. My last trip home, I went by Greyhound."

"Still vegetarian?" Bill asked.

"Yep."

Bill pushed. "Considering vegan?"

"Absolutely."

"Uber recycler?"

"Sure."

"Oh, really?" Evan eyed Bill, wary of where his friend was going with his line of questioning.

"Do you recycle your stomach contents?

"Dude, gross. No, I'm not a regurgitator." Evan chuckled.

"Composter?" Bill continued.

"Yep."

"Garden?"

"You know it."

Bill pried, "*Organic* garden?"

Evan laughed. "Probably not with that soil, though the EPA has officially completed its restoration of the battery factory land."

"Rainwater barrels?"

"Definitely."

"Own a dryer?" Bill continued.

Evan shook his head vehemently. "No way. Laundry always goes on the line—even in winter."

"Do you wash your clothes in Jordan Creek with eco soap?"

"No, but my washer is energy star."

"Solar panels?" Bill inquired.

"Saving up for them."

"Solar charger?"

"For the phone, yes, but not yet for the computer."

"Speaking of the computer, ahem, techy stuff?"

"You got me there. Not sure I'll ever be able to get totally off the grid."

"Recycled clothes?"

"Half and half. I prefer buying outdoor things new, even though this stuff is mega expensive."

"Windmill?"

"Ha ha."

They drove in silence for a minute, both taking in the scenery as they headed north.

Bill ventured into relationship territory, "Still pining after the neighbor guy's ex?"

"Anna. Yeah."

"Is she *purdee?*"

Evan smiled, "Real purdee. Great eyes and a captivating face I could stare at for quite a while."

"C'mon, what else—boobs and butt?"

"She's got a lot of boom-chocka-locka, but is definitely light on her feet, you know?"

"Nice."

Evan reminded his friend, "But we know it's not about that."

"Sure, we know it's not about that. Yet, it's still a pleasure to behold."

"I'd like to be holding them."

"Sounds like quite the crush, Evan."

"I admit—I've thought about jumping over her post office counter, lifting her up, and carrying her away."

#####

GINA GONZALEZ drove her mother the short trip to Sacred Heart of Jesus Parish at quarter past seven. The Mass in Spanish was not until eight, but the señora always liked to be super early to anything at the church.

Since the death of her father ten years earlier, Gina had Sunday morning driving duty. When Anna moved back into the house after her divorce from Eddie, she was somehow exempted from this task but, then, she cooked most nights. Gina didn't really mind. In fact, she liked the spirit of anticipation in the sanctuary before Mass, as well as the rhythms of the liturgy. And, while she never wanted to admit a need, she hungered each week for communion. It was not a physical yearning, but more like seeking a sense of rightness. If anything felt off in her life, the problem seemed to momentarily melt away after she received the wafer and wine.

Gina parked on the hill near the parish and quickly went to the other side of the car to help her mother, who clung to her arm even though the sidewalks weren't icy. Consuela covered her gray hair with a bright red scarf and wore the same coat she had worn for twenty years. She looked just like so many of the older women entering the church. Some of their backs were a little more hunched, some took steps a little more swiftly, but they all seemed pulled into the sanctuary by an invisible rope, each eager in her own way to once again make her offerings and receive hope for another week. Gina allowed herself to become captive to the positive spiritual energy, walking her mother to her favorite spot in the second pew to the left.

Promptly at eight, the priest started. "*En el nombre del Padre, del Hijo y del Espíritu Santo.*" Gina crossed herself.

#####

ANNA RAMIREZ luxuriated in her brief, every-other-Sunday-morning alone time, as Willie and Genny were with their father this weekend. She loved her kids, her sister, and her mother, of course, but she also enjoyed a quiet house for two hours.

Anna was grateful for her sister taking their mother to Mass, though she would always be confused by the two most favorite women in her life participating in one of the most anti-woman institutions in the world. It was almost as bad as her kids going every other Sunday to Church of the Living Water to hear their stepmother's father rant about all the evil in the world—not that they had a choice. Anna saw church as a place for male control freaks, and she had had enough of that growing up with her father as well as at her workplace and with her ex-husband Eddie. She had to take Eddie to court so that he would stop demanding the kids every Sunday. Her savvy lawyer had made the point that Anna could choose what spiritual influences she would provide for her children on her custodial weekends, including no religious experience at all.

The only church leader Anna could stomach for any length of time was that chunky female pastor in the neighborhood, Abigail. One day at the post office Abigail had told Anna, "You are a breath of fresh air. You minister to me every time I'm here. I stand in a long line, and just when I'm about to lose it, I come up to the counter and you treat me like I'm a person of value and I'm the most reasonable person in the world. You really do ministry every day here in this place, and for that I thank you." While she appreciated the words, Anna wasn't planning to step foot in a church anytime soon. Even with a female pastor, the church still had too many issues.

After sitting for a while, Anna flipped the television on to the Food Network. A smiling chef came on screen, preparing to cut into some luscious tomatoes.

"Now here's some ministry," Anna said.

#####

JOHNNY RAMOS locked up the church, satisfied that God had been sufficiently glorified in the worship service and the gatherings throughout the afternoon. He could not wait to return the few steps to his home, where his family would surround him and together they would enjoy a late dinner.

His wife Anita, his daughter Isabella, and his son's wives had laid out an overwhelming table of food—salads, chicken, ribs, rice, potatoes, cakes, and cookies.

Johnny bowed his head and prayed. "Lord God, in Psalm 127, You say that '*happy is the man that has his quiver full of children,* and that *children are a heritage.*' You have blessed this house so much, Father God. You have blessed this house with God-loving children. Keep growing this family and the Church, we pray. Keep us away from evil and temptation. Bless the food we are about to eat and the hands that made it."

Johnny looked up and said, "And let the family say 'Amen!'"

"Amen!"

The men filled their plates and went into the TV room to watch the National Football League's Pro Bowl game. The women stayed in the dining room and nibbled at the food items on their plates.

Johnny said, "Church and football. Sundays are the best. I'm going to miss this when the season is over after the Super Bowl." He positioned himself in an overstuffed chair in front of the big screen.

Johnny and his sons Thomas (Tommy) and Javier (Javi) had barrel chests and could have been boxers, but instead played high school football. They had been good team players and, while not gifted enough to play at the next level, enjoyed a Sunday routine of worship and the gridiron.

EDDIE RAMIREZ walked Willie and Genny to the end of the street during halftime of the Pro Bowl game. The kids would walk the half-mile back to their Mom's home with their backpacks and bags.

"Keep alert, you two," Eddie instructed.

"We won't take candy from strangers," Willie assured him.

Genny chimed in, "We'll text you when we get home."

"No slow pokes," Eddie added.

"We will stay on mission, Sir, Dad," Willie said, and saluted.

Eddie fist-bumped them and directed, "All right, carry on!"

#####

ABIGAIL BARRETT-THOMPSON tapped on her steering wheel and hummed the chorus of "How Great Thou Art." The drive home took ten minutes.

Ted heard the door close behind her. Wearing his apron, he came out of the kitchen and exclaimed, "Why, Reverend Barrett-Thompson, how is the flock?"

"They are okay—getting by—which is all we may ask for some days." Abigail kissed Ted on the cheek.

"Let me take you away from any stray thoughts of clergy burnout with some cauliflower soup, roasted beets, and leg of lamb—no offense to the sheep of the flock."

"That sounds amazing, as usual. You must've been in the kitchen most of the day."

Ted ladled soup into the bowls. "A lot of the day, yes. But I did some reading, too, trying to plow through more of the new atheist writings."

"My husband, the agnostic. My son, the Buddhist. And me, the Christian. What a trinity we make."

"Ah, the trinity—the most cherished of the shallow Christian doctrines."

"Ha ha. We'll go there another time, if it's all the same to you. Have you heard from Phil?"

Their twenty-five-year-old son lived in New York City and worked in the trenches for a publisher while still maintaining some of his youthful idealism as he developed his writing. Ted often spoke with Phil on Sundays, while Abigail exchanged texts and emails with him throughout the week.

"I talked with him this morning. He's doing okay. Have you been keeping up with his blog?" Ted asked.

"Yes. I adored the piece he called *The Empty Piety of the Hipsters.* It was funny, too."

"We sure did good raisin' him, huh?"

Abigail smiled and in a quiet voice said, "Yeah."

She sat on a stool in the kitchen and watched Ted across the counter plating the lamb and beets. She knew she was exceedingly blessed with a husband who was a thoughtful companion, a dedicated teacher, an excellent father and, on top of it, so skilled in the kitchen that she rarely needed to bother with meal preparation.

Glad to have chosen him and be chosen by him, Abigail said, "I love you."

Ted beamed and bowed. "It is an honor and delight to be loved by Abigail Barrett-Thompson."

#####

ALAN PECK exited the Atlantic City parking garage with his wife Amy beside him in the passenger seat.

"Not a bad run this weekend," he said. He stretched his right arm across the back of Amy's headrest. Tunes from an oldies station softly accompanied their conversation.

Amy replied, "Anytime we come out ahead, I'm happy. An extra hundred and fifty dollars? I'll sure take it."

"What'll you spend it on?"

"We could go out to dinner," Amy suggested.

"Sure."

With a sly half-grin, she added, "We could give it to the church."

"Very funny," Alan replied.

"I wish you would get it over with at Faith Church."

"Shutting down a church takes time. I really want to see its doors close and, as a nice treat, I'd enjoy watching Abigail twist while it all happens."

Amy reached over and patted Alan's cheek, then ran her hand over his tight bicep. "Careful, Alan. There's a thin line between love and hate. I sometimes wonder if you have a thing for Abigail."

Alan spat his words. "No way. She's a joke. The whole church is a joke, and the neighborhood is a complete disaster. You walk down any given street and it's all Spanish. It didn't use to be that way. When Pastor Paul was there, there were better people in the church. Ever since Mom and Dad died, the church—"

Amy completed his thought, "Yes, I know, the church has been going in the wrong direction. You could be like me, you know, and just leave religion and not look back. I never understood the attraction of church. It always felt so fake—people strutting around like chickens, thinking they're superior. Or, the opposite—all sorts of sad, miserable people thinking that Jesus is going to help them out. The only way out is through making something of yourself."

"You know that, and I know that. But Abigail sure doesn't know that, and neither do some of the others at the church. They talk about how everyone's equal and, for them, it's always about stooping to the level of the lowest common denominator. The people who get the most attention couldn't figure their way out of a paper bag."

"I hope it's all over soon."

Alan nodded, "I've been steering a lot of couples and families over to Cedar Beach Church. They are all really happy over there and will draw in others to go there too. And all the ones who have left Faith so far are those with the most money. It's hysterical sitting at consistory meetings. Panic rises in the room and people freak out about how the church is going to survive. It's like being at meetings at Vigor, but unlike Faith, Vigor is going to survive in all of this and we're actually going to do spectacularly well. Thank God for Obamacare."

Amy's smile was wide and revealed large, perfectly aligned teeth. "You mean the Affordable Care Act."

Their laughter was rowdy as they continued westward toward the Lehigh Valley. Amy told Alan she was going to nap a bit and let the seat back down for a more comfortable rest. He glanced at his wife as she closed her eyes. Though fifty-five, she looked barely forty in his estimation, with her fit, toned body adding to her youth quotient. She had luxurious, long brown hair, and Alan made a mental comparison. *So much better than the no-nonsense, mannish hairdos women like Abigail wore, a style that announced to the world the end of femininity.*

MONDAY, JANUARY 28, 2013

TED THOMPSON slapped off the alarm at five thirty and kissed his wife, who did not respond. Mondays were her one day off and she stayed dead to the world for most of the morning.

Abigail had packed the leftovers of the previous night's feast for Ted's lunch. He drove his 2002 Ford Explorer to his first school of the day, Washington Elementary.

"Good morning, urchins," he announced to his nine o'clock class. His blue eyes twinkled as he spoke. He was wearing an old denim smock that was covered with paint splotches, reminiscent of his favorite kitchen apron. He had gained close to one hundred pounds since he first started teaching, but remained spry in the classroom, always roaming and rarely sitting while students were present.

As the first-grade children paid varying levels of attention to him, Ted launched into the day's project description. "Today we're going to take clay and make it into something that lives. It doesn't matter if you make an animal or a plant or a person. It just has to be something that lives. No houses, no blocks, no books, no cars, no bowls, or cups. One at a time, raise your hand. What will you make?"

Rather than say a student's name, Ted stood up close to the student and asked, "Yes?" It was impossible for him to remember the names of all the students at the four schools he covered.

"Yes, young man?"

"A tiger," the student said. Ted thought the boy spoke with a bit of a growl in his voice.

"Yes. And you?"

"Barack Obama," the girl declared.

"Always good to set your sights high. Yes, next?"

"Spiderman."

"I was waiting for that. Yes?"

"A flower."

Ted encouraged the class, his youngest students of the day. "Okay, that's a good start. I'm going to be circling around the room. Start by warming up the clay between your hands. Roll it, pull at it. Work it, kids!"

For his next class, he ditched the clay. They tackled origami.

"Who here loves math?" A few hands went up as Ted handed out a diagram showing shapes they could make.

"Origami uses a lot of math. The first one we are all going to do together. And then, because we live in a free country, you will have the chance to pick what kind of origami you'd like to make. First, repeat the word after me, *origami*."

"Origami," the boys and girls in the class replied.

"It's from our friends in Japan. Origami is the art of folding paper."

Ted's third and final class at Washington Elementary was with the fourth graders who were split in two groups. The more artistically advanced kids in the class were doing a "Found Art" project, while the rest focused on an assignment with pins and string.

One of his most promising students was the Ramirez girl, Genesis. While the names of most of his students escaped him, Ted always remembered the names of those who had a heart for art. Ted thought her brother Willie had also shown some artistic promise, but, like many boys, he avoided engagement. Genesis, however, wasn't *too cool* for art, and Ted noticed she already had a bit of a bohemian look about her, with bright pink streaks in her dark hair and a funky patterned scarf wrapped around her neck. Most of her classmates played it safe.

Ted came across the table from Genesis. He looked at her lump of plastic bags and asked, "All right, what do we have here?"

"It's going to be an otter," she said, "but I don't know how to do the tail."

"Probably some braiding the bags together will do the trick and then we'll talk about attaching it to the body." Ted took two sniffs and crinkled his nose. "Kind of a smelly otter, yes?"

Genesis giggled and said, "The bags are from all over."

#####

GINA GONZALEZ looked through her files for the paperwork on two residents who, it appeared, were in the midst of a dispute. Gina's role as Assistant Director of Social Services/Admissions at Elm Pond County Nursing Home required her to deal with all roommate quarrels. Gina was looking forward to someday being director so she could delegate this task. She also frequently daydreamed about a facilities expansion so that every resident would have a private room.

Gina had done the intake for Marjorie Wagner, while the director had done the intake for Donna Allen. Both were in their eighties. Marjorie was slowly dying due to lung issues and Donna had been diagnosed with breast cancer.

Gina walked into Room 208 and addressed the woman sitting up in the bed closest to the entrance. "Good morning, Mrs. Allen."

Then she peeked around the curtain and found Marjorie lying in her bed. "And, good morning, Mrs. Wagner. I'm going to pull this curtain back so we can have a little chat about a few issues."

Gina pulled a chair between the two beds and sat. "I've heard you two ladies are having some trouble. What seems to be the issue?"

"There are a few," Marjorie said.

Donna made a dismissive hand gesture. "I have no problems."

Marjorie started. "In the middle of the night, out of the blue, Donna starts singing. Last week it was 'Tennessee Waltz,' over and over again. I also had one night full of 'Moon River.'"

"I didn't mean to upset anyone," Donna said. She looked hurt.

The paperwork for Donna had not listed dementia or any difficulties with memory. But, Gina knew, these issues sometimes manifested themselves later. During an intake interview most new residents are on high alert and their best behavior. And, sometimes, the family doesn't name such problems during the initial interview for fear of causing a scene.

"Is there anything else you'd like to add, Mrs. Wagner?" Gina asked.

"During the day there are a lot of repeats."

"Yes?"

"That's right. She'll repeat the same phrase over and over again. I would just like some peace."

"I didn't mean to upset anyone," Donna said again.

"Last night was the last straw. I woke up in the middle of the night and she was at the end of my bed! She was holding my foot. Scared me to death."

"I didn't mean to upset anyone."

Gina smiled at both women. "Thank you, both, so much for sharing. I'm going to make some notes, talk with the director, and we'll get this resolved very soon, okay?"

On her way out the door, Gina heard Donna say, "I didn't mean to upset anyone." As she walked down the hall, she heard Donna say it again. By the time she was at the stairwell, she heard it a third time. *Repeats.*

Gina stopped to see the Director of Social Services/Admissions, Sharon Chapel.

"We've got a repeater in Room 208. She needs to be transferred as soon as possible to the dementia wing."

"Who?" Sharon asked.

"Donna Allen."

"The family didn't say anything about her exhibiting dementia-type behaviors—probably too embarrassed. You'll process the transfer and notify the family?"

Gina nodded. "Yes, will do." After resolving the Donna Allen issue, Gina logged into the resident database. Every Monday, she took thirty to forty-five minutes to look through all the names affiliated with Elm Pond. It was one of her more tedious weekly chores, but she sipped on tea to keep alert. As she reviewed each name and room number she read her notes in the margins. Her entries of *sweet and funny*, or *gruff and mean*, or *wife visits daily* evoked a reminder image of each resident as she read.

#####

JOHNNY RAMOS stood just inside the entryway to a sub sandwich shop downtown. He was waiting to have lunch with Rob Handel, head deacon of Church of the Living Water. Rob worked nearby, so it was a central meeting place where they could do a regular check-in on congregational needs. Seeing a sad-looking, thirtyish man eating at a table near the entrance, Johnny couldn't help but think that when he was in his late twenties, he probably looked as pathetic and desperate as this guy.

Johnny remembered sitting in a pizza parlor one evening decades ago after yet another run-in with his father, who was drunk at the time. Johnny had berated him, telling him that his mother was working two jobs while he sat around all day doing nothing. His father smirked and said, in a long, slow voice, "Son, my life is gonna be your life." And for the next ten years, it was. He was exactly like his father, lost and living day to day without focus. At one point, Johnny had even sold what bit of jewelry his mother had to fund his drug habit. The only thing that mattered was getting high and escaping the meaninglessness of everyday existence.

Again Johnny looked in the direction of the gloomy man. He lifted a silent prayer. *Thank you, God, for reaching out to me through so many people. You, God, are the one who matters the most, above all else. I got right with You, and I'm not going to fall back. Help me reach this young man.*

To test the waters, Johnny said to him, "Can you believe this weather we're having?"

If he was surprised a total stranger would speak to him while he was in the middle of his lunch, the man did not show it. He responded, "I'm always glad for a mild winter."

"You work around here?" Johnny asked.

"Yeah, at the courthouse."

"Lot of important things happen there."

"I do filing most of the day."

Johnny knew he could go a little further with the man if he was willing to share about his workplace. "You file important information."

"I guess," the man sighed.

"It all matters. You matter. Did you know that? You matter, man," Johnny looked into the man's eyes.

The man sneered. "Let me guess. Are you some kind of church guy or is this some sort of after-school special moment?"

"You're good. Yes, I'm a church guy. But I'm not here to get you to come to Jesus or anything like that. I'm too hip for that."

"That so?"

"I see from your ID your name is Doug. Can I call you that?"

"Yeah."

"Okay, Doug, I'm just here to let you know that someone cares. I care that when I walked in here you looked kinda sad, kinda burdened, you know?"

Doug shrugged his shoulders, but Johnny saw that spark of recognition, that the man was touched in some way that another human being saw he was carrying a heavy load, that someone cared about him, even though most of his life no one ever bothered. Johnny sat down and placed a hand on the back edge of Doug's chair.

"Life does not have to be this way. There is a better way, and when you experience it, it will change everything—pow." Johnny made a fist and gently punched the air.

"Hmm..." Doug was noncommittal in words, but Johnny sensed he had made a significant opening. Well, God had made the opening, Johnny reminded himself, but he was glad to do the work on His behalf.

"Doug, no pressure, this is not a sale. I'm going to give you my card, and if you want to check out this place sometime, great. If not, no problem. God's blessings on you, man." Johnny shook his hand and patted him on the shoulder.

Johnny turned and saw Rob in the doorway. He had arrived a couple of minutes earlier and was quietly watching his pastor's masterful evangelism.

"Rob, my man! Say hello to Doug."

Rob shook Doug's hand, greeted him warmly, and the two churchmen went to the counter to order their sandwiches.

#####

EDDIE RAMIREZ was training another two patrol officers on hostage negotiation. As patrol sergeant, Eddie led and coordinated all the training for the patrol team. It was a slow process to shift the officers around to fit in the training and then track their progress on top of it.

While many of the training modules were online, Eddie preferred face-to-face instruction. It was more effective and he was firmly convinced that people learned more from a real, live person. And, besides, he had received many excellent reviews for his training sessions. He took the training seriously, and knew it was on him if patrol officers cruised the city with sub-par skills.

To the younger officers, Eddie was an imposing presence. He rarely smiled, and his conspicuous muscles were missed only by his most unobservant coworkers.

He looked at the two apparently uninterested police officers and said, "Wake up. Here we go. Your training today is on hostage negotiation. By the end of the training, you'll know some important techniques for dealing with it, how to form a crisis response team, and the policy and legal issues involved. You will also know about the psychology of hostage taking, the types of incidents, how to do threat assessments, and what needs to be done post-incident."

The officers perked up. Sergeant Ramirez made the training sound intriguing.

Eddie pointed at them, "Aha! You thought you were going to be bored, but this is gonna be good!"

#####

ANNA RAMIREZ had Monday off because she had worked on Saturday. Today she was the designated driver and interpreter for her mother, who had a medical appointment. Consuela's rheumatologist had set up a consult with an orthopedic surgeon about her arthritic left hand.

Anna and Consuela sat in the waiting room watching the television, which was set to a health channel. After five minutes, a nurse led them back to another room where Anna took a seat after helping her mother into the exam chair. Although her mother was only sixty, some days Anna felt she seemed eighty.

Doctor Brian Brooks entered the exam room with a big smile and shook hands with both mother and daughter. He appeared to be in his late fifties, with silver hair and wire-rimmed glasses. He was wearing a crisp white lab coat with a name tag and hospital logo above the pocket.

"Consuela, I'm going to share with you some of the benefits of having surgery on your hand."

Anna rapidly translated the doctor's words into Spanish.

"According to your chart, you've experienced the most pain around your thumb, forefinger, and middle finger, right?"

Anna nodded and then Consuela nodded.

"You've treated it with drugs for more than a year and have reported no improvement, so what I suggest is a surgery called a synovectomy. We'll remove the joint lining." Doctor Brooks cleared his throat and continued. "This surgery reduces inflammation, swelling, and pain."

Another translation by Anna. Again Consuela nodded.

The doctor looked at Anna and said, "The surgery would be arthroscopic and performed on an outpatient basis. It's a common surgery—very safe—and your mother would recover at home."

Consuela brightened at the word *home*.

"The nurse will give you a number of articles about the synovectomy procedure. Read them over and call back our office to schedule the surgery."

Anna was concerned. She asked, "How painful is the surgery?"

"We've really advanced with pain management during these types of procedures. It won't be pain-free, but it will not be any sort of prolonged, immovable, extreme pain."

"How long is the recovery period?"

Doctor Brooks replied, "Usually a couple of days. Physical therapy needs to start almost immediately and will continue for about two months."

"And how far ahead do you schedule?" Anna inquired politely.

"We're scheduling now for about five weeks out, early March. On your way out, if you like, you can schedule now to get on the calendar."

"Thank you, doctor," Anna said.

"Gracias, doctor," said Consuela.

Doctor Brooks kept his broad smile going and shook their hands once more. "Of course. Nice to meet you both."

TUESDAY, JANUARY 29, 2013

ABIGAIL BARRETT-THOMPSON brewed the coffee and set out hot water, tea bags, and granola bars for the attendees at the Dolly's Dollar Store Protest Committee Meeting she was chairing at Faith United Church of Christ that morning. A total of five pastors were expected to attend the planning session.

Reverends Craig Johnson and Peter Smith entered the fellowship hall together. Abigail heard Craig laugh and say to Peter, "A Lutheran, a Presbyterian, and a UCC walk into a bar, and...?"

"They respectfully debated the merits of Matthew and Luke's infancy narratives over whiskey sours," Peter said.

"Oh, boring!" Craig laughed again.

"I saw C.D. drive up. He should in any moment," Peter said.

Reverend Christopher Daniel Alexander—"C.D."—had been pastoring an independent Baptist church for fifty-one years. The church was predominantly African American, and had been toughing it out in a downtown location with no parking and adapting to twenty-first-century changes in Christianity. When people talked behind C.D.'s back, their conversation usually included the phrase "he'll die in the pulpit." C.D. was a member of just about every left-leaning clergy group in existence. He had recently turned seventy-five and wore hearing aids, but was in great physical shape and still fit into the same suits he wore as a young man. Completely on top of current events, C.D. was always ready for a protest. In fact, he viewed opposition to powerful institutions as his prophetic responsibility.

Abigail welcomed him into the hall. "C.D., so glad you could make it. We'll get started without Eric. I'll give the prayer and then we'll work through our rather hefty agenda." The four pastors bowed their heads and then gave a hearty "Amen" after Abigail had concluded the meeting invocation.

"Just a bit of history so we're all on the same page," Abigail began. "Six months ago, I read about Dolly's Dollar Stores being rated one of the worst companies to work for in the U.S. The main complaints were low wages and benefits, and also irregular scheduling. Because the workers' schedules change every week, they're not able to get second jobs or plan their lives very much in advance. This got me thinking that clergy could support the workers and hold the corporation accountable—"

C.D. interjected, "We'll have to be clear about what we're holding the corporation accountable to. Just what is it we will be calling on the corporate kings of Dolly's to do?"

"Good question," Abigail said. "We are holding them accountable to change their low wages and how they schedule their workers. In a bigger way, we are calling on them to provide fairer treatment of their most valued resource—their workers. There are nine Dolly's in our area, with three right here in Allentown. We'll protest both in support of the employees as well as against Dolly's corporate practices."

"I like it," Craig said. "It's both pastoral and prophetic. We bring the church to them, instead of attempting to get people to come to church."

"Right," Abigail responded. "Dolly's has about eleven thousand locations around the country, and have been fined by the SEC on a couple of occasions for misstating profits. They had fifteen billion dollars in total revenue last year."

"Ironic, no? So much revenue for a store where everything is priced at a dollar," Peter said.

"They sell a lot," Abigail answered as the others nodded. "I'll get a permit for protesting on the sidewalk in front of the Dolly's near Seventeenth and Tilghman. I've already spoken with a couple of the cashiers and tracked down a former employee named Tanya who is willing to share her experience. I've met with her and given her some coaching on public speaking. She'll be ready to go in April."

The four reviewed more agenda items. Fifteen minutes after the start of the meeting, Reverend Eric Windham entered the hall, cell phone in hand and texting.

"Look, he can walk and text at the same time," Craig exclaimed.

Peter smiled. "I can't even walk and sing the processional hymn."

"Hi, Eric," Abigail welcomed him. "We're on *Program* on the agenda, talking about our upcoming Dolly's protest."

"Okay."

"It sounds like we're clear that it will be three minutes per faith leader speaker, which means, of course, each will go five minutes, since so many of us clergy types tend to be long-winded. I will not speak, but instead will give the intro, do the emceeing, and wrap up at the end. We'll aim for a thirty- to sixty-minute protest. I don't think that should be a problem. Since it will be April, it should be warm enough for us to be comfortable outside for that long." Without missing a beat, Abigail kept the meeting moving along. "Our next item is *Other Invites*. Do we want to invite any political leaders to speak?"

Craig responded first. "It's really a rally for people of faith, right? While I'm not opposed to political or policy messages on the topic, they could dilute our message of this being a spiritual issue." He sat with his arms folded across his chest.

C.D. nodded and said, "Once religion is mixed with politics, what we get is politics. Religion *always* loses that contest. I suppose one politician is fine, but we'll probably want someone who is well connected in labor circles."

Craig concurred. "Yes, I agree. And Pennsylvania Citizens for Fairness has done work on the low-wage issue. I'm on their mailing list and I'll contact them about attending. They'll be able to circulate protest letters at the event that people can then forward to their legislators."

Abigail answered, "That sounds fine. And tell me what you think of this. I was thinking we could ask Johnny Ramos to be part of the event. We want to be inclusive, and none of us here is a Pentecostal, so it seems important to at least reach out to Johnny and his Pentecostal church."

"It'll end up being about him," C.D. maintained.

Eric countered C.D.'s concern. "But he's got a big church—very diverse—and whenever I've seen him at other events, he always brings a ton of people with him."

Abigail nodded and noted, "The people power really would help us. And, again, inclusion is important. How often do mainline Protestants work with Pentecostals?"

C.D. replied, "Ramos has a great track record with helping young men turn their lives around, and his personal testimony is very compelling. I've heard it a few times. He was a total scammer while he was on drugs and knew all the ways to score. He was a thief and a liar and all that, but then he had the Road-to-Damascus moment where he realized there was no turning back to the purposeless life. But just know that he tends to shy away from working for systemic changes."

"It's nothing personal. It's just the theology is so different with Ramos, as well as the ecclesiology," Craig suggested.

"Don't forget the pneumatology," Peter offered.

Abigail said, "All the *ologies* aside, I will give him a call."

"You've been warned," C.D. added.

Abigail responded to C.D.'s comment with a bright smile and a teasing chuckle. "Ooh, that sounds ominous. I'm sure it will be fine. Now, speaking of large churches, what about Pastor Davey Porterfield over at Cedar Beach Church?"

Peter opined, "A five-thousand-member mega-church really doesn't take part in events like this. We're super small potatoes. I don't see them out and about much, either."

"Progressive social justice is not on their agenda. They emphasize donations to local food banks and participation in international missions," C.D. declared.

"Okay, then, moving along," Abigail said, "but still under this item, do we want this to be an interfaith effort? You know how important inclusion is for this church. We really want to have a big tent."

"I'm all for including as many as possible, but if the four of us are speaking, we're already up to twelve minutes. Johnny Ramos will go ten minutes at the very least, so additional speakers will increase the length of the talking heads," Craig stated.

Peter tilted his head, "I always like to hear the perspective of different faiths, though my contacts are not great in the interfaith community."

"I have a connection with a local Reform rabbi. I'll give her a call," C.D. confirmed.

"I know someone at the mosque," Craig volunteered.

"And I have a Buddhist connection," Abigail said. She thought a moment more. "Peter, would you be willing to contact the Hindu Temple and give the invitation?"

Peter nodded, "Got it covered."

"And, Eric, could you contact the Sikhs?" Without waiting for a response, she continued. "And back to Christian-town for a moment, has everyone here put a 'save the date' reminder in your church bulletins?"

"Sure, but because the event is on a weekday at noon and most of our people are at work, I'm not planning for a very high turnout," Eric conceded.

Abigail pressed on. "Last item. Press release. I've given you each a copy. Let's take a look at it now."

"Abigail, you're so organized," Craig said. His tone reflected true admiration at her coordination skills. "Will you come over and manage our church's annual Stewardship Drive?"

Abigail laughed. "I appreciate the invitation, but will respectfully decline."

#####

ANNA RAMIREZ reported to work an hour early. She went straight to a designated meeting room for the Diversity Development training. The session fulfilled part of the mandatory eight-hour training requirement she had each year. Anna enjoyed almost any type of learning and hoped the teacher was at least somewhat dynamic at this early hour.

Water, coffee, tea, and mini-donuts were on a table at the back of the room. Completely unconcerned about her weight, Anna put two donuts on her plate. She never talked about diets or losing weight with Genny, as she didn't want her daughter to be like so many white girls who forever obsessed about calories.

As she poured herself a cup of coffee, her closest work buddy, Steve Palermo, entered the training room.

"Hey, Anna. Where are you sitting?"

"You ready to be diverse, Stevie?" Anna asked.

"Well, I'm as gay as a goose, have an African American partner, and I asked a Latina to sit next to me, so I think I'm starting the game in a good position."

"What makes a goose gay?" Anna set him up for his punch line.

He leaned in and whispered, "Baby, they're just born that way."

The room filled and the presenter walked in, a no-nonsense-looking woman with a severe, blunt haircut. She marched to the front of the room in her low heels and gray business suit. Anna and Steve exchanged glances and sat up in their chairs in response to the presenter's military bearing.

"Good morning. My name is Victoria Delgado," said the presenter. She then took thirty seconds exactly to share some information about her background and credentials.

Steve whispered to Anna, "I half expected her to say 'drop and give me twenty, maggots.'"

Anna giggled as the presenter continued. "Let's start with some questions. How many people here today believe they embrace diversity? Raise your hands."

Every hand in the room went up.

"How many people here identify as part of a minority group and, therefore, think they embrace diversity naturally?"

Anna and Steve raised their hands, as did a few others.

"I don't mean to burst anyone's bubble, but *claiming* you embrace diversity is very different from actually creating workplaces, schools, homes, neighborhoods, organizations, and religious groups that truly do value the differences among people. And, naming yourself as a member of a minority group does not necessarily make you any more tolerant of differences." Victoria Delgado nodded curtly as if to say her words were true without exception.

Anna and Steve were paying close attention as she continued. "Raise your hand if you know what a halal butcher does."

No hands went up.

"Raise your hand if you know how to speak any of the languages spoken in the world's most populous country, China."

There was no response.

"Raise your hand if you have ever needed someone to read a document for you because of your blindness."

The employees remained still.

"Raise your hand if you have ever been barred from entering a home or building because of physical limitations."

By now, most of the participants were fully engaged, thinking about each question.

"Raise your hand if you have ever come out as bisexual to your son's football coach."

Wow, Anna was surprised. *Wouldn't have thought of that one.*

"You are all here because you serve a diverse population. Almost every day you do your jobs really well and aim to be totally respectful of every customer, sometimes under very stressful circumstances. I'm here to tell you that diversity is a much broader category than we typically think. Yes, it's about more women in leadership, or more minority hiring, or accessibility, but it is also about developing a general awareness of the differences among people. Those differences are not bad. We are not here to become one big, happy blob of people who are all alike. This is not Stepford Wives training."

Two people in the back of the room chuckled, and Anna relaxed a little in her chair, trusting she was going to find the training completely engrossing.

The presenter continued, "We want to *honor* our differences and create a work zone where diversity is modeled. But, what in the world does that look like and sound like? I've got a whiteboard here. Let's name a few things."

ALAN PECK loved lunch meetings, especially when he was being courted. This was the fourth inquiry in the past two months from an insurance company in need of his particular skills—crunching numbers, managing analysts, and doing all the detail work that is required of a vice president at a health insurance company. Today he was dining with the Chief Operating Officer of Vigor's biggest rival, Indigo Armor, at the most expensive restaurant in downtown Allentown.

Between the salad and main course, COO Marco Flugrad launched into his proposition. "Alan, we'd love to have you join our team. What did you think of our offer?"

Alan knew how to play the game and responded the same way he had with the three other companies. "It is a generous offer and

I'm very flattered. But I'm pretty happy where I'm at. How would things be different with you?"

The executive recited his list of benefits, including profit-sharing and a two-to-one retirement match that reportedly made Indigo Armor the company that would meet one's deepest employment desires. Nearly as soon as Flugrad started speaking, Alan tuned him out. He'd toy with him some more, but in the end, stay put at Vigor. He silently replayed his own checklist. He earned a decent salary, his wife was a top earner in local real estate, and they had two fully paid late-model cars in their garage. They had long ago paid off their large, four-bedroom home in Orefield and were soon to close on a condominium in Hilton Head. There was no need to seek out other employment at this time.

It didn't even matter if the bottom fell out of the health insurance market. There was enough in his 401(k) to tide them over to retirement.

Over dessert the two men talked politics and lamented over the radicals in Washington who wanted to hand money to people who didn't work for it.

They ended the meeting with a firm handshake. Alan thanked Marco and said he would give serious thought to the offer.

#####

EDDIE RAMIREZ stood on his front porch talking to Evan, who slumped on his couch in the early evening.

"You look a little fuzzy. You okay, man?"

"Doing all right. Even though today's Tuesday, it's my Friday night, the last day of my three-day weekend. Most people see Tuesday as just a regular workday in the flow of the week, but to me, it's a reminder that I go back to work for four ten-hour days in a row. Remember, I work to live—I definitely don't live to work. Farewell, *adiós, au revoir*, weekend," Evan said with a hint of despair.

"You know there's a better way?"

"Uh oh, Eddie. You're starting to do that stealth-mutant-ninja-Jesus thing again."

"Just checking in, man. A little spirituality might do you some good. Come on over to Church of the Living Water some Sunday. It's always packed."

Evan spoke carefully, not wanting to offend his neighbor, "I've got a weekly commitment most Sundays, and I tend to go at things more with my head. I *am* interested in religion, history, and philosophy, but the whole worship shindig is not really my thing."

"Have you seen the sign in front of Faith Church?" Eddie asked.

"Sure, about their church dinners and they have scripture passages up there, too."

"They do a Bible study every Wednesday night. The pastor there, Abigail, leads a group in a historical-critical read through of every Bible book. It's free."

"I'm impressed with your fancy language, Officer Ramirez."

"My father-in-law says to stay away from historical-critical, that it gets people on the wrong track. But all those pastors think their way is the only way. They make a big fuss about other churches not having the right approach." Eddie made air quotes when he pronounced the word *right*. "Probably some of it is just trying to one-up the competition."

"Well, my Bible knowledge *could* use some expansion," Evan said.

Eddie looked at his neighbor in the dark, hopeful he had sparked some interest in him. "You're welcome. Now, I've got someone more receptive to see."

Evan watched as Eddie strolled to the end of the street to talk with Paulie, the man Eddie had put in a chokehold for his foul language. In his usual position on the front steps, Paulie wore a winter coat over a hoodie and oversized sweatpants. In spite of the wool cap covering his bald head, Paulie's neck tattoo remained visible to anyone talking with him.

"How's it going?" Eddie asked.

Paulie eyed him warily and said, "All right."

"What're you doing tomorrow morning at around seven?"

"Watching the kids."

"Take them over to my house and my wife will watch them. I'd like you to come with me to a men's breakfast."

"Some sort of church thing?"

"Yeah, but you'll like it—just men, talking about men things."

"I don't know."

"C'mon. No money needed, free breakfast, check it out with me."

Paulie shrugged and looked away.

"I'll take that as a yes and I'll see you tomorrow. Just try it this once. No need to go again," Eddie walked back down the block to his own house. He smiled the entire way.

#####

ANNA RAMIREZ and the household gathered around the table for a chicken dinner. In the next room, the television was tuned to the national news. Toward the end of the newscast, a woman with scratches and bite marks covering her face and arms came on.

The news anchor intoned, "In tonight's human-interest segment, we're going to hear about a rare California otter attack that occurred yesterday in Santa Barbara. A woman and her son are lucky to be here to tell the story."

Everyone at the table perked up and stared at the television.

The woman, apparently the mother, spoke into the microphone. "The otter just went berserk, and out of nowhere it started attacking my son, biting him all over."

She cried. "Thankfully I was able to pull the otter off him and we got him to the ER. The otter went after me, too, and cut me up. We had no idea they were so fierce."

Willie was absolutely delighted with this news story. He looked at Genny, who was not. He asserted, "Otters are psycho killers!"

Genny protested. "But they said it was rare. And, besides, that's a sea otter. I'm making a river otter."

"Doesn't matter," Willie insisted. "All otters should be killed! They all deserve to die. We need to feed them more plastic bags."

Anna warned her son. "Willie..."

He took his fork and pounded it repeatedly on the table. "All otters must die! All otters must die! All otters must die!"

"Willie, that's enough," Anna said.

Willie stopped, but then mouthed the words to Genny, "Otters must die."

"Mom, he's still saying it."

"Willie, up to your room," Anna said. Not wanting Genny's sensitivities to be met with amusement, she gave a dirty look to Gina, who was struggling not to laugh.

"Good," Willie said, apparently unfazed by his mother's discipline. "See ya."

Willie sat up on his bed and sent Genny a text message: "Otters must die"

WEDNESDAY, JANUARY 30, 2013

EDDIE RAMIREZ heard the knock a few minutes before seven. He opened the door to find Paulie with three of his four kids in tow. The fourth was already off to school to take part in the breakfast program. Eddie guessed that the two youngest children were from Paulie and his girlfriend Tenisha, while the third was probably from Paulie and another woman, and the oldest was likely Tenisha's with another man.

"Good morning. Come on in, everyone." Eddie waved the crew inside.

Isabella was in the living room holding Sofia, who looked dubiously at her potential new playmates. Isabella smiled at the children and asked, "Who do we have here?"

Paulie replied, "This is Danny. He's four. Ray-Ray is two, and Kiara just turned one. Destiny is in school." Isabella ushered them all into the living room, taking Kiara in her other arm. Ray-Ray, crawling behind, headed toward the pile of stuffed animals.

Eddie and Paulie drove the few blocks to Church of the Living Water. A half dozen cars were in the parking lot and the two men went down to the fellowship hall in the basement.

Folding chairs surrounded two long plastic tables, and fifteen men were gathered around, their voices a low rumble.

"Eddie! Good to see you." Johnny Ramos playfully punched his son-in-law on his arm.

"Hey there." Eddie introduced his neighbor. "This is Paulie."

Johnny shook Paulie's hand and put his other hand on his shoulder. "Paulie, great to have you here. Take a plate and fill up. The wives put the breakfast together. It's delicious."

The warming trays were filled with scrambled eggs, bacon, toast, and potatoes with onions and red peppers. Paulie stood behind Eddie in line and followed his lead on how much to take from each tray.

The men came from various backgrounds. All worked and were members of Church of the Living Water. The other element they had in common was a damaged relationship with their fathers. Most had had absent fathers while growing up—fathers who drifted and knew little of what it meant to be a parent or stable adult. Some around the tables had been incarcerated, many had experiences with drug addiction, and most had problems with anger and violence.

Their conversation focused on football, both the Pro Bowl of the previous Sunday, as well as prognostications about the upcoming Super Bowl.

Johnny finished eating and introduced the morning's speaker. "Most all of you know Kevin Washington. He came to Church of the Living Water about five years ago. He was stepping away from the edge, desperately wanting to leave the drugged up life. He had heard about some of our programs and decided to walk in the door. That's one of the toughest things—to just enter into the door—you know, because '*enter by the narrow gate; for wide is the gate and broad is the way that leads to destruction.*' Kevin here entered the narrow gate!"

The men all nodded and said *Amen*—except for Paulie, whose blank expression had not changed.

"Kevin took some baby steps, but he showed up, he was faithful. He went back to the drug life a couple of times, but they were just brief visits. Three years ago he gave himself over to the Lord." Johnny smiled and clapped.

"Amen!" the other men responded.

"Let's give Kevin some love," Johnny said. The men all clapped and hollered for their friend.

Kevin started, "Thank you, Pastor. I'm so grateful for Pastor Johnny. He helped me see my purpose. Everyone here has a purpose. I was dead to the world for too many years, was going down all the wrong paths—sold drugs, did drugs, slept in cars, treated women liked trash. I wanted drugs more than I wanted anything, and basically I was hoping I would die. But I kept living, if you could call it that."

Several heads nodded in recognition.

"But when I entered the door here I learned that I was created by God for a purpose, and that purpose was not to use or sell drugs! My purpose is to glorify God through my work and relationships. I've been working at Deacon Rob's construction company, praise God."

Head Deacon Rob Handel gave Kevin a wave of acknowledgement.

Kevin continued, "My language has completely changed. I used to be able to put together the longest string of curses you've ever heard and I could even make it rhyme!"

A few men laughed.

"And, let me tell you about relationships. I was a user of women. I used them and I set them against each other. I was with three or four at a time. It was all about how many women I had, and never about a real relationship. God forgave me, and I'm now married to a godly woman, Laila."

"Amen!" Johnny shouted. He loved weddings.

"The other relationships were tough. My dad was in and out of my life, in and out. One time, Dad stole all my cash and took my phone. One of his drug buddies told me that my dad was telling everyone that I was a punk and a loser, going nowhere." Kevin's voice broke.

"It's all right," Johnny said. "It's all right."

Eddie looked at Paulie, who was looking at the floor. Eddie knew the tactic—avoid getting too caught up in the emotion of the moment.

Kevin pulled himself together. "I put my fist through a few glass doors and stole a bunch of stuff from houses around town. Of course I got arrested and was in jail for a while, and I'm still paying off the fines. And now my dad wants in my life again. And you know what? If I didn't know the Lord, I would just blow him off. I would say, 'You had your chance, Dad.'" Kevin paused and took a deep breath. "But I now know that a bigger man says, 'I forgive you' not seven times but seventy times seven times. Dad may never be there for me or my family, but that's okay. Because *I'm* there for me and my family."

"Amen!" the men replied.

"Most of all, the Lord is there for me and my family." Kevin concluded his talk to a standing ovation.

Johnny gave Kevin a bear hug, then draped an arm around him and prayed. "Lord God, thank You for my brother Kevin. Thank You for Kevin's burdens by which he came to You. In Your Word, through Your prophet Isaiah we learn that '*with His stripes we are healed.*' In the precious blood of Jesus, we are made new. May all the men gathered here this morning be Your shining light to the world. May we glorify You, our Father and Lord. Amen."

#####

GINA GONZALEZ facilitated an intake while Director of Social Services/Admissions Sharon Chapel attended an off-site meeting. Poised and professional, Gina wore a black suit, collared purple shirt, and small, gold hoop earrings. Trying to ease the palpable anxiety in the room, Gina's brown eyes exuded warmth and her understated makeup aided in her approachability.

She sat with the daughter, son-in-law, and mother in the brightest room in the building. In the file Gina read that the daughter had made initial contact without the knowledge of her mother. She had been informed that no one could be placed in the facility without consent, unless the person was totally incompetent or incapacitated.

"We already have the basic information for Mrs. Burke, as well as the insurance information. Now we need to ask some questions that may seem personal, but we need to have them on file to better serve your family."

Looking quite frail and tiny in her wheelchair, Mrs. Vivian Burke nodded resignedly. Her daughter had tears in her eyes, while the son-in-law looked relieved.

"Mrs. Burke, is there a person in your family with medical and financial powers of attorney for you?" Gina asked.

"Yes, my daughter Tammy."

Gina affirmed the family. "So you've had the discussion about extraordinary measures. Good. That is a difficult conversation to have, but so important."

"Yes, Tammy knows that I don't want things carried on and on at the end."

"You have a living will and funeral and burial arrangements have been made?"

Vivian nodded and said, "Yes."

"Are there other family members that will be visiting regularly?" Gina asked.

Tammy spoke up. "My mother's sister will probably come by, but my two brothers live on the west coast so they will not be regulars."

"Okay. Now, just a general medical history of what brought you to this point."

Tammy continued, "Mother had a fall in her house, and that is really what started everything. We did home health care and then we had her move into our place, but it quickly got to the point where we realized that twenty-four-hour care would be necessary." A tear started down her cheek.

"It's all pretty overwhelming, isn't it?" Gina asked. Tammy nodded in agreement. Gina turned back to Vivian. "Mrs. Burke, we do have an opening on the second floor with a lovely lady named Mrs. Marjorie Wagner. I think you two will get along nicely. Why don't we all go and take a look at Room 208?"

RICHARD MOYER set up the table and chairs for the Wednesday Night Adult Bible Study in the Faith UCC meeting room. Then he arranged the fellowship hall for a Fundraising Committee meeting. His movements were more deliberate than they were twenty years prior, but he was still able to manage the basics of being a church sexton.

The church had tried to establish a stipend for him, but Richard insisted on performing his duties as a volunteer. He thought people should do these kinds of things for the church for free, but it seemed that nowadays everyone wanted something in return for doing just the basics. Richard often wondered, *Didn't anyone listen in Sunday School, that the reason to give is not to get back, but to honor God? Why couldn't people just give and then shut their mouths? Just do the work and don't expect anything. That's how it should be.*

ABIGAIL BARRETT-THOMPSON quickly scanned her Facebook account prior to her evening's meeting and class.

At the top of her news feed, Johnny Ramos had posted a Bible quotation an hour earlier that now had over fifty likes. She read in silence. *Philippians 4:13, King James Version. I can do all things through Christ which strengtheneth me.*

She then glanced at her own Facebook announcement about tonight's Bible study. Since posting it the day before, just one person had liked it. *Careful of the sin of comparison*, she reminded herself.

Abigail wore black to the office every day, having once heard that wearing black took the focus off her and put it on the person she was serving. She had over a dozen black long-sleeved shirts and numerous pairs of black pants and skirts. The only color she permitted herself was an occasional necklace or pair of earrings, gifts from Ted.

A young couple arrived at her office. Jacob Walker and Corinne Lake looked like teenagers, but were in their mid-twenties. Both were thin, wore small, round glasses and dressed similarly in jeans and sweaters. Abigail shook their hands and directed them to two vacant chairs.

"Tell me again how you heard about Faith UCC?" Abigail asked.

Corinne responded, "You were part of a panel at our college on religion and sexuality."

"Oh. I'm glad you thought of the church. If I remember correctly, there was a local rabbi, myself, and a very conservative evangelical pastor. I recall a bit of rancor over premarital abstinence pledges."

"Yes, that's it," Jacob said.

"You have filled out the form, and this evening is my opportunity to learn more about you and talk with you a little about the wedding ceremony. Tell me, how did you meet?"

"At college. We were in, like, three classes together our freshman year. We found that we connected over a lot of different things," Corinne said.

"What kind of things?" Abigail asked.

"The environment, movies, humor," Jacob replied.

"We're both foodies," Corinne offered.

"Black and white photography," Jacob mentioned.

"Harry Potter," Corinne said.

"Random local bands," Jacob added.

"Irony, hyperbole, satire, with just a soupçon of cynicism," Corinne grinned at Jacob as she spoke.

Then, together, "Obama, except for the targeted assassinations."

Abigail inserted herself back into the conversation, noting, "Shared things are great in a relationship. You'll never grow tired of laughing with each other and working together for a better and more sustainable world. Being open to differences is also important. In your marriage, you'll both still want to maintain your individuality. Now, what are some of your major differences?"

"Wow. I've never thought of that," Corinne said. She angled her head to the side, trying to think of an example.

"We're so compatible on a lot of different levels. Maybe our biggest difference is our backgrounds. Corinne comes from a large family, where I'm an only child."

They worked through several more differences, and then Abigail asked them the question that sometimes led her to refer a couple elsewhere. "Is there any particular reason you'd like a Christian pastor to officiate your wedding?"

"We thought you were a liberal," Corinne said.

"I'm more progressive in theology than many pastors, I'll give you that. But the service I provide is normally a Christian service. Are either of you currently attending church services anywhere?"

They swallowed before responding. "No."

"You may find you desire a neutral type of service like those performed in a hotel or a park. If that's the case, you can do that through the services of a justice of the peace. They could provide a nonreligious service."

"Oh," Corinne said, and she looked at Jacob. "The plan was to be married in a church. The Catholic church I grew up in required us to go to all sorts of classes, and we didn't want to do that. You just require the two meetings. But my parents wanted us to get married in a church. And, so, *this* church is kind of the compromise site. Jacob is from a pretty conservative Bible Fellowship background and this church seemed like a good combination for us."

"It will be an honor for me to officiate," Abigail said, "but you will need to select things like scripture readings and prayers and rituals." She handed them each a packet. "This is your homework. There are directions in the packet—things like 'select at least one scripture reading from three categories.' Bring it back in one month with your preferences and we'll plan the ceremony from there. And, you may decide that you don't want a Christian wedding after all. That's okay. But it is important that you seriously discuss it. We'll keep a spot reserved for you on the calendar. It was great to meet you both. Enjoy the homework."

Abigail said goodbye to the young couple at the front door and then hurried to the meeting room to begin Bible Study.

Five adults were gathered around. Abigail opened with prayer and started, "We're in Third Isaiah tonight. Let's review the three Isaiahs. Many Biblical scholars agree that Isaiah is actually the compilation of at least three authors. First Isaiah is chapters one to thirty-nine. Second Isaiah is chapters forty to fifty-five and third Isaiah, which we start tonight, is chapters fifty-six to sixty-six."

THURSDAY, JANUARY 31, 2013

ANNA RAMIREZ drove into work hoping her day at the post office would be steady—not super busy, not super slow, but nice and steady. She focused on ways to release the unease of those around her. Too many coworkers and customers were anxious, acting as though they had limited time, and if they didn't hurry up and finish the task at hand, somehow the world would fall apart. Anna wasn't slow. In fact, every so often, the supervisor timed all the clerks, so Anna knew she was efficient. But she detested being rushed. All these impatient people acting like they've got to go perform brain surgery in the next fifteen minutes. Brain surgeons probably don't even come to the post office. They send their minions. So there's sometimes a long line at the post office. So what? It gave people time to check out what other people were wearing, daydream a little, or ignore everyone and just text on their phone. Whatever needed to get done would get taken care of in due time—no need to worry so much. Genny understood this concept, though Willie got a little frustrated if things didn't come to him right away. But, Anna knew full well that her son was actually better than most kids his age.

#####

EVAN LEMMON MOORE picked up his fifth call of the day.

"I can't get into my BlackBox Live account," the young man on the other end said. He sounded like a teenager, and Evan wondered if he was skipping school that day. He'd know his birth date soon enough.

"Let's get it going again. What's your name?"

"Lonnie Edwards."

"Okay, just a moment here." Evan scanned his large screen. He saw two Lonnie Edwards listed, one in Paducah, Kentucky, and one in Hastings, Minnesota. "And your home address to verify?"

"3377 Lafayette Avenue, Paducah."

"Great. Thank you." Evan saw a birth year of 1991. So the guy was twenty-two, but just had a really young-sounding voice. "What seems to be the problem?"

"It says my username or password is incorrect, but to remember it, I texted it to myself," Lonnie said.

"Okay. Let's start with the username. What do you have?"

"Lonman22000."

"Yes, Lonman22000, that's what we have here. And remember that your password is case-sensitive."

"Huh?"

"If you used capital letters to set up your password, you need to use capital letters every time you sign in."

"Oh, man. Okay," he said and hung up.

As Evan waited for the next call he checked his cell phone to see if there were any new messages in his email or text inboxes. He couldn't use his computer while the BlackBox system was on, as it recorded every keystroke and every moment he was at work. Just as he confirmed he'd received no new messages on his cell phone, his next call buzzed in. "Thank you for calling BlackBox support."

"Yeah, hey, I can't play Summerall Football."

"Let's figure out what's going on with it. First off, what's your name?"

"Ronald Morris." Evan's screen lit up with forty-six other customers with the same name.

"And an address for verification?"

"8341 Fourth Street in Boston."

"Okay. Number one, have you tried turning off your BlackBox and turning it on again?"

"Um, no."

"Give it a try. Shut down the whole system and we'll start over."

"Okay, it's shutting down now. Man, I love this game! I'm a total addict."

Evan agreed. "It's a good one. Do you stick to football or have you tried any of the golf games?"

"Football's my thing. I'm a maniac on this game!"

"Glad you like it. Okay, is it on again?" Evan asked.

"Yep."

"Now log in and we'll go from there." Evan sipped his chai.

#####

TED THOMPSON arrived at his second school of the day and taught a recalcitrant third-grade class how to make sock penguins.

"I sense some restlessness in the room today, but that may be cured with our penguin project. Has anyone in the class ever seen a penguin?"

"*Happy Feet*," some of the students said together.

"Right. There was the delightful cinematic romp of *Happy Feet*, and then there was the follow-up *Happy Feet Two*, and another penguin movie *Surf's Up*, and there were penguins in *Madagascar*. That's a lot of penguins. Has anyone ever been to a zoo?"

A few hands went up.

"Often, you'll be able to see penguins at the zoo. To celebrate penguins and the winter weather, we are going to construct this bird today. So, I've given everyone a sock." Ted lifted a white tube sock. "Lift up your sock."

The children lifted their socks in the air.

After thirty minutes, most of the socks had taken on the form of penguins. As the soundtrack to *Happy Feet* played in the background, Ted offered hands-on help to the students who straggled, assisting with beak attachment and feet placement.

After the third graders departed for their next class, Ted quickly set up for the fourth graders, setting out mask-making materials.

Soon the fourth graders filed in. Ted welcomed the class, "Greetings, artists! There are Picassos in this classroom today. There are Goyas and Gauguins and Monets and Basquiats and Harings. There are Maya Lins and Kara Walkers here today."

Once the students were seated, Ted announced the assignment. "Today is a mask-making day."

He continued animatedly, "We are going to make a Biombo mask. Repeat that after me. *Biombo*."

"Biombo," said most of the class, while one joker said, "Bee-bee-bomb-bo-bo-bo."

"We have a comedian here today, I see. We'll find out soon enough who that is. In the meantime, let's look at the world map. The Biombo people are from what is today called the Democratic Republic of Congo, right here in the middle of Africa. Let's get started." The students got busy compiling their supplies and Ted turned on his portable stereo to forty-five minutes of African chants.

#####

EDDIE RAMIREZ focused on his weekly Thursday afternoon meeting with the lieutenant who oversaw his department. Lieutenant Ken Orr was just a few years away from retirement. He maintained strict boundaries in his work and never interfered in the efforts of his supervisees, letting them succeed or fail on their own terms. The lieutenant was very formal in his dealings with Eddie.

"Sergeant, we'll start as usual with incident reports. How is the compliance with your crew?"

"Over the past month, we've achieved a higher percentage of complete reports."

"Excellent. A solid start to the new year. Any trends you've been able to see?" Ken asked.

"More heroin-related overdoses in the past month. Some of the really pure stuff has entered the Allentown market, and it's lethal."

"We'll need to keep on top of it. What's the status of the evidence room?"

Eddie shook his head. "It's still not up to par. Too many things still not labeled or identified properly, definitely *not* a twenty-first-century room. But I've got one of the most organized women in the department working on it. She predicts it will be finished early spring."

"Good. We can't have that room be a mess. Too many cold cases come up in the news too often, and it looks bad for us if it's not in tip-top shape. How is the procedure change going with dispatch?"

"They made a big deal about it, but they're adjusting. The shift changes are smoother now with the new procedures."

"Let's go over the trainings that have been completed by patrol."

"Sure." Eddie pulled out the list and handed a copy to Lieutenant Orr.

Following the meeting, Eddie walked down a long hallway and briefly imagined what it would be like to have Ken Orr as his father. His mind suddenly flipped to memories of his own father. Eddie started to sweat. He entered the closest men's room and went straight into the stall, closing and locking the door behind him. He sat on the toilet and used toilet paper to wipe the drips from his forehead.

Eddie remembered the time he was seven and had to sit perfectly still next to his mother on the couch. His father was perched on a chair across from them. He called the exercise "time to learn who is in charge around here." When Eddie flinched in the slightest, his father pounced on his mother, slapping or punching her and calling her "whore" with every blow.

Or, when Eddie's mother moved, even to take a breath, his father laid into him with fists, calling him a "bad boy." Eddie's father had been abusive before, but never like this. Neither dared fight back. They were too afraid it might incite him more. After an hour of the vile game, his father left the house saying he had to get some food because his mother only cooked "garbage."

After waiting ten minutes, Eddie and his mother rushed to a clinic where they were both found to have broken ribs. They never lived with his father again and stayed with family members until his mother had saved up enough money to get an apartment. His father tried to break in on one occasion, but there were multiple locks on the door and they had piled furniture in the entryway to keep him from entering. He soon found other women to terrorize and left them alone.

Bent over with his hand supporting his hanging head, Eddie remembered what his father-in-law Johnny had told him. "We don't write our story—God does. Stop trying to write your own story. Stop writing your history. Let God take over, and then your story becomes eternal."

Eddie stretched out his neck, looked up at the ceiling, and said, "Thank you, God, that I'm not him. I'm not him. I'm not him."

#####

ANNA RAMIREZ served on the front counter fifteen minutes until closing. A line of a dozen people waited for one of the three clerks. A tall, bulky man, displeased with the speed with which the line was moving, let everyone know in a loud, raspy voice. "So much for service. Geez, no wonder people are doing all this online. There'll be no post office in another decade."

The other customers ignored his comments, and most pretended to be involved on their cell phones.

The man was unaware that the clerks received frequent instruction on dealing with difficult customers, and they were trained to handle just about any situation, though no postal employee enjoyed serving mad, loud, drunk, stoned, or harassing customers. The three clerks all heard the man, but, in spite of their training, hoped he would not end up at their station.

Anna served annoyed customers on a daily basis and dealt with an exceedingly irritated person about once a month. To defuse the more extreme situations, she thought of irate male customers as Mr. *Grumpy Pants* and angry women as Mrs. *Poo Poo Platter*. Having a nickname go through her mind helped her decompress about the overall situation later on in the break room.

In a derisive tone, Mr. Grumpy Pants continued. "Being here is like being at the downtown grocery stores—long lines all the time. There's no wait in the offices outside the city."

Anna noticed that a few people in line turned around and gave him aggravated looks, but it only emboldened Mr. Grumpy Pants more.

"You know these clerks get paid an average of fifty-three thousand dollars a year? Can you believe it? What a sweet paycheck for eight hours a day shuffling paper. And overtime also, whoa. We should all work for the United States Postal Service."

Several of the people standing behind Mr. Grumpy Pants rolled their eyes and Anna knew that victory was ensured because the crowd was on the side of the underdogs, the much-maligned-but-still-standing postal workers. Still, she did not want to serve Mr. Grumpy Pants, though the timing was looking like he would end up at her station.

Mr. Grumpy Pants continued. "Let's not forget that the Post Office loves diversity," he said, accentuating every syllable of the word. "*Die-verse-it-tee*" he said slowly, hoping to cause maximum discomfort.

Anna said, "Next in line, please." Mr. Grumpy Pants approached her counter. She saw the shoulders of the other clerks slump ever so slightly in relief that they didn't have to deal with him one-on-one. Nevertheless, her coworkers continued to be on high alert, taking care of customers, but also listening and ready to step in if this man gave Anna any problems.

"How may I help you today, sir?" Anna kept her voice steady, and even infused a bit of boredom into it, a skill she employed with the most riled up customers. The more agitated they became, the more her voice took on tones of distinct disinterest.

"These need to be mailed today." Mr. Grumpy Pants dumped a stack of envelopes on the counter.

"Right." Anna weighed each of the fifteen envelopes, announcing the price of each one calmly and slowly. "That will be thirty-three seventy-five altogether."

"Prices are always going up," the man complained as he put two twenty-dollar bills on the counter rather than hand them directly to Anna.

"Six dollars and twenty-five cents is your change. Have a good day." Anna handed over the quarter and bills. "Next in line, please."

After the man exited the building and the door closed behind him, the remaining customers gave Anna a round of applause, while the two other clerks beamed in her direction. She smiled in acknowledgment, and focused on the woman in front of her. "How may I help you today, ma'am?"

#####

ISABELLA RAMIREZ perched on a chair at the small kitchen table across from her mother Anita. Her daughter Sofia was playing in the front room and her father was at a meeting next door at the church.

Anita enjoyed constantly complimenting her children. With a hand on Isabella's cheek, she said, "I have such a beautiful daughter. I'm so blessed! Look at your ravishing hair and your great shape. With such a good heart and a beautiful daughter of your own!"

"Thanks, Mom. I get it from you."

"You're kind to me—so good to your mother. What can I give back to you, my daughter?"

"I need some more ideas for my Moms Group. I've looked all over Pinterest and need something new," Isabella said.

Anita replied, "Yes. You want to keep things fresh and keep the moms coming back. Probably a lot of them are tired and need a little pampering."

"I thought about a spa day, but they are pricey."

"How about a mini-spa day, just nails?" Anita suggested.

"Ooh, yes. We could do that."

"Have you had a Prayer Day yet?" Anita asked.

"No. What do you mean?"

"Lead a morning of prayer for husbands and then have lunch together. If that goes well, then the next week have a prayer morning for families."

"Yes, we could do that." Isabella was thoughtful for a moment. "I didn't think it would be so hard to keep coming up with ideas for the group."

"You might want to put together a program committee. They could help you with planning out activities," Anita advised.

"That's a good idea, Mom. Thanks."

"You're welcome, dear."

"You know, I still haven't heard back from Rashida. I've texted, emailed, and phoned her. I don't get it."

"Every group has members that commit for a while and then drop out. Remember the scripture passage about the seeds landing on the path, the rocky ground, and in the thorns? Those seeds did not grow. Only the seed in the good soil grows. What matters is that you have tried and reached out to her."

"I don't understand why people fall away." Isabella sounded discouraged.

"It happens, and one day it will all make sense. Jesus says, *'There is nothing covered, that shall not be revealed.'*"

INBOX

WEDNESDAY, FEBRUARY 27, 2013

RICHARD MOYER and General Ridgway returned from their morning walk and sat in matching armchairs. Daily, Richard read every section of the local Allentown newspaper: national, international, local, opinion, sports, and even the life section, which he read mostly for the comics.

#####

JOHNNY RAMOS tapped through the emails on his cell phone.

Subject: Your Daily Verse
From: YDV@YourDailyVerse.org
Date: Wed, Feb 27, 2013 4:30 am
To: PastorJohnny@ChurchoftheLivingWater.org

Daily Bible Verse – Wednesday, February 27, 2013
For the wages of sin is death; but the gift of God is eternal life through Jesus Christ our Lord.
Romans 6:23
King James Version

"Amen," Johnny said, and forwarded the message to his son Javi to post on Facebook.

#####

GINA GONZALEZ arrived early at Elm Pond County Nursing Home. Before plunging into her tasks, she scrolled through her Facebook news feed on her cell phone to catch up on the latest updates from her friends. A posting from Daisy Escobedo caught her attention. Daisy was in an on-again-off-again relationship with a player named Randi, who was a little punk. Randi had a tendency to start arguments about ridiculous issues, like parking spots at Rubies Restaurant & Bar. Gina knew just how to stir the pot a little with just a few words.

"So tired of ppl talking behind my back, making up stuff"

Gina commented, "I know just what u mean! When ppl talk behind ur back, they're just jealous, ya know?"

Within seconds, Daisy liked Gina's comment and replied,

"Yes, Gina!!! They r totes jealous!!!"

Gina liked Daisy's comment and wrote, "And they r also bored, but u have better things 2 do like go out with normal ppl"

Again, Daisy liked her comment and wrote below it:

"Yes!! Let's meet up soon, girlfriend!!!"

#####

EVAN LEMMON MOORE looked through his personal email messages fifteen minutes before the start of his shift.

Subject: Hello from IL
From: Mary.Moore@aol.com
Date: Wed, Feb 27, 2013 7:17 am
To: Evan.Lemmon.Moore@gmail.com

Dear Evan,

Greetings from IL, as always, very chilly here, hope it's a bit more temperate for you in northeast PA.

The public library expansion is almost completed and your Dad and I will be attending the grand opening this coming weekend. There will be wine and cheese and we will get to tour the new facility, really looking forward to it.

The Memorial High boys and girls basketball teams are going gangbusters, they may make it to state again this year.

Dad's term on the Church Council ended last month and I just started my term this month. A lot of changes in the ELCA, but St. Luke's is going to stick with the denomination, thank goodness. Change and progress are good things, it brings a breath of fresh air.

Love,
Mom

ABIGAIL BARRETT-THOMPSON responded to her email messages at a brisk pace, determined to clear her inbox so she could focus on other tasks. She avoided opening a message from Gordon Vanderlinden until last, guessing it would be a response to her sermon. Abigail and Gordon went back and forth on email about once a week, disagreeing politely on most issues.

Subject: Sunday's Talk
From: GordonVanderlinden@aol.com
Date: Wed, Feb 27, 2013 8:08 am
To: Rev.Barrett-Thompson@FaithUCC.org

Abigail,

Hope you're keeping warm in that drafty place.

Have to disagree with your comments on public school funding that you shared this past Sunday. Like everyone else, the schools can certainly do some belt-tightening. There was no need for any of these extras when I was going through the Allentown Consolidated School District, now it's all gimmee gimmee gimmee. As you know, I live across the street from the middle school and these teachers drive nice cars, they're not hurting at all. Summers off, a nice income and a sizable pension, we should all be so lucky.

See you on Sunday.

In Christ,
Gordon

Abigail would let Gordon know that he was heard and at the same time reiterate the need for more funding for a changing school system.

EDDIE RAMIREZ read all his departmental email carefully. The department now communicated many important procedures and policies via email. It was tough to keep on top of it all, but a senior officer once advised Eddie to "read every bit of every thing" if he wanted to advance in the department, because "the one in the know is the one who will be promoted."

TED THOMPSON clicked on a message from the Allentown Art Museum Development Office.

Subject: Support Your Local Museum
From: Development@AArt.org
Date: Wed, Feb 27, 2013 10:20 am
To: Mad.Monet@gmail.com

Dear Mad,

Support your local Art Museum by becoming a sustaining donor today.
For just $5,000 a year...
Ted laughed and clicked *Delete. Abigail and I will stick with a basic membership and let the more moneyed people of the area be the big dogs. We're puppies in the donation game—teeny, tiny puppies.*

#####

ALAN PECK spotted an email message from Faith UCC Consistory President Tim Thacker among the dozens of work emails he had received that morning. Tim had been the head of the church leadership group for over four years. Alan had served a term as president and was now a member-at-large. He used his Vigor email address even for personal communications because it could potentially result in another Vigor customer.

Subject: Thanks for the reference
From: TimThacker@yahoo.com
Date: Wed, Feb 27, 2013 11:47 am
To: Alan.Peck@Vigor.com

Alan,
A quick note to thank you for the reference to Cedar Beach. Helen and I worshiped there this past Sunday and really enjoyed it. With Faith Church's finances continuing their slide, it's time to make other plans.
Let's keep in communication.

Best,
Tim

Alan quickly replied to Tim's email.
No problem, glad it went well. Yes, let's keep in communication.

#####

ISABELLA RAMIREZ finished feeding Sofia a snack and set up the Veggie Tales DVD. While Sofia watched, Isabella checked her Twitter account. She followed 187 people and organizations—groups such as Christian Moms Everyday, Christian Mommies Online, 21st Century Christian Parenting, and Christian Wives.

She had seventy-seven followers, and was hoping to grow that number. For now, though, she felt more sure of herself on Facebook than on Twitter. Until she understood the rhythms of Twitter, Isabella stuck to re-tweeting.

Christian Moms Everyday @ChristME Feb 1
Raising Christ-centered children

Isabella clicked on the link and read the short blog item on the topic and thought it was a good article.

Retweeted by Isabella Ramirez
Christian Moms Everyday @ChristME Feb 1
Raising Christ-centered children

#####

ANNA RAMIREZ crashed on a plastic chair during her fifteen-minute afternoon break. She looked through her personal email messages, and clicked to open one from a company selling scarves.

Subject: Winter Sale!
From: Info@ScarvesGalore.com
Date: Wed, Feb 27, 2013 1:48 pm
To: Anna18102@yahoo.com

Anna,
    The Scarves Galore Winter Sale has arrived. Click on this link for gorgeous scarves at close-out prices: www.scarvesgalors.com/closeoutsale

Anna clicked and looked through the images, pausing to get a closer look at a bright blue scarf with whimsical white polka dots. *It looks a little young but I think it will work.* Anna clicked on the photo to order the scarf. Her credit card information was already stored on the Scarves Galore website, so all she had to do was click *Okay* to make her purchase.

#####

WILLIE RAMIREZ subscribed to the Best Sports Network daily digest for football and basketball. He read through the alerts on his phone every day after school.

BSN NFL ALERT: Super Bowl injury report
BSN NFL ALERT: Super Bowl predictions
BSN NFL ALERT: Come-Back City: New Orleans to be Super Bowl Host
BSN NFL ALERT: Super Bowl Quarterback Showdown
BSN NFL ALERT: Make Your Super Bowl Pick
BSN NBA ALERT: Best Defensive Players in the League
BSN NBA ALERT: LeBron's Supporting Cast

Willie clicked first on the Super Bowl Quarterback Showdown.

#####

CONSUELA GONZALEZ received her weekly Spanish-language newspaper in the mail that afternoon. *El Mensajero* covered events similar to the major Allentown daily newspaper, but from a different perspective. Consuela read every word of every page, even the classified ads.

#####

GENNY RAMIREZ stretched out on the couch in the front room of her grandmother's house, about to go up to bed. Before turning her cell phone over to her mom for the night, she exchanged text messages with her father.

"Good night dad"

"Good night, little lady. Sleep tight, no let bed bugs bite"
"Lol"
"Love u"
"Love u"

SPRING 2013

Richard Moyer walked General Ridgway on their usual route. As they passed the old battery factory, he remembered the newspaper article that mentioned construction bids were being taken for a strip mall at this location. *We'll see how quickly this all happens. First there's a heckuvalot of demolition.*

As they ambled through Jordan Park, Richard noticed another dog walker, but did not pay much attention. Moments later, he felt something grip his leg, and looked down to see a pitbull locked to his calf. He fell to his knees and heard someone yelling something indistinct. General Ridgway barked hysterically, and the last thing Richard remembered was a fuzzy outline of someone bending over him.

#####

Eddie Ramirez knew every parking lot in the city of Allentown—the busy ones, those that were perpetually empty, the lots preferred by local drug dealers, and the ones where kids rode their bikes or people cut through.

Eddie pulled into a lot that was rarely used and retrieved his private cell phone from his locked glove compartment. No one had this particular phone number, as he used a separate cell phone for work and family, and that was the number he gave out. He kept the private phone locked up, and it was protected by passcode as well as a password. No one had asked him about this extra phone yet, but if Isabella or someone else found it, he'd explain it as something related to a confidential police investigation.

Soon enough, Eddie was on the website he visited daily to view the most hardcore porn videos he could find on the Internet. He had set up an account with a secret credit card, the billing was done online, notifications went to his covert email address, and the money was transferred from a hidden bank account. Recommended videos popped up, and Eddie clicked on a twenty-minute video. That would give him enough time to watch and still get to the station to give the six o'clock briefing to the patrol officers.

The video started off with a man and a woman in army uniforms. Soon enough the two were joined by another couple in uniform and then two more couples. Various weapons on display were used as props.

The screen lit up Eddie's face like flames from a campfire.

#####

ABIGAIL BARRETT-THOMPSON pulled the signs from her car trunk and stood in front of the Dolly's Dollar Store building. She was forty-five minutes early to the noon protest and wanted to have things well organized. They would not block the entrance to a private business, but instead assemble on a nearby public sidewalk where they had been granted a permit by the city. She leaned the signs against the car and pulled out a portable microphone system. Abigail knew how to set up for photo ops and arranged the system so that photographers would catch the Dolly's Dollar Store company name behind those who were speaking.

Four of the co-planners on the committee, Reverend Craig Johnson, Reverend Peter Smith, Reverend Eric Windham, and Reverend C.D. Alexander arrived fifteen minutes after Abigail. Each brought a few congregants from their church's social justice committees. Abigail planned to see at least four members from Faith UCC at the event. Craig made sure everyone in the crowd had a sign that said *People over Profits*.

Soon enough, reporters and photographers from two local papers had arrived, along with the local television news.

Two minutes before the planned start, a bus pulled up. *Church of the Living Water* was painted on both sides. Pastor Johnny Ramos and forty congregants stepped off the bus as the cameras clicked and filmed.

Abigail introduced the event, reading notes off her clipboard. "We are here today to launch a spiritual protest. Dolly's Dollar Store and other corporations are taking advantage of their most valuable asset—their workers. We stand here in solidarity with Dolly's workers and let them know we care. We are also here to call Dolly's to corporate accountability and demand that they offer better wages and regular scheduling. You'll hear from seven local faith leaders on this issue, but before that, you'll hear from someone who just recently crawled out from under the unreasonable demands of Dolly's Dollar Store. Come forward and tell your story, Ms. Tanya Davenport."

Tanya stepped to the microphone. She started out quietly, telling her harrowing personal story of challenging transportation issues and the struggle to acquire childcare with an erratic weekly schedule. It was clear she was a resourceful young woman as she mentioned how she cobbled together childcare from a mix of family, friends, neighbors, coworkers, and a professional childcare provider in her neighborhood. She was not receiving enough hours at Dolly's, and those hours she did receive varied, which made it impossible to find a second job. She knew she had to find another job altogether. But many of the places she applied to were also low-wage employers with similarly irregular work schedules that put employees completely at the mercy of the managers. People in the audience nodded in agreement, which upped Tanya's confidence level the more she spoke. Soon her volume increased, which led to her dramatic conclusion. "Dolly's wanted to totally own me! They always wanted me to be available when it was convenient for *them*. I'm a hard worker, and all I want in return is a fair wage and a decent schedule so I can provide for my family. Thank God I was able to get out from under Dolly's! They don't own me! I have my life back!"

After the sustained applause in response to Tanya's gripping finale, Craig, Peter, and Eric gave brief statements on the essential spiritual practice of protecting society's most vulnerable people. Next, a state representative talked about the importance of workplace protections and pending pro-worker legislation in the state capitol. A local rabbi, Sarah Berger, and imam, Feisel Ali, shared cogent statements about their faiths' respective, yet similar, stances on fair wages. Next C.D. thundered for a bit about the need for all people to stand up against economic injustice and corporate powers. Then Abigail introduced Johnny Ramos. The anticipation was electrifying.

Johnny took the microphone. He shouted into it, "Let's call this business what it is!"

His congregants said, "Yes! Uh huh! Preach it!"

Johnny turned and looked at the Dolly's Dollar Store building. "It's evil! They sell stuff we don't need and take advantage of their workers. We deserve much better than this!"

"Amen!" the crowd responded.

The cameras came in for a close-up of Johnny. He continued his shouts. "We're going to take *personal* responsibility and build up our people and educate our people so we do not shop at this place that's stuffed with things that do not satisfy. Our treasure is in heaven! We'll take our business elsewhere. We will not work at Dolly's. We'll look elsewhere. What this city needs is fewer dollar stores and more prayer! What we need is a holy-ghost revival! Church of the Living Water is going to lead the city to a restoration!"

Johnny drifted more and more off message for fifteen minutes. Abigail checked her watch, then looked at the Baptist choir and nodded. She came into Johnny's line of vision, put a hand on his back, and said, "Thank you."

Johnny said, "My time's up. They're taking away the mic. You all know how I can talk!"

The choir gave its rendition of "We Shall Overcome." Abigail reminded the crowd to sign the letter of protest, then thanked everyone for giving of their time.

Abigail reloaded the signs into her car trunk and, just before turning the key in the ignition, checked her cell phone. She saw two voicemail indicators and a number of text messages from Faith Church's care team. They were all about Richard Moyer, who was in the Emergency Room.

#####

RICHARD MOYER lay in his hospital bed and choked back tears as he looked at his friend Robert Schultz. Although he dreaded the answer, he knew he had to ask the question.

"General Ridgway didn't make it, did he, Schultzie?"

"Sorry, Richie. General was chewed up pretty bad."

"Look at me—all broken up over a dog."

"General was a good one."

They talked baseball for a while until they heard a soft knock at the door. Abigail poked her head in. "Richard?"

"In here, Abigail. Word got back to you, huh?"

"Yes. I'm glad you're going to be okay."

"General Ridgway didn't make it," Richard said.

"I'm so sorry. We can have a proper burial of his ashes in your backyard sometime if you would like."

"Maybe."

"What did the doctors say about your leg?" Abigail asked.

"I'll be overnight here to be careful. Antibiotics for two weeks in case of infection. Don't know the dog or the owner, so I'll have to do the rabies shot."

"Has your daughter been notified?" Abigail asked.

"Nah. What can she do from Orlando? I'll tell her the next time she calls."

"How were you found?"

"Seems the guy who had the dog flagged down a driver on Sumner Avenue and said to call 911. Then he disappeared before the paramedics arrived."

Schultzie was incredulous. "Who walks away from something like that?"

"He could have been on parole or something. Too bad he's such a coward. Though, sometimes, people come forward later," Abigail mentioned.

"That neighborhood keeps going further and further down the tubes. I keep telling Richie to move out and get into a nice high rise somewhere. With his vet status, he'll get in no problem."

"You know what I think of those places, Schultzie. I've been in my house for over fifty years."

Schultzie crossed his arms. "Well, I hope they catch this criminal who ran off."

Richard waved a hand at Schultzie. "Ah, maybe they will, maybe they won't. It's always easier to forgive and forget. I found that out the hard way. But it's true—it does no good to hold on to things."

"Well put." Abigail smiled at Richard.

Schultzie winked at his friend. "When you'd get so religious, Richie? Could it be 'cause someone from the church is here?"

"Near the end, Ellie showed me a lot about how to let go of troubles," Richard said.

Abigail interjected, "Would it be all right if I did some prayer? And then we'll be sure to have you on the Prayer Chain, too."

Richard nodded. Abigail prayed for healing and lifted up gratitude for the many years of companionship General Ridgway had provided.

#####

TED THOMPSON endured an interminable after-school meeting about teacher contracts for the following school year.

In an adamant tone, one of the young teachers said, "We've got to fight this."

Ted had reached his limit. "It's not going to change anything. Welcome to education in the twenty-first century. The tide has turned. People don't care as much about public things. At this point, the best we can do is just buckle up for the next few months. When I started out as an art teacher, I was in one school. Now I cover four schools every week. Get ready for more changes ahead."

That got everyone buzzing. Just as the next round of thrashing and wailing began, Ted left the room. These meetings had become too tiresome—full of unspoken apprehension and people saying the same things over and over. What grieved Ted the most was that once the teachers and administrators started fighting, the students were usually the ones who suffered the most.

Ted drove west to Trexlertown and pulled into the parking lot of a gigantic discount store. He tried to space out his endeavors and had not been to this store for over a year. He mixed up his visits here with others to big box stores, just so their cameras would not get too familiar with him.

He took a cart and headed toward the electronics section, where he looked through the cheap DVDs. He found two— *Clueless*, which he placed in his cart, and *Forrest Gump*, which he slipped into his interior jacket pocket that was specially made for these shopping trips.

Then it was down the sock aisle—one pair of dress socks went in the cart, another in his jacket. Abigail needed scissors, so he went to the school supplies section and picked out a pair which he placed in the cart while also placing a package of erasers in his pocket. The last time he was caught shoplifting occurred over twenty-five years ago. At the time, he was a senior in college. A grocery store security guard had nabbed him and marched him by all the cashiers and customers, his hands behind his back. Ted had since perfected his skills and was exceedingly careful on his shopping adventures.

After paying for the items in his cart, he tossed the bag on the passenger seat and drove to a nearby church parking lot that he knew did not have surveillance cameras. He removed the stolen items from his jacket and placed them in a small trash bag. When he pulled into a gas station to fill up, he threw the bag of stolen items in the trash.

#####

ANNA RAMIREZ pulled up next to Eddie's house. Willie and Genny tumbled out of the car and raced up the steps to their father.

"Bye, my beautifuls."

"Bye, Mom."

Gina had a new girlfriend, so Anna was on her own tonight. She drove to the mall with a plan to replenish her makeup supplies. She loved sitting at the counter while the girls showed her new application tips. Mandy, one of her favorites, was on tonight.

"Anna, I can't wait to show you this new eye shadow."

"Let's give it a try."

Mandy looked like a model and had done a few gigs locally. Close to six feet tall, with a messy blonde bun and exquisite makeup of her own, Mandy was gifted at drawing out the best features of her clients, while keeping up a pleasing patter. She updated Anna on her boyfriend, her pets, and the goings-on of the other makeup artists.

As Mandy brushed shadow on her eyelid, Anna reminded her, "I'll need to be able to wear this working with the public."

"Oh, sure. It will be just exotic enough to draw out your Latina loveliness, but it will also be professional enough for customer service."

"Thank you."

"Oh, and there's a new blush, too."

After an hour and a half, Mandy packed up a small bag with a variety of makeup—eye shadow, mascara, lipstick, two types of foundation, blush, and brushes.

"That will be four hundred and fifty-four dollars," Mandy said, and Anna swiped her card.

Anna walked slowly back to her car. In her head, she calculated her credit card debt, which was probably around thirty-eight thousand dollars on her four cards combined. As long as she kept it under forty thousand dollars, she reasoned she would be fine.

#####

GINA GONZALEZ leaned across the table to kiss her girlfriend Jayla "Jay" Davis. They met two weeks earlier at Rubies, and quickly progressed to an exclusive relationship. While she would never confess it to anyone, Gina was smitten. Jay sported a close-cropped afro, and wore an aqua-colored tie with a purple oxford shirt and dark jeans.

Their server stopped by during the long smooch and barked, "Get a room!"

"Ha!" Gina laughed and asked, "What's good in the kitchen tonight?"

"The pasta dish is nice, as well as the chicken."

"How 'bout one of both?" Gina looked at Jay, who nodded. "Yep, we'll go with one each." The server took their menus and Gina turned back to Jay. "So, what're you up to this weekend?"

"I'm off, so I'm not planning a whole lot. We're on every-other-weekend shifts, so when I have one off I like to relax for most of it, you know?"

Gina purred. "Well, it looks like you're off to a good start." Jay smiled. "You work at Allentown General, right?"

"Mmm hmmm."

Gina threw her shoulders back and said, "I know a few people there."

"Yeah?"

"There's a nasty one named Tia, who dated that girl sitting over there at the bar. Tia thinks she's 'all that,' but keeps going out with all sorts of losers. She's ended up in screaming matches in the Rubies parking lot too many times to count. Do you happen to know her?"

"I think I know who you're talking about. She works in same-day surgery."

"Oh, and there's a paramedic who works there, Julie. Has probably slept with most of the people here in Rubies."

"Whoa. That's probably a bit too much information." Jay recoiled.

"Too much? I'm just getting started, 'cause you have to know that queen named Larry who works in the ER. He's hysterical, but don't ever get on his bad side. He'll spread ridiculous lies. He's great until you cross him then he takes out the big claws."

Jay changed the subject. "Tell me again where you work?"

"Elm Pond, the county nursing home."

"What do you do there?"

"I'm the Assistant Director of Social Services/Admissions."

"Do you like working with the older folks?"

"Most of the time, except when they get cranky. Like there's this guy named Ernie Goodwin, and he is always cussing out the staff. He has a metal plate in his head or something from the war. Whoever walks into his room, he just goes off on them. And there's Minnie Wasko—totally paranoid, thinks the CIA and FBI are after her, and she's always unplugging her phone. But most of them are very nice. Are you missing New York at all?"

"Allentown is different, that's for sure. But I like that it's quieter."

Gina smiled and took Jay's hand. "I'm so glad you moved here."

SATURDAY, APRIL 20, 2013

WILLIE RAMIREZ met Alex outside his apartment and they started down the hill to Jordan Park, each carrying a basketball. Families were already outside observing the unfolding morning. The two passed younger children on a variety of plastic bikes or wagons, while older kids looked up at Willie and Alex from porch chairs. They crossed Whitehall Street by way of the parking lot behind Faith Church, bouncing their balls on the pavement as they went. Right before crossing over busy Sumner Avenue to the park, they passed by a heating and cooling company with a watchful German Shepherd patrolling the fenced-in parking lot. Willie made a face at the dog, and they waited impatiently to dodge the cars with Alex yelling, "Too much traffic, all these lazy people driving cars. Walking is better." They ran down the sharp hill into the park and over to the basketball hoops.

"NCAAs are all over and now it's NBA till June," Willie said as he took a bank shot.

"Go LeBron and the Heat, yo!"

Willie demonstrated his skills by alternately dribbling the ball and thumping his chest.

"If we don't play in the NBA, we could be sportscasters."

"I'd do play-by-play. You'd do color commentary," Willie suggested.

"Listen to you with the lingo. We'd be great."

"Willie and Alex call the Pistons-Thunder game," Willie said, passing the ball to his friend.

"Gomez and Ramirez are on tonight's analysis. It's the showdown of the century as the Mavs seek redemption against the Knicks," Alex said in his best impression of a television voiceover.

#####

GENNY RAMIREZ slung the postal bag over her shoulder for collecting more plastic bags. To avoid seeing kids from school, she took deeper and deeper forays into Jordan Park, following paths until they ended and then making her own trails.

This morning she walked right next to Jordan Creek, curious about its twists and turns. Along the way she kept an eye out for growth with three leaves. Her science teacher cautioned her it could be poison ivy. She'd occasionally stop to pick up a rock and throw it in the water, enjoying the sound and watching the ripples. Her favorite thing to touch was moss. It was so soft, and she imagined what it would be like to fall asleep on a moss bed.

Something up ahead on the other side of Jordan Creek caught Genny's eye—maybe somebody fishing or a homeless person. As she walked farther in that direction, she saw a man lying on the bank of the creek. Her dad had instructed her to be alert with strangers in the park, to not give out any information, and to take in as many details as possible. The man faced away from her, and was wearing a black hoodie, jeans, and black sneakers.

Genny looked intently across creek and yelled "Hey," but the man didn't respond. She picked up a large rock, threw it into the creek, and yelled as loud as she could, "Hey, man, wake up!"

When there was no response, Genny pulled the cell phone out of her pocket and texted her dad: "Body by creek not moving may b dead?"

Eddie Ramirez recognized the special text tone on his phone as being from one of his kids. He read Genny's text and messaged her back immediately: "Go get your brother. Go now. Don't stay there. Do u understand?"

"Yes"

Genny turned around and walked back toward the main area of the park. Soon she was running and the postal bag bounced along with her. She knew Willie and Alex would be at the basketball hoops. Breathless, she reached them and said, "Willie! Dad told me to get you. There's a dead body up in there."

"Where?" the boys asked. "Let's go."

Willie, Genny, and Alex dashed off, but just before entering the wooded area by the creek, police cars appeared, one with Eddie at the wheel. The kids stopped and waited for the officers to reach them.

Eddie gave Genny a quick hug. "Okay. Show us where you found him."

Genny led everyone alongside the creek. The police radios crackled with continuing calls. They eventually came to the spot across the creek from the body's location. Two of the officers waded across the water. They pulled plastic gloves from their pockets and put them on before touching the body.

One of the officers picked up a syringe. "Looks like an overdose."

Eddie turned somber. He pivoted toward Genny, Willie, and Alex and told them to go home.

Genny followed Alex and Willie out of the park and back to the house where Isabella and Sofia were sitting on the front porch.

"Everyone okay?" Isabella asked. "I never see you before lunch on Saturdays."

"There was a dead body in the park," Alex said.

"Oh, no. Come inside." Isabella stood and motioned everyone in through the front door.

Genny, Willie, and Alex all sat down on the couch and watched Best Sports News without comment for two hours. At noon they sat down to a quiet lunch. After eating, they needed to talk. Isabella sent them outside so they would not upset Sofia.

"Let's go to my place," Alex said.

"Can I come?" Genny asked.

"This time you can come," Willie said as they walked toward Alex's apartment. "I've never seen anything like that. He just looked like he was sleeping."

Genny replied, "I know. That's what I thought."

"Maybe he was a gangbanger and the other gang members poisoned him, dragged his body there, and made it look like an overdose," Alex added.

"You watch too many crime shows. My dad says they make up a lot of stuff in those shows," Willie declared. He looked at his sister and could not resist the temptation to tease her. "Maybe it was a psycho killer otter!"

"Shut up!" Genny pushed him. "Drugs are stupid. Why do they have to do that in the park?"

The boys shrugged their shoulders. "Let's race," Alex said, and the three ran the last two blocks. Willie won handily, and then ran up the steps to the third floor with Alex and Genny rushing up behind him.

Alex unlocked the door and announced to his sisters who were watching TV, "We're here, and guess what? We saw a dead body."

"You didn't," Alex's oldest sister Daniela insisted.

"We did," Genny said. "It was at Jordan Park, back in the woods next to the creek."

"Yuck! Was he shot?"

"No," Willie replied. "The police said it was an overdose."

"Let's go back to the park and see what's going on," Alex said.

Willie and Genny looked at each other and said in unison, "Okay." Curiosity got the better of Alex's sisters, so they went along.

They ran most of the way back to the park, but the police had left the scene and a baseball practice started.

The group sprinted toward the playground where the equipment swarmed with children of all ages.

"We saw the dead body," Alex started. A number of kids gathered around him as he told the story. Willie and Genny provided the details.

#####

CONSUELA GONZALEZ looked perturbed as she sat in the living room with her two daughters for another discussion about her botched surgery. The three women were ready for fierce verbal combat—Anna and Gina taking one position, and Consuela another. Anna started the battle in Spanish. "Mamá, we contacted a lawyer who specializes in *negligencia médica*."

Consuela pursed her lips and said, "I asked you not to do that."

Gina pleaded, "Doctor Brooks damaged your nerves, and you can never use that hand again. We have to sue him. It is extremely clear that he was negligent."

Consuela responded, "Everyone makes *errores*. Doctor Brooks made a mistake. He apologized, and that's what is important."

Gina cried, "He's a butcher!"

Consuela shook her head. "That's not true. You always have to see the bad in everyone."

Anna crossed her arms. "We need to go to a lawyer."

Consuela crossed hers in response. "No. *Abogado*, no."

Anna blurted, "It's time to stop bowing and scraping to all these men in your life."

Gina was shocked at her sister's harsh words to their mother, and Anna knew she had lost the argument. Her first time verbalizing her mother's tendency to be overly subservient to the men in her life would likely be the last. There would be no changing her mother's deference to male authority figures.

Consuela narrowed her eyes. She looked slowly at both of her daughters, "*Lo perdono*. It's done. *Terminó*."

Anna tried one last time, "You don't want this to happen to anyone else."

"Stop. We're not going to talk about this anymore," Consuela said slowly and firmly.

Gina left the room upset and crying, while Anna and her mother sat across the coffee table from each other, saying nothing. After ten minutes of staring impassively at one another, Anna blinked first. "I just don't get it."

Triumphant, Consuela rose from her chair. "Someday you'll understand that money doesn't make everything better."

#####

ABIGAIL BARRETT-THOMPSON watched the local television news story of the Dolly's Dollar Store event the previous night and read about it in the local newspaper. Johnny Ramos headlined all of the accounts, and Church of the Living Water was the sole congregation named by the media. At least the news stories made clear the reason for the protest, so Abigail was confident more people in Allentown were now aware of Dolly's corrupt practices.

In her office readying herself for Sunday's service, she was also planning to walk over to check on Richard Moyer later in the day. He was to arrive back home this morning. Her preparations were interrupted by a commotion in the fellowship hall.

Abigail walked briskly into the hall and saw Richard Moyer limping around and setting out chairs.

"What are you doing here today? Shouldn't you be at home healing?"

"This has to get done."

"Someone else can take care of it while you rest."

He winked at her and said, "There's no rest for the wicked."

"Your situation was not quite what the prophet Isaiah was getting at when those words were written." Richard waved a dismissive hand at her, and she added, "I don't think anything I say will stop you."

"I'm fine," he said, and headed for the cupboard to retrieve the coffee pots.

"I guess if the Battle of the Chosin Reservoir didn't stop you, then a pitbull won't either," Abigail declared, recalling the night of testimony when local vets shared their stories with the congregation. She would never forget Richard's description of one of the coldest battles in the history of civilization. "Please, don't overdo it."

"I'm fine. Go back to what you were doing."

"God bless you and keep you. Check in with me before you go." Abigail returned to her office.

SUNDAY, APRIL 21, 2013

ALAN PECK always walked out of the sanctuary when Abigail started her sermon, as he found her preaching sanctimonious and pretty much unbearable. Five years ago, after hearing a third weekly sermon in a row about vulnerable and marginalized people, Alan stopped listening. He thought, *what about the people who are actually contributing citizens, doing their part, paying the bills?*

He wandered into one of the empty Sunday School classrooms and sat in a teacher's chair. Fifty years earlier in this classroom, he learned about Noah's ark and the Ten Commandments from Mrs. Hoyer. The thirty children in his class received juice and cookies for good behavior. Nowadays the church hosted the merest handful of children for Sunday School. Alan knew that with Abigail in charge, things would get even worse. He thought, *she is a terrible manager who couldn't lead a fish to water. If she had any skills, the church would be growing rather than dying its slow death. When the neighborhood changed, Faith Church should've moved west or north, and sold the church building to a start-up congregation.*

A text message notification from Jack Shears popped up on Alan's cell phone, interrupting his thoughts: "Letter mailed out, wheels in motion, whee!!!!" A lawyer from Charlotte and friend from college, Jack kept Alan up to date on mutually beneficial business opportunities.

Alan took delight at the speed with which the plan came together to bring down the business-hating churches and clergy who protested at Dolly's. Jack assisted SmithCo. Corporation, owner of Dolly's Dollar Stores. As SmithCo. and their multitude of lawyers worked against Faith United Church of Christ and the other congregations, Alan would watch and silently cheer as Abigail crumbled along with the church.

Alan checked his watch. It had been fifteen minutes since Abigail started her sermon. "Like clockwork," Alan said, and returned to the back of the sanctuary. When the offering plates came around he put in his customary five-dollar bill—more than he wanted to give. He knew, though, that if he wanted to maintain his leadership position on the consistory, he needed to provide a minimum amount of funding for the record.

#####

ISABELLA RAMIREZ and three other mothers departed Church of the Living Water immediately after worship. They hoped to reach the Philadelphia hotel by late afternoon, in plenty of time for the opening worship service for the National Christian Moms Conference that started that evening. Following the service, the moms were registered for a two-day conference full of workshops and presentations. None of the four moms in the car had been away from their kids for that long.

Isabella was scheduled for a fifteen-minute warm-up talk in advance of the keynote speaker, a mom who hosted a weekly radio show that was featured on dozens of Christian stations.

They reached their hotel by five and, after unpacking, Isabella disappeared to the hotel restaurant where she reviewed her notes for her talk entitled "The Lord Is With Us."

The praise singers started the service with familiar, upbeat worship songs. One thousand women made their way into the conference room, singing and clapping. After some announcements and a scripture reading, the conference planning committee chairwoman introduced Isabella.

"We're so blessed to have a word this evening from young mom Isabella Ramirez. Isabella is the daughter of Pastor Johnny Ramos and Anita Ramos. Pastor Johnny leads Church of the Living Water in nearby Allentown. Isabella is married to police sergeant Eddie Ramirez, and they have a three-year-old daughter, Sofia, along with two older children in their blended family. Isabella loves the Lord and loves leading the Moms group at her church."

Polite applause emanated from the audience as Isabella approached the podium.

"Let's start with prayer. I just pray, Oh Lord, that You bless my words shared here tonight, that they may glorify You. We want to honor You, Lord, as mothers and wives and in all our relationships. Sometimes we forget that You are with us, You are on our side, all the time. You never leave or forsake us. All praises to You, Lord. And the people said?"

"Amen!"

The *Amen!* that came from one thousand women momentarily overwhelmed Isabella, but she recovered quickly. "God is with us. God is with mothers. There are a number of moms in the Bible we could turn to and learn from their stories: Sarah, Zipporah, Rachel, Leah, Hannah, Naomi, Ruth. I could go on. It is a long list. But tonight I want to focus on Mary and her words to the angel, in Luke 1. The angel tells Mary she'll receive the Holy Spirit and conceive a son who will be Son of the Highest and His kingdom will never end! The Lord is with Mary. He's on her side. The Lord with us, He's on our side."

A few of the moms cried out, "Yes!"

"There is so much in the world today that pulls us away from the Lord—so much evil and distress, demons everywhere. They try to tell us that Christians are stupid. They tell us we're fake. They make fun of our families and our churches. There are a lot of haters out there. When we put our husbands as head of the family, they tell us we're living in the dark ages. They want us to fail. But we're not going to pay any attention to them!"

"That's right," a mom up front exclaimed.

"Yes!" other moms chorused.

"The Lord is with us! The Lord is on *our* side. The Lord is *not* with all of them who make fun and try to break us down. The Lord is with us—*not* with those who judge us and want to drag us through the dirt!"

"Yes!" the crowd responded.

"The Lord is on *our* side, not on the side of the haters! God is on *our* side, *not* with all those people who go against the church. Jesus is the only way, and we know that *our* way is the only way. We'll take the heat from the haters, and we'll be okay because the Lord is on *our* side."

Shouts of "Yes!" "All right!" "You go, girl!" reached the stage.

"The Lord is on *our* side as we honor our parents, support our husbands, care for our children, and strengthen our families!"

A handful of moms stood and clapped, hands raised toward the ceiling. "Praise the Lord," they said.

Isabella let the Spirit take the lead, and her fifteen minutes stretched to thirty. In time, the committee chairwoman motioned at her to wrap up her speech, and Isabella hastily concluded with prayer.

#####

ABIGAIL BARRETT-THOMPSON made a brief stop at the grocery store to pick up some essentials for what was sure to be another of Ted's memorable meals. The post-worship committee meetings had gone quickly, so she arrived at the store earlier than usual and had to contend with the large Sunday crowds.

Across the lettuce bins she heard, "Hi, Abigail!" and looked up to see a former church member.

"Hi, Joan. How are you?" Abigail asked.

"We're doing great. Work is going well, the kids are staying active, Billy is in baseball, and Twyla is running track. I don't know if you heard, we all joined Cedar Beach two weeks ago."

"Praise God, Joan. No, I had not heard, but again, praise God." Abigail ran through a silent, mental spiel. *Next is when you tell me about how amazing the worship is at your new church, how fabulous the programs are, and what a great pastor you have, so funny and real.*

"We love it there. The worship is amazing, the programs are incredible, and Pastor Davey is such a great guy! His preaching is so dynamic and relevant to our lives."

"Sounds like God has provided you with a great fit for a faith community!" Abigail smiled and moved away. "Take good care. I'm sure we'll see each other again soon."

Abigail walked unsteadily to the neighboring section of the store, trying to focus on her grocery list. She picked up cereal and crackers and then some frozen items. Right before check-out, she detoured to the self-serve pastries and put three blueberry Danish in a bag. She also bagged five cinnamon-sugar donuts and a dozen fresh-baked chocolate chip cookies. She ate all of the sweets as she sat in the car in the grocery store parking lot. On the drive home, she went out of her way to Faith UCC, knowing it would be empty. She unlocked the doors and ran to the church bathroom where she lurched into a stall and forced herself to vomit.

#####

EVAN LEMMON MOORE's Sunday started with trail tending and ended with his evening ritual of drinking a bottle of Mountain Delight whiskey. On Saturday nights, he walked to the liquor store to purchase the whiskey in a plastic bottle. It fit well in his backpack and he could place it at the bottom of his recycling bin so nosy neighbors would not see it.

On Mondays, Evan could barely do anything except lie on the floor and hope the spinning would stop. Tuesdays were his recovery day, and then his four-day workweek would start. The three-day weekend presented plentiful time to ruminate on his sorry history.

Evan had discovered one sure way to kill the thoughts was to drink a lot. He sat on his overstuffed living room chair, dreading the two long days ahead. Soon, images from "the events" rumbled along the edges of his mind. That's what it had become to him in recent years—*the events*—which sounded better than "Evan's massive downward spiral." His thoughts came into focus. He took a first sip of the whiskey and gripped the arm of the chair as if he was in airplane seat for take-off. He took another sip as the 2003 Spring Assembly at Edwardsville, Illinois, Memorial High School appeared in slow motion.

Evan had taught computer science at Memorial High and his girlfriend Christie Tanner taught government and coached softball. Additionally, Evan's mother and father were English teachers at the school and nearing retirement. The four grades were coming together in the gym to kick off school spirit week, which would end with the Junior-Senior prom. It was midday Monday, and Evan and his girlfriend had partied pretty hard the night before as they did most nights—they were young, frisky, and invincible.

As the school's resident computer expert, Evan was in charge of the audio/visual booth during school assemblies. At eleven o'clock, he inserted the flash drive to pull up the file titled "cheers." Instead, he blearily clicked the file directly underneath: "christie."

Evan took another sip of whiskey, remembering the giant screen in the gym where the entire school saw a photo of Christie—completely naked, legs spread, and smiling for the camera. Pandemonium ensued during the brief seconds the photo was shown. After a few moments of shock, the principal went into damage control and started the assembly as if nothing had happened. The cheerleaders and dance teams both did routines, and the pep band played a savagely loud version of the school's fight song.

Evan took a gulp. The apologies flashed in front of him. He apologized to Christie immediately. He expressed regret constantly—in writing, with flowers, countless dinners out, tickets to the Matchbox Twenty concert in St. Louis, and a long weekend trip to Chicago—but something had broken between them and remained unfixed.

The images got fuzzier, but still flickered, so Evan kept sipping. An account of an Edwardsville, Illinois, teacher's nude photo of a coworker shown at a school assembly appeared on CNN, Fox News, and all the major television networks, as did brief stories in major daily newspapers across the nation. Evan and Christie declined interviews, and the story eventually died. Evan decided not to try to weather further embarrassment at the high school that fall. He found a job in St. Louis doing computer networking, and he and Christie drifted apart. Christie managed to hold her head high for a year, but then moved to teach at a suburban Chicago school.

The bottle was almost empty. Evan's thoughts circled round to his parents, their abiding shame and their coping strategy of silence on the topic, thinking that a lack of attention would make it all go away. Evan probably could have reconciled completely with them had it not been for the DUI that winter. After work one Friday night, Evan met a college buddy for drinks in downtown St. Louis. They got plastered. Neither had any business getting behind the wheel of a car. Evan's friend miraculously made it home, while Evan crossed his car into the opposite lanes of Interstate 235 and hit the station wagon of a Vietnamese family. The parents escaped serious injury, but their boy had a skull fracture and two broken legs, and their girl had serious internal damage. Evan supposed the emotional trauma for the family would likely continue for the rest of their lives.

Just before passing out, Evan thought about his short-term salvation—meeting Samantha online and moving from St. Louis to Allentown—a fresh start and a second chance that he had ruined with more drinking. Then there was Dahlia, beautiful, patient Dahlia. They had also met online, and she moved from Seattle to

Allentown for him. When they made it to five years it was a mutual decision not to re-up.

Evan tried to stand, but he pitched forward onto the floor where he awoke fifteen hours later.

MONDAY, APRIL 22, 2013

ISABELLA RAMIREZ stared at the front page of the Style section in the Philadelphia newspaper where there was a huge photo of her, accompanied by a headline that read: *Mom to Conference: God is on our side.* She would keep a copy for her parents and get one for Eddie, too.

The photo captured something she had not seen in herself before—leadership. The shot was of her at the podium, but also included a sizable portion of the crowd. Isabella quickly lifted up a prayer. *Lord God, You are my leader and I'm in awe of You. If you are calling me to lead people, I'm sort of scared but also a bit thrilled. I want to do Your will. I want to trust You. Be clear about what You're calling me to. Amen.*

#####

GENNY RAMIREZ was on her way to Washington Elementary School when she spotted her friend Marcus half a block ahead.

"Marcus! Wait up!"

"Hey. You gonna keep going to the park?"

"Yes, why?" Genny was confused.

"'cause of that dead body."

"Oh, it didn't scare me."

"All the blood and guts?"

"No blood. He just looked like he was asleep."

"Oh."

"My dad says that when people die from drugs, they usually look like they're sleeping."

"I bet your dad has seen a lot of dead bodies."

"Probably. He doesn't say much."

"Shootings," Marcus said as he formed his hand into a gun, "and stabbings." He made a motion like he was stabbing someone.

"Beatings," Genny added, and punched her fists in the air.

"Strangling," Marcus said, and put his hands on his neck. "And choking." He made gurgling noises.

"People run over by cars." Genny flattened herself as much as possible, sucking in her belly.

"People falling off a bridge. Splat!"

"Houses on fire," Genny said, and fanned the air.

Marcus thought of other kinds of deaths. "On TV there was a woman who poisoned her husband."

The two arrived at the schoolyard. It was noisy with the normal morning kid chatter. After a minute, the principal came outside and asked everyone to form lines. As the kids filed in, they went by glass cases where the Found Art projects were on display. Genny's plastic bag otter was in between a rotary phone covered in yarn and a canvas covered with bright foil candy wrappers.

#####

GINA GONZALEZ sat at attention in the office of her supervisor, Sharon Chapel, for their weekly Monday morning kick-off meeting. It was an opportunity for the two social workers to coordinate schedules and ensure coverage.

Sharon started, "Your Spanish translation will be helpful for an intake tomorrow morning."

"Sure," Gina said.

"I'm starting the mental health wellness series next week, which, as you know, I'm able to do because of that grant we applied for last year. The classes really need to be talked up throughout the building."

"Okay. We'll try to get a good turnout."

"How are Marjorie Wagner and her new roommate, Vivian Burke, getting on?" Sharon asked.

"Looks good so far."

"Anything else to report on the residents?" Sharon was confident Gina would provide interesting and reliable news.

Gina lowered her voice and asked, "Did you hear about Janice and George?"

"Um, no. What's going on there?"

"They're back together again," Gina announced.

"Resident romances are hard to keep up with. Where are they meeting?" Sharon asked.

"Looks like they're taking it slow—eating their meals together and watching *The View* in the common room."

"Gina, you are always a wealth of information."

"I like to keep up with everything that goes on with people. If I don't make *their* business *my* business, then I'm not doing my job."

"You could start a newsletter," Sharon said.

"What?"

"Hey, I'm serious. We had a newsletter here years ago. It's probably time to start one up again." Sharon paused to think, then told Gina, "Have a draft ready for our Friday end-of-week meeting. It only needs to be the front and back of one sheet of paper. Take some photos with your phone, put the mental well-being class announcement in, and the religious services schedule. You're good with computer stuff like that. Give it a try, okay?"

"I'll work something up," Gina said. A moment later she added, "Speaking of the newsletter, did you hear about Luci over in accounting?"

"No, what's going on?"

"She is having an affair with Mike in maintenance."

"Yikes."

"She's thinks she can get away with it, but someone's going to find out. Someone always does. I don't get how a woman who is so ugly can have two men going on at once."

"Beauty does not always play a role in these sorts of things. It's more about a combo of boredom and hormones."

"Hasn't made Luci any nicer, though. She's still a meanie, treating everyone like they work for her when all she does is record payroll. She's always power tripping." Gina stood to leave, then remembered one more thing. "Oh, and you know about that aide Lizzy, right?"

"Nope. Is this the new gal?"

"Yes, the fat one. She's got some baby daddy issues, can't get a cent of child support from the guy."

"That's rough."

"Well, sometimes people just need to stand up for themselves a little more!" Gina said.

"That's probably never a problem for you."

Gina smiled and headed back to her office.

#####

JOHNNY RAMOS let his office administrator, Carla, answer the ringing phone. A half minute later, she poked her head in his office and said, "Pastor, someone named David Garcia is on the phone for you."

Johnny shrugged and said, "Only David Garcia I know is the baseball player." He picked up his extension.

"This is Pastor Ramos."

"Hello, Pastor. My name is David Garcia. You may remember me from Major League Baseball?"

"Wow. Really? *The* David Garcia who was in the World Series a few years back?"

"That's right."

Johnny could not believe his ears. "How many times did you get on base in that first game?"

The man chuckled and said, "Four times on base. Yes, it's me, though we could not pull off the championship."

"Memorable World Series that year, yessir. Your team sure had some good hitting. How can we help you?"

"It's the other way around. I have a gift for your church that I'd like to talk with you about in person. Are you available to meet tomorrow morning? I'm flying from Charlotte to Philadelphia tonight, and since I'm so close, I can just drop by. Okay?"

"Sure. Come on over. You know where we're located?" Johnny asked.

"I'll have GPS on the rental car. I'll find you no problem. How about at ten?"

"Sure. See you then."

"See you soon, Pastor."

After Johnny hung up the phone, he called Carla into his office.

"Yes, Pastor?"

"Look up David Garcia—the baseball player—online. See if you find anything about what he's doing right now. I already know about his baseball life, so I don't need that info. Print out any articles you find and put them in my box."

Johnny picked up his cell phone and called the head deacon.

"Deacon Rob, can you make it over to the church for a meeting tomorrow morning at ten? If you can believe this, David Garcia, the major league baseball player, is going to be here."

"What?"

"Yeah, David Garcia wants to give the church a gift. I don't know what's going on, but I'd like you to be a part of it. And, since you have the most flexible schedule of anyone in leadership, can you make it?"

"I have a site inspection, but I'll move it to an earlier time. Yes, I'll see you at ten."

"You're a good man."

#####

ABIGAIL BARRETT-THOMPSON heard loud banging on the front door but remained half asleep. Mondays were her day off and she rarely got out of bed before nine. In a stupor, she stumbled to her second-story bedroom window and saw a courier delivery truck. She knocked on the glass to let the driver know someone was coming. After putting on her bathrobe, she went downstairs to sign and was handed a thin envelope. The return address was from Holliday, Shears & Dowell Law Firm of Charlotte, North Carolina. It was sent overnight mail, on a weekend, which Abigail knew was extremely expensive. As she wandered toward the kitchen, she opened the envelope and quickly read the letter.

Dear Rev. Barrett-Thompson,

This is a legal notice. Holliday, Shears & Dowell Law Firm represents SmithCo., owner of Dolly's Dollar Stores.

Your protest outside of the Dolly's Dollar Store at 17th and Tilghman Streets on Friday, April 9, was an assault on lawful commerce and private business.

As a result of your actions, your tax-exempt status at Faith United Church of Christ is at risk. Be advised that we are taking all necessary actions to have your tax-exempt status revoked.

The act of demanding that corporations adhere to certain policies and employment practices is political. You should focus instead on spiritual care for your flock.

Signed,
Jack Shears, Esq.

cc: Rev. C.D. Alexander, Iman Feisel Ali, Rabbi Sarah Berger, Rev. Craig Johnson, Rev. John Ramos, Rev. Peter Smith, Rev. Eric Windham

Abigail mused, *this is an utterly ridiculous scare tactic. The letter will worry Faith Church's consistory, but surely none of the faith leaders who spoke at the rally will get sucked in by this correspondence.* She knew churches and worshipping bodies were permitted to spend twenty percent of their budget on lobbying for particular legislation. Most faith communities had scarce resources and only did the most limited advocacy on a variety of social justice issues. None of the communities that participated in the Dolly's Dollar

Store protest would be anywhere near surpassing a lobbying line item in their budgets, so the letter from SmithCo. was simply to create fear and anxiety in the congregations.

Abigail put the letter in her briefcase so she could make copies of it at the church. She phoned the pizza delivery place and ordered a large with pepperoni and sausage. She gave a substantial tip to the delivery driver and consumed the pizza quickly. *How pathetic—overeating at the least sign of trouble—as if stuffing my face is going to resolve the issue.* When she was done, she crushed the pizza box, put it in a garbage bag, and hid it in her car trunk to throw in the church dumpster so Ted would not inquire about it. Abigail went back upstairs, vomited in the bathroom, and then climbed back into bed. She'd deal with the letter tomorrow.

#####

EDDIE RAMIREZ climbed the steps to his empty house. Isabella was in Philadelphia and Sofia was with her grandmother. He glanced at the empty couch on Evan's porch. Rarely did Eddie see Evan on Mondays. He just figured his neighbor was doing marathon gaming because he always looked so bleary on Tuesdays. *Dudes who spend that much time with video games probably are avoiding dealing with something. I wonder what he's running away from.*

Realizing he could get some bonus time with his secret XXX videos, Eddie unlocked the glove compartment, retrieved his private phone, and went into his house.

In the darkened living room, he watched hardcore porn on his phone, starting with an old favorite then moving on to a new release. After an hour, he paused and shook his head. *I'm a total loser, the cop and vet who watches hardcore videos to get through the day.*

A minute later Eddie was startled by a knock at the door. "Just a minute," he shouted, and carefully logged out of the website and shut down his phone.

His neighbor from down the street was at the door, looking even more rough than usual, with bleary eyes like he had not slept or may even have been crying. "Have a seat, Paulie," Eddie said, and stepped out on the porch to join him.

"That guy in the park?" Paulie asked.

"Yeah? OD. Friend of yours?"

"My dad."

"Oh, man, sorry."

"We didn't really talk much, but it's whack, you know?" Paulie shook his head and looked up and down the street, trying to focus his thoughts as his mind was crowded with memories.

Eddie tried to help. "Sometimes this happens, and it lets you get things set in your own life."

"Huh?"

"Someone dies, and it presents you an opportunity to be different. Do you want to be like your father?" Eddie asked.

"Naw, not really. He lied a lot. And he was a scammer, but he was also kind of funny."

"Well, keep the funny but don't be a liar."

"Yeah, I see where you're going."

"Your kids need you to be a guy they can depend on."

"Yeah," Paulie said, and exhaled loudly while throwing his shoulders back. He changed the subject. "You seen a lotta dead bodies?" Paulie asked.

Eddie paused, wondering how much to share with Paulie. He decided to engage him so he could have a break from thinking about the circumstances of his father's death. "Here in Allentown, yeah. Most of them not too bad. Overdoses or old age. The worst was a guy who died after getting smashed up by a baseball bat. The bodies were much worse in Iraq. Roadside bombs, arms and legs all over the place. It's not like the movies or soldier video games."

"My uncle is with the Guard in New York."

"Good for him. You can join. How old are you?" Eddie asked.

"Twenty-two."

"Think about joining the Pennsylvania Guard. It's good money. What about Rob Handel's construction company? Rob's a really good guy. He's the head deacon over at my father-in-law's church. Have you filled out an application yet?"

"Uh, not yet," Paulie confessed.

"Where is it? Why don't you go get it, and we'll fill it out right here?"

"Who will watch the kids if I get a job like that?"

"My wife can watch them to start off until you get them in a good daycare situation. There's a woman from my church who runs a childcare two blocks from here who'd like your business."

Paulie said nothing, but Eddie knew he was thinking. "You'll have to work really hard for Rob. He's fair, but he expects an honest day's work. Have you worked before?"

"Yeah, at a pizza place. And I was a busboy in a diner. And I stocked shelves at the grocery store for a while."

"This is a long-term thing, Paulie. You can't just do it for a few weeks and then blow it off, do you understand?" Eddie asked.

"I get it, man."

TUESDAY, APRIL 23, 2013

ABIGAIL BARRETT-THOMPSON swiftly typed an email to the seven colleagues who had been speakers at the Dolly's Dollar Store protest.

Subject: Tax Exempt Threat
From: Rev.Barrett-Thompson@FaithUCC.org
Date: Tues, Apr 23, 2013 8:08 am
To: <Faith Leader Distribution Group>

Greetings Craig, Peter, C.D., Eric, Sarah, Feisel and Johnny,

By now, you all have probably received a threatening letter via FedEx from a lawyer regarding the Dolly's Dollar Store event. Ludicrous! We can meet in person to strategize a joint response. Let's plan for a meeting Thursday at noon here at Faith UCC, and if you can make it great—not a big deal if you already have something on your calendar. If you're not able to make it, feel free to share your thoughts via email.

Abigail

Then she made a phone call to the consistory president, Tim Thacker.

"Hi, Abigail. Everything okay?"

"Things are interesting. I'm going to give you and all the consistory members a copy of a letter I received from a law firm in Charlotte, North Carolina. It's regarding the Dolly's Dollar Store event, and they have sent letters to all the faith leaders who participated in it."

"Uh oh. What's it say?" Tim asked.

"They make threats about our tax-exempt status and refer to our Dolly's Dollar Store event as politicking."

"I don't like the sound of this."

"It's really nothing, but you should be aware of it, along with everyone on the consistory."

"Well, we have a subcommittee meeting tomorrow night, so I can talk with you more about it prior to the meeting."

"Sure, Tim. Take care, and I'll see you tomorrow."

JOHNNY RAMOS and Deacon Rob waited to welcome David Garcia into the office. They had agreed that Johnny would do the talking while Rob would be there as another set of ears. The two churchmen wore white button-down shirts tucked into dress pants and simple black belts. Johnny was the shorter, chestier man and, as usual, his hair was slicked back with a side part. Rob's salt-and-pepper hair was crew cut.

David Garcia was prompt. Johnny and Rob stood when he entered, and all three shook hands. The retired baseball star was wearing a substantial watch and an expertly tailored blue pin-stripe suit. It was not often that Johnny met with muscular, six-foot-five men in his office, and Garcia seemed to fill much of the room.

"It's really a pleasure to meet you. You know, Rob and I were both football players, but we don't mind welcoming a baseball player to the church. Have a seat." Johnny motioned for David to sit.

"Thank you, Pastor. And it's nice to meet you both, too. I'm sure you are probably wondering why I called."

Johnny had read through Carla's Internet research and had a pretty good idea why the retired star was sitting in his office, but he was going to let the man explain it in his own words. "That's true. It's not every day that a Major League Baseball player calls Johnny Ramos."

David smiled and said, "We saw some articles about you speaking at the Dolly's Dollar Store protest."

"Yes, this past Friday. Most of the stuff in those stores is pure junk, you know? And the low wages and crazy schedules for their workers—that's not right."

"It's a free country. People are free to work where they want, and they can resign at any time. They're welcome to get a job that pays better and has set hours. And I don't have to tell you that our communities have needed stores like these within walking distance because there's not always a big box store nearby."

Johnny maintained a polite attentiveness.

"Nine years ago, after I retired from baseball, I started with a company in Charlotte called SmithCo. We mostly focus on commercial real estate, but also own two nationwide dollar store chains—One Spot and Dolly's Dollar Stores. We also own three convenience store chains throughout the northwest and southwest parts of the country. At first I had my doubts about the dollar stores. Does anyone really need these items? But then I educated myself and realized that our people need options. Our community's needs were not being met at typical discount stores. The white folks think they know what's best for us, telling us how to run our businesses, but we're the ones who need to be making the decisions. Our demographic and our neighborhoods need the convenience of these stores."

"You could treat your workers better."

"We have management training, and I'm sure our workers will see some improvements soon. We could debate this for a while, but I've brought some handouts that summarize a lot of what I'm saying." David pulled some glossy publications from his briefcase and handed them to Rob.

Johnny said, "You've done well for yourself. I'm glad you've found success outside of baseball."

"Thank you, Pastor. Take a look over the pamphlets."

"I will."

"I also wanted to give you a gift from SmithCo. It's a check in the amount of forty thousand dollars made out to Church of the Living Water, to support all of the great programming you do here to help people rise up out of their addictions." David handed Rob an envelope.

"That's very generous of you and SmithCo. Is there something you're expecting in exchange?" Johnny asked.

David smiled. "A strip mall is going to be constructed on the site of an old battery factory just a few blocks from your church. It will be the home of a new, bright and shining Dolly's Dollar Store. SmithCo. would very much appreciate the support of you and your congregation at this new location."

"Anything else?"

"It will be publicized in a couple of days in the local newspapers. As soon as the check is deposited in your account we'll send out a press release announcing that Pastor Johnny Ramos and Church of the Living Water have had a change of heart, they've seen the light, and now understand that Dolly's Dollar Store serves the community."

"I'm sure you understand that we have to do some praying about this and determine what is best for the church."

"I understand. Do what you need to, Pastor. Thank you for your time."

"Thank you, David. Again, it has been my great pleasure to meet you." Johnny accompanied David to the front door talking World Series statistics.

#####

ANNA RAMIREZ checked her private post office box during her lunch hour. She had all of her online orders sent here due to too many prying eyes at home.

The package had arrived from the specialty perfumer in New Mexico. She would wrap the bottle in duct tape from the post office maintenance room and scratch up the glass a bit to make it look like a beat-up old perfume container. She sprayed a bit on her neck and wrists and glanced at the bill—two hundred and fifty dollars plus sixteen for delivery.

She saw Steve in the break room. "Hey, Stevie, smell me."

"Oh, my, what an invitation."

"How's the scent?" Anna inquired.

"A good match for you—nice."

"Thanks." Anna recalled that Steve and Glenn had recently celebrated their twenty-fifth anniversary. "How's your honey these days?" she asked as she set her lunch bag on the table.

"He's going cray-cray with all the outdoor work right now. But our yard and gardens always end up looking spectacular. Glad he takes care of it, because if it was me, we would just have grass—no trees, no flowers, no garden. It's all *way* too much to look after. It's like a second job for him at home. But I adore my garden guy, except for when he tracks dirt through the house."

Anna laughed. "Sounds like my kids."

"So, tell me. Are you seeing anyone yet?"

"No, not really looking. Gina has fallen head over heels, though."

"Oh, yeah? Do tell."

"Her new woman is Jay. I met her briefly and she seems okay. I know Gina's in love because I haven't seen much of her lately."

"She tends to fall quickly."

"Yes, and then she falls *out* just as quickly. I'd love for her to settle down a bit with someone who can give it back to her, you know what I'm saying?"

"Right," Steve replied, "someone who doesn't let Gina walk all over her."

"Exactly. But then look at me—I'm no relationship expert."

"So, *if* you were looking right now, what kind of guy would be on the radar of Anna Ramirez?"

Anna knew exactly what she wanted. "A man who is capable of compromise. No arrogant men, but not someone who is down on himself either. Someone who is smart, but not too much of a nerd. A man who likes kids. Someone political, but not too political. Someone who can shut it off, you know?"

"Yeah, someone who can talk on a variety of subjects and is not hyper-focused on just one thing."

Anna's thoughts were overtaken by the image of her ex-husband. "A man who is not obsessed with winning. With so many men, it's all about winning. With Eddie, it was about winning every conversation, winning the closest parking spot to the store, winning the battle, winning the promotion, winning the younger woman to be his wife. And now he's all about winning people to his church. It's an infection—this desperate need to win."

"So you want to date a loser?"

"Ha ha. No losers! I want a guy who, you know, winning and losing isn't even on his radar screen, it's not an issue. I know I'm starting to sound picky, but you asked, and I'm dreaming big." She thought a moment more. "He should also like a bit of travel— we wouldn't need to travel around the world, but exploring some places together would be nice."

"Your list isn't too long. Anything else?"

"I wouldn't mind a garden guy."

Steve smiled, "Those garden guys are keepers."

The rest of the afternoon was incident-free as Steve, Anna, and another coworker staffed the front counter. At four forty-five, Anna looked out at the line and saw her ex's neighbor, Evan.

"Next in line, please."

Anna sized up Evan as he walked toward her. *Nice haircut, trimmed beard, and tall, though not basketball player tall. High quality boots and a jacket that fits him well—he knows a little something about style.*

"Howdy," Evan said with a shy smile.

Steve noticed that Anna leaned into the counter more than usual. She asked, "How may I help you today?"

"Need to mail this to my folks."

"Okay, to Edwardsville, Illinois. Sure." Then she looked closely at the return address label. "Evan Lemmon Moore. Where do you get a name like Lemmon?"

Evan decided it was now or never. "Could I tell you over coffee or tea or whatever, after you finish work today?" he blurted. Steve glanced at Anna to see her reaction.

Anna affixed the postage and looked at Evan. "Okay. Meet me out front a little after five."

Evan walked away and Steve turned toward Anna. He whispered to her, "Could that be your garden guy?"

"Could be."

#####

ISABELLA RAMIREZ and her three companions were exhausted after attending a bounty of workshops, worship services, and prayer meetings. Each of the women had a tote bag full of brochures, idea sheets, and giveaways they had collected from the booths outside the conference hall—pens, sticky notes, and mouse pads touting the services of an array of Christian businesses.

The four young mothers sat in the car on the top deck of the Philadelphia parking garage in the soft glow of the late afternoon light.

"These past few days were just amazing. We need to do it again," said Fabiana, who was seated up front with Isabella.

"Next year's conference is in Dallas," Isabella reminded her carmates.

"We should start doing the fundraisers now so we can get enough money to go. And get more moms to come, too," Fabiana said. In her rearview mirror, Isabella saw the two women in the back seat nod in agreement.

"We could do so many things—car washes, bake sales, candle sales, a little bit here, a little bit there, and we get the money raised," Isabella said.

"And you could speak again," Fabiana said.

A chorus of "Amens" was heard from the back seat.

Isabella replied, "If it's the Lord's will that I speak again, I will say yes! We have to say yes when the Lord calls, right?"

"Right," Fabiana responded as Isabella started the car.

#####

EVAN LEMMON MOORE tried to look casual as he stood out front of the post office next to a parking meter. Finally, some follow-up on all of the glances and smiles he and Anna had exchanged. He was giddy and terrified at the same time, as it had been over a decade since he had asked a woman out in person and not online.

She is so freakin' pretty, really pretty. Warm eyes, great neck, exquisite lips, maybe a size twelve or fourteen. Even in her post office polo shirt she's delectable. Let this be a good conversation—please.

"Hi." Anna came around the corner wearing a light jacket with the Postal Service logo.

"Hey," Evan responded, smiling at the sound of her voice. "There's a place down a block on Hamilton. We could walk."

"Okay."

"Have you been working at the post office for a long time?" Evan asked, noting that she glowed just as much in the sunlight as she did in the dingy post office.

"Fourteen years. I started when I was just a young thing—twenty years old."

Evan did some quick mental math to calculate her age and was relieved that they were peers, with Anna just a year younger. Not that it mattered if there was more of an age difference, but it seemed like a confirmation of relationship potential. Evan asked, "Do you like it?"

"Most days I like helping people and giving them what they need. Some days it's not so fun. Working directly with the public can get tiring. You do customer service, right?"

"Yeah. Working from home for BlackBox now. It can get tedious, but I'm with you on it. Most days I like helping people and solving problems. And then there are those calls that I'd like to end as soon as possible."

Evan held the door for Anna. They went up to the counter to place their order and found a table by the window.

Anna continued the conversation they had started at the post office, "So, Evan Lemmon Moore, what's your story? Evan Lemmon is not an everyday kind of name. Sounds intriguing."

"My mother loved her hometown of Lemmon, South Dakota. So I became Evan Lemmon, which I didn't advertise at all until I reached my thirties, and now I feel sufficiently mature to own the name," he laughed and took a sip.

"Lemmon, South Dakota. Have you been there?"

"When I was a kid we'd drive there once a year for two weeks in the summer. Then my grandparents died, so we stopped going when I was in my teens. I remember we'd bring our bikes and I'd pedal over to the library to read or the bakery where I'd inhale this incredible cinnamon ring. Or I'd bike to the town pool."

"Good memories."

"If your middle name was your mother's home town, it would be?"

"Anna Ponce Ramirez. Or with my maiden name, Anna Ponce Gonzalez."

"Could you say Ponce twelve more times?"

"Excuse me?"

"You just sound great saying it."

Anna laughed. No one had ever told her he liked the way she talked.

"Do you go Puerto Rico a lot?"

"More when I was younger, like every couple of years, but it's been a long time since I've been in Ponce."

"And you've lived here all your life?"

"Yes, with some brief stops at army bases when Eddie was in basic training. I wanted the kids raised near their grandparents."

"Your kids are great—really smart and observant. I've been talking with Genesis about recycling and composting."

"She's my little environmentalist. Willie's my little sports guy. Well, not so little anymore. He's fourteen now. How about you? Any kids?"

"Um, no, no kids—that I know of. Ha ha. Bad joke, sorry." Evan tried to recover, seeing the perplexed look on Anna's face. "Are you a movie person at all?"

"I like the movies."

"Same here. Would you be interested in going together sometime?"

Anna replied, "Yes, Evan Lemmon Moore." Her response could not have been more direct, and he once again felt a mixture of terror and giddiness.

#####

WILLIE RAMIREZ dribbled a basketball with Alex and eight other boys in the parking lot of Church of the Living Water. They played every Tuesday night for two hours under the supervision of one of the deacons. Willie and Alex were regulars, six other teens attended occasionally, and this evening two new boys Willie had invited from his gym class had also come out to play.

Pastor Johnny came to the parking lot at exactly eight thirty, as he did every Tuesday, to deliver a brief message and send the boys home.

He saw Alex was holding a basketball. "Pass it to me," he said.

Johnny held the basketball as he spoke to the teens. Since Saturday, all the neighborhood had been talking about was the body in the park, and Johnny had learned the details of the death from his son-in-law Eddie.

"You all know about that body found over there in Jordan Park?" Johnny asked the boys.

No one said a word.

"I know you all know because Willie and Alex saw it, and Alex here definitely has the gift of gab, so I'm sure he shared it with you."

Some of the boys smiled and said, "Yeah."

"That guy died because of drugs. All he cared about was getting drugs. What a waste." Johnny looked at the boys and asked, "What do you care about?"

His question was met with silence once again.

"Let's try this one more time. What do you care about?"

"Basketball," one of the boys responded.

"That's a start. Basketball. You are all here because you love shooting hoops. You would do it all day if you could. Better to do basketball than drugs any day! Keep coming here Tuesday nights to play. Now, before you go, I want to share with you someone who cares about you no matter what. His name is Jesus."

The two new boys had blank looks on their faces, while the ones who participated occasionally knew they had to listen to the pastor's message if they wanted to keep playing.

"This man will care about you every day. And if you ever have any trouble you can 'cast all your care on Him, for He careth for you. That is from the Bible, First Peter. And right before those words, it says 'younger, submit yourselves unto to the elder.' This means you don't act out in school or anywhere. You obey the teachers and coaches because they are your elders and they care about you. I care about you, okay?"

Most of the boys were feeling uncomfortable at this point, shuffling their feet and avoiding looking at each other or at Pastor Johnny. "Okay, I know. It's not cool to talk about these things, but you need to know it. Let's pray and then you can go. And remember to bring a friend with you next Tuesday. Father God, bless these young men. Give these young men a positive vision of their future, help them to cast their cares on Jesus, their Lord and Savior. Amen."

WEDNESDAY, APRIL 24, 2013

TED THOMPSON parked in the lot of his first school of the day. He sat in his car and checked his email on his phone. In his early teaching days, when he taught at just one school all day, he would sit in the teacher's lounge and chat before classes started. But now he was unable to get into a rhythm covering four schools, and felt like an interloper at each. He quickly exited from his email as he saw the subject headings blaring more bad news from the teacher's union as well as interminably dry headings from the administration.

Suddenly another teacher appeared at Ted's car window—a young guy Ted recognized from some of the meetings he attended.

Ted rolled down the window. "What's up?"

"Hi. It's Ted, right?"

Ted nodded, and the young man said, "I'm Darren, Darren Long."

"Hi, Darren. Everything all right?"

"Yes, sure. I just thought I'd say hi because it's always good to meet other male teachers. I feel a little outnumbered, you know?"

Ted narrowed his eyes and asked, "Do you have a problem with women?"

"What? No, I'm good with women."

"Feel emasculated by feminism?" Ted asked.

Darren became defensive, "I'd like to think I'm a feminist."

"Was your mommy a little hard on you?"

"Huh?" Darren was confused.

"I'm just messin' with you. Come, have a seat in my chariot for a moment."

Darren climbed into the passenger seat and Ted looked at him closely, trying to guess what he needed. *A little mentoring, maybe? A listening ear? A buddy? A father figure?*

"So, what grade do you teach?" Ted asked.

"Fourth grade."

"An excellent vintage."

Darren smiled and said, "It is. They're not old enough to have an attitude and not too young so that it's all shapes and numbers. I don't know how the kindergarten and first-grade teachers do it."

"Different skill set."

Darren found Ted trustworthy. "I just get concerned sometimes."

"Concerned?"

"Are they learning what they need to learn from me? Teaching is a much bigger responsibility than I thought before."

Phew, he just needs a mentor, not a daddy.

"You're very conscientious, and that's commendable. Most teachers don't get to where you're at until they're halfway through their careers. I get the feeling you're not one of those guys I can share a few platitudes with and you'll be inspired—you know, just do your best, put your heart into it every day."

"Uh, you're right. I'm not one of those guys," Darren affirmed.

"How long have you been teaching?" Ted asked.

"This is my second year."

"You seem like a smart guy. Why not go for a graduate degree? There are a lot of programs to choose from, and it might help you get deeper into your issue—do some really focused research on how kids learn best."

"I've got a lot of loans from undergrad."

"Now's the time to be in debt. You won't want to do graduate school in your thirties or forties. Suck it up, take out more loans, and know you'll pay them off sometime before you retire from here."

"Something to think about. How do you know if your teaching is getting through to the students?" Darren asked.

"It's hard to quantify, but, number one, I always view the students as bright and capable of learning a great deal. Number two, I see teaching as a vocation, not an occupation. This job does not occupy my time. It is a calling. It's not a religious calling, though my wife would argue all callings are spiritual in nature. Teaching is simply what I am supposed to do. You, also, Darren, have been summoned by the universe to do what you do. And every student you've taught or will teach is part of a great sea of humanity that will keep the universe ticking. If you don't do what you are supposed to do, a part of the universe will die a little death, as it does every day when people give up on it. I'm serious."

Darren was surprised at Ted's response. "You're not as burnt out as they told me."

"Oh? And who told you this?"

"Some of the other teachers warned me that you're burnt toast and that you don't care anymore."

"But, look at you, an independent thinker, investigating before accepting an opinion. Let's do something more manly sometime and go out for beer, okay?"

"Cool."

#####

CONSUELA GONZALEZ and her friend Marta sat on the padded metal chairs on her front porch. The two were conversing, as usual, in Spanish. They kept an eye on the variety of activities happening on the block—the neighbor working on his car, the young woman sitting on her front steps talking on a cell phone, the toddler children playing on the porch three doors down under the supervision of a watchful grandmother.

Marta was sympathetic regarding Consuela's failed surgery. "But your hand! What are you going to do?"

"What can I do? What's done is done," a stoic Consuela stated.

"I'm so sorry, so sorry. Did you know Maria Arroyo has the diabetes?"

Consuela nodded and said, "Y Antonio Benitez *también*."

Marta leaned in and lowered her voice. "And now Fatima Nieves was diagnosed with breast cancer."

"And José Prado with lung cancer."

"Your hand, your hand!" Marta repeated.

Richard Moyer came out his front door and stood on his porch, interrupting the women's conversation. Like them, he eyed the activity on the street. With a small half wall in between his and Consuela's porches, they ran into each other frequently, though rarely communicated due to the language barrier. They could, however, pick up on each other's moods and understood each other's personality.

"This one got bitten by a dog," Consuela said, looking first at Richard and back at Marta.

"Oh, dear," Marta clucked.

"Tore up his leg," Consuela said.

"Oh, dear!"

The women smiled at Richard and gave him a look of concern.

"I'm fine," he said, and stepped down to fuss with his tiny front yard, picking up a gum wrapper and a cigarette butt.

#####

EDDIE RAMIREZ regarded his participation in the Latino Leaders of Allentown as an important part of community policing. The group gathered monthly at the county government building on Seventh Street. The meeting was chaired by a lawyer named Luis Abreu, which made Eddie happy, because Luis always made sure to move things along. Abreu looked like a bit of a slob—Eddie had never seen him in anything but an unkempt, aging brown suit with a stained 1980s-era blue tie. But the lawyer caught everything, never missing an agenda item, and rarely allowing a comment go without a response.

Each committee gave their report: Education, Fundraising, Outreach, Health, and Government.

Then Luis moved to the last part of the agenda. "Next we have our Police Liaison. Sergeant Eddie Ramirez is here. What do we need to know today?"

Eddie stood and addressed the five people on the Executive Board as well as the nineteen in the audience.

"You probably saw in the paper or on the news that there was a body recovered in Jordan Park this past Saturday. Looks like it was a drug overdose. Too many drugs continue to move through Allentown. The police department has applied for funding from the federal government to add another program in our fight to reduce drugs in the city." Eddie spoke about additional police programs and then took questions.

"What's being done about the gang situation?" a local business owner asked. "My cameras keep picking up groups of shady-looking guys at two or three in the morning. My locks and alarms are too good for them, but they're some scary-looking dudes."

"Yes, they are scary, and I hope everyone here understands to contact us immediately if you have a problem, because we have a specially trained police task force focusing on local gangs. While we've seen a reduction in some of the gang activity, this problem continues to need more resources."

"How about hiring more Latino police officers?" a retired teacher asked. "How can the Latino community feel safe and protected by the police if there are so few officers who can really relate to us?

"We recently hired two. While we're still not where we need to be, I'm sure we'll be doing more Latino hiring in the future."

After Eddie responded to questions about police profiling and community policing, Luis Abreu moved to wrap up the meeting. "We're glad you could be here today Sergeant. Latino Leaders of Allentown appreciates your support. Thank you for your time."

#####

ABIGAIL BARRETT-THOMPSON looked up from her Bible to see consistory president Tim Thacker at her office door.

"Tim, hello. How're you doing?"

"I'm good, thank you, Abigail. I read the letter from the lawyer about the Dolly's Dollar Store thing you did. It's pretty menacing."

"A multi-million or billion-dollar company can hire lawyers that are good at making things as adversarial as possible. The protest was entirely legal, ethical, and in no way called our tax-exempt status into question. They're just blowing smoke."

Tim folded his arms and said, "I'm not so sure. Maybe we should have a lawyer look it over."

"I wouldn't waste the money. Churches are allowed to spend twenty percent of their budget on lobbying for legislation, and we are a long way off from even one tenth of one percent of the budget. If it would help people feel better, I'd recommend getting a response from the Conference Minister."

"That's a good idea. I'll ask for someone to get in touch with Reverend Ben and get his take on the situation."

Inside, Abigail tried humor to cope. Whenever her authority was dismissed, she imagined herself emerging victorious from a cage match with a clergyman possessing a Chippendale-type physique. *It's the lady pastor versus the manly, masculine, big, strong, tall, ripped, muscular man pastor. And the lady pastor triumphs!!!*

"And, Tim, the social justice committee will continue in other efforts like this. In fact, there is a minimum wage demonstration coming up that a number of our people will be participating in. And immigration reform efforts. As the song goes, we've only just begun."

"Good to know."

"I've got to start the Bible study. Have a good consistory meeting." Abigail carried her Bible and notes to the classroom where she was delighted to see another person in addition to the five regulars. She had seen this thirtyish man walking around the neighborhood on numerous occasions. He was nice-looking and didn't appear to have a car.

"Greetings." Abigail shook the man's hand. "I'm Abigail, Pastor of Faith UCC."

"I'm Evan."

"Great to meet you, and welcome to the Wednesday night Bible study. Let's go around the table."

"I'm Keith," said a young man with a goatee.

The young man sitting next to Keith also had a goatee, "I'm Jerry. Keith is my husband. We were legally married in Connecticut."

Evan responded, "Congratulations!"

"Hi, Evan. I'm Sherry."

"I'm Katie."

"I'm Chuck."

Evan gave a wave to everyone seated around the table, "Howdy."

Always moving things along to keep the class on track and on time, Abigail started, "Tonight we're in the middle of our study of the prophet Ezekiel. He's a little tough and weird, but I think we'll all end up liking him in the end."

Abigail offered prayer, handed out the study packets for Ezekiel 19-20, and gave her introduction of the prophet. "Ezekiel was in the first group of Israelite exiles to Babylonia, around 597 BCE. He was active as prophet from about 593-571 BCE. Let's help our newcomer with some of this. What does *BCE* stand for?"

"Before the Common Era," Sherry said.

"Right. We use *BCE*, Before the Common Era, and *CE*, Common Era, instead of *BC* and *AD* to keep in alignment with Biblical scholarship. And what Bible translations do we use for this study?" Abigail asked.

Katie replied, "NRSV, New Revised Standard Version and KJV, the King James Version."

"Yes," Abigail affirmed. "We use the NRSV Bible at Faith Church as it is often acknowledged as the most precise scholarly translation. However, we also use the King James Version because of its literary impact through history. And, what was the Exile?" Abigail asked.

Chuck answered, "It was a big event that happened when Israel was defeated by the Babylonians, and then the Israelites were exiled to Babylonia."

"A very good summary, thank you, Chuck," Abigail said. "So we have this guy, Ezekiel, who was from a priestly family. As a priest, Ezekiel spent a lot of time hanging around the great temple in Jerusalem—the temple was his life! But then what happened around 586 BCE?"

Keith responded, "The temple was destroyed."

Abigail replied, "Right. The temple was torn down by the Babylonians. Ezekiel had already been living in exile, but when he heard the news about the temple he must have been completely devastated. This thing Ezekiel had centered his life on was completely razed. Gone. Imagine how painful that would have been. So, Ezekiel was angry and he spent a lot of time sharing God's judgment on Israel. A little later on, we'll hear through Ezekiel how God judges other nations, and then the book will end with a good word about restoration for Israel. Phew! Before we start our read-through tonight, we really need to understand this concept of exile. What is a modern-day concept of exile?"

"People thrown out of their countries for political or religious reasons," Jerry offered.

"Yes, that is the most important way to understand it. And we might also spiritualize it. What are some ways an average person in the United States may be in exile?" Abigail said.

"Being on the outside of current politics," Katie suggested.

"Being exiled from your family for some reason. For being different," Keith said.

"Not wanting to participate in consumer culture," Chuck submitted.

Sherry added, "If you don't know how to do tech and social media very well, it's isolating and feels like exile."

"All good, thank you," Abigail said. The class worked through their first assigned chapter and continued diligently through the next. "Sherry, read verse fourteen in chapter twenty."

In a clear voice, Sherry read, *"But I wrought for my name's sake, that it should not be polluted before the heathen, in whose sight I brought them out."*

Abigail said, "God *wrought* for God's name's sake, meaning God acted for the sake of God's name. Ezekiel is sharing a little history. The Community of Israel was liberated from slavery in Egypt so that God's name would not be polluted. The notion of pollution occurs throughout Ezekiel. It's about not letting God get dirtied through worship of idols or profaning the Sabbath. What are some of our modern forms of pollution? How do we pollute God's world and sacred space?"

"With drugs," Jerry answered.

Abigail responded, "Yes. The body found in Jordan Park this past weekend showed the effects of drugs and how they pollute a community."

"Operating out of self-interest rather than common interest," Sherry offered.

"Idolatry of any kind," Chuck said, "when we put something above God."

"Like putting relationships above God," Katie said.

Keith added, "*Isms*—you know, things like racism, sexism, heterosexism."

"How about literal pollution?" Evan asked.

Abigail urged him, "Say more, Evan."

"The way we have let corporations pollute the water and the air just so we can have a hamburger, and then drive to get that hamburger instead of walking. I guess it could be called the pollution of convenience."

Keith pretended to sound an alarm, "Activist alert!"

"But don't worry, Evan. We love activism in this room," Abigail assured him. "Let's continue through this chapter."

#####

ALAN PECK, President Tim Thacker, Vice President Francine Dunning, and four other at-large members of the church's consistory assembled around a conference table for their monthly meeting. They were in the Peck Memorial Meeting Room, named after Alan's father, who had been a devoted member of Faith Church for decades and given a significant contribution to the church through his estate. Alan did most of the talking at the consistory gatherings owing to his decades of experience with leading and participating in meetings at his workplace. Due to his family's imprint at Faith Church, Alan was handily reelected to the consistory every two years. With the exception of Francine, the consistory members deferred to his opinions.

Tim glanced at the agenda. "Our next item is the financial update. Any comments?"

Alan spoke up immediately on a topic he brought to the consistory's attention every month. "Clearly, with this crazy dollar store rally, it's time to fire Abigail. The church continues to go downhill. She's done nothing to increase the finances or bring more people to worship here."

Francine had readied herself for this moment. She decided it was finally time to put a different vision in front of the group. Taking a deep breath, she replied to Alan, "I'm proud of Abigail and the church members who were at the dollar store rally. We've had this firing discussion many times before, and it has gone nowhere. So I'm offering a different idea this evening. I would vote to pay for Abigail to take Spanish classes so our church could communicate more effectively with the people in the neighborhood."

Alan slammed a hand on the table and raised his voice, "No way are we going to start speaking Spanish at this church!"

The other consistory members gasped at Alan's over-the-top reaction. Francine, however, was relieved that some of his true personality was being exposed. She had long suspected Alan to be a closeted racist, but had found it hard to navigate around his manipulations. *Perhaps something had changed. Maybe ol' Alan was no longer able to be as careful as he once was, using only coded references to how the neighborhood around the church had changed. But now it appeared he could no longer hide his xenophobia. It must have been taking too much energy and work to keep it concealed.* With narrowed eyes and tilted head, she said, "Well, well. We seem to have hit a nerve, Alan."

Tim cleared his throat and tried to take charge of the meeting, "Okay, folks, I think we're starting to get off track here."

Francine was not put off. "No. I think we're finally *on* track here and getting to the bottom of a few things. I'd like to make a motion to provide funding for Abigail to attend Spanish immersion courses at the local community college."

One of the quieter consistory members seconded the motion, and Tim asked for further discussion but there was a long pause. Everyone around the table looked at Francine and then at Alan. Finally, Tim again asked for comments and a few members briefly debated the cost of classes, but the motion failed to pass in the end.

Alan regained his composure and suggested the consistory focus on reducing expenses through the elimination of Internet service at the church. "I don't see a need for it for just one staff member. None of the volunteers need it while we're here. If Abigail needs to get online, she can use her 4G or go to the library or use it at her home."

THURSDAY, APRIL 25, 2013

RICHARD MOYER shortened his daily walk, omitting the portion through the park. He shuffled a bit as he journeyed down Greenleaf Street and left on Meadow. He paused in front of the vacant battery factory, hanging his right hand for a moment on the chain link fence that surrounded the property.

Even when it employed three shifts, the place always looked bleak. No landscaping, just a massive parking lot with a low brick building set at the back. The walls were falling, weeds were plentiful, and bricks were piled haphazardly around the building. The Environmental Protection Agency's brownfield restoration took decades, but the land under and around the building was apparently finally healthy enough for new construction. *I may see what comes of it or I may croak before they take away the first pile of bricks. Funny how I used to think that I'd see everything. Now it's a countdown to the end. At least I'll be with Ellie again.*

Richard turned around and slowly started back home.

#####

EDDIE RAMIREZ was transfixed by another hardcore video when a call on his other cell phone interrupted his viewing. He unthinkingly slipped his private phone in his suit jacket pocket.

"Hey, beautiful." Eddie turned up the charm as he greeted his wife.

"You forgot your reports on the table."

"Oh, wow. I'll be back in a few minutes. Thanks, babe." He stuffed his phone into the same pocket as his private phone.

Eddie started the car, sped out of the empty parking lot, and headed back to the house. He shook his head at his forgetfulness. *Too much going on, too much to keep up with every day. I'm slipping.*

He bounded up the steps to the house and found his reports on the dining room table where Isabella was seated, sipping on her morning coffee.

Eddie's cell phone rang. He reached into his pocket and inadvertently pulled out his private phone.

"I've never seen that phone," Isabella said.

Eddie responded smoothly, "It's for a special police investigation." He reached into his pocket again for the other phone.

He glanced at the caller ID and saw it was his night desk sergeant. "Hey, Sarge. What's up?"

"Two call-outs so far today. Some kind of plague going on."

"Understaffing, my favorite thing," Eddie joked.

"Thought you'd want to know."

"Yeah. See you soon."

Isabella looked up at her husband from her chair. "You missed our last two date nights 'cause of work. When are we going to make it up?"

"Oh, babe, we'll make it up, believe me." Eddie bent down and kissed Isabella. "You have to know that I want to take my gorgeous wife out on the town."

Isabella crossed her arms. "Friday night. No cancellations."

"Friday night it is. Gotta go. Running late."

#####

ABIGAIL BARRETT-THOMPSON arranged the agenda and handouts for the clergy meeting to strategize a response to the threatening letter from the Charlotte law firm.

She heard noises from the fellowship hall and walked in to find Richard fussing with tables and chairs.

"Good morning, Richard. How are you feeling today?"

"Better." He came toward her carrying a section of the local newspaper.

"I know you don't get a paper copy of the newspaper anymore, but I thought you would be interested in this article." He pointed to the headline in the Business section.

Abigail read it aloud. "*New Strip Mall to Include Dolly's Dollar Store, Tobacco Store and Pizza Shop*. Blecch."

"It's going to be just two blocks away from the church. I know you had protested them and thought you'd want to know about this."

"Yes, thank you, Richard. This will be a part of our meeting today."

"I was wondering what kind of stores they were going to put in that strip mall. At least they're going to tear down the battery factory. It's falling apart over there."

"Replacing one pollution with another," Abigail said.

#####

GINA GONZALEZ checked her text messages again. Nothing from Jay, which was strange. Jay usually responded to her texts quickly and flirtatiously, but she had not replied to any texts from the day before. *Maybe she had a long shift at work.* Gina decided to send one more text: "Jay, darling, u ok?"

Gina walked into the nursing home, cheerily greeting the residents who lined the front entrance. She continued straight to her office where she started on some paperwork. After an hour, she peeked at her phone and saw Jay had sent a text in reply: "I'm good"

Gina texted back: "didn't hear from u 4 awhile. just miss my jay jay"

By lunchtime, there was still no reply. Gina forced herself to focus on resident issues throughout the afternoon. On her way to her car at the end of the workday, her phone pinged. She read Jay's message: "U talk 2 much about other ppl, I'm done, Peace"

Gina couldn't believe it—a breakup by text message? *How dare she!* She couldn't type fast enough: "Not cool 2 do on text. Could we talk in person?"

This time Jay's reply was immediate: "Nope"

Gina was barely able to concentrate on the road as she drove home. Hurt and angry, she ran to her room where she let her emotions run freely.

By dinnertime, she had pulled herself together. She was still puffy, but presentable.

Anna asked, "You okay?"

"Sure. I'm good. What's for dinner? Smells delicious."

"Mofongo."

"Yum! How's e'rybody doin'?" Gina went into life-of-the-party mode as she took a seat. "Willie, how's basketball these days?"

He shrugged. "Fine."

"Fine? That's all you got for me? I'm sure you made, like, four hundred shots today."

"Did layups mostly."

"Any bags today, Genny?"

"No. Went to the park with Marcus and we played this game with rocks in the creek," Genny said, not thinking.

"Marcus. Who is this Marcus?" Gina smiled and raised her eyebrows.

"Just a friend."

Willie giggled. "He's a munchkin."

"Shut up!" Genny turned to her aunt and explained, "He's kind of short."

"A dwarf," Willie said.

"Shut up! Mom!" Genny looked at her mother.

Anna said, "Willie, come on. Don't call someone names. You know better than that. And, Genny, no more of the 'shut up's."

"Why have I not heard about this Marcus before?" Gina asked.

"Mom said not to share stuff like that with you because you go and tell everybody," Genny replied.

Anna and Consuela sucked in their breath and looked at Gina, who put her fork down, left the table, and exited the house out the back door.

"You need to talk to her when she gets back," Consuela said to Anna.

"What's wrong with Auntie Gina?" Willie asked.

"She probably had a tough day at work," Anna said, "so we're going to be extra nice to her the next few days, okay?"

#####

ALAN PECK met Amy at the gym. It was the busiest time of the day, but they enjoyed being out and being seen, both trim in their tight exercise gear. While Alan spent a half hour on the treadmill, Amy was on the elliptical, and then both undertook a series of weightlifting exercises.

Back home after their workouts, dinner was salmon salad, which they ate while debating weekend plans.

"I'd like to get back to the casino in Bethlehem. It has been a few weeks," Alan said.

"They do love us there, don't they? It's nice to be regulars some place. Or we could go into New York, do some shopping or take in a show."

"We haven't been there for quite a while, have we?" Alan acknowledged.

"Almost six months now."

"Well, then. Sounds like it's New York, New York, for us."

After cleanup they went into the home office where they both caught up on work email. Then Amy spent the next two hours on social media while Alan watched a Knicks game on the big screen television with surround sound. During a commercial break Alan muted the sound for some reflection. *This really is my castle. My life couldn't be much better—everything I've ever wanted, I have. No one gave me any of this—I earned it all. It's all a result of my labor. On top of it, I've got nice lookin', hard workin' wife and two great kids. Anyone can do it. Equal opportunity for all.* Alan's mind wandered to his nemesis, Abigail. *She talks about people on the margins, but these so-called marginalized people did it to themselves. And all these other clergy whine on behalf of the Dolly's Dollar employees, forgetting that they chose to work there. When are these religious types going to stop being busybodies? Telling someone how to run their business? Insane! Imagine if a group of people from Dolly's came over to protest at Faith Church, telling Abigail how to run the church?*

#####

JOHNNY RAMOS looked across his desk at Deacon Rob. "Forty thousand dollars, now that's a generous gift," Johnny said.

"He'd own you. They'd own us," Rob replied.

"Of course. Who is doing demolition and construction?"

"Some contractor out of Philly, probably in possession of a long-standing friendship with SmithCo. They're even seeking LEED certification."

"What's that?" Johnny asked.

"A greener, more environmentally sensitive approach to construction. The project will get points for restoring a brownfield."

"Sorry you lost the bid."

"You win some, you lose some. I've been in the construction business for thirty years and it's always been up and down, feast or famine."

"You know, with that extra forty thousand, we could hire another person to help with counseling to get more addicts clean."

"If it's supposed to be, the money will manifest itself from the people, or so a certain pastor always says," Rob reminded Johnny.

"Or we could put the money in savings for when we need roof or boiler repairs."

"At what cost?"

Johnny waved a hand at Rob, "Right, right, I know it. *'For what shall it profit a man, if he shall gain the whole world, and lose his own soul?'*"

Rob said, "This was a test and you have passed it."

Johnny shook himself and said, "Okay, I'm going to snap out of this. Here's what we'll do. I'm going to have you record me as I put the check through the shredder. You can use your phone. I'll have you start off from far away, then come in for a close-up on me, then a close-up on the shredder."

Rob found this amusing. "What are you, some sort of movie director?"

"My sons show me this tech stuff all the time, and videos can really have an impact if they're filmed well."

"No pressure on me, your amateur cameraman."

"You'll do fine. Okay, start over there." Johnny pointed to the far corner. "Let me know when you have everything ready."

Johnny moved to sit on the edge of his desk with the shredder next to him.

"Five, four, three, two, one, and, we're rolling," Rob said.

Johnny looked into the phone, "Hi. I'm Pastor Johnny Ramos, Church of the Living Water, Allentown, Pennsylvania. It's

Thursday, April 25, 2013. We recently received a visit from retired Major League Baseball player David Garcia. Garcia now works for SmithCo., which owns Dolly's Dollar Stores. You may remember that Dolly's sells a lot of junk, pays their workers scandalously low wages, and gives them inconsistent work schedules so they can't make personal plans in advance. The business is doing well, and Garcia presented us with a check in the amount of forty thousand dollars to support our church's addiction programs."

Johnny paused to hold the check next to his face, and Rob moved in closer with his phone camera.

"I'd really like to accept the gift—forty thousand dollars is a lot of money—but it comes at too high a cost. In exchange for the forty thousand dollars, we'd have to support Dolly's employment practices and encourage people to go to their new store that's going to be built a few blocks from the church. So, this check is going in the shredder. Jesus said, '*It is easier for a camel to go through the eye of a needle than for a rich man to enter into the kingdom of God.*' I'm going to stay on the side of Jesus. Johnny Ramos and Church of the Living Water cannot be bought!"

Using his best theatrics, Johnny held the check over the shredder. Rob went up to Johnny and filmed the check as it ground through the teeth. Johnny then reached into the basket of the shredder and let pieces filter through his hands. "We're going to pull together and take care of our own. We don't need other people's money. We don't need SmithCo.'s money. We know that the Lord will provide in due time! Come over to Church of the Living Water, Sundays at ten. Join us for worship—you will be blessed."

Rob stopped filming and the two men watched the video together.

"Not bad," Johnny said as he lightly punched Rob's shoulder. "Send it to Javi. He'll put it on YouTube and he'll make it blow up all over Facebook and Twitter." Tech-related matters were capably handled by Johnny's eldest, Javier Ramos. He managed all of the church's social networking, the recording of worship services, and any random tech need of the congregation. Javi had built a large network of loyal friends and followers of Church of the Living Water, and the video would be reposted and shared by hundreds.

#####

ABIGAIL BARRETT-THOMPSON flipped on the local evening news at ten, wondering if there would be a piece on Dolly's Dollar Store. The clergy meeting that afternoon at Faith UCC had produced a well-written press release, though Abigail had not received any phone calls from print or televised media in response.

The lead story was a fire in downtown Allentown, and the second story started with the somber anchor stating, "A local pastor says he cannot be bought." Abigail sat astonished as she watched the video of Johnny Ramos shredding a check and listened to the story of the attempted forty-thousand-dollar payoff.

Good for Johnny. It's a bit showy, but all in all the right thing to do. He'll probably get fifty new church members as a result. Meanwhile, I'm the one who started this effort, got it off the ground, did all of the coordination, and Faith UCC will probably lose members. She reached for a bag of candy bars.

INBOX

WEDNESDAY, MAY 8, 2013

GINA GONZALEZ awoke from her troubled sleep at four o'clock. She tried to fall back to sleep, but could not. She finally gave up and propped herself up on her pillows. *Let me see what's happening on Facebook.* She grabbed her phone and scrolled through her news feed. A friend, Heidi Jacobs, had posted that she was in a new relationship and had received numerous congratulatory comments. Gina searched more and saw that Heidi's new love interest was Jay—her Jay Jay. Figuring that Heidi would unfriend her anyway, Gina wrote a comment under the announcement: "Congrats Heidi & u better watch out cuz jay jay is a supah dupah playah"

#####

EVAN LEMMON MOORE re-read the message he drafted to his mother.

Subject: re: Hello from IL
From: Evan.Lemmon.Moore@gmail.com
Date: Wed, May 8, 2013 7:01 am
To: Mary.Moore@aol.com

Hi Mom,

Sorry to take so long to write back to you.
I'm still working for BlackBox customer service. It gets a little dull sometimes but it pays the bills. I'm also volunteering with the Trail Tenders once a week and it has been a good way to stay connected with nature. A lot of the guys are former scouts, so that's good too that we have some shared memories of things like scout camp.

I followed the Memorial High boys and girls basketball teams online, what a year! Playoffs for both and quarterfinals for the girls, I bet the school went wild, along with the town.

Congratulations on Church Council. One thing I remember from the pastor when I was a teen is that we are supposed to live "in" the world and not be "of" it. I try to do that. Say hello to Dad and Happy Mother's Day, you are a great mother,

Evan

JOHNNY RAMOS paused in the sanctuary to read his daily devotional email message.

Subject: Your Daily Verse
From: YDV@YourDailyVerse.org
Date: Wed, May 8, 2013 4:30 am
To: PastorJohnny@ChurchoftheLivingWater.org

Daily Bible Verse – Wednesday, May 8, 2013

Be ye therefore merciful, as your Father also is merciful.
Luke 6:36
King James Version

"Amen," Johnny said, and forwarded the message to Javi to post on social media.

ANNA RAMIREZ thought about the text before sending it to her ex-husband. She had to be careful or he might try to bust her on a technicality with the custody agreement. She typed: "Hi

Eddie, this is a reminder that the kids will be picked up early Sunday morning for a previously scheduled family gathering for Mother's Day. This had been arranged with you last month."

So glad we're no longer married. I was always so stressed out being with Eddie, constantly giving in to his schedule and his needs. He's got his new wife under his thumb, and apparently she's fine with Eddie making all of the decisions. I guess some women actually like being controlled by a man. Thank goodness Willie and Genny aren't in that 24/7.

#####

ABIGAIL BARRETT-THOMPSON caught up on thank you notes. Mostly she sent them through the mail, but if she was far behind, she would send thanks via an email message.

Subject: Your ushering
From: Rev.Barrett-Thompson@FaithUCC.org
Date: Wed, May 8, 2013 10:19 am
To: Dana45883@gmail.com

Dana,

A quick note to thank you for your ushering at Faith UCC. Ushers fill such a critical role at the church, welcoming first-time visitors, ensuring a smooth worship service, and keeping the sanctuary in good order. Your service to God through the church is much appreciated! I hope you are enjoying this marvelous spring weather – I'm sure your flower gardens are spectacular right now.

Peace,
Rev. Abigail Barrett-Thompson

#####

TED THOMPSON waited for his last class of the day to begin and was efficiently working through his school-related email messages. He clicked on a message from the young teacher he had spoken with recently in the parking lot.

Subject: Appreciated
From: Darren.Long@AllentownConsolidated.edu
Date: Wed, May 8, 2013 11:01 am
To: Ted.Thompson@AllentownConsolidated.edu

Ted,

Appreciated your teaching pep talk a few weeks ago, thanks. How's about a brewski soon? I'm headed home for the Mother's Day weekend, but could meet you sometime in the next week.

Darren

Ted smiled and clicked on the calendar on his phone, to check availability.

ALAN PECK opened the message from his buddy Jack Shears, knowing it would be in the code they had talked about the last time they got together. Jack had instructed Alan to delete his emails after reading them. The attorneys at Holliday, Shears & Dowell had a computer genius on their payroll, and Jack was confident that once the messages were deleted it would be nearly impossible to retrieve them. Jack had been burned once with recovered emails in a case that ended with a payout to a client's opponent and, while the amount was not large, he was determined that it not happen again. Both Jack and Alan carefully deleted every email, chuckling at the drama they had created and thrilled with their little cloak-and-dagger escapades.

Subject: Juice squeeze continues
From: Jack.Shears@HollidayShearsDowell.com
Date: Wed, May 8, 2013 12:02 pm
To: Alan.Peck@Vigor.com

Squeeze continues, it's healthy to drink juice.

JS

The plan was to "squeeze" the antibusiness churches financially by pursuing legal action and then making a case that would force the congregations to pay lawyers' fees. Alan quickly replied:

Excellent. To your continued good health!

ISABELLA RAMIREZ cleaned the kitchen while Sofia worked on a coloring book. Afterwards, Isabella sat at the table with her daughter and checked her Twitter feed. After the National Christian Moms Conference, Isabella now followed 256 people and organizations, had 504 Twitter followers, and her number of Facebook friends had almost tripled to over a thousand. Earlier in the morning Isabella had sent out a tweet.

Isabella Ramirez @Mom4Christ May 8
    Day 8 of 12 Days of Things My Mom Taught Me: My
Mom Loves Jesus

A photo of her mother was included, and it had been retweeted seven times.

#####

WILLIE RAMIREZ texted Alex on his walk home from school.

> Willie texted: "Where were u 2day?"
> "Home sick"
> "Sorry"
> "Meet u at park for bball?" Alex typed back.
> "R u sick?"
> "I feel bttr"
> "Ok c u soon"

GENNY RAMIREZ stepped onto the front porch of her grandmother's house and texted her mom: "Home now"

Anna was on her afternoon break and wrote back to her daughter: "I'll b home soon. Love u my smart and beautiful daughter"

Genny texted back: "Love u"

CONSUELA GONZALEZ and **RICHARD MOYER** sat on their respective living room couches and flipped on their TVs at five o'clock for the first round of Lehigh Valley evening news.

EDDIE RAMIREZ read Anna's text about returning Willie and Genny to her for Mother's Day. He typed back: "The kids will be ready for pickup at 9 AM Sunday May 12. They will be at my house the next two Sunday mornings (May 19, 26) due to missing worship service May 12."

SUMMER 2013

FRIDAY, JULY 19, 2013

RICHARD MOYER took his usual early-morning route down Greenleaf, then left on Meadow. General Ridgway had not been replaced, so Richard walked alone. He stopped to catch his breath at the former battery factory property. The building was demolished in late May and then in June the weed-strewn parking lot was ground into pieces. Now there was a new cement parking pad, looking very smooth, along with a pad for the strip mall stores. *Here we go. Once they get started, it'll all go very quickly.*

#####

JOHNNY RAMOS rarely sweated a decision, but fretted with Deacon Rob during their early morning meeting. Until Office Administrator Carla arrived an hour later at eight, things would be quiet in the church.

"It's a big risk," Johnny said. "It's private property."

"Yes, but you know it's evil."

"Rob, Rob, Rob-a-lob, I didn't know you were such a radical."

"I'm not, but this thing has me worked up. We need to draw the line. And when did you get all revolutionary?"

Johnny nodded. "I'm with you. This needs to stop. We need to be the ones to determine what stores come into our neighborhoods. I'm tired of these corporations making decisions and taking advantage of our people."

"I'm glad we informed all those other pastors about what we're doing. They'll rally their people and it won't be just about us," Rob suggested.

Not one to shy away from the spotlight, Johnny asked, "What's wrong with it just being us?"

Rob replied, "This is bigger than us and we're going to need as many people there as possible. We have charge of the hours where we are most likely to get on television, probably nine to eleven in the morning and four till seven in the evening. We may need to pull in even more churches for additional coverage. Have

Carla contact every one of the churches in at least the immediate neighborhood. She can give them the details for Sunday night."

"Yeah, yeah, you're right. That's the way to go. Let's pray on this, Deacon." Johnny paused, then offered one of the shortest prayers of his pastoral career. "Father God, we're heading into the unknown. We will not fear because our trust is in You. Amen."

#####

GINA GONZALEZ led nursing home resident Vivian Burke through a review and evaluation. For the first year, Social Services did a quarterly check-in with new residents to follow and ease their transition. They were in the room where Gina had previously conducted the intake with Vivian and her daughter and son-in-law. Vivian still looked small in her wheelchair, but her emotional health had improved. Gina knew that a move to Elm Pond often increased a person's conviviality due to more daily interaction with others.

"Mrs. Burke, this is our first check-in of the year. I have a series of questions to ask you that won't take too long. It will help our facility provide the best care possible to our residents."

"Anything to help, dear."

"First off, is our facility clean?"

"Yes."

"Does it smell clean?"

"Most of the time. Accidents do happen with some people—it can't be helped. But the housekeepers are fast to clean up."

"How would you rate the food? Excellent, good, fair, or poor?"

Vivian shook her head. "It's not good! I'd definitely say poor. I know they work hard in the kitchen, but the food has no taste most days."

Gina asked thirty-five more questions, concluding with, "Are there any other comments you'd like to provide at this time?"

"I can't think of anything, except, dear, there is something I need to tell you."

"Oh, okay, Mrs. Burke. Go ahead." Gina held her pen above the paper.

"You don't need to write this down."

Gina tilted her head, curious as to what Vivian could possibly tell her. "What is it?"

"The nurses call you *Gossip Girl* behind your back."

"They do? Well, that's... interesting." Gina looked down at her notes.

"One thing you might want to think about is saying only good things about people, putting them in the best possible light."

Gina smiled at Vivian. "Yes, sure, but I don't want to lie about people."

"You don't lie. You find the good part of people and share it."

"But people have bad things happen or they're negative or they're mean and they need to be called on it," Gina insisted.

"But why would you want to share that with others?"

"I'm a good person. I really am." Gina was convincing herself more than she was Mrs. Burke.

"Of course you are, dear. But we all have something to work on in our lives. And, guess what? It never ends. Even when you're my age there will be things in your life to keep working on. You are such a pretty young lady with a lot of potential."

Gina switched the subject, "Time to get you to your next activity. It's arts and crafts morning!"

Gina wheeled Vivian to the activity room. "Have a good day, Mrs. Burke." Her emotions running high, Gina rushed to the nearest stairwell and sat on the top step. Memories of that traumatic day back in eighth grade knocked her over and she had to withdraw from her coworkers and Elm Pond's residents. First, the smell of lunch returned—the ground beef the cafeteria cooked and served in tacos had always made her gag. That day she ate only applesauce and salad and chatted with her best friend Ruthie. When she retrieved the books for her afternoon classes from her locker and clicked the combination lock, she turned to see a herd of girls gathered behind her.

Startled, she saw Ruthie among the group that inched closer and said, "Ruthie, what's up? What's going on?"

One of the bigger girls at the front stared intently at Gina and said, "Shut up. Just shut up, *dyke*."

Gina felt her face getting hot. "You shut up. I'm not a dyke."

Another girl came up and pushed Gina hard against the lockers. "Big dyke. Ruthie told everyone. She said that almost every day this week you told her she looks pretty."

Gina looked frantically for an escape. "So what?"

The larger girl pinned her against the lockers and the punches and hair pulling started. A hall monitor heard the ruckus and broke the fight up moments after it had started. Gina escaped serious physical harm, but for the rest of the school year—four months—she endured constant whispers in her ears. Someone would lean over during class and murmur "hey, dyke," and others snickered. Boys mumbled "dyke" as they passed her in the hall, and the power-hungry, status-driven girls pushed her into the lockers while the quiet girls looked at her sympathetically but did nothing. Ruthie would not make eye contact with her and they never spoke to each other again.

That summer, Gina devised a plan. During her first week in high school, she ingratiated herself with three other freshman girls from a different middle school. They quickly became the power girl group on campus, and for the next four years, Gina and her crew were the main source of rumors, misinformation and all varieties of salacious gossip. *In high school, there was no more talk about me. It was always a lot more fun to initiate the talk than be the subject of it.*

One of the doors to the stairwell opened. Gina shook off her disturbing recollections, cleared her throat, and continued down the steps.

#####

ISABELLA RAMIREZ smoothed her skirt and leaned against her mother's kitchen counter. Sofia busied herself with toys in the living room.

"I shared the good news with Eddie last night, Mamá, and I want you to be the next to know. I'm pregnant!" She was exuberant.

"Another grandchild. I'm so blessed." Anita clapped her hands together. "You will be so blessed."

"Oh, yes, we are absolutely blessed. But Eddie will probably want to stop with two."

"We'll see about that."

"I never thought being a mom was going to be so hard, but I never thought it would be so rewarding."

"My greatest honor was raising children and keeping the home. The most important gift anyone can give the world is the godly raising of children. You are carrying on the tradition, and I'm so proud of you. In Proverbs, the virtuous wife looks after everything and fears the Lord. That's what we try to do."

For just a moment, Isabella stood straighter and became serious. "Would you like to buy three candles so *more* women could learn to be a mom like you next year when I go to Dallas?"

Isabella pulled out the order sheet and the two women giggled. She had raised twelve hundred dollars so far toward the trip to the National Moms Conference in Texas.

#####

ALAN PECK couldn't hide his smile as he took a seat at the table with executives from Care2Trust, a Charlotte-based health insurance company. A merger between Vigor and Care2Trust would increase revenue for all parties. The merger had come about through a connection via Jack Shears. Care2Trust was a newer company and highly Internet-integrated. Vigor would benefit from their advanced technology, and they would profit from Vigor's loyal customer base.

Persuading Vigor's executives to consider the merger had not been easy. Some wanted things to stay the same, but Alan had carefully and indefatigably built a solid case for why Vigor and Care2Trust should come together. In the end, Vigor's executives found releasing themselves from the company name the most difficult part of the merger. But Care2Trust was already an established Internet brand, so it would be less confusing for Vigor's customers to acclimate to a name change.

Every executive around the table was able to keep their job as part of the merger agreement, though four were conveniently opting for early retirement. For now, they would maintain their locations in Charlotte and Allentown, and rely on weekly teleconferencing and daily emails to keep things running smoothly. Jack's law firm would complete the final paperwork by the end of the day, and by Monday morning, everyone would arrive at work to find contractors removing the Vigor sign from the front of the building.

As last-minute details about the merger were worked out around the table, Alan reflected on potential weekend plans. *Tonight we'll celebrate at the casino. Tomorrow we'll make an appearance at the gym. And tomorrow night, dinner at our favorite steakhouse.*

#####

EVAN LEMMON MOORE rocked in his chair while on the daily noon conference call with eight other BlackBox customer service reps and their supervisor, Soren Hendrick. Because they all worked from home and never gathered together in a bricks-and-mortar building, BlackBox insisted they have a brief daily check-in.

Soren started off, as usual, with a slide show on the latest metrics. "If you'll all look at the first slide, you'll see the latest average wait time and average length-of-call. And then look at the comparison of our team results to the others. We land in the middle. We want to reduce those wait times, and we do that by resolving our incoming calls with more speed. I have confidence that our team will improve. It's all about customers being satisfied with the entirety of their BlackBox experience. They may think our games are awesome, but if they have a bad experience with customer service they will have no qualms about switching to a game system offered by one of our competitors."

And that's less money for the executives, Evan thought, crossing his arms and frowning. *Meanwhile, customer service reps have a paltry five personal days annually to use for vacation or sick days, bare-bones health insurance, and certainly no retirement benefits.*

Soren continued with the instructional portion of the conference call. "Our training today is about a change we're making to our script. Starting today, you will be required to ask at the end of every call 'Is there anything else we can do for you today or any purchases you'd like to make?' This puts in the customer's head that they can buy additional games or services while they're on the line with you. We've done a test run of it, and it has been shown to increase revenue. Think of it like those items right next to the cash register in the grocery store line—gum, candy, magazines, batteries—stores receive a nice revenue stream from these impulse purchases. Because our calls are recorded, we'll be checking to make sure you're using this phrase at the end of every call. The line will be sent to your email inbox, but I'll say it again. At the end of every call you are now required to ask 'Is there anything else we can do for you today or any purchases you'd like to make?' Any questions?"

Evan couldn't resist. "So you want us to reduce the average length-of-call time while at the same time add this phrase about purchases which makes the call longer?"

"Our old timer Evan always has a juicy question," Soren said. "The phrase is not that long, and remember, it's all about helping people have a better customer service experience along with providing them with an opportunity to purchase more BlackBox products."

That wasn't really an answer, Evan thought.

Soren wrapped up the call, "I'm not hearing any other questions. Okay, team, keep it up! Talk to you tomorrow at noon."

#####

ANNA RAMIREZ ended her shift and immediately checked her private post office box. The earrings she ordered two weeks earlier had arrived. In the empty breakroom she carefully opened the package. The hoop earrings were so rich looking—none of that discount store gold-plated junk—these were solid gold, baby. She'd wear them for tonight's date with Evan. Anna glanced at the bill—four hundred and ninety-nine dollars, plus twelve for delivery.

Steve popped in just as she was trying the earrings on. "Well, what do we have here? Some new earrings? I smell a date night."

"Yes. Gotta look good, you know?"

"Those look good and expensive. What'd you pay for those babies?"

"A lot."

Steve went into an infomercial-type voice. "Have your debts now or ever been unmanageable?"

Anna put her hand on her hip and scowled. "What?"

"Just making fun. But it looks like I touched a nerve. You do seem to order a lot. That's all, I guess," Steve shrugged.

"I guess it's none of your business." Anna tried hard to make her voice sound playful.

"My sister went to credit counseling and it really turned things around."

"I should have been a counselor. Everything these days is 'see a counselor for this,' 'see a counselor for that.' I'd be making some *good* money. I could start by counseling all those people in line every day about how to get happy and get over themselves 'cause the wait isn't nearly as long as they think!"

Steve laughed on his way out of the break room and wished Anna well, "Have a good date. Let's double-date sometime—you and Evan, me and Glenn. The garden guys can talk gardens and we can counsel one another about all our problems."

Anna threw the packaging in the trash and sat on one of the time-tested orange plastic chairs. *Maybe if Dad had said yes to me just once or twice. I'd ask for new shoes and it was no. I'd ask for a new top and he'd say no. Even for just a dollar to go to McDonald's and it was "No. Your mother's food is fine." And with Eddie, every purchase was a battle, an opportunity to win a dispute. Well, they don't control me any longer. It's my life and my credit card and I can spend whatever I want, whenever I want.*

#####

GENNY RAMIREZ spent barely ten minutes at her father's house after being dropped off before she was out the door and galloping down to Jordan Park, trailing her brother by a block. Willie raced to the basketball court to meet Alex while Genny headed to the creek. The park was packed with kids and families out for a summer's evening—some enjoying a picnic, others lying on blankets. Genny had on her old shoes so she could walk through the shallow areas of Jordan Creek to look for smooth rocks.

"Hey, Genny."

Genny looked up and saw Marcus walking toward her with a towel draped around his neck. "Hey, Marcus. Were you at the pool all day?"

"All afternoon. Going to the movies tonight with my uncle—probably *Lone Ranger* or maybe *Man of Steel* again."

She handed Marcus a small rock and they tried to skip their stones as many times as they could. Earlier in the month, Genny had reached an all-time high of five skips, while Marcus had been stuck at two since May. They were taking turns with a handful of stones when suddenly something moved on the opposite bank.

"What's that?" Genny looked at Marcus.

"I thought it was a big snake, but that's an *alligator.*"

Genny squinted at the shape across the creek. "I've never seen one before."

The two stared at the alligator for a moment and then Marcus yelled, "Gator!" The people nearby looked up. Again Marcus yelled and pointed, "Gator! Gator! Gator!"

Several people headed toward the creek, the adults more excited than the kids. "An alligator in Allentown?" "That's a first." "What the—" A few kids picked up rocks, but one of the adults said sternly, "Don't throw anything. I'm calling Animal Control."

Genny texted her dad: "Alligator in creek"

Eddie wrote back: "Lol"

Genny texted back: "Really"

Upon seeing the large crowd rushing to the creek's edge, Willie and Alex jogged over.

Willie glanced at the alligator and asked, "Did you tell Dad?"

"Yeah, I just texted him," Genny replied.

"Good thing you were out of the water." Alex gave Genny a pseudo-serious look. "He could have bit your foot off."

"Bloody stump dragging around." Willie pretended to limp.

Before Genny could reply, they saw a police car and animal control van enter the park. The crowd watched, fascinated, as the valiant workers corralled the alligator. The rare event of an exotic animal in Jordan Park had people getting raucous and shouting jokes about alligator shoes and purses. The alligator appeared to be grinning with all the attention, showing off its dangerous bite. After ten minutes, the animal control experts had captured the alligator and placed it in the van. When the excitement was over, everyone dispersed back to their picnics and blankets.

Marcus said to Genny, "That was a long gator!"

"Really long. What if it has kids?"

"More gators in the creek," Marcus said as Genny squinted at the water, looking for gator family members.

Marcus left and Genny sat at the water's edge texting with her dad.

"It was big!"

"Genny the gator slayer"

"No killing animals"

"U r right, the gator will go to a nice home somewhere with other gators"

"In a wild place?"

"Up to animal control now. U did good. I'm proud of u, my brave daughter"

"Love u"

Eddie shook his head and wondered how and why an alligator would be in their city park. He'd get the details later. He then thought about how his kids would never have experienced seeing an alligator in Allentown if they had been glued to a TV or playing games at a computer. *They're learning and seeing real things every day. All these other kids with their blank looks from sitting in front of screens all day. Not my kids!*

#####

ANNA RAMIREZ took Evan's hand as he led her along the rocks to North Lookout at Hawk Mountain. It had been a short but steep hike, and she was glad to take a seat on a massive rock with a magnificent view of the valley. About twenty other people were at the lookout, many with binoculars to get a better view of the hawks. Evan sat behind Anna with his legs wrapped around her. He occasionally kissed the top of her head, and she responded by snuggling closer. They both could have remained on top of the mountain overnight in each other's arms but knew they had to hike back down to the car before nightfall.

They had kept their relationship quiet. It was too early, and they did not want others nosing around, asking questions and offering advice. Anna shared with her coworker Steve, while Evan let his friend and fellow Trail Tender Bill know about his new relationship. On their date nights, Anna picked up Evan at a diner parking lot on Seventh Street. At the end of their date she dropped him back off in the same place and he'd walk home so as not to arouse Eddie's suspicion and to keep the kids unaware.

Anna guessed that Eddie already knew about their relationship. He had always been highly intuitive, which served him well in police investigations but sometimes caused Anna to be extra cautious in her comings and goings. Her activities with Evan were none of Eddie's business. Surely Anna's sister and mother suspected there was something or someone new in her life, though they did not know the specifics. And others would figure it out soon enough as she and Evan started spending more and more time together. For now, Anna loved the affection and the hikes. She especially looked forward to cooking with him, researching vegetarian recipes and even secretly testing new side dishes for family dinners.

The one thing Anna didn't understand was Evan's whacked Monday-caveman-communication black-out. He had been so vague with her, saying that from Sunday evenings till Tuesday mornings he had other commitments and wasn't available to talk. *Whatever. Maybe it's some geeky male thing—fantasy football or weekly video game competitions.*

ABIGAIL BARRETT-THOMPSON watched the local news in the evening with her husband. The first story featured the alligator found by Jordan Creek. She guffawed and turned to Ted, declaring, "I guess there won't be any river baptisms there anytime soon."

SATURDAY, JULY 20, 2013

RICHARD MOYER slouched in the passenger seat of Robert Schulz's 1994 Chevy Cavalier. Both front seats were as far back as they could go. Richard didn't really need the extra leg room, but Robert's belly would only fit behind the wheel with the seat in its outermost position. Senior Day at the Allentown Fairgrounds started at eight o'clock. Richard checked his watch. Seven thirty. They were parked outside the main hall keeping an eye on everything until the doors opened. Always out of bed before most, and perpetually early for events, Richard and Robert sipped coffee they had purchased from a nearby donut shop.

"You know they're going to try to get us to sign up for all sorts of things," Richard said.

"They think we have lots of money, Richie."

"That's what the newspaper says. The old folks have the money while the young ones coming up are scraping by."

"Most young ones have to scrape by at some point."

"Who has all the money, Schultzie?" Richard asked, ready to launch into his speech.

"You know who."

Richard had said it all before to Schultzie and he couldn't resist another exhortation on the topic, "Yeah, those Wall Street guys and corporate kings aren't interested in helping anyone out but themselves. Bunch of crooks! Even when the business fails, the CEOs take home bags full of money. They bail themselves out, but screw everyone else. They think they earned that money or got to the top 'cause of brains, but it's all luck, nothing but luck. It used to be hard work could get you far, but now it's all on the computer. How do you make something on the computer?"

"Who knows? But there will always be a need for men like us—people who can make things with their hands."

"We were makers."

"Now we're takers, Richie."

"We worked hard. We deserved our pensions. Those poor people who worked at the sewing factory next to the church? That company shafted them. No pension. Unbelievable. Anyway, we paid into Social Security. I'm going to take. It's time to take."

"Yeah, yeah, but no one's applauding us for our time as makers. It's the bosses who got the glory and sit in their nice houses. And then they get home health care, and when things get really dicey they go to a nice assisted living facility with a private chef. We're going to be at the county home."

"Could you see us at one of those fancy assisted living places? We'd scare them, Schultzie. None of those people with money want to mix with the likes of us."

"Ah, well, the county home ain't bad."

"They were so good with my Ellie. My neighbor's girl works over there and she's really with it—very sharp. And doesn't let anyone mess with her."

"Speaking of her, look over there."

Richard turned and nodded at Consuela and Gina as they walked past Schultzie's car toward the entrance. "I thought they might come to Senior Day."

GINA GONZALEZ felt relief to be at Senior Day with her mother. It would be good to get out after a self-imposed confinement most of the summer. She would circle the hall, drive her mother back home, and then return to work a shift at the Elm Pond booth in the early afternoon.

The hall was packed with booths and people. Gina carried the bag that her mother stuffed full of brochures, magnets, letter openers, pens, and other giveaways. In addition to tables promoting elder care facilities, they saw booths occupied by every local officeholder or officeholder hopeful in pursuit of the coveted senior vote.

Gina and Consuela stopped by the Elm Pond booth which was staffed by Gina's supervisor Sharon Chapel and the big boss, Director Stan Stein. Sharon and Stan were standing on opposite sides of the table to address attendees coming from either direction.

"You've both met my mother, right?" Gina put her arm on her mother's back to urge her a step closer to the table that was covered with brochures and a display board.

Sharon and Stan both brightened, smiled broadly, and shook Consuela's hand. They said all sorts of complimentary things about Gina, most of which Gina translated into Spanish for her mother.

The cheerleading of her managers boosted Gina's mood. She and Consuela moved on to a funeral and cremation services booth, and Gina waited while her mother looked at the display. Gina glanced at the booths down the line and was taken aback to see her old flame, Jay, staffing the Allentown General Hospital booth. Gina had not seen Jay since before receiving her breakup text, and decided that the best strategy would be to ignore her completely.

Consuela went next to the Allentown General booth while Gina pretended to be on her phone. Thankfully her mother did not spend much time picking up their information, and they moved on to a booth displaying medical equipment. Then it was on to knee replacement surgery and walk-in bathtubs. Gina walked slowly, her right arm linked through her mother's left arm.

"You okay? You look a little upset," Consuela observed.

"Some people I will never understand," Gina replied.

"What do you mean?"

"I mean, some people just play games or change their mind all of the sudden or cause drama."

Consuela squeezed her daughter's arm and asked, "You've never done any of those things?"

Gina paused and replied, "Well, maybe."

"Maybe? Have you stopped with the gossip mouth?"

Gina halted abruptly and exclaimed, "Mother! Why does everyone think that?"

"Because you talk about people."

Gina resumed their stroll, "Everyone talks about people. You and Marta talk about dead and sick people all the time."

"Because that's news. You need to share less of *tu opinión de la gente.*"

"Is that *your* opinion?"

"Now you are a smart mouth. Less of your opinion and less information about people."

"Most of what I share you can read on the Internet or you hear it from someone else. Why not be the trusted source?"

"Trusted source? People will just use you for information. They won't want a real friendship with you because they know you'll do the same about them. And if it's all on the Internet, let people go to the computer and get their own information. You don't have to do it for them. When talking about people, talk only about when someone was born, when they marry, when they get sick, when they die. Then talk about cooking or something nice."

"Why do you share things like this only when we're in public and I have to be polite?"

"You usually are *muy respetosa de mi*, but sometimes it is easier to be in a crowd for difficult conversations. Your bosses just said wonderful things about you, and I am very proud that you are my daughter and do such a good job. That softened you up to hear something hard from me."

"Ah, I see. So, how about I share something hard with you?"

Consuela eyed Gina, uncertain what she might say. "Like what?"

"Like about suing Doctor Brooks for your messed up hand."

"Oh, no. We are not going to talk about that."

"So you can dish it out, but you can't take it, huh?"

"*Yo soy la mamá.*"

Gina sighed as they moved on to a booth advertising a health food store.

#####

ISABELLA RAMIREZ looked across the breakfast table at Eddie and nodded. He cleared his throat and said, "We have an important announcement to make today."

Willie, Genny, and Sofia looked up from their bacon and pancakes.

"You found another alligator?" Genny asked.

"No, no gators. We think the one you saw yesterday was someone's pet that escaped."

"Weird pet!" Genny asserted.

"Not too weird for you," Willie teased.

"You're the weird one," Genny retorted.

Exasperated with the interruptions, Eddie raised his voice, "Okay, enough. Let your father speak!"

Genny and Willie sat straight in their chairs and looked directly at Eddie.

"You are going to have another brother or sister."

"Oh," Genny and Willie said at the same time, surprised with the news and wondering how it would affect them.

Eddie commented, "This is where you say congratulations to both of us."

They looked at their stepmother then back to their father. "Congratulations."

Impressed, Willie observed, "Dad, you'll have four kids."

"Look how great I've done so far," Eddie said, and winked at Willie and Genny. "What shot are you working on today?"

"Reverse layups," Willie replied.

"And what are you doing in the park today, Genny?" Eddie asked.

"Exploring."

"Dora the Explorer," Willie chortled, and Genny rolled her eyes at him.

Eddie dismissed his children from the breakfast table. "Go forth and conquer, children. Run around, keep in shape." Willie and Genny bustled out the door to the park.

Sofia went to focus on her toys in the living room. Isabella took advantage of the moment and softly observed to Eddie, "You seem distracted lately. Anything you want to tell me?"

"Nothing wrong. A lot going on in my mind."

"Hmm. Like what?"

"Like providing for another child and working on getting promoted," Eddie said.

"Remember, the Lord will provide."

"Yes, the Lord will. I'd just like to keep up *my* end of everything."

"You put a lot of pressure on yourself."

Eddie kissed his wife. "I just want the best for my woman and my children."

Isabella reminded him, "Don't forget to take care of yourself too."

#####

TED THOMPSON heard the mail drop through the front door slot. It was late morning and he was preparing a Thai soup for lunch. He finished chopping an onion and scooped up the mail from the floor, his eye drawn to an envelope from the school district superintendent. The brief letter informed Ted that he would no longer be teaching at only four schools in the coming academic year. Instead, he would be responsible for covering six elementary schools.

After eating and cleaning up, he headed toward a busy discount store on MacArthur Road in Whitehall, just north of Allentown. On weekends, the lines at this location stretched longer than any Ted had seen, including on a presidential election day at his precinct. Thankfully, they also had four self-serve registers, so checkout wouldn't take forever.

Ted searched for the kitchen supplies aisle to pick up glass measuring cups, dish towels, and containers for leftovers. He was not wearing his special jacket—just khakis and a polo shirt. He knew it would arouse suspicion to enter with outerwear on a hot summer day when guards trained on security cameras looked for the out-of-the-ordinary. The kitchen aisle was busy, so Ted couldn't resist pocketing measuring spoons. *Their cameras will never catch me in a crowd.* With his well-honed speedy thievery only another skilled thief standing right next to him might notice.

As Ted headed to the front registers, someone behind him said, "Excuse me, sir."

Ted did not turn around, figuring he was not the one to whom those words were directed.

"Sir, excuse me. You took something from the store. What's that in your pocket?"

Ted froze next to a large bin piled high with inflatable swimming flotation devices. He slowly turned around to see a store employee looking in his direction.

"Sir, you'll need to come with me."

The employee looked beyond Ted and addressed a man who had been walking just in front of him. The man wore baggy sweatpants with side pockets, a perfect hiding place for a number of items. Ted breathed a sigh of relief. *Phew, that was close.*

#####

ALAN PECK blew a kiss across the table to his wife, and they clinked their glasses of Pinot Grigio.

"To mergers!" Alan said.

"To mergers!" Amy repeated, and took a quick sip of her wine. "What's the package look like? You said you'd share more of the tidbits over dinner."

"Increases in salary for everyone and, like before, no charge for health insurance, of course. No changes in retirement benefits."

"Good work on this, really good work," Amy said.

"It took a lot of persuading, but in the end they all saw it was going to be the most profitable course."

The server came to take their orders, and they chose their usual meals—a filet for Amy and a New York strip for Alan. They enjoyed dinner at Andre Reed's Steakhouse three times a month. The restaurant was named after a local high school football star who went on to have a long professional career in the NFL. Flat-screen TVs tuned to anything sports-related covered up much of the wood paneling. On the first Sunday of the month Alan and Amy always met their two twenty-something sons for dinner at the steakhouse as a way to regularly check in on their lives.

"Any new news on the church?" Amy asked.

"Not really. Jack and his firm tried to nail them on tax-exempt status, but the clergy got together and hired some Spanish lawyer—can't remember his name—Abu, Ablew, something like that. Anyway, this guy works for barely any fee and goes in front of some sympathetic woman judge for a hearing—probably some hippie dippy from the 60s—and the whole thing gets dismissed."

"You'll need another tactic, but you'll find one."

"Yes, I was hoping Faith Church would be closed by the end of the year. Now I'm not so sure. These other churches seem to be hanging on too. They're like cats who have endless lives. Wish some of them would have do-not-resuscitate orders."

"You're close to being over-the-top. You can pull back at any time, right?"

"Not to worry. I'm not going to bother going to church tomorrow morning. Taking a summer vacation from it. I haven't even been reading Abigail's endless emails over the past two weeks. They go directly into the delete file. Haven't bothered with any of the messages from the other church folks either."

"Good. And remember, we always keep each other in check, right? We never let things get out of hand at the casinos. We dial back the workouts if we feel they're getting too intense—you know, like branches of the government, checks and balances."

"Ooh, I'd like to be the Supreme Court," Alan said.

"And I'll be the Legislative Branch."

Alan asked, "But who is the Executive?"

"God," Amy said, and they burst out laughing.

"We are really bad, mocking God. Isn't that blasphemy?" Alan gasped.

"It's not blasphemy if you never believed in any of it in the first place," Amy said.

Alan nodded. "True, all of it really does border on being childish, like believing prayer actually makes a difference. Or that worship provides any value in a person's life. Or that studying the Bible will change anything. The more I think about it, the less sense it makes."

SUNDAY, JULY 21, 2013

EVAN LEMMON MOORE knew that Abigail arrived to the church at around six on Sunday mornings because he'd see her Honda Civic in the lot on his walk to catch his ride for his Trail Tenders work. He had enjoyed the Bible study Abigail led, found her approachable, and thought she might offer some new thoughts on an old problem.

The front door at the church was unlocked, though the second door in the foyer was locked. Evan knocked loudly, hoping Abigail would hear. Soon enough he saw her walking down the hall.

"Good morning, Evan. Everything okay? It's very early."

"Uh, hi. Yeah. Could I talk with you for a minute?"

"Sure. Let's go to my office." He made himself comfortable in a chair next to a coffee table. Abigail started the conversation. "Looks like there is something on your mind?"

"There is, yes. But what I share with you, you can't share with anyone else, right?"

"Right, unless you threaten to harm yourself or others."

"Okay, uh, I'll just say it. Once every week I drink myself into oblivion."

Abigail maintained her typical steady composure at this admission. "That's a lot to drink."

"I want to get away from doing it."

"Have you tried a support group?"

"Yes. I went once, but when I got out of the meeting, I felt an overwhelming need to get smashed. I think support groups probably work for many, many people, and I'm not trying to slam it, but it had just the opposite effect for me."

"Done any one-on-one counseling?"

"It's not covered by my insurance, and would be pretty pricey on my wage."

"You don't strike me as the kind who would be interested in our transformative weekly worship, although it could help you keep on track and accountable on a weekly basis."

"I'm not really into worship, though I have learned a lot in the Bible study."

"Well, besides worship, there are other spiritual practices, like tithing, fasting, or prayer."

"Um, those don't sound like my kind of thing either."

"The pastor at Church of the Living Water, Johnny Ramos, has led a really successful addictions program there for men."

"I've heard of it, but they're pretty clear on requiring men to 'take Jesus Christ as their Lord and Savior.' That's not really my kind of gig either. I'm not a raging drunk. I only drink on Sundays. I have a three-day weekend every week and the thought of having two completely empty days on Monday and Tuesday puts me over the edge. So I drink and think of stupid things."

Abigail offered some gentle direction, "It sounds like you're holding on to something pretty tightly. You've made a weekly date with oblivion, as you call it, scheduling things around it. I believe you can change, but it is a process. The spiritual practice is called *surrender*."

"That sounds defeatist."

Abigail was quick and firm in her reply. "Surrender is actually the only way to true victory. Some radical rescheduling may be in order. You may need to find something to fill your time on Mondays and Tuesdays—another job, some classes, or something like that. You need to find something that really engages you, Evan."

"I've got to go to catch a ride. See you at Bible study. Thank you for your perspective."

#####

EDDIE RAMIREZ parked his car in the Faith UCC parking lot and walked to the front door. He missed seeing Evan by ten minutes. Abigail heard a knock and guessed Evan had returned to ask another question or had forgotten something. She was surprised to see Eddie at the door.

"Good morning, Sergeant. How are you today?" Abigail knew Eddie from his community work and neighborhood watch efforts. She also knew him as the son-in-law of her clergy colleague Johnny Ramos.

"I'm good. Do you have a minute?"

"Sure. Come on in." Abigail led the way down the hall. "How are things at the police department?"

"Busy. Summer is our busy season. Temperature goes up, crime goes up."

They entered Abigail's office and each took a seat. "And how are things at Church of the Living Water?"

"Real good. Lots of people getting saved—you know, committing to the Lord."

"Praise God. So, what brings you here this morning?"

"I've got a problem."

"I'm sorry to hear that. What kind of problem?"

"You won't tell anyone about this?"

"No. I don't share what people tell me in this office unless they threaten to harm themselves or others."

Eddie shifted in the chair. "I, uh, I watch a lot of porn."

Abigail nodded. "A lot of men have that problem. Did you know there's a really active program over at Cedar Beach Church? That's that huge church? They've had a lot of success in helping men overcome addiction to pornography."

"Yeah, I've heard of it. But, with my father-in-law being a pastor, for me to go to another church would be like a slap in the face to him. Also, I'm kinda known out in the public, so I can't really do a program with all sorts of guys from around town."

"Your wife doesn't know?"

"No. Neither does Johnny. No one knows. Well, my ex-wife knows—it made issues between us. But even though we don't get along, Anna's not going to go telling anyone about it. She doesn't blab about that kind of thing because she knows it could hurt the kids."

"You are being faced with one of the biggest spiritual tasks of your life. Addiction is all about putting something before God.

You'll need to come to an understanding that, apart from God, you are nothing and you can do nothing. It may sound harsh, but you cannot do this on your own. You are completely dependent on God. That may be especially hard for someone like you, because you have spent your life being indispensable and fixing situations."

"I have fixed a lot, but I can't seem to fix this."

"Have you tried your employee assistance plan? Surely, like most other police forces, they offer confidential counseling?"

"I really want to go someplace that has no connection to work or my church. There's too much of a chance that someone would start talking and I don't want to have to explain anything."

"Well, I have a list of counselors I could give you. It would be private sessions. All the ones on this list are quite good and they'll really try to help you get out of this rut. They're expensive. But I'm guessing you won't want it on your insurance and so you'll pay cash?"

"Yeah. I don't want a paper trail."

"I'll get you the list. You can beat this, I'm confident of that. Just talking about it with someone is a really big step."

Eddie nodded. From his own police force training he knew that admission of a problem was an important first step.

"Until your first counseling session, try replacing the porn with something else. Look at sports highlights twenty minutes a day, or whatever. Busy your brain with other things." Abigail walked to her desk and pulled out a list of counselors from one of her files. She asked, "Will I see you tonight at the site? I know I'll see Johnny. It's good to have so many churches coming together again to take a stand."

"I'll be at the perimeter for a while, but will not enter into the site. It's not a good idea for me to get too involved, given my position."

"Oh, yes, that might get awkward. So, I'll see you tonight in passing, but know that you will be in my prayers." Abigail walked Eddie to the door.

Instead of driving the two blocks directly home, Eddie drove to one of his regular parking lots. He pulled his private phone out of the glove compartment and went to the YouTube website, plugging in the words "kobe bryant highlights." Thousands of videos came up and Eddie tapped on the most viewed one at the top of the list. As he watched Kobe's flair on the court, he thought, *It's not the same. Man, this is lame.*

#####

GINA GONZALEZ genuflected, crossed herself, and sat next to her mother for the eight o'clock Mass at the Sacred Heart of Jesus Parish.

In his homily that morning, the priest talked about the Samaritan woman at the well and mentioned that it was the longest recorded conversation Jesus had with anyone in the gospels. "Apparently the woman had quite a past that included a lot of husbands." Father Enrique went on to say the Samaritan woman was scrappy, and bold enough to ask Jesus questions so she could understand the spiritual teaching. Although Gina was normally at her most alert during the communion liturgy, she perked up for the homily. *This might be interesting, 'cause I'm kind of scrappy too.* Gina put herself in the woman's place as the priest retold the story.

The priest started by describing how Jesus and the woman at the well went back and forth. Gina thought, *yes, I would do that with Jesus. I'd want the answers. If it was me at that well, I'd want to know more. I'd pester Jesus. I'd bother him. And he'd love me.*

The Samaritan woman asked Jesus where to get some of that living water. *Yes, where? Where can I get the stuff that will make me feel alive again? I thought Jay-Jay was the one, but that ended with a bad taste. I have all this bad luck with women. Why? I'm a good person. I have a good job. I take care of business at home and at work. Maybe it's 'cause no one can keep up with me. Ha!*

The priest talked about how people constantly focus on physical needs, but forget about spiritual needs. *Yep, that's me. I get really into the day to day, all the drama. I get pulled in and can't get out. I go really fast at the start of a relationship and then it just sort of fizzles out—I get bored or something.*

Love of family and, most of all, God's loving presence in our lives are what really sustain us, the priest concluded his homily. *I'd be so lost without my family. Mamá, Anna, Willie, and Genny. They love me despite my craziness. And without God, I don't know, I think I'd lose so much energy. Life would just be blah—no zing, no hope.*

#####

ABIGAIL BARRETT-THOMPSON came out of her second meeting following the worship service. Consistory President Tim Thacker and Vice President Francine Dunning were standing outside her office. *Uh oh. What's this all about? Does it have something to do with the announcement I made this morning about supporting the direct action at the tent where the new Dolly's Dollar is going to be built?*

Abigail forced some perkiness in her voice and asked, "How's it going, all?"

Tim replied, "Doing all right, Abigail. Do you have a minute?"

And before Abigail could respond, Francine inquired, "And when you're done with Tim, could I have a minute?"

"Sure, yes," Abigail said. She and Tim entered her office and they sat across the coffee table from each other.

Tim cleared his throat. "I have something difficult to share with you."

"Nothing is impossible with God," Abigail said with calm assurance.

"I've been giving things a lot of thought, and my wife also. You've probably noticed we have not been here for most of June and July."

Abigail nodded.

"That's because we have been attending worship at Cedar Beach Church."

"I see."

"We've really enjoyed our time there. Pastor Davey is a real powerhouse. That church is hopping. Helen and I have just started the membership classes there."

Abigail made sure there was no change in her facial features—no surprise, no disappointment—just a simple response, "Thank you for letting me know."

"We have been with Faith UCC for fifteen years now, and feel it is going in a direction we can no longer support. There's a lot of emphasis on liberal politics and not enough on what a church should focus on, like personal responsibility."

"I'd disagree with you on that. Faith Church doesn't practice or promote liberal or conservative politics. But we do focus on prophetic social justice, which is a Biblical mandate. We'll just have to agree to disagree on it."

"Yes, Abigail, we'll agree to disagree."

"God bless you and Helen on this next part of your journey," Abigail said, and stood to walk Tim to the door. "We'll get your membership transfer in the mail tomorrow. Take good care, Tim. You are always welcome here. Okay, come on in, Francine."

Francine was a bulky woman, and she started hesitantly, "I've been needing to tell you something for a long time."

As with Tim, Abigail projected her usual calm. "You're safe here. What's on your mind?"

"I'm no longer identifying as a Christian. I've thought and thought about it, and the whole Jesus thing is not in me anymore. Although, I don't know if it was ever in me or was just something I did because it's what my family did."

"A Christian walk is quite a commitment. And it's really very courageous of you to be able to name that you are no longer able to keep that commitment. Are you pursuing an interest in another faith?"

"No. I'm going to step away from all religion, maybe forever. I no longer see a benefit with any type of spirituality."

"And what are you going to do for community?"

"I'm involved in some sci-fi writing groups, and other things will come up. I'm not worried."

"We'll remove you from membership and an official letter will be sent out tomorrow."

Francine hesitated again. "I'd like to be de-baptized."

"I'm not able to help you with that, Francine. The church's stance—and mine—is that once baptism is done, it cannot be undone. You might find someone in a secular or atheist group to assist you through that process."

"Oh."

"Thank you for all of your service. I will miss you on the consistory and I will miss you at worship." Abigail started to rise to signal an end to their meeting, but then sat back down when Francine spoke again.

"One more thing. You need to know that Alan Peck is working against you."

"Alan has been working against me for a long time. I don't think it's about me, but I keep him in prayer daily," Abigail replied.

Francine leaned in and said, "He wants you gone. He's telling people to go to Cedar Beach Church and he's been successful at persuading a number of people to become members over there."

Abigail had suspected Alan all along but did not feel there was much she could do about it. "Alan's entitled to his opinions."

Francine shook her head. "It's extremely disloyal."

"It's the times, Francine. Churchgoing has become very much about consumerist choice. People choose Cedar Beach because something there attracts them. My hope is that all current and former Faith Church members are growing in spiritual maturity whether they're here or a part of some other community."

"Watch your back, okay? You sometimes have a bit of magical thinking and don't always keep on top of stuff like this—"

Abigail interrupted, "I'm not sure there is anything to keep on top of. Also, I try mightily to avoid magical thinking and aim more for the mind of Christ."

Francine shrugged, "We see it differently, and that's okay. Everything's always okay with you. That's why I knew I'd be okay coming and telling you about my journey out of Christianity."

Abigail smiled. "Thank you for the heads up. I'll be careful." She stood and walked Francine to the front entry doors. "I'm going to lock up now, since I'm not expecting anyone at the church. All the best with everything. I mean it, Francine. I'll miss you!"

Abigail returned to her office and sat down at her desk. She reflected just a moment, then opened her lower right desk drawer, which contained three bags of peanut butter cups. She ate one full bag and staggered toward the church bathroom where she forced herself to throw up.

After splashing water on her face, she entered the sanctuary and slid into the front pew. She stared up at the cross, pulpit, and communion table, and sorted her thoughts. She understood why people transferred their membership to other churches. It happened frequently in a competitive religious marketplace.

She also recognized that Faith Church was certainly not going to be a good fit for every person or family. And, besides, she had years of experience—being married to an agnostic—so people renouncing their Christianity was neither shocking nor disconcerting to her. No, some people just moved on. What was hard for Abigail to digest was the cumulative loss. Francine, Tim, and Helen were just three of a long line of people to say farewell. *Pretty soon it's going to be just me and Richard Moyer.*

#####

EVAN LEMMON MOORE unscrewed the cap on the bottle of Mountain Delight whiskey. *I'm a weak, weak man. I guess I can't surrender. It's got me, and I want it too much.* Just as past events tickled at the edges of his consciousness, but before taking his first sip, Evan heard a loud sound outside his door. *Sounds like construction. That's strange for a Sunday.* He put the cap on the whiskey and went out on his porch. The noise sounded as though it was coming from the old battery factory site. He jogged around the corner, saw a gigantic tent, and spied a bevy of construction vehicles lining up at the front of the site to prevent other vehicles from entering.

Evan was intrigued. People were walking into the tent, where there appeared to be at least five hundred folding chairs. They were filling up quickly with people of all ages. A band was playing loud music, and groups of people swayed to its rhythm. *Uh oh, looks like a worship service. I think that's my cue to turn around.* But he didn't. Instead, he approached the tent and stood at the back as Johnny Ramos took to the microphone. "What we have here, folks, is a piece of land where they are going to put up an abomination."

"Yes!" a handful of people in front said. Evan looked more closely at the stage and saw Abigail Barrett-Thompson sitting with other clergy wearing collars as well as other religious-type leaders.

Johnny gathered steam. "We know this is private property. We know that we are on disputed ground here. But the time has come to stand up to these corporations. SmithCo. wants to build another Dolly's Dollar Store in Allentown—right here on this property! They've already got eleven thousand Dolly's around the country. Do we really need one more?"

"No!" scattered audience members responded.

Johnny continued, "Dolly's sells a bunch of junk and they treat their employees like dogs! These corporations have to start learning that they don't own people."

Evan found a seat in the last row. The chairs had informational papers on them.

"Amen!" shouted some in the crowd.

Johnny continued, "We'll be here till they drag us away! Deacon Rob and his construction company are taking some time off from business to do work here. We've blocked the site to keep the strip mall from going in. Our efforts are not for the faint of heart. They may put charges against us. But we're going to have to roll with it all. Are you ready to roll with it?"

Some clapped and gave a hearty "Yes!"

"We're going to keep the sound system as loud as possible," Johnny said, "to cover the sound of all the generators we brought in here. Those of you with sensitive ears may have to bring earplugs. But, you know, all of us from Church of the Living Water are used to a louder service."

People laughed and nodded.

"Deacon Rob brought over ten of his porta-potties. Let's keep things as nice and clean as possible. We'll have some food available around six, but food donations are always welcome, by the way."

Evan looked through the papers as Johnny announced other details of the site. The first page was a basic fact sheet outlining what was happening. Corporate power was taking over and it was time for people to take back the city. *Amen to that.* The next sheet was a schedule of when the supporting organizations would be on the property. Church of the Living Water was covering the most hours. Faith UCC, some other churches, a synagogue, a Buddhist meditation group, and a political group were also on the schedule. A half sheet of paper advertised Church of the Living Water and their worship times, and another sheet listed volunteer opportunities. Overnight security team volunteers were directed to Paulie. *Is that Paulie from down the street? Wow, he's really made some changes in his life.* Volunteer tech squad members were sent to Javi Ramos, as were volunteer media management team participants. At the bottom of the list Evan saw they were looking for a food preparation team and to contact someone named Joyce Taylor of the Independent Baptist Church. Evan turned around and saw a separate tent with tables, warming trays, and a group of women bustling between stations. *Ah ha! I could help with that.*

Johnny Ramos kept talking, and Evan ambled to the food tent. He noticed a line of eight large grills just outside the tent. "Is Joyce Taylor here?"

A woman pointed. "Down there."

Evan walked toward a diminutive African American woman at the end of the line. She was wearing a baseball cap adorned with the words *Jesus is #1* spelled out in fake pink diamonds.

"Hi. Are you Joyce?"

The woman nodded and gave Evan a dubious glance.

"I'm Evan, and I'm a good cook. I'd like to sign up to be your right-hand man."

"Well, well. We could use a man around here, though we've been doing a lot of the heavy lifting just fine on our own so far. You can start by getting the burgers laid out on the grills. Once they're cooked, we'll put them in the warming trays."

"Will do. Any veggie patties by chance?"

"Not a chance. Are you one of those?"

Evan laughed. "Yes, I'm a vegetarian. What's the menu?"

"It's burgers and beans for a light supper. Then we'll have to figure out the water situation, because all we have is a hose. The closest church is Faith Church, so we're going to have to carry all the dirty cookware over there, wash it up, and bring it back. We'll get all of this running smoothly, but for now it's going to be a little loosey goosey, okay?"

"No problem. I'll get the burgers started." Evan donned the plastic apron Joyce held out for him.

EDDIE RAMIREZ could hear everything that was being said because Javi had set up the sound system so well. He stood outside the site and saw Isabella with the three children seated in the front row. Sofia was putting her dolls in a pile on a chair, while Willie and Genny were playing games on their phones and would be sent back to their mom soon. Normally Eddie and Isabella did not permit the children any sort of distraction during worship, but the kids had already been at Church of the Living Water for the morning service and the tent seemed more informal.

As his father-in-law spoke, Eddie thought about the ramifications of what these people were doing. *Trespassing on private property is serious business. What they're doing is edgy and radical, and legally, they're on really shaky ground. A takeover of private property never ends well, and it sounds like SmithCo. gets a kick out of crushing people who get in their way. But there's no stopping Johnny when he gets something in his head. And Dolly's Dollar is shady in how they treat their employees.*

Eddie texted Willie and Genny that it was time for them to meet him outside the tent. They picked up their bags and exited out the side.

After sending them off to their mother's house, Eddie walked the perimeter of the tent. It was a good turnout—mostly Church of the Living Water members, but also a lot from other churches and communities.

As Johnny introduced the next speaker, Eddie scanned the crowd and the property for potential problems, but saw none. He had advised Johnny to not alert city officials or the media in advance about their plan so the church could leverage the element of surprise a bit. *Never a dull moment with Johnny.*

MONDAY, JULY 22, 2013

RICHARD MOYER slipped through a narrow entryway in the fencing between a bulldozer and a dump truck to check out the morning crowd at the tent. Someone was speaking without the microphone to a group of twenty or so people gathered near the front. Richard quietly worked at straightening the chairs in the big tent, lining them up in precise rows. After fixing the chairs, he went to the kitchen tent where he saw volunteers—mostly women—assembling egg sandwiches. Richard recognized a young bearded guy from the neighborhood and, more recently, attending Abigail's Wednesday night Bible study. Seeing the kitchen responsibilities were well orchestrated, Richard grunted and moved toward a cart piled with dirty cookware from the breakfast preparations. He wheeled the cart toward the entrance and then over the sidewalk two blocks to the church.

#####

ANNA RAMIREZ was shocked to receive a text message from Evan before the start of her Monday morning shift. *I guess he does* *come out of his Monday cave sometimes.* She smiled as she read the words: "Have u heard about the tent? I'm on cooking crew, help me out tonight?"

She quickly texted him back: "Yes, kids told me about tent & yes will help"

"U r da bomb"

Steve caught Anna smiling as he passed her on his way to the front counters. "Someone got a happy message this morning."

Anna laughed. "It's Evan. He's cooking at the tent."

"The tent?"

"Some people and some groups have taken over a property in north Allentown where they are putting up another one of those dollar stores. You know, those places where it's all junk and the workers always look overwhelmed?"

"Yeah, those are bad news."

"So, they put up a tent and have blocked off the property to prevent the developer from building the strip mall where the dollar store is supposed to be going in. The people who are protesting are there all day and all night, and so, they need to eat. Evan's on the cooking crew. I'm going to help him out tonight."

"Occupying private property? You're such a radical."

"Not usually, but it's time to stop all this corporate stuff taking over our country. Corporations need to get the consent of the people, and not just come in and do whatever they want. And then they get tax breaks, trash things, take all our money, and pay their workers terrible wages."

"Power to the people?"

"Yes. Those of us who are awake need to shake things up, you know? How about it, Stevie, will you come out to the tent?"

"I am a rules-compliant kind of a guy."

"What?"

"Really. I find it hard to break the rules, except, of course, for heterosexuality."

"But these corporations break the rules all the time."

"I'm not a protester, but I support the right of my radical coworker Anna to protest. To each their own."

"Think about it. The tent is going to be there a while."

"You are persistent."

"I'm going to put flyers everywhere. You'll see them in the break room every day and eventually you'll realize that you and your honey Glenn need to be at the tent."

"We must put the tent to the side, dear, for it is time to serve the postal needs of the great people of the great city of Allentown." Steve and Anna lifted their shutters at the same time and looked out at a long line of people already waiting.

#####

ALAN PECK nodded to the crew tasked with removing the Vigor sign from the front of the building. By afternoon, the Care2Trust sign would be installed, and Alan's efforts would be validated with some amount of finality.

He looked away from his computer when he heard the text tone on his phone that identified a message as coming from Jack Shears.

"Have u heard?"

Alan texted back: "???"

"Go online to the newspaper now"

His curiosity piqued, Alan clicked on the bookmark he set up for the local newspaper website. At the top of the screen a headline announced: *Faith Communities Stake Out Dolly's Dollar Store Site.* The article went on to describe how different churches and other groups had taken over the cement pad at the building site in protest over Dolly's business practices.

Alan was infuriated and said aloud, "They can have whatever kind of business practices they want to have. We don't live under communism or socialism or anything like that."

He quickly scanned the rest of the article and saw the reporter had highlighted quotations from Pastor Johnny Ramos and his deacon Rob Handel, who provided construction vehicles from his contracting business to block the site. Rather than texting Jack back, he phoned him so there could be no written record of their conversation.

"Jack, what a fantasy life these people lead. I'll do whatever you want me to do to help destroy them."

"Number one, call the Lehigh Valley state representatives and senators, and then go to the federal level. Call your members of Congress and two senators, okay?"

"I'll make the calls this morning."

"You have an idea of the messaging, right? Emphasize private property and that these radicals need to be removed as quickly as possible."

"Looks like this guy Johnny Ramos and his deacon Rob Handel are the ringleaders of this circus. I don't know either of them, but is there something I could do there?"

"Handel has his own construction company, and he's the one providing the equipment out there. He'll be easy enough to deal with. We just make sure other companies underbid him on every future job. Johnny will be harder to handle. His congregation adores him, and they're a bunch of holy rollers. I don't mess with super religious people—they're dangerous and unpredictable. The tactics you've been using with those other churches wouldn't work over at Johnny's church. His congregants wouldn't be interested in attending a mostly white, middle-class mega-church. I'd stay away from Johnny and focus more on people from the smaller churches that are involved at the tent. They seem more vulnerable. Mess with their membership, sow division, and eventually they'll dissolve. They're barely surviving as it is."

"I'm on it."

After ending the call, Alan remembered he had been ignoring and deleting every email message he received from Abigail. If he had opened them, he would have been on top of what was happening. He shook off the regret, looked up the legislative phone numbers, and started down the list, identifying himself with every phone call as "Alan Peck, business executive." He left messages on most of the legislator's lines, making it clear he expected a phone call in return.

JOHNNY RAMOS met with Deacon Rob before heading over to lead things at the tent from nine to eleven. Carla always took care of the day-to-day tasks of the church, so his absence wouldn't have much of an effect. In fact, Carla preferred that Johnny be out every day, as she was able to get a lot more done with the pastor away.

"Just one article in today's local paper," Johnny said.

Rob replied, "It's going to pick up all week. You'll have local television here and, in no time, Philly and New York stations, and then national media coverage will happen. It will be a nice buildup."

"Wonder how long we can keep this up?" Johnny asked.

"From what I understand, SmithCo. can get nasty, so we won't be able to sustain everything for very long. And it *is* their property—we're squatters."

"I hadn't thought of it that way. Pastor Johnny Ramos, squatter. Deacon Rob Handel, squatter."

"It's the only way to get people's attention anymore. SmithCo. normally would try to get their way by force, but we've blocked everything off. Their vehicles can't bust in anywhere. But then they'll use the courts and we'll be carried off. I don't see the tent lasting longer than a few weeks. Are you ready for talking five hours a day?"

"Five hours is nothing! I could easily cover ten hours a day."

"Yes, you could. You do have that gift," Rob chuckled.

EVAN LEMMON MOORE returned to the tent mid-morning with a cart full of washed cookware from Faith Church. It had been decided that for Monday and Tuesday, Joyce would be the lead for breakfast and lunch, and he'd be in charge of dinner. He wore hiking boots, cargo shorts, a t-shirt, and a St. Louis Cardinals baseball cap.

In the kitchen tent, Evan stood at attention and saluted Joyce.

"What's the food situation?" he asked. Joyce was again wearing her sparkly *Jesus is #1* hat.

"More burgers and bags of chips for lunch. For dinner, canned corn and green beans in the warming trays and chicken on the grill. There are dozens of packages of cookies from the food bank. They're expired, but not too stale. That can be dessert for both meals."

"Anywhere else we could get fresher food? How 'bout I find some gardeners to donate some produce?"

"We could try sell-off at the Farmer's Market, and maybe some local restaurants."

"We may want to start having regular meetings for those who want to help with the planning. If this grows, it's going to take a lot of organizing."

"When do you work?" Joyce asked.

"Wednesday through Saturday, eight to six. But I live just right over there. I could do a seven o'clock check-in meeting every morning with a food crew and keep track of supplies. And then I could also check in early evening."

Joyce delegated, "Well, you sound like an organizer, so I'll let you do that."

"We'll need a few days to see who we can depend on, who shows up consistently, who'll be our go-to people."

"People will prove themselves. It's going to be hard to figure out how many people we need to feed day to day. The weekends will probably be big."

"Right. Wow, this is quite a project."

Joyce stood next to the grill and testified to Evan. "Nothing's too big for God. You know, when I first started cooking over at Allen High School, I'd get so worried about if there would be enough for all the kids. Would there be enough potatoes that day? Would there be enough hamburger buns? Would there be enough meat? What I found out is that there is always enough. There is always enough. Of everything. There's always enough food and there's always enough money and there's always enough love. It's just that some people take too much, you know? Like these corporations. Now, I'm not saying all of them are bad, but a lot of them just take and take and take, and that gets me mad."

"You're preaching to the choir. Are you a preacher over at your church?"

"Oh no, I let Pastor C.D. Alexander take care of that. I am on the Deacons Board and the Ladies Auxiliary. We do all the meals for church events."

Evan chatted with Joyce about salad dressing options and got to work separating the stack of frozen hamburger patties.

#####

GENNY RAMIREZ entered the tent right before lunch and saw a large group of people seated close to the front. They were listening to a preacher. She walked to the kitchen tent and saw her dad's neighbor, Evan, flipping hamburgers on a grill. She liked sitting with him on his front porch or in the garden behind his house, talking about environmental issues. He always took an interest in her projects. She went up beside him and asked, "Can I help?"

"That would be awesome, Genny," Evan said. "Do you see how I'm filling up this tray with burgers? You can hand them out to people coming through the line, but you have to wear gloves. And, just to warn you, the plates are Styrofoam." They both made a face. "Maybe we can find some plates or old school trays for people to use instead of this nonrecyclable junk. Then, after you're done serving, you can help me clean up, okay?"

"Yeah." Genny took the tray from Evan and put it on a table next to the other food trays. She joined the elderly women behind the table who were also handing out food. Twenty minutes later, all the people had come through the line. Three burgers remained in her tray, which she returned to Evan.

"Let's chow," Evan said, and they sat down to eat next to Joyce and the Independent Baptist Church Ladies Auxiliary. Evan had brought a vegetarian lunch, while Genny munched on a burger. Reverend C.D. Alexander was speaking, as the Baptist Church was to cover the lunchtime hours of eleven to one every day.

"You know the hymn 'I Shall Not Be Moved'?" C.D. asked the crowd.

"Oh, yes!" Joyce and the ladies said.

"Sing it with me," C.D. encouraged, and a number of people joined in. "Just like a tree that's planted by the waters, I shall not be moved."

C.D. stood in front of the makeshift pulpit, his well-thumbed Bible in hand. He shouted, "We will not be moved!"

"Amen!" the ladies around the table said.

"We keep being moved here and there by the powers and rulers. Well, sometimes we've just got to stay put and say, 'enough!'"

"Mmm hmm," the ladies nodded.

"God is the mover and shaker—not anyone or anything else!"

"Yes!" the ladies said.

C.D. opened his Bible. "Let's take a look at chapter seventeen of the prophet Jeremiah, where we hear more about this tree planted by the water."

Evan noticed that some in the crowd had brought their Bibles and were following along.

"God has planted us here. *All* of us. We've come together because that's the only way we can do something like this—*together*. They'll push us around, they'll threaten us, they'll send lawyers after us, oh, yes. We've ignored their letters because we know we have done nothing wrong! Isn't it funny how the biggest violators of morals and ethics always go after the people who take a stand?"

C.D. continued preaching until twelve forty-five, when the Independent Baptist Choir Director went onstage to lead people in singing well-known gospel songs.

As the singing started, Evan motioned for Genny to follow him back to the food staging area. He pointed to a soapy tray containing four sponges. Evan handed Genny a sponge and a dish cloth, and they cleaned off the tables where people had eaten lunch. Then they stacked the dirty cookware on the cart and set off toward the Faith Church kitchen.

ABIGAIL BARRETT-THOMPSON opened the door for the dishwashing crew and returned to her office to prepare remarks for her time in the tent that night. Faith Church would cover the seven to eight o'clock hour. Abigail knew she would not be able to fill an hour every night with just her own words, so she had invited the Bible study crew to participate in a public Bible study each night. She would also spend time encouraging people to sign letters to their legislators requesting a raise in Pennsylvania's minimum wage. Additionally, she selected prayers and scripture readings related to social justice to share with the crowd. Ted was planning to be there as many nights as possible that week, and their son Phil was even coming in from New York on Friday night to participate.

ANNA RAMIREZ changed quickly out of her uniform and hurried down the stairs.

"Come over to the tent tonight for dinner," Anna called to her mother, sister, son, and daughter who were in the living room watching TV.

"I was there for lunch. Burgers," Genny said.

"What's for dinner?" Willie asked.

"Chicken," Anna replied. "Okay, everyone?"

"Do we have a choice?" Gina asked.

Anna smiled. "No," and she rushed out the door to her car. Evan had suggested she park behind Faith Church and walk the few blocks to the site.

At the tent, Church of the Living Water members were amening Johnny Ramos. Anna saw the kitchen tent and found Evan cooking the chicken on the grills.

"A vegetarian doing the chicken. You are impressive," Anna complimented him.

"Hey, there. I just happen to have another set of special tongs for Anna Ponce." He handed her a long set.

Overwhelmed, Anna said, "I've never worked this many grills before."

"We just need to keep moving," Evan encouraged.

Anna turned the chicken on one grill. "I should have brought spices. I'll remember tomorrow. This looks pretty bland."

"We're learning a lot as we go along. I'd like to figure out how to use real plates and how to set up a sink system so we don't have to lug our dirty cookware over to the church. We'll build our empire bit by bit."

Anna added, "An empire that's not about stiffing workers and getting every little darned dime. What a refreshing thought."

GINA GONZALEZ drove toward the tent thinking the whole protest was a bit dramatic, but supported the general idea of trying to stop a corrupt corporation. The line by the kitchen tent was long, and Gina, Willie, and Genny inched closer to the food, doing a lot of people-watching at the diverse crowd as they waited. Consuela sat at a table, saving their seats and taking in the scene. Gina saw her sister standing behind the table scooping green beans onto people's plates. She also noticed Evan right next to her, and recalled her conversation with Anna from months earlier. *Hmm, wonder if there's something up with my sister and this guy. I've never seen her look happier. She's glowing, and all she's doing is dumping food on people's plates.*

Gina filled her mother's plate first and returned to the line. She was surprised to find herself behind Dante Washington, whom she recognized from Rubies Bar & Restaurant. The two women were not close, but knew enough about each other's exploits. Dante was wearing baggy plaid shorts and an oversized t-shirt. Her afro escaped from under a blue baseball cap.

"Well, Dante, what're you doing here?" Gina asked.

"My brother's involved at Church of the Living Water. He told me what was going on, and I decided to check it out. How about you?"

"My sister is one of the servers." Gina pointed at Anna, who waved at them both.

As they went through the line, Dante shared, "Sometimes people just have to get together and say 'this ain't right, this has to stop,' you know?"

"Yeah, it has reached that point."

"I've got to go and sit with my brother and his family, and it looks like your family is waiting for you," Dante nodded at Consuela, Willie, and Genny. "Let me give you my card. Maybe we could get some flyers up at Rubies and get some more people down here to the tent."

Gina took Dante's card and, unable to check her enthusiasm, burbled, "Great idea."

#####

ANNA RAMIREZ helped Evan wash the dinner cookware in the church kitchen, with Evan scrubbing and Anna drying.

"We did it!" Anna said.

"We did," Evan agreed, and playfully squirted Anna with the sink sprayer.

"Hey, punk," Anna teased, splashing him with soapy water.

Within five minutes they were both completely soaked and unable to stop laughing. Evan landed on the floor and Anna tumbled on top of him, their kisses long and damp. As much as they enjoyed their wet mess, they knew they had to complete their chores for the night. They eventually returned the cookware to the tent, and Evan walked Anna to her car. He watched her drive off.

Back home, Anna entered into a quiet house. She saw a light on in the living room. *It can't be the kids. Maybe it's Gina.* She walked in and saw her mother reclined on the easy chair. She appeared to be asleep. Anna turned to tiptoe away, but Consuela spoke. "Maybe it's time to put your own house in order before telling off some corporation."

"Excuse me?" Anna asked.

"You know what I said. Put your own house in order." Consuela leaned her head back as she spoke.

"What do you mean?"

"You think I don't know about all the buying? All the makeup and the perfume and the scarves, all the things? You think you could hide that? I know you and Eddie fought about it all the time. You'd spend, he'd yell. You didn't have the money for it then, and you don't have it now."

"This is none of your business."

"None of my business? *Ésta es mi casa*. You're doing this in my house."

"You know it all started with Dad, all the time saying no."

Consuela sat up straighter to emphasize her words. "Don't you blame your father. You're not a teenager anymore. That's ancient history and you could have done far worse for a father. He really loved you. He just had a lot of fear about not having enough money. He came from a very poor family, barely any money, and he worked hard and provided for us—maybe not exactly how we would have all liked, but we got by. You should be ashamed, a grown woman still saying it's her parent's fault."

Anna knew she had gone too far. "I'm sorry, Mamá. It was wrong of me to say that about Dad. I've got a handle on it."

"No, you don't."

"I do, Ma. I do."

"No, you don't. You're a mess. Stop buying. Just stop buying. That new man you're seeing isn't a buyer. I can tell by looking at him. He's frugal. It's going to be a disaster."

"What new man?" Anna tried to frown, though a tiny smile escaped at the thought of Evan.

"A mother knows. I saw how you were standing next to him tonight and that silly grin on your face. You've been bouncing around the house lately, humming. *Estás enamorada*. You better be careful and stop with the buying if you want to go with that guy. He is not a spender."

"We've *definitely* entered into none-of-your-business-land now. I've got to go to bed so I can be half alive for work tomorrow."

"You better be careful."

"*Buenas noches*, Mamá."

TUESDAY, JULY 23, 2013

EVAN LEMMON MOORE grabbed a stack of papers and a half-dozen bamboo kebab sticks from his kitchen counter. He walked to the protest site and through the main tent where about a hundred people were listening to a speaker. He saw the old guy from Faith Church fussing with the chairs in the back.

In the kitchen tent, he'd soon lead the seven o'clock organizational gathering of the meal crew. He saw Joyce, who had already been there an hour or more. He saluted her and said, "Boss, Evan Lemmon Moore reporting to serve."

"Evan Lemmon?" Joyce asked.

"Lemmon, South Dakota. My mother's hometown."

"I like it, Evan Lemmon. Now, since you're reporting to serve, for lunch we've got hot dogs for the grill with potato chips again. Not sure what we'll pull together for dinner yet."

"I brought these paper calendars so we can plan out meals and supplies through next week."

"Look at you, Mr. Organization," Joyce said. She turned to the other ladies working at various places in the kitchen, and announced, "Time for a team meeting, y'all. Gather over here, except for Della and Macey. You two keep an eye on those sausages on the grill."

The larger group brainstormed meal ideas and Evan started a grocery list on his cell phone. "I'll type out the menus and drop them off tonight after my BlackBox shift."

#####

TED THOMPSON filled the kitchen counters with food dishes in various states of readiness.

Abigail sat at the kitchen table, still groggy at the early morning hour. She took a sip of coffee and said, "You were inspired. That's quite a spread you've got going there. Care to introduce me?"

"Delighted to," Ted replied, and started at the far end. "Ladies and gentlemen, over here we have carrot cake in a cupcake form, along with mini zucchini breads. Healthier and tastier than those stale, old cookies they were giving away last night, though I did bake some standard chocolate chip cookies. Here we have four large trays of blueberry buckle. They'll last through dinner time. Fruit salads will go in the cooler in a minute. I'm also working on a Middle Eastern dish."

"I'll have to taste test them, of course."

"Of course."

"You're amazing."

"Go on," Ted joked.

"You really are."

"I'm going to contact a few artists. We'll make some large dolls to place in various parts of the tent as a statement against Dolly's. The venue could use a little more art—it's pretty blasé. Only a few more weeks till school starts, so I want to get as much done as possible before things start up again."

"The tent has reenergized a lot of people."

"A community coming together is a good thing, though it's too church heavy."

"Hey, could be our last gasp as churches, so give us our time."

Ted mashed chickpeas for fresh hummus and said, "Too bad you're not more conservative. The progressive churches seem to be the ones having the most problems."

"Yes, but the labels get fuzzy sometimes. Johnny Ramos and his elders have surprised me by taking such a strong stand on this. And they really know how to do big events. Two different theologies and worldviews can, sometimes, come together. Well, maybe not 'sometimes,' but more appropriately 'on rare occasions.'"

"Still, we both know that religion is definitely on a downswing these days. The fastest growing religious group in America is..."

Abigail filled in the blank with some resignation, "... the non-affiliated."

"Who'd a thunk it? And what did that French social scientist say?" Ted asked.

"You're referring to Oliver Roy?"

"Yes, Roy. Something about how religion these days surrenders so much to the secular world that it is no longer able to offer the average Joe a transformative option."

"Ouch."

"Good to know what you're up against."

"I'll fight the good fight with the Lord and eat carrot cake to sustain me."

Ted kissed Abigail and stated, "You are and will always be my number one favorite leader of lost causes."

#####

ALAN PECK again called local and national representatives, urging them to dismantle the tent site immediately. The night before, Amy had warned him to not go overboard, and so he decided to focus on the issue for just one hour now and wait until night to do more.

In between calls, Alan looked out the window and thought about the tent scene. *These people are totally unbelievable, thinking they can get away with a stunt like this. What SmithCo. is doing is perfectly legal and lawful. Where is this country going with people thinking they have some sort of right to tell private companies how to run their business? Maybe we should trespass on their private property so they can see how it feels.*

Just as he was about to dial the office of the next Congressman on his list, he had an incoming call. *Ah, the Harrisburg area code.* "Hello?" Alan said.

"Hey, it's Charlie, calling from your beautiful state capitol."

Charlie Connell was Vigor's lobbyist in Harrisburg, though now he was lobbying for Care2Trust's interests. He was an effective advocate for the corporation and had long-standing relationships with legislators.

"Charlie! Great to hear from you. What's up?"

"A little birdie told me you've been making some phone calls."

"Oh yeah? Who was that?"

"Actually it wasn't a birdie, and the guy wasn't little. It was a staffer from the Majority Leader's office—he wrestled at Penn State. Shared that you were making phone calls about a Dolly's Dollar Store building site, is that right?"

"Yes, wow, you guys sure do talk around there."

"Hard to keep anything a secret here. Don't know why everyone thinks government isn't transparent. Everyone seems to know everything. So do you want some help?"

"Absolutely."

"Keep your phone calls coming and I'll also talk to folks here on the ground. The law firm that put together our merger also is connected to Dolly's, yes?"

"That's right."

"Well, Alan, I'm happy to help out. Things are a little slow around here anyway. We'll all keep talking till it gets taken care of—and it *will* get taken care of. What a bunch of idiots, parking their butts on private property."

"It's an embarrassment for the city and for the churches that are taking part."

"We'll win this one no problem. It's about the most cut and dry thing I've seen in a long time. They're in the wrong, and they'll be gone."

"Really appreciate your help, Charlie." Alan was jovial as he dialed the next number on his list.

#####

GINA GONZALEZ worked on a resident transfer to the dementia wing. She paused and pulled Dante Washington's business card from her purse. Dante's original name was Dierdra, but Dante was a much better description of her personality. She wore only men's clothing and was not caught up in presenting herself as one particular gender.

The card was thick and glossy, and showed Dante's email, Facebook, Twitter, and cell phone information. On the back it advertised her services as a DJ. She worked a full-time day job at a hardware store, but hustled DJ gigs on the side. She was good— Gina remembered one wedding with a packed dance floor, the best indication she was skilled at her work.

I think a text message would be the least intrusive and noncommittal approach to take with her. "Hey dante, it's gina, u at rubies tonite?"

Twenty minutes later Gina received a text back: "I'll b there if u r there & i'll bring flyers"

Gina replied: "C u tonite"

#####

EDDIE RAMIREZ looked at his phone and calculated he had a bit more than an hour until his next training session. The streets of Allentown appeared incident-free, at least for the moment, so he stepped out and phoned Luis Abreu, the lawyer who had moderated the Latino Leaders of Allentown meeting.

"Hi, Mr. Abreu. It's Eddie Ramirez, from the Latino Leaders meeting."

"Eddie, yes. What can I do for you?"

"You do labor law, right?"

"Part of my practice covers employment law, yes. But you'd be covered by your police union. They have lawyers."

"This is something I don't want to run by the union."

"Okay, then, come over and we'll talk."

"What's the charge?"

"First hour is free because of your service to Latino Leaders of Allentown."

Eddie drove to Luis's office at the corner of Sixth and Chew Streets. Reminiscent of Abreu's sloppy manner of dressing, the paint to the door of his first-floor office was splotchy and peeling. Eddie reminded himself that Abreu's reputation was solid and he was known for his astuteness. There was no office administrator and Eddie went right into Abreu's office. The two shook hands, and Eddie noticed the lawyer was wearing his usual brown suit and blue tie. He didn't appear to get outside much, and slouched at the shoulders. Although his face was unsmiling, his bright eyes flickered with amusement.

Luis sensed agitation on Eddie's part, and wanted to set him at ease. He initiated the conversation combining sarcasm and humor. "What brings you here today to the fabulous law office of Luis Abreu?"

"You heard about the tent that went up in North Allentown?"

"Yes, on the property where they're going to build another Dolly's."

"I was there this past Sunday night for the kickoff. Didn't go in, just stood on the perimeter. Word from the higher-ups at the police department this morning is that we'll go in on Thursday and make arrests for trespassing."

"With the occupy movement in New York a couple of years back, a handful of people were convicted on trespassing charges, but that was far along, months after it started."

"They want to kill it here quickly. It is private property, owned by a gigantic corporation called SmithCo., and they're politically well-connected."

Luis smiled and asked, "Are you worried about being arrested, Officer?"

"Nah, I'm not going to be at the site. But I'm going to call out on Thursday, and I know other officers are calling out, too. There's a group of us that doesn't want anything to do with clearing the site."

"How's your record with the department?"

"Close to spotless. No complaints. I've never been late, and have taken only two sick days in ten years."

"And you're a vet, right?"

"Yeah, Army National Guard."

Luis waved his hand at Eddie. "You'll be fine. No worries. It's pretty hard to get fired from any police department. Recent cases I can think of were for drug use, which isn't a problem for you. Three NYPD officers were fired for robbing tourists. Extreme stuff."

"And what if I have to call out additional times?"

"They can't ask you why you're calling out."

"Yeah, but they'll figure it out."

Luis shrugged. "You won't be at the protest site. You're good."

"Okay. I just wanted to go over it with someone, you know?"

"Always good to check it out with your friendly neighborhood lawyer. Just curious, why so much heat around Dolly's? I'm all for what is happening over there. It's great a tent was staked and all those construction vehicles are blocking it, but why now? I mean, this kind of thing has been going on for decades and no one ever responded in any way at all."

"Sometimes things just get to a place where people say 'enough.'"

#####

ANNA RAMIREZ and Steve entered the break room with their bag lunches.

"Let's see what delicacies Glenn packed me today," Steve announced.

"I want Glenn to live with me and pack my lunches," Anna said.

"I could loan him out for very short amounts of time, as long as he fills my freezer with meals before he leaves."

"A househusband would be a wonderful thing."

"Well, this Evan is shaping up into one, from what I've heard." Steve opened a container of spinach salad with walnuts and bacon dressing.

"He's sweet," Anna said, recalling the image of her and Evan on the floor of the church kitchen the night before.

"You have that faraway look in your eyes. Good times?"

"Yes, very good times." She smiled, then returned to the present moment. "Um, hey, you know how you said that your sister saw a credit counselor? Could you give me that person's name?"

"I don't remember their name, but I'll give you my sister's phone number and you can ask her. Tell Patty I told you. She'd be happy to pass the info along to you."

Anna tapped the number into her cell. She was glad to have a friend like Steve who wouldn't rub her face in it. He just wanted to help her out and didn't need all sorts of acknowledgment for it.

Recalling Evan's comment about wanting to serve fresh food at the tent, Anna asked, "Does Glenn have any extra veggies right now?"

"Does Glenn have any extra veggies? Is the Pope Catholic? Does the U.S. Postal Service have unfunded liabilities? Is Congress gridlocked? He has a *ton* of vegetables. Truckloads. Well, maybe not truckloads, though it seems like it."

"Do you think he'd consider donating some to the tent?"

Steve made air quotes. "To 'the tent'? This is starting to sound sort of cult-like. Are you all going to start speaking in a different, made-up language or wear matching t-shirts?"

Anna laughed. "We're not that unified. It is a lot of church folk and worship services, which I'm steering clear of, but overall it's a really good cause. Evan and I are working in the kitchen. I'll be there most nights this week."

"I'll check with Glenn tonight and put some things together. He'd probably love to contribute to your radical gathering."

"Thank you, and thank you to Glenn, too."

"See, you did get me involved in this. Your persistence has paid off. I just better not be arrested as a coconspirator or something like that."

"No worries. I'll bail you out if it comes to that."

"But you'll be locked up too!"

"Mr. Paranoid, they're not going to arrest you for transferring vegetables to my car."

"You never know."

#####

GENNY RAMIREZ and Marcus bounced through the tent close to lunchtime. The number of people present had doubled from the previous day with most gathered near the front for the current stage presentation.

In the kitchen tent, Genny saw Joyce Taylor. "Mrs. Taylor, could Marcus and I help serve lunch?"

Joyce looked at the two and said, "Go squirt some of that hand sanitizer on your hands and put on gloves. Marcus can be the main bun man. Genny can be the dog lady. The church women will spoon the beans and the fruit salad."

"Fruit salad? Yum!" Genny said.

"A teacher dropped off some things earlier today—Mr. Thompson—I think that was his name."

In unison, Marcus and Genny said, "He's our art teacher!"

"He brought fruit salad and some other goodies. Look over there." Joyce pointed to a table behind them.

Genny and Marcus's eyes widened as they turned to look at the table full of treats.

"Most of it you wouldn't like—things like carrot cake and zucchini bread."

Joyce was right. The two made faces and were clearly disappointed, but Joyce continued. "See? I knew you wouldn't like it, but Mr. Thompson also brought homemade chocolate chip cookies, and if you serve the whole lunch time I'll make sure you get some. How about that?"

They nodded energetically, and Joyce turned and yelled, "All right, people. Time to line up. You can start over here."

Willie and Alex came through the line and stuck out their tongues at Genny and Marcus as they were being served.

Joyce had planted herself next to the treat table and occasionally yelled, "One treat per person. We want them to last for everyone." She kept a close watch on Willie and Alex as they came by, making sure they didn't snatch extras.

Genny enjoyed looking at all the people and serving them hot dogs. She planned to be here every day. There would be plenty of recycling to do when this was done.

#####

ALAN PECK and Amy dined at an upscale Italian restaurant in the far western suburbs of the Lehigh Valley. They were semi-regulars, eating there once a month after workouts. Amy enjoyed the shrimp risotto while Alan usually ordered the veal.

Looking up from her plate, Amy updated her husband on her phone calls. "I called everyone on the list again today. I also emailed their offices, just for an extra push."

"You're my favorite lobbyist. Thank you."

"They're all about power, so I just come at them with my own power voice and power attitude. Act powerful, and eventually you *are* powerful."

"This tent thing will be over super fast," Alan proclaimed.

"You know, as I make these calls, I wonder if you have ever thought of one of us running for office?"

"Not really."

"Seriously, think about it for a moment. We would be great. We are both successful at business. We know how to run things and manage people and make a profit. Either one of us could run. And we'd make the Lehigh Valley better for people like us—people who work hard and contribute to society. We could do things like put a stop to these kooks at the tent, lower taxes, take away incentives for people to sit at home and watch television all day. Help to get the government smaller and leaner."

Alan pondered Amy's words for a moment and said, "I'd never thought of it. Public service always seemed to me to be a bit boring—long meetings and huge amounts of reading to do to make sure someone didn't slip something into a committee report."

"We both already endure a lot of boring stuff with all the paperwork we do on our jobs. You, especially, know how to sit through boring meetings. We have a lot of connections. I think a lot of people would support a Peck candidacy."

"Or we could fully retire to Hilton Head and live out the rest of our days taking morning walks on the beach and eating fresh seafood every night for dinner," Alan mused.

"Alan, I'm serious. I think we could really do this. Either one of us. We're a great team and our boys would totally step up and help. They're the perfect age—mid-twenties—with tons of extra energy to burn. And think of all the connections they would build for themselves.

"Hmm..." Alan considered Amy's idea. "You know me—I'm pretty cautious. Let's put some feelers out there, talk so some people in the local political party apparatus and go from there."

"We already know the party's county chair, remember? I sold him his house out in Macungie."

"Let's start with him."

#####

GINA GONZALEZ dropped her mother back at the house after dinner and headed for Rubies. She checked her makeup in the rearview mirror and put on another coat of mascara. As she pushed through the heavy front doors, she immediately saw Dante seated at the bar, apparently keeping an eye on the entryway.

"Hey there, Dante. You got the flyers?" Gina was nervous. Her hands were shaking so much she kept them by her sides. *What is up with me? I'm way too old and experienced to get all worked up about this. Dante and I would be ridiculous together, anyway. Too much crazy relationship history plus too much crazy relationship history equals a super-psycho relationship.*

"Check it out." Dante fanned a hundred brightly colored flyers. "I cleared it with the owner. We can go from table to table."

"Okay, what's the pitch?"

"I'm going to talk it up as a rare chance to say no to these businesses that squeeze their employees and sell junk. You could add in something about how important it is to be unified. Be prepared for rejection."

Gina took a deep breath, "Okay, here we go."

The two women headed to the area by the pool tables. Dante started at a table of four, smoothly setting flyers in front of each patron. "Good evening, all. Could we have just a moment of your time?"

One person at the table gave a slight nod, which Dante took as acquiescence. She swiftly jumped into her invitation. "There is a once-in-a-lifetime opportunity happening in north Allentown right now. A developer is building a strip mall with one of those Dolly's Dollar Store places that treats their employees like dirt and sells trinkets and stuff we don't need. We need people out at the construction site to protest the building of another Dolly's."

Gina stepped up to the table and said, "It would be so great to see more of our community be a part of this event. The people of the city are really coming together."

They received flinty looks and Dante concluded. "All the information is on the flyer. Give it some thought and come on out some night this week."

As they moved to the next table, Dante whispered to Gina, "Whew, tough crowd here tonight."

"Yeah, a lot of people come here and just want to drink and not be bothered."

Dante saw the couple at the next table were holding hands. "Hi there, lovebirds," she teased, and gave her pitch.

Together, Gina and Dante covered twelve tables and the bar on the first floor. They skipped the restaurant so as not to upset people dining, then moved to the basement where they spoke to people at twenty tables as well as those seated at a long bar. They were often met by awkward pauses, though with her years of experience as a DJ, Dante expertly dealt with the silent moments. A handful of people expressed some level of interest in coming to the tent, dependent on work schedules or childcare coverage.

As soon as they completed handing out the flyers, Dante turned to Gina and asked, "Could I buy you a drink?"

While Dante drank a beer, Gina sipped on a martini and asked, "So your brother got you involved in the tent?"

"Yeah, Kevin told me about it. His life got really turned around by Church of the Living Water, and there's nothing he wouldn't do for that church."

"Do you go there too?"

"I'm not very religious, and the whole gay thing has been sort of don't-ask-don't-tell at the church but, look at me—you don't even have to ask—my whole persona screams that I'm gay!"

Gina laughed.

"I've been there for Christmas, but I do a lot of gigs on Saturday nights so I'm barely with it on Sunday mornings. When the church has projects or special events I'll go sometimes. How about you?"

"I go with my mother on Sundays to Sacred Heart of Jesus."

"Every week?"

"Every week. I seriously don't think Ma has *ever* missed Mass. My sister got involved with the tent and we all support the cause. Though if it comes down to arrests or anything like that, I'm outta there. I've got to work."

"Yeah, same here. Work just gets in the way sometimes. But we gotta do it, gotta pay the bills. But I'll be there tomorrow night. How about you?"

Gina smiled. "Yeah, I'll be there." She felt her hands shaking again.

WEDNESDAY, JULY 24, 2013

ISABELLA RAMIREZ cooled off in her mother's air-conditioned kitchen while Sofia investigated a doll house in the next room.

"Mom, he is hiding something. I know it. Maybe he's having an affair," Isabella whispered so Sofia wouldn't hear. Though she knew her daughter would not understand the conversation, she didn't want Sofia exposed even tangentially to adult issues.

Anita gave her daughter a serious look. "Don't even think that. Once you go down that road, you are just going to think more and more negative things."

"He clams up and all we end up talking about is my day and things here at the church."

"Sometimes you have to take a longer view. Not everything is solved with a snap of the finger, but it will eventually get figured out."

"I want this fixed now."

"Of course you do, my impatient one. But some things cannot be taken care of in an instant. Some things take years."

"Years!"

"You love Eddie?" Anita asked.

"Yes!"

"You said 'I do' for your whole life. You are twenty-four and have a lot of marriage ahead of you. Give up on overthinking things and just be there for him."

Isabella pointed back and forth between her mother and herself, and said, "We talk about everything, why can't Eddie and I?"

"It's different. Men aren't always interested in having the kinds of talks we have."

"I want him to trust me."

"He does trust you, and he'll trust you even more if you just love him through whatever's going on."

#####

EDDIE RAMIREZ arrived at the counselor's office at noon. He fidgeted in the waiting room, hoping to go unrecognized. There were two other people in the room, listlessly paging through magazines.

A tall, wide woman opened the office door and stepped into the room holding a clipboard. Eddie guessed she probably outweighed him by thirty pounds.

"John Doe," she bellowed.

Eddie stood and answered, "Yeah, that's me."

The woman gave Eddie a knowing smirk. "Follow me."

They went into a gray office that contained several pieces of cheap ratty furniture.

The woman extended her large paw and introduced herself, "I'm Doctor Lianne Chandler, and I'm guessing you are not going to share your name with me?"

"You guessed right. Call me John."

"And you'll pay cash?"

"Yeah."

"You're aware that it will be one hundred and twenty dollars?"

"Yeah."

"Okay, what brings you here today, *John?*" The doctor made air quotes as she pronounced his name.

"I'm having some trouble quitting porn, and you were one of the counselors recommended by Abigail over at Faith Church."

"Your neurons are more interested in porn than anything else. Once those neural pathways are established it's really difficult to go in a different direction."

"Neurons?"

"The cells in your brain that deliver messages to other parts of your body. Neurons are related to impulses."

"Right. I've tried replacing the porn thing with sports videos, but it's not enough."

"You seem like a guy who is pretty much in control of himself."

"Yeah."

"You're in control on the job. You take care of business, right?"

"Yeah."

"You're in control at home, provide for the wife and kids, right?"

"Yeah."

"Well, it looks like you are always in control except for this one thing. Porn has captured and captivated you. You can't control it."

Eddie thought, *Am I crazy or is she taunting me?* He sat up straighter in the chair and said, "I could control it."

"Oh, really? Then why are you sitting here?"

"Listen, I just need a little bit of help."

"A little bit? Uh, *John*," she said, again with air quotes, "you've got a major, runaway problem. You've tried everything else. I'm guessing you've tried everything from anonymous Internet support groups to Jesus. And you're still out of control."

"You're starting to sound offensive."

"I'm here to whip you into shape. Reverend Barrett-Thompson refers people to me because she knows I'm not interested in long-term clients. I don't want to hear about your problems for years. I don't want to suck your bank account dry for the next decade. I'm here to work with you for a few sessions—maybe five or ten at the most. I have no desire to be liked. In fact, most clients really *dis*like me. But I don't seek recognition. I just get the job done, and I do it well. The first thing we're going to do is get you back in control of this part of your life. I'm your boot camp instructor, and if you want to change, you will."

#####

EVAN LEMMON MOORE tried to focus on his calls, but found it a challenge. He was eager to get back to the kitchen tent and help with dinner. Although he was staying at the tent past midnight, Joyce and the ladies from the Baptist church stayed later.

"You've reached BlackBox customer support. How may we help you today?"

"Yeah, I got double charged on my credit card."

"I'm sorry to hear that. We'll get that resolved as soon as possible. What's your name, so we can enter your account?"

#####

TED THOMPSON joined Allen High School art teacher Jorge Paredes in the art room of Trexler Middle School art teacher Annie Sims. The three were working on various art forms of play dolls to put on garish display at the tent. Annie was painting a canvas. Ted wrestled with wire mesh for a large, trophy-like doll head. And Jorge was pasting fake dollar bills onto one of two gigantic papier-mâché dolls. An art teacher from the nearby Bethlehem school district had heard about the effort and dropped off the papier-mâché dolls that morning. Graffiti font on the doll's stomachs read "stop worshiping corporate power."

#####

ABIGAIL BARRETT-THOMPSON drew her papers together and shut down her computer. She paused for a moment before leaving the office to pray and ask God to work through her during the evening's study.

She walked to the tent, hearing Johnny Ramos's preaching from two blocks away. A few steps from the tent she saw the art installation of various dolls, and grinned at the display. *Ted is the best.* Before entering the tent, she noticed Jacob Walker and Corinne Lake standing off to the side.

"Whoa. Hi there, guys. You have a wedding this Saturday. No last-minute details to get set?"

Jacob replied, "We just feel it's really important to be here." He spoke in earnest.

"I'm looking forward to meeting both your families."

"We're pretty organized. And it's not one of those big, blow-out weddings, so we're glad to be here tonight," Corinne said.

"This is great. Are any of your friends planning to come here? We especially need young adults for the overnight hours."

"We'll ask around and put it on Facebook and Instagram," Jacob volunteered.

"Wonderful!" Abigail said, and made her way to the stage area, noting that the crowd had grown yet again, to nearly three hundred. Most were from Church of the Living Water, but Abigail was counting on at least twenty from Faith UCC to come out, including most from her Bible study group. When it was her turn to speak, she would lead a Bible study, figuring she could fill much of the time with a teaching on the prophet Amos. The Bible study crew was pretty flexible, so she expected a good turnout.

As seven o'clock arrived, Abigail was introduced while most of the Church of the Living Water members departed for the food tent for dinner. She spoke into the hand-held microphone. "Thank you. We are so glad to be here with all these great churches, groups, and organizations. I'll be leading a Bible study on the prophet Amos. All are welcome—we had some extra packets made. We go at things a little differently at Faith United Church of Christ, and I thank you in advance for your openness."

Alongside her on stage was the regular crew seated in folding chairs and holding microphones—Keith and his husband Jerry, plus Sherry, Katie, and Chuck. They'd take turns reading sections of Amos, and then Abigail would interject with her teaching. Jacob and Corinne were in the second row, and thirty or forty others sat scattered throughout the space. Abigail had never led a Bible study with over twenty people and tried to calm herself.

"We're using the King James Version tonight and we'll start with a little bit of background on Amos. He was active in the eighth century BCE. That stands for *Before the Common Era*—some may know it as *BC*. If it seems like Amos is kind of an angry guy, well, he is! Amos isn't mad for any sort of petty reason or personality difference with someone. Amos is angry about all the injustice he has witnessed his people take part in over the years.

Like the twenty-first century, there was income inequality during Amos's time."

The audience was not rapt, but they were paying attention and taking in the information. The Bible study crew read through the various sections and went back and forth with Abigail in an easy-to-follow discussion. At chapter five of Amos, Keith read aloud. *"Forasmuch therefore as your treading is upon the poor, and ye take from him burdens of wheat: ye have built houses of hewn stone, but ye shall not dwell in them; ye have planted pleasant vineyards, but ye shall not drink wine of them."*

After Keith finished the chapter, Abigail posed a question, "Does anyone remember the three vulnerable groups that again and again the people of Israel are directed to protect throughout the Hebrew Bible?"

"Widows, orphans, foreigners," Keith quickly answered.

"Yes. These three groups were financially vulnerable, as well as socially marginalized. They didn't necessarily have the family system to provide stability and needed society to step in and ensure their safety and prosperity. Is anyone able to see a tie in between the words of Amos and what we are doing inside this tent?"

Chuck spoke into his microphone, "Sounds like Amos is announcing repercussions for people who have taken advantage of the poor. Dolly's takes advantage of their employees with low wages and tough schedules. Big corporations tend to not have a lot of concern for vulnerable people."

Abigail affirmed, "Right. We always have to remember that for most corporations, maximizing profit is their number one goal. What does Amos say will happen to the powers that be?"

Sherry said, "Those with power and wealth won't get to live in their fancy houses or drink booze from their private vineyards."

"Does this happen in our time?" Abigail asked.

"Well, I guess it depends on how you define time," Katie said.

"Say more," Abigail encouraged.

Katie bent forward with her microphone close to her mouth. "Sometimes corrupt people live a great life, have a sweet house, plenty of wine, women, and song. They may never get caught or be brought to justice. So, I guess some do not really experience any type of punishment or repercussions for their actions, but instead live what they believe to be the *good life*. Only it's not the good life because it's a life that shows no concern for others. Time extends to beyond this sphere, and so if these corrupt, stingy people do not understand their sins in this life, they will in the life that is to come. Time catches up to everyone."

"Great summary, Katie." Abigail smiled and some people scattered throughout the tent applauded.

Abigail continued. "Dolly's may keep trying to put up stores in this area and across the country. We may not be able to stop them. The people who run Dolly's may continue to get richer off the backs of their employees. That does not mean we are released from speaking about them and advocating for better business practices. We are here to take a visible stand and we must believe that our presence here is transformational, that it changes things. What we have to let go of is the specifics. We don't know *how* our action here will make change, but we may be assured that it *will* make change! God will take care of the next chapter. Speaking of chapters, Sherry will continue for us in chapter six of Amos."

#####

GINA GONZALEZ and her mother finished dinner at the tent and returned home. Rather than go inside with her mother, Gina told her she had to do some grocery shopping. However, Gina went back to the tent and found Dante at the end of a table tapping on her phone. She was wearing a bright red Washington Nationals baseball cap, a short-sleeved collared shirt over a t-shirt, baggy black shorts, and black high-tops.

"See anyone from Rubies?" Gina asked.

"Naw, not tonight. Maybe tomorrow?"

"Yeah, maybe tomorrow." Gina's hands were shaking again so she kept them on her lap under the table. *This is crazy. Why am I so freakin' nervous?*

"Want to go for a walk? The park is just a block away."

"Okay. We'll probably see my nephew Willie over there. All the boy does is play basketball at the park. Every day, almost all hours of the day."

Sure enough, as they entered the park, Gina saw Willie on the court playing basketball as usual with Alex. She waved. "That's his best friend Alex with him."

"Keep 'em busy is what I say. Keep kids busy. Keeps 'em out of trouble."

They walked along Jordan Creek, going deeper into the woods as the sun set lower in the sky.

Gina asked, "Should we go much farther? Isn't it a little spooky down there? That's where my niece discovered a dead body. Some guy who overdosed."

"You'll be safe with me," Dante assured her.

"It's kinda pretty in here, peaceful."

"We can sit by the riverbank." Dante removed her collared shirt and spread it on top of the overgrowth next to the creek.

They tossed branches into the water and watched them drift downstream. Gina was unable to restrain herself any longer and burst out, "You've been with a lot of women."

"So have you," Dante retorted.

"Maybe we should say we've both been around."

"Does it matter?" Dante asked.

"Maybe."

"Maybe not. Gina, I like you. You're smart. You're hot. I've asked around about you, and some people told me to watch out 'cause you'll talk a lot of smack, but that's a young person's game. I'll have to believe that you're talking less these days and letting the young people take that over."

Gina crossed her arms, annoyed, "Well, I'm sure you've got some history too—you know, negative stuff."

"Lots of it—some things I'm not too proud of—but I'm still here, trying to be older and wiser."

"We've moved on to our wiser years, huh?"

"I sure hope so."

Gina leaned close to Dante, her lips a mere millimeter away from her ear, and whispered, "So are you wise about kissing?"

Dante nodded.

"Well? Prove it!" she challenged, and removed Dante's baseball cap from her head.

#####

ALAN PECK downloaded the document from Jack Shears onto his personal computer. Amy was at a house showing in Saucon Valley that evening and he hoped to get his project half completed.

That morning, Alan had made his customary daily phone calls to the Lehigh Valley legislative offices and Congressional representatives. His focus now was on the church memberships. Jack had forwarded him documents from each of the churches that were participating in the tent action. The tech employee at Holliday, Shears & Dowell knew how to hack into just about any computer, and since the churches didn't have even the lowest level of security on their machines, it was easy to appropriate their address lists.

Earlier, Alan had stopped at Cedar Beach Church and picked up two thousand large postcards from the church receptionist. The cards had an eye-catching design, with the church building on the front, and a map and the church's slogan on the back. "Be a part of the Cedar Beach community. We will meet your family's needs in every way!" Alan intended to mail a card to every member of the antibusiness churches.

Figuring his employer would support his efforts in a general way and want to keep the Lehigh Valley safe for corporations by ridding it of extremists like Abigail and the other so-called faith leaders, Alan had taken a supply of labels from the Care2Trust offices, along with ink cartridges for his home printer.

He had looked up instructions for a mail merge and customized it for his project, deciding it would be more prudent and look more like a random mailing if he used the word *Resident* instead of specific names on the postcards. One by one, Alan sent the postcards through his printer, starting with Faith Church's members, but being careful to leave Abigail's address off the list. Next, he printed out postcards to everyone on the St. Paul's Lutheran Church list, but tore up the postcard with Rev. Craig Johnson's address. While Hanover Avenue Presbyterian Church's list was merging, Amy came in the office and kissed Alan's neck.

"Quite an impressive load of work, Alan."

"One little way to help steer people toward sanity and get away from those socialistic churches. I'll send out another mailing next month."

#####

ANNA RAMIREZ helped Evan move the cart of cookware to the church for washing in the industrial-sized kitchen. As Evan washed, Anna asked, "If it comes down to arrests for trespassing, are you going to 'stand your ground?'"

"I've thought about it and, yes, I'm willing to get arrested. It's that important to me. If I get fired from work, that's fine, really. I've been ready for a change. Although I don't know why they'd fire me—I'm a great employee and never call out of work. How about you? Are you going to let yourself be arrested?"

"It's just too risky with my job and two kids at home, and my mother would be really freaked by it. But I completely and totally support you, Evan Lemmon."

Evan bent down and kissed her on the cheek. "Thank you, Anna Ponce."

They were startled by a loud voice. "What's going on here?" Joyce Taylor, wearing her trademark sparkly Jesus hat, entered the kitchen, her arms full of trays.

Evan gave a clumsy salute and said, "We're taking care of business, boss."

Joyce shook her head and said, "Looks like you're taking care of *something*, Evan Lemon n' Lime."

Joyce put the trays in the sink. "That's the end of it."

Evan asked, "Don't you ever sleep or take a rest?"

"Who can sleep? Besides, there will be a season for rest. Now is a season for going. I'll see you tomorrow. Till then, be sure to behave." Anna blushed.

THURSDAY, JULY 25, 2013

EDDIE RAMIREZ followed the call-out procedure, phoning into the department at 1:00 a.m. The night desk sergeant said, "I hope this isn't a trend." Eddie knew that most of the officers on the day and evening shifts would be calling off throughout the night. The trespassing arrests at the tent were planned for eleven the next morning, but there was no way there would be enough personnel to take everyone into custody. The mayor of Allentown would not step in because he was supportive of the protestors. However, the conservative governor might stick his nose in and call in Pennsylvania state troopers or the National Guard.

#####

JOHNNY RAMOS met with Deacon Rob to review site management before his morning coverage in the tent. "It's growing every day. More people coming," he stated.

Rob started down the list. "Paulie's done a great job with overnight security—no problems to report."

"His woman Tenisha works overnight too, so Paulie takes the kids over to my daughter's house." Johnny looked up from the paperwork and announced, "Paulie and Tenisha are going to get married in September."

"That's great. It's always a good thing when young people want to take vows. Music is going well, and your son has done a great job with all the tech stuff. Javi knows what he's doing."

"He sure does."

Rob added, "I'd say the food has been pretty good."

"Yeah, always let the Baptists be in charge of the food! But it's still a pretty primitive setup for the kitchen area," Johnny noted.

"It's going to take a while to get better water flow at the site, but my construction crew is aware and brainstorming it. Media coverage gets bigger and bigger every day."

The conversation took a serious tone. "Rob, how much money are you losing?"

"Some, but it's not that bad. I didn't want the men to go without pay, so I'm paying them like they're on a paid vacation. They're doing a lot of invaluable work around the site, including security and all the maintenance headaches that come up with an event like this. Speaking of security, what's the police situation? Any word from your son-in-law?"

"Eddie tells me arrests were supposed to happen at eleven, but most of the force is calling off. They don't want any part of it. With the callouts, they won't have enough personnel to make arrests."

Rob looked at the schedule. "Eleven is when Pastor C.D. Alexander is on. Does he know about this?"

"I let him know yesterday. He was kind of looking forward to being arrested, so I'm sure he'll be disappointed."

Rob chuckled. "He's a legend."

"Eddie warned me, though, that we may not have much more time at the site. The governor is looking to send folks in to make arrests and clear the site as soon as this weekend."

"I've been listening to some of the political talk from that group at the tent, Pennsylvania Citizens for Fairness. They've done a lot of research and they know the enemy. Apparently SmithCo. has really skilled lobbyists and they're probably blowing up the phones and emails of all the state legislators and the governor's office. One of the activists at the tent put together a list of all the political donations SmithCo. has made to Pennsylvania elected officials. A disgrace."

Johnny nodded, "I saw the list. Whew, they have deep pockets."

#####

TED THOMPSON was stirring the apple muffin batter when he heard the mail fall through the front door slot. After placing the next batch in the oven, he retrieved the pile of letters from the floor. *Another envelope from the superintendent's office.* The brief notice informed Ted that, in addition to his six elementary schools, he would be responsible for the sixth grade art classes at Trexler Middle School for the coming academic year. *Annie's school.* Allen High School art teacher Jorge Paredes would take on the seventh and eighth graders. Ted immediately dialed Annie Sims who gave a teary hello.

"Annie, I'm so sorry."

"Last hired, first fired."

"You're a terrific teacher. Don't ever forget that," Ted insisted.

"With no students."

"Can't you apply elsewhere?"

"We're not that mobile. My husband's work is steady and the kids adore their days with their grandmother. Why move for a job for me when I could be laid off again?"

"If I hear of any opportunities, I will let you know, okay? Again, I'm so sorry, Annie. This is an injustice. Hang in there."

Ted set the muffins on a rack to cool. He had made ten dozen to nourish the troops at the tent. After dropping them off at the site, he headed to the gift shop at Tilghman Street and Cedar Crest. He needed an anniversary gift for Abigail as they would be celebrating twenty-seven years together on August 2.

The shop was crammed with expensive knickknacks and jewelry. He decided on earrings for the gift and went to the counter where a friendly saleswoman set him up with an arty pair of silver and turquoise hoops.

"Can I box these and ring them up for you?"

"I'm going to browse a bit."

"When you're ready, they'll be at the front register."

Ted wandered through the store, passed a display of fancy necklaces, and slipped one into his right pants pocket. He saw tiny, handmade wooden boxes on another counter and swiped two, placing them in his left pants pocket. He feigned interest in the gift book section, then peered at the wind chime collection. He finally went to the counter to purchase the earrings, and was startled by a man who suddenly appeared by his side. Ted had not heard him approach.

"Sir, you need to come with me."

Ted blustered to the security guard, "I'm in a hurry. Can we talk about this later?"

"No, you need to come with me now."

"What's this about?"

"The items in your pockets."

Ted turned back to the saleswoman and said, "I'll be back for the earrings."

The security guard had his hand on Ted's shoulder and directed him to a back room. Television screens lined one wall—the store must have had at least two dozen hidden cameras. *Duh. All the mirrors on the walls out there, the perfect place to hide cameras behind. Too much on my mind to be thieving today, too many distractions, too much anger.*

"We'll wait back here until the police come," the security guard said.

"Police?"

"The boxes you took are worth thirty dollars and the necklace is two hundred and fifty. You should have taken something cheaper. It's a first-degree misdemeanor in Pennsylvania to shoplift anything valued between one hundred and fifty and two thousand dollars."

At least it's not a major felony, so I can keep my job. But how will I explain all this to Abigail? How pathetic.

"How'd you see it?" Ted asked.

"I stole stuff from stores for fifteen years, but then I reformed. My pastor helped me take a different path. Anyway, I know every trick when it comes to retail theft."

"Who's your pastor?"

"Pastor Ramos at Church of the Living Water."

Ted sat in the back room with the man for almost six hours. A police officer finally came to the store at five o'clock.

"Wow, the longest we've ever had to wait for an arrest is forty-five minutes," the security guard said to the officer.

"We're way understaffed today—an insane amount of callouts from the officers."

"Here's the guy—retail theft, first degree misdemeanor. I've written everything down for you."

The officer cuffed Ted and they headed downtown for booking.

#####

EVAN LEMMON MOORE pushed the cart full of cookware toward Faith Church for the nightly washing. Anna walked alongside him, strangely thrilled to again be doing this arduous task together.

"No arrests today," Anna said.

"Rumors abound that the big guns may be coming in this weekend. We'll see."

"Still planning to be arrested?" Anna asked.

"Yes." Evan stopped the cart. "Um, this wouldn't be my first arrest."

"Oh? You've been arrested for other protesting, Mr. Radical?"

"No." They maneuvered the cart into the church kitchen and Evan said, "I know there's a classroom nearby where we could talk."

Evan pulled out a chair for Anna. He started, "About ten years ago, I was arrested for DUI. It had never happened before and has never happened since, but I thought you should start knowing some of the not-so-great stuff in my past.

"We'd all like to do some things over. What happened?"

"Went out with a buddy and drank way too much. I never should have gotten into a car. I plowed into a family's van. Everyone survived, but the two kids had some bad injuries. The fines were heavy duty, as they should have been, and it's forever on my record—and in my memory."

"Thank you for telling me, Evan, for trusting me with it," Anna said and reached out to hug him.

#####

WILLIE RAMIREZ was with Alex, squeezing out the last moments of daylight at the basketball hoops in Jordan Park. They did not see the group of older boys approaching until they were on the court.

Alex said, "Oh, hey. What's up?"

"Get off the court," the bulkiest boy demanded.

"What's your problem?" Willie asked.

"What's my problem? My problem is that you're still on this court. Go home and play your video games, little boys," the bruiser ordered. His cronies laughed.

Willie figured that two against four was not a good idea, and remembered his father's stern words. *With big thugs and when you're outnumbered, do not engage. Just walk away. Pretend like it doesn't matter.*

Alex blustered, "We can take them."

Willie feigned indifference. "Whatever. Let's go, man."

The two boys walked to the kitchen tent to see if any snacks remained.

#####

ABIGAIL BARRETT-THOMPSON checked her cell phone after her hour-long session at the tent. A call had come in from a number she didn't recognize. When she tapped the voicemail, she was surprised to hear Ted's voice.

"Hello, love. Well, this is quite the awkward call. It's your favorite husband. I'm in a holding cell downtown. I need you to spring me from this joint and I'll fill you in on all the details."

He gave her directions where to go, and Abigail headed downtown in a daze. After a disorienting back-and-forth process, Ted was finally released and seated next to Abigail in the front seat of her car. She remained parked in the city garage.

"What on earth is going on?" she asked.

"I'm an idiot, that's what's going on," he replied.

"I said 'for better, for worse' twenty-seven years ago and meant it, but I never pictured myself bailing you out for petty theft."

In jest, Ted corrected her, "It's called *retail theft*."

"You know what I mean. Why not get arrested for something that matters? Like, trespassing at the tent? But no, you stole stuff."

"There's no explanation. I'm an idiot."

"You've done this before?"

"Uh, yes."

"How many times?"

"I was down to around once a month or so, sometimes more, sometimes less. I was handcuffed years ago, in college, right before we met. They let me off and just told me never to come in their store again."

"Why do you do this?"

"There's a thrill involved. The heart races, and it's really quite easy to do in most stores. I picked the wrong one today. I have been getting sloppy lately, and that is a sure sign that I have to stop. Have to. It's wrong, and if any of my students did it, I'd tell them to shape up, get right, and knock it off."

After a long pause Abigail declared, "Daddy issues."

Ted didn't understand. "Excuse me?"

Abigail pursed her lips and repeated, "Daddy issues."

"I thought I had Dada issues."

"Not funny. Is there any man alive who doesn't have daddy issues?"

"That's a bit of a stretch to apply it to every man."

"Then I'll just apply it to you. This is about you never dealing with how your father regimented every moment of your life. The same meals for breakfast and dinner for weeks on end, like being in the military. The constant curfews and disdain for anything creative or out of the ordinary. You say you've forgiven him but you still carry him with you. You thought that by majoring in art you were your own man. You thought that by teaching instead of going into the trades you separated yourself from him. You thought that by being a feminist and marrying a feminist you'd dealt with it. Instead, it never left you, and even after he died, you're still clueless and wrapped up in it."

"That hurts."

"I don't know what to say."

"Say that you love me, that you're disappointed in me, that we'll get through this, that you'll support me as I seek some kind of professional help."

"Yes, all that," Abigail replied, and started the car. They drove in silence to the parking lot of the gift shop where she dropped him at his car.

Ted waved. "I'll see you at home."

Abigail ignored him and drove to the nearest fast food restaurant. At the drive-through she ordered the largest burger and fry combo possible, a sugary soda, and a chocolate shake. She shoveled the food into her mouth and on the drive home stopped in the lot near the entrance to Trexler Park where she vomited into a trash can.

#####

ALAN PECK continued with his postcard project after a quick dinner, having dropped the first batch off at the post office before arriving at work in the morning. Postage was on Cedar Beach Church's bulk mail designation, though through a private donor, SmithCo. had kindly and helpfully provided a generous donation to Cedar Beach's general fund.

Alan printed out the postcards to St. John's UCC, making sure Reverend Eric Windham was not a recipient. While some church members were likely to share with their pastors about the mailing, there was also a chance it would go unmentioned as congregants sometimes didn't want to upset their pastors.

The next two lists were for members of Church of the Living Water and the Independent Baptist Church. Alan had mixed feelings about sending to them, knowing the unlikelihood of their members switching allegiances, but even if just a handful of people checked out Cedar Beach, that would be a triumph. He removed the postcards for Reverend C.D. Alexander, Reverend Johnny Ramos, and Rob Handel.

By eleven, Alan had completed the project and made some notes that would speed the process in the future. One postcard mailing per month was planned for the next five months. He concluded his night's work with a brief message:

Subject: 1ˢᵗ Project Complete
To: PastorDaveyPorterfield@CedarBeachChurch.com
Date: Thu, Jul 25, 2013 11:14 pm
From: Alan.Peck@Care2Trust.com

Pastor,

The first postcard project is complete. I hope it brings in many more members to your freedom- and private-property-loving church! Thank God for you and your congregation. You're so needed in this crazy world.

Best,
Alan

RICHARD MOYER bolted upright in his bed. *Sounds like tanks.* He looked at his clock—eleven forty-five—rushed to get dressed, and clambered down the stairs as quickly as he was able. His next-door neighbors Anna, Gina, and Consuela were on their front porch. Other neighbors were out and everyone was staring north to Sumner Avenue as the tanks paraded down the street toward the site. *Must be National Guard. SmithCo. really wants to* *stop this tent. Who's really running the show here? The people we elected or the corporations?*

"I'm going to check it out," Richard said.

"I'll drive you," Anna offered, and turned to her mother and sister. "We'll be right back. I promise." The kids slept like rocks, and Anna always confiscated their cell phones before bed, so she was certain they wouldn't be roused.

Richard and Anna climbed into her car to drive the five-and-a-half blocks to the protest area, but the streets were blocked off closer to the site. Anna pulled into the Faith Church parking lot, and they walked closer to the tent site to join a fast-growing crowd that was watching one tank pushing against a backhoe and another against a loader.

"Not sure why they need tanks. It's not like there's a whole lot of people in the tent overnight," Richard said. "Some sort of security team and maybe some of the kitchen folks—they seem to be around all the time."

Trying to keep her anger manageable, Anna muttered, "I have an overwhelming need to start throwing things at these tanks."

"Yeah, me too."

"But then we trade violence for violence."

Richard commented, "This crowd is on the edge, that's for sure. They could riot, but can't say I blame 'em. Sending tanks into a neighborhood, that's ridiculous." He looked around and saw men and women of all ages and races chattering, pointing, and gesticulating. The volume increased when one of the tanks turned toward the crowd. A group of young men started toward the tank and it rumbled forward ten feet.

"Don't mess with that tank," someone in the crowd yelled. "We need you to stay alive."

"Pull back. It's not worth it," another shouted, and the young men returned to the large crowd.

A line of state troopers took their places, standing in a row between the tent and the crowd and pointing guns at the ragtag assembly of neighborhood people.

Anna shook her head. "What a bunch of cowards, in their big tanks, with their big helmets and huge guns."

"I never thought I'd see tanks like this in my own neighborhood. I thought I was done with 'em in Korea," Richard said.

Finally, a television crew arrived from the local station to catch the event for the news. Additionally, people in the crowd were videotaping or snapping photos with their phones and immediately posting on social media.

One of the tanks had made a large gap in the fencing, and military officers wearing plastic gloves escorted arrestees to a massive military truck. Richard and Anna moved closer. They saw the head of the security team, Paulie, in handcuffs, along with four other men on his overnight security crew. The crowd applauded as the arrestees were loaded onto the truck. When Joyce Taylor appeared in handcuffs along with three ladies from the Independent Baptist Church, the crowd went berserk, jumping and cheering them on. "You go, girls!" "You're my heroes!"

A shower of taunts was rained down on the officers. "Arresting old ladies, you should be ashamed!" "That make you feel powerful, cuffing the cooks?" "Get out of our neighborhood!" The officers carefully lifted the women onto the truck. Evan Lemmon Moore was the last to follow them on.

AUTUMN 2013

Friday, October 18, 2013

RICHARD MOYER guided a small, white Pomeranian on his route down Greenleaf, then left on Meadow past the gleaming new Dolly's Dollar Store on the end of the strip. Sal's Pizza, Nina's Nails, and Tobacco Time were the other stores that sprouted up seemingly overnight. Richard looked down at his dog and said, "Princess, that, over there, is all that's wrong with America. No respect for the will of the people." He then he spat in the direction of the Dolly's store.

Richard had no plans to get another pet, but the fluff ball kept showing up in his backyard without tags and he couldn't help but feed it and brush it daily.

ABIGAIL BARRETT-THOMPSON heard loud voices and soon identified the sound as a couple's quarrel. She went to her window when the voices increased in volume and saw the couple going back and forth, leaning in and then withdrawing in an almost elegant dance. Occasionally, opera happened at the intersection of Fourth and Whitehall Streets, right next to the church, dramas that were a mix of comedy and tragedy. *Another aria.* Abigail knew when to stay at her desk and let it be background music, when to stand up and observe through the window, and when it was necessary to go outside, be a witness, and call the police.

The couple was having an argument aria—that so many do—about the claim they had on one another, how much they really belonged to each other. Abigail had heard arias on the topics of fidelity, children, money, level of involvement from exes and, one of her favorites, a couple who raged over the level of spiciness to put in a chicken dish. There were angry gestures, head shaking, finger pointing, and then the man and woman abruptly walked away from each other. *Praise God. Just walk away and give it another try after cooling down.*

Abigail went back to her work preparing for the New Member Welcome and Blessing to take place on Sunday. Two new members would be welcomed into Faith UCC—hardly enough to replace all the members lost to transfer or death, but, she thought, a way to stave off closure for just a bit longer.

#####

JOHNNY RAMOS and Deacon Rob devoured turkey sandwiches at the sub shop downtown and then rehashed the summer protest.

"I'm still wondering what, exactly, came out of staking the tent on the property of powerful developers?" Johnny asked.

"The satisfaction of knowing we took a stand."

Johnny scowled. "Yes, and that we got a bright, shiny Dolly's."

"Let's hope the new Dolly's is a total failure and people shop elsewhere. Give it time. We'll see."

Focusing on the positive, Johnny said, "I'll praise God for the forty-five new members we've taken in since August."

"Praise God indeed. We could keep announcing at services that people should not shop at Dolly's and have the Youth Group do another leafleting of the neighborhood to tell people to stay away from the place."

"Have you done a final accounting of your losses?" Johnny inquired.

Rob nodded. "The equipment loss was the worst—a backhoe and loader were destroyed with no insurance to cover it."

"Sorry about that, man. That hurts."

"We're scouting out used equipment for purchase, or we may rent. The paid vacation wasn't a big deal, and the bailouts of everyone arrested wasn't a big deal. We've covered court costs and the modest fees for Luis Abreu."

"Really glad you were able to do all that."

"But I don't know the long-term effects for the business. We haven't received a bid for quite a while. I'm wondering if something underhanded is going on there with SmithCo. They may be messing with my bids. I've been thinking about bidding further afield, up to Stroudsburg, or bidding under a different name."

"I wish you didn't have to do that. It really upsets me," Johnny stated.

"They're playing hardball, but I've dealt with corporations like this before and they're never going to get to me again. Did I ever tell you about my parent's house?"

"No, I don't remember anything about that."

Rob cleared his throat and disclosed, "My folks, me, and my three brothers lived in a little house in New Jersey, right in the middle of where they wanted to build a big, new shopping mall—one of the largest in Jersey at the time, though much larger ones have been built since."

"Uh oh."

"Yep, uh oh. Through the county redevelopment authority, the developers bought up all the houses and, while they paid a fair price, that's not the point. We wanted to stay in our house. It wasn't much, but we had a gigantic yard with a huge garden and plenty of running space for four rowdy boys. Too many of the nearby residents sold, so my parents didn't have enough support to stay and fight. We make a big deal out of private property in this country, but corporations and the government stick their nose in a lot more often then we think, and they have a big advantage over unorganized ordinary people. It all belongs to God anyway, right?"

Johnny concurred, "Right. If more people got that, we wouldn't have as many problems. We're just here for a bit on earth. God owns it all."

"But I do have to say some good actually came out of it. My parents moved us to Allentown, where I eventually met my wife, and together we raised two Christ-centered kids. I run a good, ethical business and I get to serve with people like you."

"Sounds pretty spiritually mature of you."

"Well, I was angry for a number of years—really angry. And you know how much boozing I did in my younger years. It took a while but church and, most of all, God, helped me turn things around."

"God is good! That explains why you had such a passion for stopping the Dolly's store. Sounds like your family got burned in Jersey. But even if that hadn't happened in your past I'm guessing you probably still would have done it."

"Probably so. But imagine if we had tried it while I was still drinking all the time and you were still drugging. What a mess. I think the powers that be want us to stay drunk and high so we don't take a stand. I'm proud of the church for taking the lead on this."

#####

ANNA RAMIREZ beckoned the customer, "Next in line."

A young woman approached her counter and asked, "How do I get my mail forwarded?"

"Fill out this form. Here's a pen. Just step to the side and I'll keep serving customers while you put in all the information. Next in line!"

An elderly man stepped forward with a large envelope. "I need to mail this."

"Certainly. Do you need delivery confirmation?" Anna asked, turning to weigh the envelope.

#####

EVAN LEMMON MOORE announced, "BlackBox customer service. How may we help you today?"

"Yeah, hey, I can't get my game to load."

"We'll try to fix this right away. What's your name?"

"Ray Nelson."

"And, Ray, where do you live?"

"Phoenix."

"Okay, just a moment while I pull up your information." Evan saw eleven Ray Nelsons listed for Phoenix.

#####

GINA GONZALEZ texted back and forth with Dante while waiting for a family intake meeting to start.

"What up dan dan?"
"Morning contractor rush over, phew. Can't wait 2 c my sexy grl tonite"
"Haven't seen u 4 5 days, that 2 long!!!!"
"I know, I miss my sexy grl"
"Miss u 2, u r my sun n moon n stars"

Gina didn't care anymore how silly her texts were. And, besides, Dante was goofy too.

"U r in my dreams & on my hrt"
"Can't wait 2 touch u, grrrrrr"
"Grrrrrrrr, can't wait 2 look in ur eyes prtty lady"
"Aw, tks u like me?" Gina asked.
"Yes!!!"
"I like u 2. I like ur STYLE"
"Tks, i try 2 look GOOD 4 my lady"
"U always look GOOD. Gotta go, mtg ppl here. Ttyl"
"Ttyl"

#####

EDDIE RAMIREZ pulled the car up to the curb to drop off Willie, Genny, and Sofia with Grandpa Johnny and Grandma Anita. The grandkids would eat a big dinner and play with other Christian youth at Church of the Living Water next door. Eddie and Isabella were going on a long-awaited date—out to dinner and then maybe a movie.

"You look more and more delicious each day. I mean, you always look delicious. You've just got that glow workin' right now."

"Aw, thank you. And you look handsome." Isabella squeezed Eddie's muscular bicep.

"Come up with any new baby names?"

"I have a ton of baby names, so many great names that we need to have lots more babies."

"Babies are great, but a ballooning expense."

"What?"

"They get older and cost more."

"God will provide," Isabella proclaimed.

"Yes, definitely. But we probably don't want to push our luck with God."

Isabella put a hand on his cheek, "It's not about luck. It's where the Spirit leads."

Eddie stretched his arms out in prayer, looked up toward Heaven, and joked, "I feel the Spirit leading us to two children."

Isabella put on her best pouty face and replied, "But I feel the Spirit leading us to five children."

They both smiled as Eddie escorted his wife into the Cuban café, turning the heads of most of the patrons at the restaurant.

#####

ALAN PECK and Amy were pursuing the support of another member of the county central committee. This was the seventh committee member they had taken out to Andre Reed's steakhouse for a "conversation about the future." They had made their decision—Amy was preparing a run for the state senate. The election was a year away but they were slowly and tirelessly lining up the support of the local party decision makers ahead of the May primaries. It was a big reach, but a new senate seat had been created right in their area due to all of the population growth and redistricting.

Central committee member Ian Ehrlach was the toughest sell so far. He refused an alcoholic beverage, seemed unimpressed by his surroundings, and didn't appear to be listening as Amy outlined her platform.

"I think you'll be pleased to know that, as a candidate, I'll run as pro-life, pro-marriage—with marriage understood as between one man and one woman. I'm also pro-firearms and, as I already mentioned, pro-private property."

"You said you'll *run* as a candidate that way, but are these your actual positions?"

"Sure," Amy replied. She was getting nervous.

Ian looked hard at her and asked, "Where do you go to church?"

Alan quickly replied, "We are taking on membership at Cedar Beach Church this Sunday."

Ian looked dubious. He grumbled, "Well, that's convenient."

In the friendliest and most authentic voice he could muster, Alan said, "Not *convenient*. It had been a long time coming. Amy and I reached a point in our lives where we wanted to be at a church that teaches people to develop a personal relationship with God as well as take personal responsibility for their lives." *Phew!* Alan thought, *Glad I've been paying attention during the Cedar Beach Church membership classes.*

"Why weren't the faith-based items first on your list?"

Her nerves recovered, Amy said "We need to appeal to a broad range of voters in the general election, and a lot of voters are not as interested in the faith-based issues."

Frowning, Ian said, "If they're not first, you won't have my support."

Alan replied, "That's good to know, Ian. We really appreciate your willingness to be clear on where you stand."

Both Alan and Amy were skilled with customers who said "no" or "not yet," and they finished out the meal focusing on the political issues Ian was passionate about, decrying reality television and how society no longer cared about those who worked hard.

SATURDAY, OCTOBER 19, 2013

ABIGAIL BARRETT-THOMPSON unlocked the front door and ushered Jacob Walker to her office. They sat in their respective chairs and Abigail asked cheerily, "How is married life?"

"I didn't think I'd feel much of a difference, but something did change."

"It was a memorable ceremony. You two will have many great adventures together. What brings you here this morning? Your email was pretty vague."

"I'm thinking about going to seminary."

Abigail was baffled. "Have you lost your mind?"

"Excuse me?"

"Religion is not exactly a growth industry these days. Churches that focus on social justice are having an especially difficult time. You were thinking of pursuing ordination with the United Church of Christ?"

"Uh, yes."

Abigail put her thumb and forefinger to the bridge of her nose. "I'm going to start by telling you all the reasons to *not* get ordained. First and foremost, you're going to have to let go of the idea of making a good wage. If you were planning to be the sole wage earner for your family, it will be a huge stretch to support a spouse and kids. You'll need to do a lot schooling for very little money in return. Doctors, lawyers, and other professionals get a much higher return on their educational investment."

"I've thought about the financial issues and talked with Corrine about it, and we feel prepared to manage."

"You'll need to develop a very thick skin. Criticism for the pastor is constant in faith communities, and you'll need to respond to it graciously and kindly on a daily basis."

"I'm sure I'll have some instruction on how to develop that skill."

Abigail would not let up. "Pastors are the cleanup crew. Most people don't understand that Christ is all they need until they have hit absolute bottom. Clergy help pick up the pieces of broken lives and dashed dreams, and it is extraordinarily hard work."

"I think I'm ready for it."

"The job of a pastor used to be low-pay, low-stress, high-status work. Now it's low-pay, high-stress, low-status work for most faith leaders. Pastors of evangelical churches tend to have higher status, but only within their circles. Since the Catholic priest pedophilia scandal and the televangelist shenanigans, even the most ethical of pastors are viewed with immense amounts of suspicion. There recently was a national study of clergy, and it found that many of them have chronic health problems, depression, and emotional damage from dealing with constant budget issues, personality clashes in congregations, and trying to keep up with increasing technological innovations."

"I'm not going to go into it for money or status, and I know there are difficulties in any profession. But I do know I'm definitely not where I'm supposed to be working right now at the auto dealer."

"Well, that leads to the most important question. Do you feel called by God? Do you feel like your soul will die a slow death if you do not pursue this?

"Yes."

"You are named after the God-wrestler. You'll certainly be doing some spiritual grappling in the years ahead, Jacob."

"I can't wait, actually. The membership classes really got me thinking about where I'm going and what I'm supposed to be doing with my life. The Bible Fellowship church of my youth was too constricting, and I didn't think there was any sort of alternative to conservative Christianity, so I was really excited to discover a place like Faith Church."

Abigail smiled and said, "Well, Jacob, welcome to the luxurious life! Luxury in terms of the depths and richness of God's gifts, grace, and challenges you will experience. Would it be all right if I announced it tomorrow when you and Corinne become church members? The congregation will be ecstatic for you."

#####

GINA GONZALEZ arrived at Dante's apartment on Twelfth and Chew Streets with take-out Italian to share.

"Food! You are the best," Dante said as Gina entered holding the take-out bags. "What do I owe you?"

"Lunch is on me."

Dante laughed. "My assistant is paying for lunch. Shouldn't the boss be the one who pays?" Dante was set to DJ a wedding reception at a southside Allentown fire hall that evening. For the third time, Gina would be her assistant. Dante didn't have much specialized equipment to load anymore, with her laptop as the main music generator, but she still needed large speakers and lighting pieces for effect. Gina would receive the song requests from the wedding guests.

They opened containers of salad at the small dining room table and Gina asked, "How many are you expecting?"

"It's not going to be huge. Probably around a hundred."

"Think you'll ever get married?"

"I had a commitment ceremony with one of my exes."

"Oh yeah? Which one?"

"Rhonda. We were really young, too young, and it was before so many states were doing legal marriage. I don't regret it, but we should have waited."

"Rhonda. You haven't talked much about her. I saw her at Rubies once or twice this summer. She had a skirt up to here," Gina put a hand on her waist, "and a shirt down to here." She poked at her belly button.

In an attempt to steer Gina away from her gossipy tendencies, Dante said slowly, "Careful now. We probably don't want to go down this conversational path."

"Conversational path?"

"I heard it on some talk show the other day."

"Well, well, impressive words," Gina said. She changed the topic of discussion, having picked up on Dante's preference to focus their dialogue elsewhere. "So, anyway, no other ceremonies?"

"No. How 'bout you?" Dante asked.

"I don't know if I'm the marrying kind."

"It would have to be someone pretty special, huh?"

"Yes, very special," Gina smiled.

"Well, I'll have to work on my specialness."

"You do pretty good," Gina conceded.

"*Pretty* good?"

"Yes, pretty good. We all have room for improvement, right?"

"Yes, we *all* do," Dante suggested.

#####

GENNY RAMIREZ strolled through Jordan Park looking for plastic bottles to put in her old postal bag. She had taken a break from collecting over the summer, but when the school year began, she started back up. She washed and kept the empties in her grandmother's basement where she would soon start tying them together to make the longest possible chain. *I wonder if I could stretch it all the way to downtown Allentown.*

Genny was always surprised by how many people threw plastic away rather than recycle it, or just left their bottles under picnic tables and benches, too lazy to retrieve them. Wearing gloves, she dug through the trash can and found three sports drink bottles, then circled the Jordan Park pool. Lastly, she walked around the MacArthur Road businesses and then back to the basketball hoops at the park. Her bag was full.

As usual, Willie and Alex were on the court taking practice shots. Both boys had made the freshman basketball team at Allen High School. They practiced after classes Monday through Friday in the school gymnasium, and on Saturday mornings continued to use the park courts to sharpen their skills. They were nervous and excited to play against area freshman teams starting in November.

Willie saw his sister approach and said, "Baggy Genny is here!"

Alex greeted her with the same moniker. "Hello, Miss Baggy Genny."

Genny put a hand on her hip. "I don't collect bags anymore—it's now plastic bottles." She held one up for the boys to see.

Willie bounced his ball and took a shot. "You'll never get every bottle in this town recycled."

"Did you know that enough plastic is thrown away each year to circle the earth four times?"

"You always have your little facts," Willie said.

Genny disputed his adjective, "They're not little."

#####

ANNA RAMIREZ met Evan at their designated spot at six thirty. Evan got in Anna's car and joked, "We've got to stop meeting like this." He leaned over to give her a quick kiss and then belted himself into the front passenger seat.

"It is starting to feel a little *young* of us," Anna admitted. "It's time I tell the kids. We've been too cautious because of Eddie, but you know what? He probably already knows. He'll deal with it—he has to deal with it. Keeping it on the down low sends the wrong message, like it doesn't matter."

"I'd like to cook for you sometime while you sit in my kitchen."

Anna was surprised. "You've thought about that?"

"Sure. Do you ever think about things like that?"

"I've thought about making a home together, yes. It's a big deal. Lots to figure out. But I like thinking about it."

They pulled up to a Mexican restaurant known for its use of fresh and local ingredients. After being seated in a quiet corner, Evan ordered a vegetarian entrée while Anna chose a chicken dish.

Evan took a sip of his water and then his tea. "There's something I need to tell you."

"Uh oh."

Evan shuffled in his seat. "Since we've both mentioned some interest in something long-term between us, there is something I need to come clean about."

"You already told me about your DUI."

"But I haven't told you about what happened *before* the DUI."

"Oh."

Evan laid the foundations of the story. "Back in my home town, I was a teacher at the high school. One day, I was putting together the technical gear for a pep rally."

"Teacher?"

"I taught computer science for two years at Edwardsville Memorial High School in Illinois."

Anna's heart beat faster, unsure where Evan was going with his story. *I can't imagine what he's going to tell me. Is it that bad?*

"Just as the rally was about to start, with hundreds of teenagers were gathered in the gym to kick off School Spirit week, I put the wrong image up on the giant screen." Evan looked around the room and took a deep breath. "Instead of clicking on the cheers the school would be shouting, I put up a photo of my girlfriend."

Anna let out a dubious "Okay?"

"She was naked, and she also happened to be a teacher at the school."

"Oops."

"Yeah, big oops. It hit the national media."

Anna's mind raced. "Now that you mention it, I think I did hear something about that. That was years ago."

"It was everywhere, but, thankfully, for only a really short time. My girlfriend's situation aside, it completely devastated my parents. They taught at that high school and were so proud to have their son teaching there too. And then I go and do something that caused them endless heartache—the naked stuff, embarrassing my girlfriend, clicking on the wrong picture because I was fuzzy from partying the night before, the students thinking it was hilarious. I quit teaching that summer."

"Sounds like you haven't forgiven yourself for it, even after all this time. I'm sure your parents have, and the girlfriend too. Haven't they all moved on?"

"Depends on what you mean by 'moved on.' Seems like it's still a source of pain for my parents, and I haven't heard from Christie since she moved to the Chicago area ten years ago. Things didn't end well."

"Then that's on them, right? We can only hold stuff over people for so long."

"I suppose."

"Everything's forgivable," Anna declared.

Evan detected some authority in her tone. "Everything?"

"That's what I've found for my life. I don't have the energy to hold on to everything."

"Listen to us—we almost sound religious," Evan chuckled.

Anna smiled. "Spiritual, not religious. Thank you again for trusting me, Evan."

"You deserve it."

"Hey, um, while we're talking this way, there's something I need to share with you."

"Okay."

"I'm having some problems with money."

"Oh?"

"It's, uh, gotten out of control at times," Anna confessed.

"Like with spending money?"

"Yes. I have four credit cards and about forty thousand dollars' worth of debt."

Evan straightened in the seat. His eyes grew large and his voice rose, "That's not *some* problems with money. Sounds more like *a lot of* problems with money."

Anna looked down in embarrassment at Evan's reaction. She took a deep breath, then looked Evan in the eye and said, "When I was married to Eddie, I'm ashamed to say it reached eighty thousand. With the divorce, we split the debt exactly in half, even though ninety-nine percent of it was mine."

"Bet he wasn't too happy with that."

"He was enraged. I worked hard to pay it down and pay it down some more, but then it goes back up again."

Their entrées arrived and Evan said, "Thank you for letting me know."

"Do you think less of me now?"

"What? No, absolutely not! It doesn't seem you think any less of me after what I just shared."

"No, I don't."

Evan continued, "It's just a lot, isn't it? Every person just has a lot to deal with or not deal with."

"I'm seeing a credit counselor."

"That's a good step."

"It was one of the harder things to do, to go to a meeting with her, but I needed to do it. I had to develop a budget and stick to it. And I'm recording every single purchase I make, even if it's a pack of gum."

They sat with their dinners in front of them, not eating for a moment, and each nodding absentmindedly. Evan suddenly exclaimed, "Whew, we did it!"

"What do you mean?"

"We did it. We shared some pretty ugly stuff. Neither of us screamed and ran away and the world is still spinning. Confession *is* good for the soul."

Anna replied, "Sounds like we're getting spiritual again."

SUNDAY, OCTOBER 20, 2013

EVAN LEMMON MOORE climbed the path with Bill and the small group of Trail Tenders on a portion of the Appalachian Trail. As the crew walked along, they cleared brush out of the way. Evan occasionally raised his head and took in the dazzling view. *The fall leaves are stunning.* They were headed to a remote portion of the route to respond to a report of a tree across the trail.

One of the Tenders started to sing, "Hi ho, hi ho, it's off to work we go."

#####

GINA GONZALEZ received communion, returned to her pew, and prayed silently alongside her mother. The craving for Divine forgiveness was once again satisfied, and she felt a pulsing spiritual energy flow in, through, and around her. It had color and shape, hundreds of thousands of bright curvy lines that pulled her along on a warm and exhilarating excursion closer to God. She smiled, and thought, *Up most of last night at the wedding and helping Dante, and here I am super early Sunday morning going to Mass with my mother. No one and no thing will ever get in the way of this.*

#####

ALAN PECK drove into the half-filled Cedar Beach Church parking lot on his and Amy's day to officially become members.

He turned to his wife. "Sure you want to do this, Amy?"

"Are you kidding me? Yes, yes, yes, I'm very sure! Five thousand members, so many of them potential Amy Peck voters. This place is an absolute gold mine."

Alan turned off the ignition and threw his head back. "Compared to *fifty* people at Faith Church. That place would be no help at all."

"The only thing that feels a little strange is that neither of us believes any of this."

"But we're pretty darn good at faking it, and it's not like every single one of the five thousand members believes in everything either."

Amy agreed. "True. I think there are probably more nonspiritual people here than anyone would care to admit."

Alan looked through the windshield toward the Cedar Beach entrance. Attendees streamed in. "I don't think I *ever* understood the spiritual stuff—it never computed. Most of my life I just went through the motions to please my parents."

"There's no shame in living one's life for oneself rather than spending all sorts of time trying to figure out some long-dead religion. We're here for practical purposes and we'll stay at Cedar Beach for practical purposes. It's one of the easiest networking places in town with a sweet demographic that we'll need in May and again in November."

"Pastor Davey will definitely help move things along toward victory for you and for us."

#####

JOHNNY RAMOS expected over five hundred in the sanctuary that morning. The church needed to soon add a second Sunday service to accommodate everyone.

The musicians tuned their instruments, and congregants flowed into the sanctuary where Johnny now stood. He slapped the backs of the men and gave as many people as possible his heartiest "Good morning."

After two hours of music, announcements, prayer, testimony, and an offering, Johnny stepped up to the pulpit.

"God has been good to us!"

"Amen!" the people responded.

"Let's all take out our Bibles and turn to the Gospel of Matthew."

#####

ABIGAIL BARRETT-THOMPSON stepped up to the pulpit. She was uplifted by the positive energy in the sanctuary after the New Member Welcome and Blessing and the announcement of Jacob Walker's pursuit of ordination.

She looked out and guessed there were sixty people present at Faith UCC this morning. "We hear the prophetic voice of Jesus today in Matthew's Gospel. We'll focus on two questions for today's message. First, what is the interpretive framework for our own personal life? And second, what is the interpretive framework for our lives in the larger context?" Abigail paused and scrunched her brow. "What in the world does that mean? One thing Biblical prophecy gets us thinking about is, what is *my* life about? And since we do not want to remain in just an individualistic frame, we also want to think about, well, what *our* lives are about as a community of faith."

Abigail glanced at the right side of the sanctuary and noticed Jacob and Corrine nodding as she spoke. The couple appeared to be glowing, perhaps from their joy in making a commitment to a new beginning.

#####

TED THOMPSON put the chicken in the oven to roast. He hoped it would be spicy enough—this was his first time trying the smoked paprika recipe. He started on the red potatoes, picking them out of the strainer in the sink. They were small enough to cut in two for bite-sized pieces which he tossed in a large bowl with olive oil, salt, pepper, and rosemary. A self-proclaimed "oven whisperer," Ted knew the precise moment the potatoes would be browned and crispy on the outside and sufficiently soft on the inside.

Abigail walked into the kitchen and Ted turned to greet her. "Good afternoon, Reverend Barrett-Thompson. How is the flock?"

Abigail kissed Ted on the cheek and said, "Two more sheep were officially welcomed into the flock."

"Huzzah! That calls for some of the good wine." Ted poured two glasses.

"Well, before we toast, Faith UCC lost seventeen members this past year to transfer, death, or atheism."

"So, it's a small victory, but a victory nonetheless," he said, and clinked Abigail's glass.

"What's for dinner?"

"Paprika-roasted chicken, potatoes, carrots with caramelized ginger, sautéed spinach with pine nuts, and something chocolatey for dessert."

Ted continued the meal preparations.

Abigail asked, "What reading did you do today?"

"I started some heavy-duty reading in psychology. I had not read much Freud, so I'm doing that, but switching it out with three different books on shoplifting that I ordered online."

"Good for you—on the road to recovery."

"That's part of the title of one of the books. You know me, I read my way to a better place. It's how I get at things. Sitting in a counselor's office an hour a week would be torment—I just don't think I could do it."

"You've never tried."

"It's a man thing."

"Nah, it's a Ted thing."

"Well, we all have our *things*. Let's talk about some Abigail things."

"I'd rather talk about someone else. How's Phil?"

"We chatted this morning. He is still blocked with his novel, but continuing to blog. Work is going okay. He's not thrilled with it, but is plodding along."

"His mother and father are plodders so he was bound to be a plodder too. Poor guy, the writer's block is probably very hard on him."

"Yes, I told him to come down here for a weekend, and that might get him unblocked. He's done meditation and tried yoga, but it's not loosening anything."

"Sometimes you just have to ride it out for a few months or years—just hopefully not a few decades." Abigail watched as Ted scrubbed the carrots under running water. She asked him softly, "Have you shared it with him yet?"

"No. Can't bear it."

"Wouldn't you rather he heard it from you than from some random source?"

"The arrest never made the newspaper, and the only people who know about it are some higher ups in the school district offices and teacher's union. Misdemeanors apparently aren't a big deal, even some felonies. I didn't realize there were so many employment protections for teachers—something for which I'm feeling a lot of delayed gratitude."

"Speaking of gratitude, maybe Thanksgiving? I can sit with you when you tell him about it."

"'Happy Thanksgiving, Son, your dad's a thieving imbecile.' It's so deflating, for son and father. Too bad we're not sports guys. We could just watch a football game in resentful silence."

"It would be good to just get it over with."

"You Christians with your impatience for confession and repentance."

#####

EVAN LEMMON MOORE pulled the plastic bottle of Mountain Delight whiskey from his cupboard. The Trail Tenders day had been productive but, once again, Evan faced two empty days ahead. *Why didn't my conversation with Anna last night help stop this? Maybe there's no helping me. Some people observe the Sabbath once every seven days. I do this once every seven days.*

He sat in his chair and sipped, thinking of past events. He became increasingly disoriented—not by the liquor, but by images of Anna interrupting his regular chain of thoughts. He also had images of Joyce Taylor and their time at the tent. Evan kept sipping. He had no idea how he could *not* sip a bottle of whiskey on Sunday nights. The bottle was almost empty when he pitched over on the dusty hardwood. Instead of curling up as he usually did, Evan crawled across the floor. He kept crawling all the way out the back door and into his garden.

#####

EDDIE RAMIREZ looked adoringly at Sofia and said, "You know, little one, you're going to have a baby brother or a baby sister. How about that?"

In a tense voice Isabella interjected, "Eddie, there's something you need to check out next door. Look out the kitchen window."

Eddie quickly moved next to the stove, and Isabella continued the conversation with Sofia as if nothing was awry. Through the panes he saw Evan on his hands and knees crawling around his backyard. *Dude is totally smashed on something.* "I'll be back in a minute," he barked, and threw on his jacket.

Eddie saw Evan's breath in the air. He called out to him over the chain link fence, "A little cold to be hanging around out here tonight." Evan did not respond. Eddie yelled again in a louder voice, but again, received no response.

Eddie walked to the back entrance of Evan's yard. Before entering the gate, he texted Anna: "Evan in bad shape at his house, better come over"

Anna replied within seconds: "Coming now"

Eddie leaned over Evan, who had stopped crawling but remained on his hands and knees near what remained of his tomato plants. The smell of alcohol momentarily overwhelmed Eddie. "Dude, phew. You're on quite a bender."

At that, Evan rolled on his side and assumed a curled-up position. Eddie said, "I don't think you want to sleep out here."

Anna arrived ten minutes later and ran to Evan when she saw him on the ground in his backyard. She thanked her ex-husband, but wanted him gone. "Really appreciate you letting me know. You'd better get back to Isabella and the little one."

Eddie looked back and forth between Evan and Anna, and thought, *Glad my relationship isn't messed up like that.* He eagerly returned to his warm home.

"Everything okay?" Isabella asked.

"It's being taken care of. Sorry you had to see that—very disturbing. We're really blessed to have each other. Let's never forget that."

#####

ANNA RAMIREZ roused Evan slowly. She shook him gently and said over and over, "Evan Lemmon, c'mon. We gotta' go inside. Wake up." After a few minutes Evan finally asked, "Is this Anna Ponce?"

"It is."

"What's going on?"

"You're in your backyard. It looks like you passed out."

"Oh." He tried to sit up, but his head landed in Anna's lap.

"C'mon, let's go inside. It's getting cold out here." Anna helped Evan first sit up and then stand. They slowly walked toward the back door, with Evan bent over almost completely at the waist. He turned to Anna and said, "I've got to use the bathroom."

Anna heard him turn on the water. *I guess he needs his privacy.* She looked for two glasses in the kitchen and found a pitcher of water in the refrigerator.

She wandered around the living room, her first view of it. In avoiding Eddie, they had not spent any time at Evan's house. Two bookcases held a wide variety of books, the furniture was serviceable, and the coffee table was covered with magazines. She saw an empty whiskey bottle near an overstuffed chair. *Did he drink the whole bottle? So that's what he does on his days off—he nurses a mega hangover. My deep, sweet Evan is a boozer. Is this where everything turns sour, where we have an epic fight and walk away from each other forever? Where we decide there's just too much to overcome, like what happened with Eddie with his porn and me with my spending? We just walked away. No, there was a lot of other stuff too. We were too young and too different when we got married, and Eddie was a hothead, though I was a bit of a hothead too. I thought Evan and I had a lot in common— I thought we had a connection.*

Evan finally appeared in the living room. "I'm so sorry, Anna Ponce."

"I poured us some water." Anna pointed to the glasses on the coffee table. "Do you drink like this a lot?"

"I'd been doing it once a week, but then we had the tent and I stopped for a month. I picked it up again a few weeks ago."

"That's a lot of booze for one kinda skinny guy—a whole bottle of whiskey. Wow."

"I thought I could quit. That's why I didn't tell you."

"Well, you did quit for a bit when the tent was running. What made you start again?"

"The futility of it all. Seeing the Dolly's Dollar store sign being attached to the building. The unfixable emotional distance between my family and me. The damage I've done to others. The lame jobs. The serious relationships with great women that have crashed and burned. The potential of a serious relationship with a great woman named Anna Ponce and how it might end up like everything else."

Anna was annoyed. "Thanks a lot."

Evan pointed out, "You have your doubts, too."

"Maybe, but it's okay to be scared."

"You're starting to think less of me."

"No, not at all. But seeing you super smashed and on the ground in your backyard is a lot to digest. No, Evan, I don't think less of you. I'm just trying to fit it all together."

They talked until three, when they both drifted to sleep.

MONDAY, OCTOBER 21, 2013

JOHNNY RAMOS was seated next to Anita on a couch at his doctor's office, waiting for his annual check-up appointment. A middle-aged woman in a business suit was seated nearby, flipping through magazines with a desultory attitude.

Johnny leaned toward her and said, "Waiting is a pain, right?"

The woman looked up, startled. "Huh?"

Johnny spent the next ten minutes in an evangelism attempt, until a nurse entered the waiting room. She checked the name on her clipboard. "John Ramos."

Before going with the nurse, Johnny looked at the woman in the business suit and said, "I'd like to give you my card. Check us out sometime. We would love to see you."

Johnny offered his card, but the woman responded with a firm, "No thanks."

ABIGAIL BARRETT-THOMPSON fiddled with the buttons on her jacket as she sat in the office of Renee Moss, a longtime spiritual director and retreat leader. Renee was an ordained Presbyterian pastor, but had focused on counseling for the duration of her thirty-year career. Through various channels of communication, Abigail had heard of her and thought it might be time to be on the receiving end of some spiritual guidance.

"What brings you here?" Renee asked.

Abigail stopped fussing with her buttons and replied, "I'm teetering on the edge of burn out, but not quite there. Pretty crisp around the edges. So I'd like some tools to get healthier and stay well."

"Okay. You're probably familiar enough with spiritual direction to know my role can be one of counselor, friend, instructor, coach, clinician, sergeant, pastor. Is there any model of interaction that works best for you?"

"I'd lean toward instructor."

"What are some of the issues?"

"You name it. Probably the number one issue is that the attendance and giving at the church continues to decrease. We've done every type of program under the sun to grow the church— bring a friend, progressive evangelism training, community organizing on social justice issues. For instance, we started the Dolly's Dollar Store protest."

"I thought that was Church of the Living Water?"

Abigail sighed. "No, I led the organizing for the first effort. Johnny Ramos and Church of the Living Water joined later and received a lot of media attention and a real boost in their membership."

"Your sweat, your coordination, and someone else gets the credit and the good results. That bites."

"We know it's not about who gets the credit, and Johnny knows it is not about credit but about glorifying God."

"Sure, we all know that, but the reality is that the church you serve is not budging in terms of its attendance. So how are you dealing with reality?"

"Not so well." Abigail disclosed her truth. "I'm binging and purging. It's sin, and I just keep sinning."

"You're really stressed. How long have you been doing this?"

"Off and on for the past five years as things have kept diminishing at the church."

"So we'll need to look at some ways to enhance and reframe your reality."

#####

GINA GONZALEZ coordinated the week ahead with Sharon Chapel. They worked swiftly through their agenda. "We are two organized women," Sharon declared.

"Disorganization makes me nauseous," Gina replied.

"Same here. The newsletter continues to be a rousing success. You've done a great job with the layout and photos, and including clients and staff."

"Thank you."

"Is there still enough information to warrant it being a weekly thing?"

"There seems to be—between six hundred and fifty residents and all our staff. We'll keep doing the three 'Getting to Know You' columns, as they fill the space nicely."

"Anything else going on around the building?" Sharon prodded.

"Nothing that I know of. It's been pretty quiet."

"You used to be my information connection, but these past couple of months, you've been giving me bupkis."

Gina smiled. "I'm just not as much in the loop as I used to be."

"Oh, well, moving on, let's analyze the dementia transfer percentages."

#####

TED THOMPSON welcomed the students into the classroom. "*Entre vous*, artists, dreamers, and the East Coast glitterati of 2040."

The first graders settled into their seats. Two students put a leaf and a sheet of paper on every desk.

Ted led them through the lesson, "Now, take your leaf, put it on top of the sheet of paper, and trace around it with a pencil, crayon, or whatever writing utensil you like. See my example?" Ted held up his own drawing of a traced leaf. "We'll decorate the leaf, cut it out, and then attach the real leaf and the decorated leaf to a long garland we'll hang around the room. This is how we'll celebrate the change of seasons."

Ted walked up and down the rows, encouraging individual students as they traced their leaves.

#####

CONSUELA GONZALEZ looked across her immaculate front room at Marta Colon. Their mood was somber. "What have we done for our children?"

Marta waved her hand dismissively. "Everything. Raised them, took care of them, loved them. That's a crazy question."

"They just seem to go through so much struggle. I don't remember that much struggle. So many difficulties, up and down, up and down."

"We did what our husbands said. That's part of it. We didn't struggle because we didn't question. They don't want to live that way anymore," Marta said.

"Their way also has problems. Things are complex now, so many choices."

"Yes. We did our best as mothers, okay? Don't worry. What did you say about your hand? What's done is done."

"Yes, what's done is done. We did our best. I'm glad we didn't have that many choices."

#####

ALAN PECK staffed the table near the front entryway of his home. The Pecks were hosting a dessert fundraiser for Amy's state senate campaign, and Alan was collecting the fifty-dollar-per-person donations. Their catering company had set up stations throughout the house offering assorted desserts, coffee, tea, and cheap wine. The turnout was great with guests throughout the house and backyard. Amy worked her way around the clusters with expert timing, thanking people for coming and sharing a soft-sell of her platform. Many of the guests were former real estate clients as well as a good turnout of Cedar Beach church members.

Due to some population shifts, Amy was running in a newly drawn district. She had a good chance to receive her party's nomination in May given the low probability of anyone well known entering the race. The County Chair had shared with her that the district leaned conservative, and if she survived the primary process, stayed on message, and avoided major gaffes, she could triumph in the general election.

Alan stood when he saw the next couple come through the door.

"Pastor Davey!" Alan exclaimed, "and Sally, too. How great to see you!" Alan shook their hands and took their one-hundred-dollar check. "There are about forty church members here, and we expect more throughout the evening."

Davey grinned and patted Alan on the shoulder. "Wouldn't have missed this."

Sally Porterfield said, "We're so happy for you two. Amy is a great candidate. The church ladies are so excited to support her. She's helped so many purchase a home. What a blessing to be able to provide that kind of service."

Alan nodded and said, "Amy loves to help people."

Sally continued, "I've had so many people tell me that Amy really went above and beyond in finding the right house. She showed one couple forty-three houses. Another family needed a home to accommodate a child with special needs, and Amy was totally on top of it. She made all sorts of calls to make sure everything was taken care of."

Alan nodded. "Amy's work ethic is unparalleled, which is why she'll make a great state senator."

"We're glad to affirm her in this new calling," Davey said.

"I don't know where we'd be without Cedar Beach Church," Alan replied.

TUESDAY, OCTOBER 22, 2013

EVAN LEMMON MOORE stood on the spotless front porch of a row home near the intersection of Fourth and Liberty Streets. He took a deep breath, centered himself, and knocked on the door. Joyce Turner soon appeared, wearing a pink hat with *Jesus = Love* spelled out in sequins.

Evan said, "Hi, boss."

"You look a little green around the gills, Evan Lemon n' Lime," Joyce responded.

"A little out of sorts, but I'll be better soon. I haven't seen you for a couple of months. I miss you. I got your address from your pastor at the Baptist church."

"He must trust you with your scraggly looks to give out a widow's address."

"Could I talk to you for a moment about an idea of mine?"

"An idea? Sure, why not? Come in." Joyce held the door. "Glass of water? Soda? I've got 7-Up and ginger ale."

"Ginger ale sounds good, thank you."

Evan sat on a recliner in the front room, and Joyce on a love seat. Evan asked, "Any issues with the arrest?"

"Nah. Wasn't it great to have Church of the Living Water pay all the fines and look after the legal stuff? Glad that wasn't on my plate. I'll always be a Baptist, but those Pentecostals are all right. Had a New York reporter up at the church about a month ago to interview me and the other church ladies."

"I saw that in the New York Times, with a great photo, too."

"I'd do it again even if it got no attention."

"Same here."

"Looks like something's on your mind, something's agitating you."

Evan plunged in, "I've been thinking about this for a while. Years ago, I read about a similar effort somewhere in the United States, but I can't remember what city and I don't even remember where I read it. Anyway, I was thinking of starting a restaurant. Just two days a week to start and just for lunch. We could run the restaurant out of your church or out of Faith Church. It'd be different from other restaurants, but it wouldn't be a soup kitchen. Instead, it would bring together people who go to restaurants and people who go to soup kitchens. People would pay whatever they're able to. Those that have more contribute more, those with less, pay less. What do you think?"

"Where are you going to get the food? Through donations?"

"I was hoping you could help with that. We would use donated food at first, and in time we'd self-fund. We'll supplement donations with the cash people pay. Ask to use kitchens and social halls at the churches and pay some rent to help them out. We'd need a volunteer bookkeeper to keep it all on track."

"So some people pay full and others give a little? You know that some who could pay more, won't, and some will give too much."

"It will all even out. I know I'll need a lot of help, and I was hoping to secure volunteers from your church and Faith Church and some other organizations."

"So, two days a week and only lunch to start?"

"Yes, Monday and Tuesday lunch."

"Why just Monday and Tuesday?"

"It's a long story, but those are my days off right now. Well, I have Sundays off too, but I'm already committed. Hopefully, we'd expand at some point, like to Monday through Friday."

"You put a lot of thought into this."

"I think it can work. We pulled off the tent. That was for less than a week, but this would be, well, for as long as possible. Cooking in the tent was rough, but it'd be a breeze in these big church kitchens."

Joyce was convinced. "I could do two lunches a week, no problem."

"I'll talk to Abigail at Faith Church. Could you talk to your pastor?"

"Yes, he shouldn't have a problem with it."

"I'd love to have it ready to go by the first of December. I'll work up some flyers and get help handing them out to the people who work in the big buildings downtown. I'm sure Abigail could pass information along to other churches. And I'll do some Internet stuff to get it out there."

Joyce smiled at Evan. "You look less green around the gills."

"I think this can work."

"It will. Not sure how long, but it will. Let's hold it lightly, okay? If we hold it too tight and squeeze the life out of it, we could get in trouble. These types of inspirations can go off the tracks if they're messed with too much. We'll do it for as long as we're supposed to. If it's for a few months, great. If it's for a few years, it's all good."

"It's all good," Evan said.

#####

ANNA RAMIREZ stared at the wall of the break room, pondering the many cracks in the paint. Steve soon joined her. "You look a little bewitched, bothered, and bewildered today. Everything okay?"

Anna replied, "Sort of distracted. Things on my mind, trying to sort them out. Have you ever thought less of Glenn because of something he did?"

"Thought less of him? No. Thought I was better than him? No. Thought he was a jerk at times? Yes. Thought he was careless? Yes. Thought he was uncouth? Yes. Thought he was offensive? Yes. Thought he was indifferent? Yes. Thought he was a psycho driver? Yes. I could go on and on."

"Relationships take a lot of letting go," Anna said. "A lot."

"Tons of it. I don't think the couples who are together for decades have any big secret. They just don't let things get to them. Many times I've plotted Glenn's murder for cluttering the dresser or leaving towels on the bathroom floor, but somehow I could never carry through with it."

"You crack me up."

"Remember, I'm rules compliant and find it totally bizarre when Glenn breaks everyday-normal-American-set-in-stone rules and just drops a towel on the floor. Who would do that? Only trolls and teenagers—not grown men. And then I had to stop thinking like that. Just because I wouldn't do that and was raised not to do that, doesn't mean everyone was—though sometimes I think Glenn was raised by a pack of wolves."

"Family of origin seems to play a role in everything."

"Don't get me going on Glenn's family of origin! Entire psychological studies could be done on them. Have you met any of Evan's family?"

"No. They live pretty far away in Illinois and we're still so new, you know?"

"The fragile first months of a relationship—you'll never forget them. Delicate strand upon delicate strand until you weave together a strong bond."

"Listen to you, so sensitive. We are learning a lot about one another right now—a lot of strands coming together."

#####

GENNY RAMIREZ started the walk home from school carrying both her backpack and postal bag to store the plastic bottles she picked up along the way. Three classmates passed her, pointing and taunting, "Baggy Genny, baggy Genny."

Genny corrected the girls. "Actually, they're bottles, now."

A voice behind her said, "Hey, leave her alone." Genny turned around and saw Marcus.

The three girls laughed even louder and said, "Genny and Marcus are boyfriend and girlfriend. Genny and Marcus are in loooooovvvvvveeee."

"No we're not!" Genny shouted.

"You're crazy," Marcus muttered and he turned to Genny, "They're dumb. What are you doing with the bottles?"

"Stringing them together. I want to see how long I can get it— maybe stretch it into downtown Allentown, to the PPL Building!"

"Or to New Jersey! How many do you have?"

"I haven't counted them. There's a pile in the basement."

"Can I see?"

"Sure," she agreed.

At home, Genny's grandmother was in the front room watching a *telenovela*.

Genny introduced her friend and Consuela nodded. "*Abuela*, this is Marcus."

Marcus gave a small wave and said, "Hi."

The two friends went into the dining room to drop off their backpacks. Marcus asked, "Does your grandma speak English?"

"A little, not much."

"Do you speak Spanish?"

"A little, not much."

Genny led Marcus to the basement and showed him the pile of bottles. Half had already been strung together with twine. "So, I take twine and stick it through the holes in the bottle and then go to the next one. Wanna help put holes in the plastic?"

"Yeah." They punched holes in the bottles and strung them together. After an hour's work, they had an impressively long garland of plastic bottles.

WEDNESDAY, OCTOBER 23, 2013

ISABELLA RAMIREZ left Sofia with the two dozen other toddlers in the care room at the church, then headed to the moms group. For many, the group was their weekly oasis—a respite from daily domestic issues and an opportunity to refresh with other like-minded women who wanted strong and faithful families.

Isabella worked the room, going from one small gathering to the next, checking in and giving encouragement and praise. Two moms were in attendance for the first time, so Isabella connected them with two other longer-term members. She eventually made her way to the front of the room.

"Okay, okay, ladies. Time to get in our circle," Isabella said, and the women took their seats. "We have a lot to talk about, don't we? But first, let's pray." The women all closed their eyes and bent their heads. "Father God, we want our lives to reflect your light. Pour out your blessings on us. Bless our motherhood, bless our children, bless our husbands, bless our relationships with one another, that our friendships may strengthen us to do Christ's work. Keep us away from the ungodly, the haters and the baiters, those who hate clean living and those who try to bait us and tell us that we're wrong to live life this way. Father God, we know you're going to keep growing our group because that's your will for us. Amen."

"Amen!" the moms responded.

"A few announcements before I introduce our guest speaker," Isabella began. "I have good news to share about the fundraising for the Dallas National Christian Moms Conference. We have now raised over four thousand dollars!"

The women clapped enthusiastically, and two or three shouted, "Praise the Lord!"

Isabella continued, "It's going to be amazing! Keep the candle sales and donation solicitations going, and we'll be at five thousand dollars in no time! Alleluia!"

"Alleluia" the moms responded.

"Our guest speaker this week is Mrs. Meagan Foley. Meagan belongs to a moms group in Philadelphia and speaks throughout the northeast on the topic of healthy and holy communication. She is mother to four children and is delighted to be a grandmother to one baby boy. Let's show Meagan some love."

The moms applauded warmly as Meagan walked to the podium. She asked, "How many of you grew up in a home where the communication was mostly negative?" Half the women raised their hands.

"I grew up in a home where the police were frequent visitors. My parents fought constantly, screamed at each other, and worse. I ran away more than once—unsuccessfully—but left for good at seventeen. Soon after, I married. At first, my marriage seemed to be going down that same unhealthy road as my parents'."

Several women nodded.

"And then I was invited to a Christian moms group. I had two children in elementary school and two at home. I thought, 'Christian moms?' What could *they* possibly teach *me* about being a mom?" There were laughs.

"I was so prideful. But something stuck, and I checked out the group, expecting it to be a bunch of loser moms." More laughter from the circle of women.

"You know what happened? God used those women to reach me. Little by little, I shook off my fears. I was desperate to change my marriage, but I really didn't know what to do. In time, though, I opened myself up to learning. I studied scripture with a small group. I took the children to church. Eventually my husband attended too. Over time, we grew together. We became really solid, and continue that way now." Meagan smiled as a chorus of *Amens* echoed throughout the room.

"Today we focus on communicating respect for self, for husband, and for others. Our husbands very much need our respect. Their workplaces are full of disrespect—they don't need to hear it at home too. We can be respectful of our husbands in so many ways, and not even use words. Just listen, for instance."

Isabella took notes and then looked around at the circle of moms. *Praise the Lord for their engagement and interest in the topic.*

#####

TED THOMPSON met Darren Long for beer and wings after work, and they caught each other up on their fall assignments.

Ted asked, "How are your fourth graders?"

"A real mix of kids from a real mix of backgrounds, so it's a challenge."

"Diversity in the classroom keeps you on your toes, keeps you alert as a teacher."

"I do feel pulled in a lot of directions."

"Glad you didn't receive a pink slip," Ted said.

"Don't know how I escaped."

"You're not in the arts or ESL or the libraries."

"How many schools do you cover now, Ted?"

"Six elementary schools and sixth graders at Trexler Middle School."

"Man, how do you do it?"

"You just find a rhythm and go with it. I have to trust that the bit of art instruction they're receiving is somehow making a dent in their developing souls."

Ted asked, "Any movement on the Master's degree?"

"I decided to dip my toes in the water ever so slightly. I'm taking one class this semester for the MEd program at Lehigh."

Ted raised his glass, "Hurrah!"

"They have a blended online and classroom Master's program. We'll see. It's a lot of work so far."

Ted assured Darren, "You're up to it."

#####

EVAN LEMMON MOORE arrived at Faith Church thirty minutes before the start of Bible study. He wanted to catch Abigail before class to share his idea for the Monday-Tuesday lunch.

Abigail wholeheartedly endorsed it. "Sounds great to me. Write up a blurb and email it to me for the church bulletin. I'll also send it on to some of my church contacts. You can also hang posters around the church. I'd prefer the Tuesday slot for Faith Church if you haven't settled on days yet. I'd require one thing, however. So, you're aiming for a start date of December first?"

"Yep."

"That's about five weeks away. It'd be nice for us to get into a rhythm, so I'd like to see you every Tuesday leading up to your start date. Just come at the time you plan on starting lunch preparations and stay until whatever time you think it'll take to clean up, so we have an idea of what we'll be accommodating."

"We'll eventually want to pay rental money."

Abigail waved a hand. "Build up the ministry and then we'll touch base about rent."

"Ministry?"

Abigail clarified. "Oops, using my churchy language again. Build up your lunch project and then we can talk about funding. Of course you and Joyce will need to come up with a name for your travelling restaurant."

#####

ABIGAIL BARRETT-THOMPSON completed a brief social media check after her conversation with Evan. At the top of her news feed was Johnny Ramos's smiling face, with a Bible quote from Deuteronomy 31:6: *Be strong and of a good courage, fear not, nor be afraid of them: for the Lord thy God, he it is that doth go with thee; he will not fail thee, nor forsake thee.* It had been posted fifty minutes earlier and already had ninety-three likes and a number of short comments, such as "Love this" and "Thank you Pastor." Abigail's Bible study posting from the previous day had one like.

She hurried to the classroom, where six of the usual attendees were gathered around the table—Keith, Jerry, Sherry, Katie, Chuck, and Evan.

Abigail began, "We're almost through the prophets. I will certainly miss them."

THURSDAY, OCTOBER 24, 2013

EDDIE RAMIREZ moved deliberately through the agenda with Lieutenant Ken Orr, following up on the previous week's business, discussing crime trends, touching base on management issues and, finally, going over the training lists.

Eddie thought the meeting was concluded and started to gather up his papers.

"When are you going to apply for the lieutenant's position?" Ken asked.

Surprised, Eddie responded, "I had been thinking about it, but it looks like the lieutenant roster is pretty full right now."

"I'm retiring soon."

"Oh?"

"I've made suggestions to the captains and chief that you'd be a great candidate. You're a careful cop, but not overly cautious. You're well regarded by the patrol officers and the other sergeants. Your training, overall, has been effective. And you handled the Dolly's tent issue smoothly, Sergeant. Impressive."

"Thank you." Eddie was speechless at the strong support, as Ken was normally not an effusive kind of guy.

"Is there anything that would prevent you from applying? Any skeletons in your closet? No hidden reports or excessive force complaints that may have been misfiled?"

Eddie replied quickly, "No, not at all."

"Nothing in your personal life that would get in the way?"

"Like what?"

"Affairs with coworkers, addiction issues, unresolved anger management issues?"

Eddie paused before responding. "Uh, there is one thing."

"Yes?"

"I *had*—emphasis on the word *had*—a porn addiction. No child stuff—hardcore adult porn. I saw a professional about it and have not looked at it since."

"A lot of the men in the department should do as you have done."

"It was pretty bad."

"There's a lot of stress on the job, and that seems to be a release. But it becomes a crutch and is not usually helpful to a marriage. I'm glad you took care of it. You're active in a church?"

Eddie nodded, "Church of the Living Water."

"I'm Catholic and know that being part of a church puts life in a proper perspective."

"Definitely."

"I'll be happy to help you with the lieutenant's application, the needed documentation, and references."

"Thank you, Lieutenant."

"Thank *you*, Lieutenant," Ken winked.

#####

GINA GONZALEZ was on the fourth floor of the nursing home, attempting to resolve a roommate dispute between residents Marvin Holmes and Leo Grantley. Both men were in their late eighties. Marvin struggled with a heart condition, while Leo was recovering from cancer.

Gina started her discussion with a positive we-can-fix-this tone. "Mr. Holmes and Mr. Grantley, I have been told that you two are having some problems."

Leo said, "You betcha," while Marvin hollered, "What?"

#####

Evan Lemmon Moore and **Anna Ramirez** arrived on time at Steve Palermo and Glenn Conover's home in the West End of Allentown.

While Steve fussed with *hors d'oeuvres*, Glenn, whose graying afro was covered with an ancient straw hat, gave a tour of their extensive flower and vegetable gardens which contained the last remnants of the summer season. Herbs, cruciferous vegetables, root vegetables, vine vegetables—each had their own section. Fall flowers were throughout the yard. There were even a few rows of corn. A biology professor at Lehigh University, Glenn loved to observe the growing process. At the end of his tour, he ushered Anna and Evan to a gazebo in the corner, where they sat on handcrafted benches. Steve joined them, carrying platters full of hummus and pita, deviled eggs, and cheese and crackers.

"Appetizers have arrived. Dig in," he said.

Evan turned to Glenn, "Have you ever tried fruit?"

Glenn scrunched his face at Evan. "What're you calling me?"

"No, no. I meant, have you ever grown fruit trees?"

Steve guffawed. "He's joking with you. Glenn, don't scare the guy. Evan, we know you're cool with the gays and that you'd never call us fruits."

Glenn said, "I tried some fruit trees, but it didn't work out. I leave it to the farmers around the Lehigh Valley. Pests really like fruit trees, so if you don't want to do pesticide, it's a bit of a conundrum."

Between bites of vegetable quiche, Evan said to Glenn, "Thank you for the vegetables you donated during the Dolly's protest. We made vegetable kebabs as part of our last supper."

Glenn replied, "I was sorry I couldn't get over there, but glad so many took a stand."

Evan was reminded of his restaurant concept. "I shared with Anna a couple of nights ago my idea to start a restaurant with a friend." He continued excitedly, "Just lunch, and limited at first to Mondays and Tuesdays. People will pay what they're able to."

"Some will stiff you," Steve commented.

Anna quickly interjected, "Sure, but some will *overpay*. The whole idea is to bring people from different economic backgrounds together—the soup kitchen crowd and the downtown lunch crowd."

"I like the idea," Glenn said.

"Would you be interested in donating any produce?" Evan asked.

"Absolutely!"

Steve stood to replenish their drinks and teased, "I'm hanging out with a bunch of commies."

"No," Glenn replied, "it's about changing one little part of the world in one small way—so we can come together just a little bit more. Our country has become too separated. We're all in our own little worlds. I'm for any attempt at crossing artificial boundaries. Count me in, Evan."

#####

"**ABIGAIL BARRETT-THOMPSON** and those Lutherans just need to pack it in," Davey Porterfield chuckled. Following an evening meeting, the senior pastor of the five-thousand-member Cedar Beach Church was in his office with associate pastor Jeff Harrison.

"Right. How many members has she lost to Cedar Beach?" Jeff asked.

"A bunch. Tim and Helen Thacker—apparently he was a major leader at the church, board president or something like that—Alan Peck, the Sundeen family. I could go on and on because it's a long list. And we've had a ton of Lutherans join recently."

"These small church pastors are a joke. You can't pastor fifty people. At that point, you're ushering them to a slow, painful death. Get big or get out," Jeff said.

"The friendly neighborhood church has gone the same way as the friendly neighborhood store. Bigger is better."

Jeff shook his head. "These pastors are living in the Stone Age."

"And too busy getting in trouble with the law."

"I'm surprised Johnny Ramos got wrapped up in it."

Davey reflected for a moment. "It made him a hero in the neighborhood and he got a lot of members out of it. From what I hear, Church of the Living Water is growing pretty fast. Good thing our demographics are different so we're not competing for sheep. He's great with the addicts and thugs and all the city folks. I'm happy to stick with the suburban crowd."

"That tent thing was crazy, like they had some sort of right to take over private property." Jeff shook his head again.

"That's the problem with these people—they're way too focused on rights over responsibilities. They're takers, and that's why we have to keep up with our message of accountability and ownership, which is really what people need to hear. People are desperate for someone to model how to be accountable to authority and how to take ownership of their life in partnership with God. People don't want chaos, they want order in their lives—a path and a plan."

"It's been a great sermon series. You'll definitely want to get it out on DVD and streaming services. Thousands will benefit from it."

"Definitely. This series will be our fifth DVD production. Seems like we just completed the first one yesterday. Speaking of that, we need to make sure we've got the A-Team on hand to film the Leaders Forum next week."

"I'll make sure of it. How's the governor these days?" Jeff asked.

Davey smiled at the thought of his connection with the state's highest officeholder. "I talked to him earlier this week. He's a good man. We have a good rapport. I lend him an ear, I pray over him, help him work through all the stress on his job."

"It will be good to see him again at the forum."

"I'd like to announce how many political leaders are currently members at Cedar Beach. Do you know off the top of your head?"

Jeff counted on his fingers, "Let's see. Congressman Bach, State Representatives Yessell, Dowd, and Jensen, and three County Supervisors. Seven total. And, there's new member, Amy Peck, who's running for state senate, and probably some other potential candidates amid our *great congregation*."

Davey exclaimed, "Excellent! And do you have the latest list of the featured speakers for the Forum?"

"Three governors, three congressmen, and a former vice president."

"It's been made clear we don't want any controversy?"

"Very clear," Jeff responded. "Specifically, each knows we don't want any surprises. They're to speak thirty minutes on the importance of family and how their Christian walk has been a comfort to them as leaders. No campaigning. We'll do our best to have the media frame the forum as an informational and devotional gathering for people wanting to know more about voting their values. Looks like we'll have at least two national media outlets here."

"Good work on this, Jeff, and good press for Cedar Beach. All of the guys are clean?"

"Yes, from what we can tell, the seven political leaders are all practicing Christians—no skeletons in any closet. All are pro-life and support marriage between one man and one woman, and they all champion free markets. They've all made statements about how our country needs to stop the spread of radical Islam."

SPRING 2014

WEDNESDAY, JUNE 4, 2014

JOHNNY RAMOS scrolled down his cell phone to check his email.

Subject: Your Daily Verse
From: YDV@YourDailyVerse.org
Date: Wed, Jun 4, 2014 4:30 am
To: PastorJohnny@ChurchoftheLivingWater.org

Daily Bible Verse - Wednesday, June 4, 2014

Ask, and it shall be given you; seek, and ye shall find; knock, and it shall be opened unto you

Matthew 7:7
King James Version

"Amen," Johnny said, and forwarded the message to his son to post on social media.

#####

GINA GONZALEZ saw a new message in her Facebook inbox from an old acquaintance, Karina Vasquez. "How come I never see you at rubies anymore? Heard ur seeing Dante, but ur FB doesn't say anything. What's the 411?"

Gina kept her response brief. "Been so busy. See you soon I hope! Miss you Karina!"

Then she scrolled through her news feed to catch up on all her friends. She had not been commenting or liking lately—just looking. *No need to get involved anymore. Just stand back and know as much as possible.* She let others get into spats and online squabbles, and was now simply an observer who was keeping her distance.

#####

EVAN LEMMON MOORE was surprised to see an email message from his former girlfriend Christie.

Subject: Some news
From: Christie.Rockland@gmail.com
Date: Wed, Jun 4, 2014 7:31 am
To: Evan.Lemmon.Moore@gmail.com

Dear Evan,

I was able to track down your mom and she gave me your email address. Are you the only one on the planet who doesn't have a Facebook page? Ha ha. She didn't share much, except that you are in Allentown. Heard about some demonstrations happening there last year about a dollar store and googled your name. Unless there is another Evan Moore in Allentown, looks like you were arrested, you radical punk! Ha ha.

I have been happily teaching in Niles, Illinois, for the past ten years and was married three years ago to my great hubby Joe. We're expecting a girl next month and as the birth comes closer I've been reaching out to some people in my past for various reasons.

In case you don't know, it is all forgiven. Stuff happens, you know? It's all okay. When you have a moment, let me know how you're doing.

All the best,
Christie (Tanner) Rockland

#####

ANNA RAMIREZ waded through a number of personal email messages as directed by the credit counselor she had recently started to see. Her weekly assignment was to unsubscribe from retail email lists or, because they sometimes made it difficult to be removed, she clicked the spam button so those emails went directly to her Bulk Mail folder to be automatically deleted. She'd report the list of unsubscribes to her counselor at their next appointment. Even though she had been focused on the task of deletion, numerous messages continued to slip through every day. First was a message from a jewelry website she had often used:

Subject: New Designs In!
From: Julie@JuliesJewels.com
Date: Wed, Jun 4, 2014 7:32 am
To: Anna18102@yahoo.com

Anna,

We have some great new designs in for charm bracelets and earrings! Check out the great deals on this link: www.juliesjewels.com/charmearrings

I'm sure I unsubscribed from this list. Anna searched for the unsubscribe button, clicked it, and removed herself from the list. Then she clicked the spam button. She recorded the company name, date, and time. Next was a message from Cleopatra Makeup:

Subject: Free Sample
From: Info@CleopatraMakeup.com
Date: Wed, Jun 4, 2014 8:01 am
To: Anna18102@yahoo.com

Anna,

Daily Deal
Free sample of eye shadow with purchase of mascara!

Free is great, but then I'll end up spending even more. Anna looked for the unsubscribe button and followed the process for removal. A message from her favorite perfume company in New Mexico was also in her inbox:

Subject: 2 Samples with 2 Orders
From: Info@SimpleSmells.com
Date: Wed, Jun 4, 2014 9:10 am
To: Anna18102@yahoo.com

Anna,

Happy Hump Day!

This week's offer is two free samples with two orders of our new desert blossom series.

Anna had not said she would unsubscribe from *every* business, so she merely deleted the message. Someday, when she was out of debt, she'd want to buy their perfume again.

#####

TED THOMPSON sat in the parking lot at his second school of the day, reading through email messages.

Subject: Weekly Update
From: Superintendent@AllentownConsolidated.edu
Date: Wed, Jun 4, 2014 9:41 am
To: Ted.Thompson@AllentownConsolidated.edu
To all teachers and staff:

Allentown Consolidated School District faces another year of economic challenges and we are waiting to hear if there will be any additional state funding. We're expecting a decision within the next few weeks. Without funding, the district faces cutbacks in several departments in order to maintain fiscal viability.

#####

ISABELLA RAMIREZ had Diego down for a nap. She called him her Valentine's baby as he was born on Valentine's Day, weighing a healthy 9.2 pounds. Sofia was concentrating on an art project, so Isabella took a moment to check the Facebook moms group, a private group for all the moms who regularly attended the church. She scanned the comments and saw that one of the moms had recently posted about feeling overwhelmed with twins in addition to her older child.

Kelly Goode: I don't know if I can do this anymore. So many diapers and so many feedings. So tired.

Fabiana Morciglio: YOU CAN DO THIS GIRL!! YOU GOT THIS!!

Laila Washington: Every mom feels that way sometimes, u r gonna grow from this, God is refining u!

Jen Slater: Let's do a play date soon, I private messaged you some dates/times.

Patty Dowd: Kellygirl, you were meant to be a mom! God is giving you what you need right now.

Tenisha Crim: Sending you good thoughts, you will get through this.

Raylene Smith: Oh Kelly, there were times when I just wanted to pack up the kids, leave them at their grandmother's and move to a deserted island somewhere and drink daiquiris for the rest of my life. But I miss the kids so much even when I'm away for just a couple of hours. Maybe you could hire a babysitter and do a mini getaway for half a day.

Angelica Solis: We've got your back, girl! So blessed to have this group and everyone helping each other out. This storm will pass.

Sonia Mora: U r a great mom!!! Ur babies love u so much and so does ur husband and all of us moms!! Praying strength and rest for you.

Kelly Goode: Awwwwww ... thanks everyone, u really picked me up!

Isabella thought of what to post that would inspire Kelly and the group and decided on a verse from Deuteronomy.

Isabella Ramirez: *Fear not, neither be dismayed* (Deuteronomy 31:8). Kelly, you are in the right place at the right time for God to use you for His glory!

ALAN PECK had worked on the draft of his resignation for over a week. He finally clicked *send* and delivered the message to the fifteen people on Care2Trust's Executive Team.

Subject: Alan Peck Resignation
From: Alan.Peck@Care2Trust.com
Date: Wed, June 4, 2014 11:33am
To: ExecTeam@GroupDistributionCare2TrustExecTeam

Dear Executive Team,

This letter is to inform you that I am regretfully resigning my position as vice president with Care2Trust, effective June 20, 2014. I have nothing but praise for the entire Executive Team and will be forever grateful for the professionalism enjoyed between team members.

Our accomplishment of merging two companies has set the standard for other health insurance companies considering sharing operations. We were effective and efficient in joining together and it was an honor to be a part of the process.

Care2Trust will continue its growth and, as a result, more Americans will lead healthier lives with the insurance we provide. I'm confident that the private insurance industry will continue to thrive in the years ahead as more consumers realize that business will always do a better job than the government in providing for the well-being of people.

As you all know, my wife won the primary this past month and is a candidate in the general election for the Pennsylvania State Senate. I was just named Amy's campaign manager and the election requires my full and undivided attention. Over the next two weeks I will do everything needed to ensure a smooth transition.

Sincerely,
Alan Peck
Vice President, Department of Research & Analysis

#####

CONSUELA GONZALEZ and **RICHARD MOYER** were sitting on their front porches when the letter carrier came by and handed each their mail.

Consuela looked through the envelopes and groaned, "No *hay nada bueno hoy, solo correo basura.*"

Richard looked through his envelopes, sighed, and said, "Nothing good today, just junk."

#####

GENNY RAMIREZ arrived home from school and sat on her grandmother's front porch texting with Marcus.

"Hey Marcus"
"What r u doing this summer?"
"At the park a lot"

"Me 2"

Genny asked: "Pool?"

"Yes! Can't wait 4 summer 2 start!"

"Yes c u 2mrw"

"C u"

#####

WILLIE RAMIREZ walked out of Allen High School and checked his text messages.

BSN NBA ALERT: See warm-up photos and videos of San Antonio & Miami players as they prep for Game 1 of the finals

BSN NBA ALERT: Read predictions of who will prevail in finals

BSN NBA ALERT: All-NBA First Team selections

BSN NBA ALERT: Participate in NBA Mock Draft

BSN NFL ALERT: Rosters taking shape

BSN NFL ALERT: Vick comments on quarterback situation

BSN NFL ALERT: The art of returning punts

While Willie waited for Alex, he clicked first on the All-NBA First Team selections.

#####

ABIGAIL BARRETT-THOMPSON saw thirty-seven unread emails in her inbox. *I've got to get off some of these mailing lists. I don't have time to read through every one of these messages, but these causes are all so important.* She clicked on a message from Faith & Food, a faith-based nutrition advocacy group in Washington:

Subject: School Lunch Legislation

From: Info@FaithandFood.org

Date: Wed, Jun 4, 2014 1:42 pm
To: Rev.Barrett-Thompson@FaithUCC.org

Waiting on Funding Decisions

Dear Abigail,

The stakes are high.
The kids need your help and your voice.
We keep fighting for healthier school lunches for kids across America, but we are up against some very powerful special interest groups. The food industry spends millions of dollars lobbying Congress for favors that end up hurting our kids and contributing to the obesity epidemic.
Isn't it time to stop them? Encourage your representative to support bipartisan legislation requiring more fiber and less over-processed sugars in school lunches.
Click here to donate:
www.faithandfood.org/donate
Click here to send your representatives a message:
www.faithandfood.org/legislativemail

Abigail clicked on the link to send her representative a message, changing some of the words in the letter and subject line so hers wouldn't look exactly like every other message.

Next she read a message from a statewide gun control group, and followed up by sending a message to her state senator and representative requesting they support common sense background-check legislation.

She saw a forwarded message from her colleague C.D. Alexander and clicked on it. It was an invitation to join the mailing list for the Clergy Concerned on Climate Change (CCCC) group. *Another important cause.* She quickly typed in her information to get on the list.

SUMMER 2014

Richard Moyer walked with Princess past the Dolly's Dollar Store strip mall. He always tried to perform one disobedient act while walking by—sticking out his tongue or spitting—but nothing too drastic because of the security cameras. He remembered Abigail talking about the "cursing Psalms" and muttered, "God curse those who curse others." He looked at Princess and said, "The captains of industry may get their way sometimes, but it's not forever. All that over there will die too sometime, just like everything and everyone."

#####

Alan Peck waved to the crowd and threw candy while volunteers behind him handed out campaign literature. The rain probably lessened the crowd, though they were still three deep in some spots. Amy walked in the center of the street, regularly crisscrossing from side to side to shake hands. They were marching in Slatington's annual Fourth of July parade and had received their requested placement behind a loud brass band on a truck. Amy and Alan had recently attended the Conservative Candidates Training Academy in Fairfax, Virginia, and learned things like advantageous parade participation, setting up calling centers, and successful door knocking. They learned they needed to walk near a musical group so they wouldn't walk along the parade route in silence. They remembered to throw candy first and then hand out their brochures. Many found the announcement catchy: *Pick Peck: A New Voice, A Fresh Approach, Ready to Serve*.

Alan paused momentarily to locate Amy. She was not too far behind, and he felt a tremendous amount of pride at seeing her wave to the crowd and shake hands with people seated in lawn chairs in the front row, her slim limbs on display in a collared tank top and skirt of appropriate length. She was a natural with people, looking them in the eye, taking an interest and saying

"Vote Peck" with her gorgeous smile. *How could you not vote for Amy Peck? You'd have to be crazy or brain dead.* Getting to their place before the parade started, they had to maneuver around Amy's election opponent, Vincent Palazzo, a retired teacher and longtime peace activist. Alan chuckled at the thought of the Amy-Vince matchup. *Vince and his bunch of dumpy liberals are no match for in-shape Amy and her fit team of parade helpers. We've got this election thing sewed up as long as we don't make any major mistakes.*

#####

JOHNNY RAMOS sat under the tent in the church parking lot, munching on salad and giving testimony to a new church member. Church of the Living Water was hosting a festive Fourth of July picnic for its members and, as usual, turnout was great, with people of all ages milling around the tent. Johnny would hold a revival service that evening and the next night.

"By the grace of God, my doctor noticed my elevated PSA levels and, boom, next thing you know, I'm in surgery," Johnny said to the new member, a middle-aged man. "I had a scare, definitely, a scare. God shook me up. So now I'm telling every guy, keep an eye on that prostate, you know? Make sure your doctors are testing you, okay? In August, we're going to do a big awareness campaign at the church. Get your prostate checked! Then in the fall we'll start our obesity awareness campaign."

#####

EDDIE RAMIREZ worked the July Fourth holiday, his last as a sergeant. Next week he would be Lieutenant Eduardo Ramirez. *Check me out! Lieutenant Eddie Ramirez. Captain Ramirez next? Then Chief? Whoa, don't get too far ahead of yourself, but all things are possible. Wish my mom was alive to see this. God has really blessed me. Promotion at work. Fine-looking and godly wife at home. Four great kids. And a church family too.*

Eddie liked working holidays and weekends because things were quieter at the department and he could get more done. And the day shift today meant he didn't have to deal with the traffic headaches later on after the Allentown fireworks display.

He was moving through a stack of paperwork at a steady pace until Detective Gary Schlegel sat on the corner of his desk. They had served together in the Pennsylvania National Guard in Iraq, providing convoy security.

"Eddie! My man." Gary placed his hand over his heart, bowed, and said, "I want to thank you for your service to your country."

Eddie leaned back in his chair, smiled, and saluted. "Thank *you*, Shlegelmeister."

"Congratulations on the lieutenancy. Well done." They did a fist bump. "Look at us, two hometown boys movin' on up in the world. The PA Dutchboy and the Puerto Rican serving and protecting the people of the third largest city in the state."

"You going to the Guard reunion next weekend?" Eddie asked.

"Probably. Lots of good food and beer—what's not to like? How about you?"

"Yeah, I hope so. Busy here, though."

Gary rolled his eyes and said, "Dude, you can take one weekend off a year and hang out with the men and women you served with to bring freedom and democracy to a place that never wanted us there."

"We did what we had to do. Glad it's over, you know?"

"Can you imagine being in Syria right now? That place sounds like a nightmare compared to Iraq. The whole region is a mess. I prefer dealing with the messes here in Allentown. They seem a little more fixable."

"Yeah," Eddie replied, "Always better to focus on what's winnable."

#####

TED THOMPSON removed the kebabs from the grill and carried them inside. "Dinner's ready."

Abigail and Phil appeared in the kitchen from different corners of the house.

"There are chicken kebabs for the meat-eaters and seitan kebabs for the vegan," Ted announced. "The corn salsa is vegan, as is the salad."

"Thanks, Dad."

"It's good to cook vegan every now and then—keeps me limber and on the hunt for interesting recipes."

Abigail carefully liberated the chicken, peppers, and onions from the bamboo stick. "Anyone interested in a movie at the Nineteenth Street Theater tonight?"

"What's playing?" Ted asked.

"Some thought-provoking, independently produced gem."

"Gem? The last one we saw there was a dud. But, of course, you know I'll go."

Phil responded, "I'm meeting up with some old friends, probably going to see the fireworks or partaking in some variety of hijinks unique to the millennial generation."

"I thought the boomers invented everything and there was nothing new left under the sun?" Ted teased.

Abigail turned to Ted, "I love it when you quote scripture, even if Ecclesiastes is the favorite of atheists and agnostics." Then she asked Phil, "How is meditation these days?"

"A lifesaver in a lot of ways. It's a regular thing, so it keeps me grounded and in touch with a group of spiritual people in the city."

Ted said, "The physiological benefits of meditation can do wonders. Are you feeling any more unblocked or should I not bring it up?"

"It's okay," Phil said softly. "It has definitely been a frustrating year, but I think it will help in the long run. I'm not comparing my suffering to people in really horrible situations, but I think that the blockage is teaching me something about character."

"That's a very wise assessment," Ted beamed at his son.

#####

JOHNNY RAMOS clapped along with the Praise Him Wholly Band as they wound down their last song of the set. "Because it's the Fourth of July," he began, "I want to start off tonight's message by talking about how we live in an exceptional country."

A scattering of congregants responded with "Yes!"

"America *is* exceptional. We live in an exceptional country. God has indeed blessed America. Look at me, I got cancer and I'm standing up here in front of you, healed. God bless America for the doctors and medical people we have. I was a young gun, always looking for trouble, and I started a church. Look at us now! God bless America!" Johnny scanned the crowd, guessing there were well over five hundred in the tent.

"We give thanks for our nation tonight. We live in a great country and you know what? We have a great faith! Christ is exceptional. Without Him, we are nothing! With Him, we become exceptional people. The meat of tonight's message is: 'Five Ways to Becoming Exceptional.' We start with number one: 'Put Christ in the Center of Your Life.'"

SATURDAY, JULY 5, 2014

ALAN PECK flipped two pancakes on the griddle at the American Legion Post in Fleetwood. Amy worked the early morning crowd, dutifully asking each person where they or their family member served. In turn, she shared about her father's service in Korea.

Alan grinned at his wife. She excelled at one-on-ones, skillfully making a sale and closing the deal. *This crowd is on her side. Most would vote for her without reservation. She says the right things, comes across as caring. Her real estate buddies always said she could sell a flood-damaged home to even the pickiest buyer. She keeps people focused on the positive, not the negative.*

As Amy's campaign manager, Alan had events scheduled every day through Labor Day. Beyond that, the calendar was going to be on overload until Election Day, including meetings with potential donors and church every Sunday at Cedar Beach to maintain those critical votes.

#####

ABIGAIL BARRETT-THOMPSON received the phone call from Anna Ramirez at ten. Anna said she was talking with her neighbor, Richard Moyer, and all of the sudden he had a massive heart attack.

"Is he at Allentown General?"

"Yes," Anna replied.

"Thank you for letting me know, Anna. I'm headed there now."

"We'll watch the dog."

"I'll let him know Princess is in good hands."

#####

GINA GONZALEZ helped Dante load the speakers, lighting, and portable dance floor into the car. Dante was wearing black high tops, black pinstripe pants with a matching vest, a black collared shirt with a shiny white tie, and a black baseball cap. Gina decided on black too—black three-inch boots, dress pants, and a silk top. She wore her hair in a simple updo with a jeweled barrette. They arrived an hour and a half ahead of the start time for Steve and Glenn's wedding ceremony in Allentown's West End. They found the two grooms setting out the folding chairs in their gorgeous backyard.

"The DJ has arrived." Steve welcomed Dante and Gina. "You'll do a good mix, right? For the oldies and the young ones?"

Dante assured him, "We've got it covered—all types of music to get people out on the dance floor."

"Dante's got it down, no worries!" Gina added.

Steve took a step back and eyed the women from head to toe. "You two look fabulous."

Gina replied, "We wanted to look *good* for your special day! What are you and Glenn wearing?"

"We thought it would be too hot for tuxes, so we're wearing white linen shirts over khakis."

"Nice and cool," Gina said.

"For two cool dudes," Steve laughed. "Actually, I'm not cool at all. I'm pretty flustered. You'd think after twenty-six years together, a legal wedding ceremony would be no big deal, but this is a *really* big deal!"

Gina grunted, "About time Pennsylvania got legal marriage for us."

"Amen, sistah."

#####

ISABELLA RAMIREZ was to give her "Exceptional Families" talk just before her father's closing sermon for the two-night revival.

Johnny introduced his daughter. "The next speaker is an anointed young woman. She is the wife of Lieutenant Eddie Ramirez, and mother of Diego, Sofia, Genny, and Willie. She loves to talk about strong marriages and strong families and she isn't afraid to put up a fight against people who try to pull us away from living right. She is the daughter of fine parents—I should know, because I'm one of them," Johnny laughed. "Let's show some love for Isabella Ramirez!"

Isabella came forward to the microphone through loud, sustained applause. "Praise God for revival! Let's pray." She bowed her head and led the crowd in prayer. She took an extra moment to steady herself. Though she had spoken in front of large crowds at the Philadelphia and Dallas conferences, the experience continued to intimidate. She took a deep breath and started her presentation. "Praise God for this opportunity to continue an important message. Last night, my dad talked about becoming an exceptional person. Tonight he'll talk about being an exceptional church. I'm here to talk about becoming an exceptional family. I'm so blessed to have grown up in an exceptional family and, with my husband, to have started an exceptional family of our own. Every family has the potential to be exceptional. There are five ways to be an exceptional family. We start with number one: 'Put Christ in the Center of Your Family's Life.'"

#####

EVAN LEMMON MOORE wore an oxford shirt, khakis, and his closest thing to dress shoes—hiking boots. Seated on his front steps, he waited for Anna to pick him up, and sweated a bit about dancing in front of others. He had told Anna he didn't put himself in the category of "terrible, horrible, unredeemable dancer," but he did designate himself as a "pretty bad" dancer, "not quite ready for public viewing." Anna was terrific on the dance floor, a natural with a surplus of smooth moves that appeared to connect with some sort of universal rhythm. Evan sensed that, though patient with him, she was baffled by his rigid dance floor maneuvering.

At six thirty, Anna pulled up, and Evan bounded down the steps.

"You're in good spirits," she said.

Evan leaned in for a kiss, "Anna Ponce, it's a good day. Our friends are getting married. And tomorrow we move in together."

Anna looked sideways at him. "I didn't think men got into weddings."

"Everyone loves a party, and this is a party these two guys have been waiting twenty-six years to have."

"I'm happy for them. And happy for us, not doing the marriage thing."

"Have I told you yet that you look ravishing? That dress is killing me, killing me!" Evan faked being slain.

They found parking and walked into Steve and Glenn's yard holding hands. They waved at Dante and Gina in the DJ booth, and took in the full summer's bloom on display. The tables were decorated in red, white, and blue, and flowers were everywhere they turned. Classical music played softly in the background as the forty guests took their seats.

A photographer moved unobtrusively around the yard and took photos. Earlier, guests had been asked to shut their phones off and put them away, as the grooms did not desire any cell phone photos.

Halfway through the service, the minister, secured from the Metropolitan Community Church, started the vows. "Glenn, if you could repeat after me, 'I, Glenn, take you, Steve...'"

Glenn paused for a long moment, pulled himself together, and said, "I, Glenn, take you, Steve..."

The minister continued, "To be my lifelong partner in marriage."

The very reserved and stoic Glenn paused again. He finally pushed out the words between tears, his voice breaking, "To be my lifelong partner in marriage."

Steve cried too, and soon everyone was sniffling—except for the minister, who smiled. They exchanged rings, were pronounced legally married, and directed to kiss. Dante blasted high-energy music during the lip-lock, after which the two men walked animatedly down the aisle.

Evan and Anna sat at a table with other post office employees. They chatted about the ceremony and the holiday weekend while passing food around the table. Brie and bread, stuffed mushrooms, mini quiches, potato puffs, and crab rangoon. At the end of the meal, Evan turned to Anna and asked, "Would you like to dance with your friendly neighborhood robot?"

"Let's go," Anna took Evan's hand and led him out to the dance floor, swaying to Kool and the Gang's "Celebration."

Evan did his best as they laughed through several songs. Dante mixed up the music and put on a Salsa. The dance floor cleared except for Gina and Anna, who were the center of attention until Anna motioned to Steve and Glenn to join them. Each sister took a hand and valiantly provided the men with a quick tutorial in Latin dance. Evan went to the DJ booth, caught

Dante's eye, and made the motion of closing his gaping mouth in awe over the sisters' dance skills.

"I know," Dante smiled. "We're with two fine women."

"We are lucky."

Dante eyed Evan carefully, and added, "Don't forget, they're lucky to have us too."

"True," Evan agreed softly.

#####

ANNA RAMIREZ and **GINA GONZALEZ** arrived home at the same time, a little after midnight. They entered the home quietly and saw their mother sleeping in the recliner. Their neighbor's dog Princess was nestled on her lap.

SUNDAY, JULY 6, 2014

ABIGAIL BARRETT-THOMPSON turned on the air conditioning in the sanctuary and fellowship hall. Normally Richard Moyer would have turned it on the night before, but he remained immobile in the intensive care unit at Allentown General. Abigail had prayed for seventy people to attend—*Or what? Or I'll stuff my face with something? Get over yourself, Reverend Barrett-Thompson and just do your job excellently, glorifying God, no matter what the results.*

She stepped into the pulpit and guessed there were forty seated in the sanctuary. After a brief prayer, she started. "In light of the Independence Day holiday, I want start today with some words on church and state. Throughout the centuries people have used and tried to use religion as a means to achieve political power. We must always remember, though, that God is above all states and nations and governments and powers and principalities."

The congregation listened courteously.

"While we have responsibilities as citizens of the land we live in, our ultimate responsibility is to God. This past week, our nation's Supreme Court issued a ruling on Burwell versus Hobby

Lobby. This case, on its surface, was about the practice of religion. Hobby Lobby's Christian owners filed suit against the Department of Health and Human Services to challenge the contraception requirement of the Affordable Care Act, or Obamacare, as many call it. Hobby Lobby argued that protections for nonprofit religious groups should extend to for-profit businesses. We need not be fooled by this ruling. It is not at all about religion, but about the expansion of corporate power and protecting business owners. The decision in favor of Hobby Lobby is not a victory for Jesus. The clear winners are private corporations who keep receiving more rights while the vast majority of Americans must constantly, constantly, constantly fight to maintain even the most basic rights, like voting access, affordable health care, and a living wage."

Abigail heard a pair of quiet but firm "Amens" from the middle rows. They caused her to almost lose her place. It was the first vocal response during her ten years of preaching in Faith Church.

#####

ANNA RAMIREZ looked around at the boxes stacked and ready to be moved later that morning. Evan was taking a Sunday off from Trail Tenders so they could complete the move-in process today. He was not to arrive before ten, when Gina and her mother would be back from Mass and grocery shopping. The kids were with their father at Church of the Living Water. Anna needed some time alone before making the short but significant move to the row home they had bought some ten steps across the alley.

It was too good to pass up. Still next to Ma and Gina so we can help with medical appointments and transportation. And Evan will still be a Garden Guy in that big yard. I know there'll be some issues at first with Willie and Genny, but it will be okay. She was armed with patience, as was Evan, who was sensitive to the needs of her beautifuls.

Anna took a deep breath. *Here we go—a new man, new life, new house. My name on the deed and the mortgage when I get my debt cleared up. The monster's down to thirty thousand. I just wish it wouldn't take so long. But good things take time to develop. Evan is a good man. I'm a good woman. There's not going to be any other for us.* She felt strongly. She had no concept of life without Evan. *He has his shaky times and I have mine. We're old enough to know there will be both smooth and rough times ahead.*

She looked at the clock. 9:59. *Shoulders back, girl. Time for courage. Time to show everyone a healthy new start.*

#####

ABIGAIL BARRETT-THOMPSON landed at the fast food drive-thru after visiting Richard Moyer in the I.C.U. She ordered their largest burger and fry combination and a chocolate shake.

After worship, the ushers told her the attendance count was thirty-nine. "Wow, that's the lowest we've ever had," she observed.

One of the ushers replied with a shrug, "A lot of people had plans for the long holiday weekend."

One month had passed since Abigail's last binge and purge, and the fast food smell emanating from the bag was so nauseating she didn't want to open it. She parked the car in the restaurant lot and opened all four windows to remove the stench. After ten minutes of reflection and prayer, she threw the uneaten meal and shake in the closest garbage can. *Now it's time to talk to Ted.*

She found Ted in the kitchen preparing one of her favorites—pasta primavera.

"Why, Reverend Barrett-Thompson, how is the flock?"

"Can a congregation be dwindling, yet more deeply committed at the same time?"

"Pope Benedict did call for a 'smaller, purer' church, wanting to rid the church universal of doubters, skeptics, and the sorta-kinda Catholic. You've always welcomed doubters, skeptics, and the sorta-kinda Christian, so it's not about ridding. People are being refined. Maybe those who remain at Faith Church are having epiphanies and transformations too wonderful to put into words. Perhaps this is your core group of people with which to rebuild."

"Perhaps. Thank you for that and for driving Phil to the bus depot. I miss him already." Abigail sat on a kitchen stool. "Um, Ted, I have something hard to share with you."

"Uh oh, this sounds serious. I'll put everything on simmer."

Abigail watched him turn down the burners and then started. "I don't know how to say this any other way other than I have had a problem with binging and purging food. Eating tons of it in a hurry and then throwing it all back up again."

"My food?"

"No, no! Your food is absolutely divine! I mean crappy food—fast food, pizza, candy—things like that."

"Well, you're quite the stealthy woman. I had no idea. How long have you been doing it?"

"Five years."

"Five years? Abigail, that's a long time to stuff down pain."

They sat in silence for a few moments. Ted's expression was full of concern while Abigail focused on the tree outside the window.

Ted moved slightly, standing right in Abigail's line of vision, and asked, "Anything else you're hiding from me?"

"No. I'm sorry I didn't tell you sooner. It's a pretty heavy-duty sin, and I admit I wasn't ready to confess. There's a lot of shame attached to it too. It's kind of like you not sharing the shoplifting with me until you were arrested."

"No need to bring that up now."

"You're right, it's not a tit-for-tat thing. The only reason I'm sharing it with you is because I had my first episode of being able to stop it, and that means I may get past this thing. I don't know if I could have let you know if I was still so deep in it."

"Well, we're a quite the potpourri of a family right now. Son has an obstinate case of writer's block. Father is working through shoplifting addiction. Mother is working through binge-purge issues."

"We're all trying to overcome."

"I thought binging and purging was a young woman's disease?" Ted asked.

"Same with shoplifting."

"Ahem, again, let's focus on Abigail and not Ted for a moment."

"Right, right."

"You've never struck me as being obsessed with body image."

"I had some years of it as a teenager. It was definitely about body image back then. This recent bout has been about the pastor image, and the pressure to be so successful at what I do that no one will ever question the wisdom of ordaining women."

Ted quietly added, "And your mommy issues."

"Excuse me?"

"Oh, Abigail, you're good at seeing other people's deep-seated, ugly little issues, but when it comes to your own, you're nearly blind."

"How so?"

"Your mom's desire that you be a beauty pageant contestant and her disappointment with your pursuit of a crunchy granola, hippie-ish style."

"That wasn't that big of a deal."

"Oh, really?"

"Truly. I think the big thing was the withholding of food."

"What?"

"Mom withheld food. She was terrified I'd be a fattie, so she put locks on cupboards and kept the portions tiny. How weird to be a middle class kid walking around hungry all the time."

"You've never shared that with me."

"I never thought of it till my last session with the spiritual director. We can easily push memories like that away for a long time."

"Well, I'm glad you were able to stop it today. Here's to many more stoppages—a lifetime of them," Ted raised a wine glass.

Abigail clinked it and said, "To many more stoppages. And here's to our potpourri of a family."

They clinked again, and Ted looked deeply into her eyes, "*For love is strong as death.*"

Hearing Ted quote from one of their wedding scripture passages, Abigail cried and replied through tears, "*Many waters cannot quench love, neither can floods drown it.*"

#####

ANNA RAMIREZ unpacked the final box in the kitchen just as Willie and Genny entered through the back door.

"Hello, my beautifuls! How was your weekend?"

"Fine," they both said, and Genny asked, "Can we go up to our rooms?"

"Of course," Anna replied, and they ran up the stairs to the third floor. She and Evan had worked hard to have their rooms ready by the time they returned from their father's. She wanted her children to feel as "at home" as possible. The kitchen was not quite ready and the front room was still cluttered but everything else had a settled feeling.

Evan approached Anna from behind. He wrapped his arms around her and kissed the back of her head. She leaned back into him and said, "Looks like we're just about moved in here. Is your office set?"

He leaned on the counter and rattled off the tasks he'd completed. "Yes, and the game room too. Genny's plastic bottles were successfully moved from one basement to another. The clothesline has been attached outside, and I told the kids to watch out that they don't choke on it."

"I'll try not to cheat and run across the alley to use my mom's dryer. Only on *really* damp days."

Evan laughed. "I promise I won't be the Green Police." He formed his hands into a gun and teased, "Freeze! Pardon me, ma'am, it's the Green Police, and we have a report of you using a dryer."

"Thank you for being patient with me."

"Your room is set too."

"My room?" Anna had no idea what Evan was talking about.

"I lied when I said the game room was going to be on the second floor. Gaming is going to be in the basement with my old couch, so when the kids have friends over they're not right next to my office when I'm working. I don't want to be grumpy, shushing them all the time. When Steve and Glenn were over earlier, we switched it all while you were working down here. Steve was our distracter. C'mon, let me show you." Evan led Anna up the stairs. Before entering, he said, "May I introduce you to Anna's room—your space for reflection and restoration."

She entered and raised her hands to her cheeks in surprise upon seeing the overstuffed chair, small end table, and bookshelf with inspirational books. Bouquets of flowers from Glenn's gardens were placed strategically around the room, filling it with their fragrance. A bed sheet hung on one wall. "What's with the sheet?"

"I consulted with Steve and Glenn about a good quote to put on your wall. We couldn't come up with just one, so we picked three." Evan removed the sheet to reveal the three quotes artistically painted across the wall. At the top in a fancy cursive script:

"Don't mistake politeness for lack of strength." - Sonia Sotomayor

In the middle in block letters:

"AND I AM NOT ONE OF THOSE WOMEN WHO TRIPS TWICE OVER THE SAME STONE." - ISABEL ALLENDE, INÉS OF MY SOUL

And close to the bottom in all lowercase:

"it is much more important to be oneself than anything else." - virginia woolf, a room of one's own

Anna sat in her chair and looked at the wall. She smiled and said, "It's perfect."

MONDAY, JULY 7, 2014

WILLIE RAMIREZ and Alex reported to Deacon Pat Haugen in the Church of the Living Water parking lot. The church planned to host four basketball camps over the summer, and Willie and Alex were scheduled to serve as helpers.

"Good morning, basketball wizards," Pat said. "We're going to start off the camp with dribbling. You'll need to go from boy to boy and help them with their form, just as we showed you in training last week. Remember what we *don't* do on the court?"

"No texting or checking phones," Willie said.

Pat unlocked the fence and the boys waiting with parents and guardians ran toward the bins of basketballs.

"Hold up!" Pat bellowed. "First, we pray. Gather round and bow your heads." Deacon Pat prayed, "Father God, bless our basketball today. Everything we do, may we do it for you. Amen. Okay, *now* go run and get a ball."

Pandemonium ensued as the dozens of boys got their balls.

"Hold up!" Pat bellowed again. "Hold your basketballs. Stop bouncing! Today we start with the most basic skill—dribbling. Keep your eyes up here. This is how you dribble a ball." Willie and Alex demonstrated how to dribble, and then went up and down the lines, commenting on each boy's skills.

Willie said to one, "Hey, little man, you're looking good. Try keeping the ball lower to the ground." Willie showed him his technique. The boy watched Willie with awe and admiration. "Keep it up," Willie said, and moved to the next boy. *Maybe I could be a coach when I'm done with my playing career.*

#####

ABIGAIL BARRETT-THOMPSON stepped into Richard's hospital room and joined Richard's daughter Clarice, his best friend Schultzie, a nurse, and a young doctor. Richard had not spoken or opened his eyes since being admitted, and Abigail guessed he would soon attain a long-awaited reunion with his darling Ellie.

The doctor explained that when no directive exists, they always do everything possible for the patient.

Abigail asked, "Richard didn't have a living will or medical power of attorney?"

"Nah, Richie never bothered with any of that," Schultzie replied.

Clarice said, "My dad never talked about it with me."

"I know this for sure—Richie'd never want all this fuss," Schultzie said. He crossed his arms in front of him and looked at the medical staffers with disdain.

Disregarding Schultzie's comment, the doctor announced, "We'll put the feeding tube in now." As he and the nurse started to put the tube in Richard's mouth, with the last bit of strength left in his body, Richard bit down on it.

Schultzie shouted, "There you go, Richie! That's the way to do it. Do it your way, not theirs!"

The two medical professionals briefly debated policy and procedure, with the nurse repeating, "It's done, Doctor. There's no more for us to do." They finally left the room.

"Would it be okay if I said a prayer?" Abigail asked. Clarice and Schultzie nodded solemnly. This would be the start of the official farewell to Richard Moyer.

"We give thanks to you, oh God, for your faithfulness is from generation to generation. We give thanks to you for Richard Moyer and the many ways he touched our lives and the lives of people we do not know. He was a faithful husband to his beloved Ellie. He was a faithful father to Clarice. He was a faithful friend to Robert. He was a faithful church member, faithful to his work, and faithful to his country. We know Christ will soon meet Richard with the words, '*Well done, good and faithful servant.*' While it hurts to let him go, we rejoice that Richard will be forever in your embrace, God, redeemer of us all. Amen."

#####

GINA GONZALEZ held her pen over her paper and started the conversation with the wife of one of Elm Pond's residents.

"Mrs. Edmonds, you have been a great caregiver for your husband."

Mrs. Edmonds shrugged. "You're married to someone over fifty years, you just do it. I get tired sometimes, but I know Norm would do the same for me. You're a beautiful woman—I'm sure you keep your husband happy too."

Gina gave her standard response, "I'm not married yet. I'm happy to remain focused on my work here at Elm Pond."

"Don't forget to live a little, dear."

"I won't, Mrs. Edmonds. You said you needed to talk with someone in charge?"

"Yes, I need to report someone stealing." Gina listened as Mrs. Edmonds recounted her observation about one of the floor's residents.

"We've had reports of all sorts of missing items in the dementia wing. This explains a lot. Thank you for letting us know."

"I don't like tattling, but it was so strange seeing this man poking in dresser drawers—that's people's property."

"You did the right thing. We really appreciate it." Gina walked Mrs. Edmonds to the elevator. After seeing her out, she headed to Sharon Chapel's office.

Sharon looked up from her desk. "You're swaggering."

"Caught the thief in the dementia wing," Gina bragged.

"Excellent! Thank you, Detective Gonzalez!"

#####

ALAN PECK and Amy were at their lunch booth at Andre Reed's steakhouse. They smiled and shook hands with the largest commercial real estate owner in the Lehigh Valley, Charles Chaput. They had arrived to their lunch meeting fifteen minutes early to ensure there would be no delay in their gathering, just as they did with every other large donor appointment. As Amy's campaign manager, Alan held fast to the phrase "never make big money wait."

They settled in at the table, and Alan asked, "What's the big news in the biz right now?"

Charles cleared his throat before speaking. "There's a lot of play in downtown Allentown, as you know. We're looking to expand more both east and west. East to capture the Jersey crowd and west to capture everyone in Macungie. But, again, you already know this," he winked, "because you two are on top of who's who and what's what."

Amy kept the conversation focused on Charles. Her early work experience was at Chaput & Dingman Real Estate. "I learned from one of the best. I really appreciated your mentoring those many years ago."

Charles looked up from his menu and said, "But you stayed in residential. I could never persuade you to dive into commercial."

"I didn't have the stomach for commercial—too many long waits—but it sounds like things continue to go well for you. You're adding more agents, and I see one Chaput & Dingman sign after another on buildings around the area."

"Things are good," Charles said.

A server appeared at their table. Charles ordered wine and a seafood dish. Alan and Amy always followed the lead of the donor, and Alan said, "Make it three."

Charles rubbed his jaw and was ready to talk business. "Well, I think I know why we're having lunch."

Amy nodded. She knew that Charles, and business owners like him, preferred things clear and to the point. She said, "Yes, you know why we're meeting. My campaign for state senate is in need of substantial financial support. I'm a relative unknown in political circles and it is going to take a lot of cash to pull together a professional series of ads and mailers that will introduce me to as many voters as possible over the next four months."

"What about PAC money?" Charles asked.

Alan jumped in, "Amy has received some PAC money, from a realtors' PAC, from the PAC that SmithCo.'s a part of, from a Chamber of Commerce interest group, and some conservative groups. She came out as pro-fracking and will receive some money from a pro-fracking PAC. But we would love to have a connection to the builders and contractors' PACs."

Charles said, "I can help you there."

"Thank you," Amy said. "Is there a chance you'd be able to provide an individual contribution?"

"Sure."

Amy reached out and touched Charles's right arm. "I'm so grateful. To the allowable limit, twenty-six hundred dollars?"

"That was my plan," Charles said.

Alan was next. He placed his hand on Charles's left arm, and said, "Thank you. We couldn't do this without you."

"I know you'll protect the interests of business owners, right?" The tone was more of a low-key threat than a question.

Alan and Amy nodded vigorously, "Yes!"

"Well, then, no need to thank me. I'll write the check and thank *you*," Charles said.

#####

EVAN LEMMON MOORE hurried to the sink to pour the last of the penne pasta into the strainer. They would keep it warming until an order came through so they wouldn't need to make pasta over and over again throughout the lunch rush.

Ezekiel's Eatery was going strong on Mondays and Tuesdays. Plans were underway for additional days, with two Lutheran churches and Church of the Living Water also interested in hosting. The lunch menu was limited to three entrée options: vegetarian, vegan, and meat. They were hoping to add gluten-free options and incorporate more organic and locally sourced produce soon. Several local musicians expressed interest in providing live music during the lunch hour in exchange for free advertising for upcoming concerts.

"Order up," Joyce barked at Genny and Marcus as they scrambled to the counter. "Careful with the plates. Walk slowly!

Smile and thank the customers. Don't forget to ask them if they need anything else. I've got my eye on you."

Evan saw the order for two vegetarian pennes. He filled two plates with pasta, added zucchini, squash, and tomatoes that had been sautéed with garlic, then drizzled on a creamy basil pesto sauce. He topped each with cracked pepper and a garnish of fresh basil.

He twirled effortlessly between stove and sink and counters. While he focused on the food prep and cooking, Joyce concentrated on taking orders, accepting payments, acclimating customers to the uniqueness of Ezekiel's Eatery, and directing the volunteer wait staff. One portable whiteboard listed the day's menu choices and another the possibilities for payment.

Pay What You Can - Here Are Some Suggestions:

Fully employed:	$10
Part-time employed:	$ 5
Fixed Income (Social Security, etc.):	$ 2
Unemployed (receiving benefits):	$ 2
Children:	$ 1
Unemployed (benefits ran out):	$ 0
Homeless:	$ 0

Word had gotten out around the neighborhood that the food at Ezekiel's Eatery was good, and at times patrons had to wait for a table. Genny and Marcus started volunteering after school let out in June, and had quickly learned how to bus a table.

At two o'clock they closed the restaurant, and Evan, Joyce, and the volunteers sat down for a late lunch.

"Next week will be here soon. Are menus set?" Joyce asked Evan.

"Summertime is picnic time. We should probably do some picnic-themed lunches—chicken salad, egg salad, cucumber-watermelon salad, stuff like that."

"I make a pretzel-coated baked chicken that tastes almost as good as the fried I used to eat till the doctor said to cut back."

"We could do that for the Monday meat entrée."

Joyce noted, "Not too many vegetarians or vegans have been coming through the line."

"I know, but I still want to have everyone be aware of the options. I've got to evangelize a bit about vegetarianism."

Joyce shook her head, "I don't get the all-vegetable thing, but I know it's important to you."

After final clean up and thanking the four adult and two children volunteers, Evan walked with Joyce to the front entry.

"Evan Lemon n' Lime, this has really taken off. Have you thought about how you're going to add days?"

"I'm not sure how to work it at this point—maybe assign a main cook for Wednesdays, Thursdays, and Fridays?"

"It would have to be a *good* cook."

"Yes! We could do some sort of tryout to make sure their cooking is tasty. I was thinking, too, that the time has come for a volunteer who can get us running in a more business-like way so we can concentrate on the food and that person can handle those kind of details, like bookkeeping and maybe even grant writing."

"I'll put it on the prayer chain. Let's request it of the Lord and see what comes back."

"You do the prayer part, I'll put an announcement online, and between the two of us something will come of it. Come to think of it, one of my Trail Tenders buddies might be interested or could refer us somewhere."

"Still holding this all lightly?"

"I'm trying to."

"It could come to an end tomorrow or it could last fifty years. We're not in charge of the timing," Joyce reminded him.

"That's actually a relief," Evan said.

TUESDAY, JULY 8, 2014

JOHNNY RAMOS finalized plans with Deacon Rob over breakfast. In the fall, there would be a new youth football league organized by Church of the Living Water.

Johnny couldn't help but feel disappointed. "It's starting out pretty small."

Rob replied, "All good things start small."

"Just three teams—they'll play each team twice for a total of four games."

"These are fourth and fifth graders. They don't need a bunch of games. Give it time. It's going to grow."

"Yeah, everything else sure has! We'll build it slowly. Who'd have thought, 'Church of the Living Water starts a Christian football league'?" Johnny held up his hands in a mock headline gesture.

"Kids and parents are all about sports these days. And, it's another opportunity for evangelism."

"Think of the great environment we're providing, with prayer and godly coaches. I'm getting the coaching covenant finalized for the three head coaches and six assistant coaches. No cursing is at the top."

"Unbelievable how most coaches scream profanity at their young players all the time."

"I'm really pumped about this. I think it may explode."

"Yep, this is going to be big, Johnny."

"I hope I can get the school off the ground while I'm still on the earth."

"If not you, then your children will make sure it will happen," Rob assured him.

"Right. Moses never entered the Promised Land, though he did get to look at it."

#####

ABIGAIL BARRETT-THOMPSON was facilitating a clergy meeting to organize an immigration reform rally. She had gathered the usual gang to assist with planning—Reverend Craig Johnson, Reverend Peter Smith, Reverend Eric Windham, and Reverend C.D. Alexander. They had just agreed on including a dramatic visual, the release of hundreds of butterflies to symbolize the beauty of migration.

After the group moved swiftly through the agenda, Abigail asked Eric to close the meeting with a prayer. Following a resounding "Amen," Eric inquired, "Off topic, what is that delectable odor wafting into my nostrils and causing my stomach to grumble?"

"Faith Church hosts Ezekiel's Eatery every Tuesday. If you don't have lunch plans, stay and try it. It's quite good. Pay what you're able."

Craig said, "Speaking of food, it's probably time for our next action to be about the food industry."

#####

GENNY RAMIREZ bounded to Jordan Park with Marcus after helping with Ezekiel's Eatery. They split off as Marcus ran to the pool and she took the path next to Jordan Creek. Genny loved the lush green above, below, and around her, and she found a spot fifty yards down from a family doing some fishing. She removed her empty postal bag, placed it on the bank, and sat on it, where she contentedly watched the creek and let her thoughts wander. *That's what I could do. I'll make a raft out of plastic bottles. I saw a video about a guy who made a big boat out of plastic bottles from the ocean. Mine won't be as big, but Evan could help me. So could Marcus. That would be fun and we could collect other plastic bottles from the creek while we float on the raft.*

#####

TED THOMPSON wasn't interested in what the school administrators thought of his idea—he was here as a courtesy, not to get approval. He looked at the three blank faces in front of him. "I'll start advertising next month, in early August, putting out flyers in teacher's lounges. It's called ATM, Allentown Teacher Mentors." He handed each administrator a flyer.

"ATM?" one asked.

"Right. You get cash when you go to an ATM, right? In this case, you get wisdom when you contact a mentor. The overall purpose is to improve classroom instruction so students reach their learning potential. The secondary purpose is to connect rookie and veteran teachers. I'm not looking for you to endorse or fund it, though that may happen eventually. This is purely a grassroots effort. It may take off like wildfire or it may fizzle. We'll see."

"You don't want anything from us?"

"I'd appreciate being able to announce it via every teacher's email."

"Ted, I'm impressed with the program. No problem with the email. We'll make sure it gets out. Keep us posted."

Ted shook hands all around and headed to his car. *This is probably my last big effort as a teacher. Why not put a bit of the rage to some practical use?*

WEDNESDAY, JULY 9, 2014

ABIGAIL BARRETT-THOMPSON's name appeared in the appendix of the report from the Holliday, Shears & Dowell Law Firm. Along with the names Joyce Taylor, Independent Baptist kitchen volunteers, Evan Lemmon Moore, Paulie and the Security Crew, Eddie Ramirez, Rev. John Ramos, Deacon Rob Handel, Rev. Peter Smith, Rev. Eric Windham, Rev. Craig Johnson, Rabbi Sarah Berger, Imam Feisel Ali, the Buddhist group meditation leader, and membership lists from all faith communities with a connection to the tent. Also in the appendix was a membership list of Pennsylvania Citizens for Fairness, a list of pro-SmithCo.

Pennsylvania state legislators, and a list of anti-SmithCo. politicians.

The CEO of SmithCo., Casper Upshaw, was in SmithCo.'s top-floor conference room with two SmithCo. executive vice presidents, Zane Fraser and Cooper Reynolds. Also present were two lawyers from Holliday, Shears & Dowell Law Firm, Kingsley Holliday and Jack Shears. This group comprised the Executive Working Committee on Project #173-174. The sun shone brightly in Charlotte, North Carolina, so the shades were drawn on the windows.

CEO Casper looked at the lawyers. "Impressive work on the report—very thorough."

Attorney Kingsley responded, "Amazing how quickly and easily it was all retrieved from the Internet. We've got a computer whiz who can find just about anything online."

Casper continued, "Let's first review Project Number 173. It's been about a year. I don't want to do too much Monday-morning quarterbacking, but let's see what could have been done better."

Jack Shears cleared his throat and began, "We got off to a good start on the property itself, but things went sour with Dolly's Dollar Store. We were able to contain the damage, however, due mostly to our skilled lobbyists in Harrisburg. The ridiculous tent lasted less than a week. Our polling of citizens across the state found little sympathy with a group of people squatting on private property. It was a rogue minority group that got some attention. These antidevelopment yahoos prefer a city that's crumbling around them rather than have access to decent services."

Casper said, "I don't get it. We take these burned-out, busted properties and make them usable again. What's not to like about that?"

"The problem wasn't with the redevelopment in general, but that some of these radicals got a bee in their bonnet about Dolly's. Because Dolly's was part of the deal, they went crazy," Jack said.

"It's a free country. People have choices. They can shop there or shop elsewhere," Casper said.

Jack replied, "A lot of these people think they have a right to tell private property owners how to run their business."

EVP Cooper added, "We sure got socked with bad publicity with the whole check-shredding episode. That pastor got a lot of play for destroying the forty-thousand-dollar check and we looked shady."

"In the report we've recommended a change in strategy for future Dolly's locations. Instead of giving cash gifts to potential friends, we would partner with local organizations for free rental space for after-school programming, like tutoring. SmithCo. writes off the free rent as a donation while the local orgs get nice, new space for their events," Jack said.

"If this tent occupation thing happens again, what's our best approach?" EVP Zane asked.

Jack spoke with confidence, "I think we demonstrated the best strategy just as the tent thing was gaining momentum. We lobbied state government officials, and because the local police force couldn't be trusted, the bigger guns were sent in—earlier than we expected. We thought the tent might be up for a couple of weeks, but it was over quickly. We'll be fine if it ever happens again, with an even more rapid response."

EVP Zane asked, "How can we thank the governor?"

"I'd suggest a large donation to his PAC."

"Any movement on the nonprofit status of those rogue churches?" EVP Cooper asked.

Jack replied, "We're no longer pursuing the tax-exempt status revocation. What we found out in that process was that most of the churches were small and barely had any sort of budget to keep their doors open, let alone pay for effective political action against us or anyone else. It really is amateur hour with that group of pastors—local yokels. There's nothing to worry about with them, with no money, no leverage, and few people. They'll be gone long before SmithCo. will. In the next few years, we'll probably be redeveloping the land where their churches stand today."

"And the trespassing arrests?"

"There were five guys on a so-called 'overnight security crew.'" Jack made air quotes with his fingers. "Every one of the five had a police record. Another guy worked in the kitchen—Evan Moore—and he has a sketchy background. A few years back he flashed a naked photo of his girlfriend during a high school pep rally. There were four church women who also worked in the kitchen, and they got sympathetic publicity through some major news outlets, but the media moved on from them quickly. Church of the Living Water took care of all their court fees, and a sleepy-looking lawyer, a Luis Abreu, represented them all. He took advantage of a fluke and was able to get them all off on a technicality—some bit of arcane minutiae about processing and arresting authorities. We decided to stay out of that legal process and instead just focus on getting the building up and open. In the end, people saw that private commerce always rules the day."

"How are the numbers?" CEO Casper asked.

"The property management team reports that rental monies are solid—not spectacular, but solid."

"And the Dolly's returns?" EVP Cooper asked.

"At property number 173, the returns are the lowest in the city of Allentown, though it's still profitable, of course" Jack said.

Casper changed subject. "Thanks, Jack. All in all, it looks like we came out of it all right with no lasting dents in the SmithCo. armor. Let's move on to the next property. Give us a summary and analysis of any legal issues we might encounter with 174."

Kingsley provided an overview of the property. "It's an old paint factory on the north side of Allentown, about a half mile from property 173. Remediation first, then redevelopment into food shops and some housing. No major legal issues."

"Any chance of a rerun of the tent with this new property?" EVP Zane asked.

Kingsley said, "Unlikely, given the small sizes of the churches that participated, their lack of resources, and minimal impact they'd have on the city. Our connection inside Church of the Living Water—the church that played the largest role—says that the pastor and deacons are focused right now on building up sports programming and eventually a school. They're pouring all their energy into that, so we don't think we'll be on their radar for this next site. Besides, 174 doesn't have a dollar store—just a pizza place, ice cream shop, fast food restaurant, and convenience store, so people don't have to schlep as far to eat. Why would anyone protest more food options?"

#####

EDDIE RAMIREZ met his father-in-law for lunch at the sub shop down the block from the police department. They talked about Eddie's promotion to lieutenant, Sofia and Diego, the growing Sunday School at the church, and the Men's Group.

"We're looking for more volunteers for the new basketball program this winter. Turnout will be high. Kevin Washington is organizing it but I've been scouting for volunteers too. Could you ask around in the department? Maybe some of the officers could spare a night for the program."

"Yeah, I'll ask around. There'll be at least a few who might give it a try."

"They'll need to sign a covenant, so we have coaches and supervisors with high-quality character. Hey, how are the new neighbors?" Johnny asked.

"I'm going to miss having Evan next door. Had only one incident with him. Other than that, he was a good neighbor. Looks like a family's moving in—a couple with three kids. They're still unpacking, but you know I'll tell them about Church of the Living Water when they seem more settled."

Johnny smiled, "Thanks, man."

#####

ABIGAIL BARRETT-THOMPSON concluded her last-minute review for Bible study. The group travelled through the gospels slowly and had only recently reached Luke. The regular crew was present—Keith, Jerry, Sherry, Katie, Chuck, and Evan.

Abigail announced, "We start off tonight with the eleventh chapter of Mark and we'll talk about prayer. Anyone here ever had unanswered prayer?"

Sherry offered, "I no longer pray for things or outcomes or results, so I haven't had an unanswered prayer for quite a while. I pray now only to be in communion with the Divine. God can sort out my needs better than I can. When I was praying to God for certain things or successes, it seemed like an almost consumeristic approach. I'm not saying it's wrong to pray to God for specifics—it was a way of prayer that stopped working for me."

Abigail nodded, "There are different types of prayer for different types of people. Glad you could find a way that worked for you. Whatever the type of prayer—silent, meditative, intercessory, prophetic, improvisational, prepared, praise, lament, centering, sung, individual, communal—and I'm sure I'm missing some, they all help us to not lose heart, to stay in this life. Could someone read the first verses?"

THURSDAY, JULY 10, 2014

CONSUELA GONZALEZ sipped iced tea on the front porch with her neighbor Marta Colón. Clarice was going in and out of the house next door.

"*Quién es esa mujer?*" Marta asked.

"She's Richard's daughter from Orlando. So sad."

"She's cleaning out the house?"

"Yes, it's quite a job. Richard lived in that house a long time and things accumulate."

"She said you can keep the dog?"

Consuela looked at the fluff ball at her feet. "Yes, *Princesa* is such a pretty dog."

The two looked down opposite sides of the street to take note of any activity. Marta then asked a delicate question, "You miss Anna and the kids?"

"So much, but they are right behind us. We will see a lot of them."

Marta pried her friend for information. "How is this Evan?"

"He is a good man and good with Anna and for her."

"So different than when we were young."

Consuela nodded. "Can you imagine if we had moved in with a man when we were young? So much judgment. But these younger people, they don't judge each other as much about those things. The only thing they're judgmental about is our generation's way of doing things."

The two women laughed and sipped their tea.

#####

TED THOMPSON was in the art room at Trexler Middle School putting together the frame for the butterfly they'd use as a backdrop at the immigration rally. The soundtrack to Puccini's "Madame Butterfly" was blaring, but was soon interrupted by Jorge Paredes.

Ted jogged to the stereo to turn down the volume. "What brings you to this up-and-coming studio today?"

"Better light. And I'm working on a piece for my cousin up in New York."

"Your art dealer cousin?"

"Yep."

"Here's hoping for a monster sale for you."

"I'd settle just for a sale. What're you working on?"

"This is for an upcoming immigration rally. I'm thinking of making additional butterflies for more of a sense of a group migrating."

Jorge asked, "À *la* Favianna Rodriguez?"

"Yes, of course. Her work inspired me."

The two men continued on their pieces, talking about their plans for the rest of the summer.

Jorge was the first to bring up work. "What if you are assigned more schools?"

"They'd be insane to pile more on, but nothing surprises me anymore. We're really cut all the way to the bone. These kids need *more* art, not less!"

"I've been thinking, if they *do* make more cuts to the arts, we could do a sit-in, kind of like the tent thing last year."

"Put a tent up by the superintendent's office? I like it. What would be the theme?"

"Why not what you just said? *More Art* or maybe *More Art for Kids*."

"Even if it's status quo this year and nothing changes, they still need more art."

"Right. We could still do a display by the administration building no matter what happens. We could also do temporary installations around the city—you know, sidewalk chalk somewhere, eco art in the city parks so that when it falls apart it just gets recycled back to park land. Sand art."

"I like it. Bold and creative with just a tinge of radicalism."

#####

ALAN PECK drove while Amy spoke on her cell phone to a potential donor. They were on their way to a luncheon with the Small Business Owners of the Lehigh Valley—SBOLV. Amy was scheduled as the keynote speaker and they would stay afterwards to network and gather more contacts. Alan thought, *I didn't think I'd enjoy political work this much. This is really fun. Why didn't we do this when we were younger? We could have been making many more years' worth of real change for people like us.*

Amy ended her phone conversation and turned to Alan. "Okay, remind me again. It's the small business owners for lunch, and then a coffee meeting with a big donor named Doug, and I know we had a dinner meeting?"

"LEPA—the Law Enforcement Political Action group. You're going to be talking about how you'll always fight for full state support and funding for police and sheriff's deputies. There will likely be media there."

"Oh, right. When were we going to go door-knocking?"

"We may have to wait until tomorrow—before we go to the LOT meeting."

"LOT?"

"Lower Our Taxes. You'll knock their socks off with your tax cut ideas."

"It's a whirl."

Alan warned, "It's going to get more whirly the closer we get."

#####

ANNA RAMIREZ called out, "Next in line," and one of her regulars stepped up to the counter. Not all postal clerks enjoyed the chatterboxes, but Anna didn't mind them, nor did Steve. They helped pass the time.

"Good morning, Mrs. McNeil. How are you today?"

"I'm fine. It's a little muggy out there, but I'll take this time of year over snow on the ground anytime."

"I'm with you on that. Are you looking to buy some more stamps today?"

#####

EVAN LEMMON MOORE took a quick sip of chai as he looked up the woman's name in the BlackBox system. "Okay, let's see... Miranda Reece in Boston... Here we go. I've found your account. How may we help you today?"

"We're having trouble opening the Summerall football game. My son and I play this game every day—amazing he lets me play with him! I had to learn it so I could connect with my son. He's off with his friends right now, so I thought I'd try to get it fixed by the time he gets back."

"Gaming gets a bad rap for isolating people, but it does have the potential to bring families together. Glad you are connecting with your son. Let's go through a few steps and see if we can get you two gaming again soon."

#####

ABIGAIL BARRETT-THOMPSON reflected on the funeral service for Richard Moyer, which would be at Faith Church on Saturday morning. It would be a simple liturgy, followed by a burial with military honor guard. She put together prayers, selected scripture readings, and considered appropriate hymns.

He's irreplaceable. Middle-aged and young people don't have the time to come over to the church and do set-up and watch after the property the way Richard has done for so long. Richard was one of a kind— irreplaceable here, but, more importantly, also irreplaceable in the universe. Praise God for the gift of each unique life.

#####

ISABELLA RAMIREZ sat with her mother in the backyard, with Diego on her lap and Sofia engrossed with a coloring book.

"All those basketballs bouncing over at the court, that program is really big."

"Last day is tomorrow for these youngest boys. They'll do another week-long camp next week for the next age level."

"Dad's really excited about it."

"Yes, and about starting a school."

"I wish it could be ready for Sofia and Diego."

"My impatient one, it takes a lot to build a school!"

"I know, and I'm almost done with the homeschooling certification. I just don't want them to have to go near the school system."

"You turned out all right and so did your brothers."

"We had strong parents."

"You all are strong parents."

"Yes, but it's getting even worse. Christian kids mocked all the time. I don't want our kids to have to deal with it. Sofia and Diego will not be like all those other kids. I'll be sure of that! They will not be disrespectful and God-hating—no way. I pray God's protection for Willie and Genny every day in those schools, and then not having a Christian home to go to... I feel so bad for them."

"You get them every other weekend. That's your chance to fill them with your values. Sometimes God gives us different timetables to work with people."

#####

EDDIE RAMIREZ reviewed his keynote speech for the Latino Leaders of Allentown scholarship breakfast. Isabella, Johnny, and Anita had all read through Eddie's notes the previous week. They all agreed his speech, entitled "Get Ready," was good. He practiced again from the beginning.

"Congratulations to all of the scholarship winners this morning. Your hard work and focus has paid off. Now you are on to the next stage of life and you need to *get ready*. Preparing well is half the battle in life. My mother and my teachers and military commanders and supervisors at work all helped me prepare. Now I want to help you prepare. There are five ways you can get ready for life—

Number one: 'Get ready with hard work. No slacking!'

Number two: 'Get ready with focus. Eliminate distractions!'

Number three: 'Get ready with determination. Make up your mind!'

Number four: 'Get ready with strength. Be a winner!'

Number five: 'Get ready with goals. Aim high!'

Now, starting with number one..."

#####

GINA GONZALEZ was seated at the dinner table with her mother and Dante, the first meal together for all three. Consuela and Dante had been introduced only briefly on one other occasion.

They were eating dinner quietly when Dante suddenly set her fork down and glanced mischievously at Gina. She said, "I think I'm going to tell your mother her daughter is a super hottie."

"Dante!" Gina blushed.

Dante smiled, and directed herself to Consuela, "Your daughter is beautiful and smart and I am glad to be with her."

Gina translated for her mother and then translated the response to Dante. "Her exact words were, 'She is a good girl. She has her problems. Everyone does, but she is a good girl.'"

"Could you tell your mother that her house is very nice?"

Gina translated the compliment.

After the meal, Gina shooed her mother to the television as she and Dante took care of the cleanup. Gina washed the dishes and Dante dried. "Well, how'd I do? Did I pass?"

"She likes you and thinks you're funny. What she was most looking out for was to see if you respect me. You passed that test."

"Phew! I did it!"

Gina leaned in for a quick kiss. "You were great! More tests will come soon."

"There's another test?"

"There are endless tests in the Gonzalez household."

"That's kinda intimidating."

"But you're such a natural, they won't even feel like tests."

REPRISE

FRIDAY, JULY 11, 2014

TED THOMPSON and ABIGAIL BARRETT-THOMPSON sat across from each other nibbling breakfast, reading the news on their respective tablets, and murmuring random phrases to each other. Ted had salvaged a loaf of rock-hard sourdough bread and made French toast, pairing it with Canadian bacon from the Allentown Farmer's Market.

"Date night tonight?" Abigail asked. "We haven't been out and about much lately. Maybe a documentary?"

"There's bound to be one showing somewhere in the Lehigh Valley." Ted pulled out his phone to check.

"Well, we may get enraged about the broken political process, environmental degradation, prison industrial complex, corporate welfare, or any number of issues."

"Isn't that the point?" Ted asked.

"But what to do with the rage?"

"In our case, art or worship."

#####

WILLIE RAMIREZ ambled with Alex and Genny toward a crammed Jordan Park. People wanted to enjoy another clear summer day outside.

Alex feigned horror at all the people. "Get out of my park," he said as the trio approached the play equipment. "I am King Alex and this is *my* park."

Willie amended his best friend's statement, declaring, "King Alex *and* King Willie."

"*And* King Genny."

Willie scoffed at his sister. "You can't be a king."

"I can be anything," Genny insisted.

Willie teased, "Yeah, okay, you're king of the geeks."

#####

JOHNNY RAMOS led a second training session with Ray and Todd, two potential evangelists he had handpicked from the congregation. They were doing a role-play and the two trainees stumbled over much of the lingo.

Johnny said, "Don't worry about the exact words!"

"But I want to say the right thing," Ray said.

"When you evangelize, it's *got* to be natural. People will see right through you if they think you're going through a script. They'll think it doesn't mean anything to you, and then it really won't mean anything to them. And remember, this is about winning people to Christ, helping them to meet a need they've had all along. Church of the Living Water is third on the list. First, it's Christ. Second, it's the person. Third, it's the church."

#####

GENNY RAMIREZ tossed rocks into Jordan Creek with Marcus.

"Maybe we'll see another gator," Marcus ventured.

"I saw ducks here yesterday."

Marcus said, "They probably got eaten by the gator!"

Shouts to the north interrupted their conversation. Some teenage boys were swimming at a popular spot up the creek. Genny and Marcus were not allowed to swim in the creek, but knew that kids swam in and out of a two-foot diameter metal pipe that went under a walkway.

Along with some adults, Genny and Marcus sprinted toward the shouts where they saw a boy with his foot caught in the pipe.

"I'm stuck," he shouted over and over. The current was fast and the boy was having trouble keeping his head above water. Genny texted her dad and someone else called 9-1-1. Two adults and Marcus jumped in to support the boy so he could keep his head above the water.

Fire rescue arrived quickly. Eddie came soon after and stood beside Genny as personnel devised a strategy to loosen the boy's leg from the pipe. By now, a large crowd had gathered. When the boy was finally freed, everyone gave a collective sigh of relief and applauded the rescuers.

When Marcus came back on the bank, Eddie shook his hand and said, "Good job, young man. You might think about someday becoming a first responder." Marcus nodded solemnly.

Eddie turned to Genny. "And *you—you* are a crackerjack dispatcher."

Genny and Marcus headed toward the pool, and Genny followed up on her father's comment. "You could be a lifeguard, Marcus."

"Maybe the Coast Guard."

"Like that guy in the rescue boat after the Titanic sunk. Remember all those dead frozen bodies? This guy goes looking for people who are still alive."

"Or we could be pirates!" Marcus exclaimed.

Genny brightened, "Pirates of the Caribbean, Pirate Genny and Pirate Marcus, yes!

"We could find sunken treasure."

Genny sighed. "We'd be rich."

"We'd have our own island."

"Where everything is recycled."

#####

GINA GONZALEZ neared the end of a meeting about another roommate dispute.

Sharon hesitated, and then stated, "I want you to be among the first to know—there are some changes ahead."

"Everything okay?"

"Everything's okay, but it looks like in the next few months my family will be making a move to the Jacksonville area."

"Florida? Wow. That's a big move."

"It's time for a change. We love the idea of warm weather and being closer to the ocean. The winters here are getting to be too much. It is going to be announced on Monday that I'm accepting a new position as Director of Social Services at a facility in Jacksonville."

"Just like that? I'll miss you!"

"I'll miss you too. You know, you would be great in my position here. In fact, I have highly recommended you."

"Thank you."

"Are you interested?"

Gina nodded vigorously, "Yes, absolutely."

"Over the weekend, you'll want to brush up your resume a bit. You sure you want to keep working with this population? You could work with teenagers, families in crisis, drug addicts, just about any demographic. What keeps you here?" Sharon asked.

"It's a good fit for me. I was raised to respect my elders, and the residents see that I treat them with respect and that I'm here to help."

"I think that wherever you work you'd treat others with respect and in turn be respected. But, what makes seniors special for you?"

"One big thing I've learned from seniors is that they *look* at you—at least those in good health. They *see* you, because they're not in a hurry and they really observe. It's not like kids who look everywhere and want to see everything. It's not like young adults or the middle-aged with their heads down, going from here to there. Seniors take it all in—they have the time. Well, we all have the time to take it all in—we just don't take the time. I like their stories and their corny jokes and the way they carry history with them. Everyone here has done a lot of living. I don't like to see the pain that seems to come so often with the end of life, but we do a lot to relieve it."

"Funny that we don't talk about this as often as we need to. It's a good reminder about why we do what we do."

"One of the things I can do here is help them see they're not *stuck* here, that this is a necessary stop on their journey to the next life. We get to give to them and receive from them—they get to give to us and receive from us."

"Gina, I didn't know you were so spiritual."

"I've been thinking of some things differently lately, really getting serious about how my mind works. It has been hard work. I mean, my brain seriously *hurts* sometimes, but it's been worth it."

#####

ISABELLA RAMIREZ strolled to her parent's house with Sofia and Diego, grateful for a chance to stretch her legs. Anita had prepared a light lunch.

"Dad, I was telling Mom yesterday how I can't wait for the school!"

"I know. Can you see it?" Johnny was ebullient. "Church of the Living Water School. It's going to take a long time, though. It might be ready by the time Sofia's in high school. There's a lot to put together, more than I thought at first."

Isabella nodded. "Think of all those families at the church who want something different for their kids."

"The school committee is going full speed ahead," Johnny shared. "They want this to happen. In the meantime, they brought up something about a homeschooling support group here at the church."

Isabella was intrigued. "Oh? What would that do?"

"This would be the core group of families the school would eventually serve. All the moms who are homeschooling would get together on a regular basis to pray and talk about the nitty gritty, like what curriculum is working best." Johnny paused. He looked at Anita and then back at his daughter. "You are anointed, Isabella. God has made you a leader and I think you would be wonderful to head up this new group."

Isabella was hesitant. "I'm not sure I'd be able to juggle moms group *and* the homeschool group." She looked at the ceiling while pondering the idea.

Anita pointed out, "The moms group keeps getting bigger. Surely God will lift up a person to take your place. Others could take on the scheduling and programming for the moms while you concentrate on the homeschooling group. And you'd attend conferences and workshops on homeschooling too. You'd still attend the moms group, just not take care of all of the details."

"It's all so important," Johnny contended. "It all matters. We are building an alternative for people."

Isabella was determined. "I'll do it. I want to show these families they don't have to give in and just put up with the ways of the world. They can keep their kids safe and in a Christian environment."

"What got you so fierce on this?" Johnny asked.

"Well, my parents," Isabella smiled at them both, "but also I look around the neighborhood and hear the girls with their trash mouths and see the boys disrespecting, and that's not going to be Sofia and Diego's world. They're not going to be like everyone else."

#####

ALAN PECK leaned back on a metal folding chair at the back of the fire hall. The group had just finished a lunch of hoagies, potato chips, and chocolate chip cookies. Twenty Alliance for Freedom members peppered Amy with questions about her approach on the issue of school choice. They were an anti-public-schools and anti-teacher's-union group that supported religious schools, homeschooling, and some charter schools. As usual, Amy handled the questions skillfully, not overpromising and not under-committing, but rather, making it clear she would give voice to their concerns at the state capitol.

#####

ABIGAIL BARRETT-THOMPSON worked on Richard Moyer's eulogy. She had plenty to share about Richard and his servant's heart, and she'd also include remembrances from Clarice and Robert. Abigail often sought a family member or friend to speak at a funeral, but there were no volunteers for Richard's service. Not everyone was a public speaker and sometimes people were just too overwhelmed with grief to put something together. Abigail always considered it an honor to officiate a funeral—to pull together a person's past, present, and future was a holy moment. Making sure the service was more about the resurrection than the person who had passed was tricky, but survivors needed theological reflection in addition to the celebration of a life.

We'll see what happens now. With Richard gone, Faith Church loses the person with the longest institutional presence. It's either a new day or one more step toward demise.

Abigail said a private prayer in her office. *Loving and gracious God, let the passing of Richard Moyer be for Faith Church an opening up to your new thing. For in death there is new life. It is not an ending but a beginning. Show us a path we have not yet taken, arouse in us a way forward and help us turn to You at all times as our GPS. Let not past triumphs and tragedies impede us or any present dysfunction dismay us. Let us not get too absorbed in dreaminess about the future but let us plan well and boldly. We want to be Yours. God, remove any barrier from us that would keep us from giving ourselves over to You fully and wholly. You are indeed our rock and our fortress. Into Your hands we now commit our spirit. You have redeemed us, O Lord, faithful God. Amen.*

#####

EDDIE RAMIREZ was sprawled on the couch with Isabella watching a movie. The kids had been put to bed a few hours earlier. Suddenly, they heard loud voices coming from the house next door.

Eddie looked at Isabella and sighed, "The new neighbors—sounds like they're arguing."

"Be careful," Isabella entreated.

"I will." Eddie got up and went to his neighbor's house. The front door wasn't locked, so he went inside and stood in the entry. He looked up and saw three children seated at the top of the stairwell. The shouts were getting louder, and when he heard the sound of glass breaking, he dashed up the stairs. He found a man and woman standing on either side of a couch. Remains of a broken lamp were shattered all around.

The man stared at Eddie and asked, "Who are you?"

"I'm your neighbor and your friendly neighborhood cop."

"We got a cop next door?" the man asked incredulously.

Eddie smiled and said, "Aren't you lucky?"

The woman said, "You can't just come into our home."

"You can't just scream at each other and upset the neighborhood. I can call in backup if you'd prefer, and you can sort this out downtown. Or you can tell your kids to go to their rooms while we talk for a minute."

#####

ANNA RAMIREZ went to her mother's house for flour, as her new kitchen was not yet fully stocked. On her way out, she touched base with Gina while their mother watched television in the front room.

"Date night tonight?" Anna asked Gina.

"Later, maybe a movie. How about you?"

"Quiet night at home."

"You guys are such homebodies."

"Still getting settled in right now. Trying to get rhythms established and everyone working toward a family flow."

"Well, go flow now, yo!" Gina laughed and pushed her sister out the door.

Anna returned to the chicken parmesan for her and the kids and eggplant parmesan for Evan. They were going to split kitchen duties, though Anna enjoyed cooking and didn't mind doing it, especially on the days Evan was cooking for the restaurant.

After dinner, the kids loaded the dishwasher and then returned to the table for Friday-night game night. Anna insisted they all hang out together to bond more as a family.

"Everyone will pick the game they want to play. I'm the mother, so I'll go first," Anna said. "We'll start with a card game."

"How do we know who wins?" Willie asked.

Anna responded, "We're all winners because we're doing this just for fun." She shuffled then dealt the cards.

Willie declared, "At church, Grandpa Johnny says there are winners and losers. Winners hang out with winners, and losers hang out with losers."

Anna figured the winners were the conservative, judgmental Christians, while the losers were everyone else, but she decided not to mention it. "Grandpa Johnny is entitled to his opinion and so is your mother."

After a boisterous game night, Anna and Evan headed upstairs and readied for bed. "Tonight went really well," Evan said.

"A good way to come together in our new home as a family."

Evan rubbed Anna's shoulders, kissed her neck, and said "There's no one I'd rather form a family with than you."

She cupped Evan's face in her hands. "Evan Lemmon, here we go. Almost one week together and thousands more to go."

"I may mess up."

"I may mess up, too."

Evan wanted to reassure her. "I don't want to. Just know I'm still working through some things."

"We all are. But we'll talk things through if it gets weird, right?"

"Yes. We seem to be the type of people who want to make things right if they get off kilter. I need you to know that sometimes I look over at you, I steal a glance in the kitchen, or I watch as you walk to your car or talk with your mother, and I almost cannot breathe. I used to go to the post office and I would be speechless standing at your counter. You must have thought I was a psycho."

Anna laughed, "No, I just thought you were quiet."

"You'd drop the kids off at Eddie's, and all I wanted was for your car to break down right there—anything—so I could see you for just a bit longer. And now we're sharing a bed."

"And sharing a life, for however long life lasts."

"Uh oh, you're not going to tell me now that you have a terminal disease?"

Anna said, "No, nothing like that, but seeing our sweet old neighbor Richard have that heart attack was a reminder we don't have all the time in the world."

FALL 2014

Monday, November 10, 2014

Evan Lemmon Moore now walked the neighborhood in the early mornings. He usually walked for an hour and then joined Anna for breakfast. When he first started in April, he walked solely for fitness purposes. He felt he was slowing on the Trail Tenders outings, and didn't want to be a drag on other crew members who all had memberships in fitness centers and kept in good shape with daily weightlifting and time on the treadmill.

Most mornings, Evan walked by Faith Church, past his old house, up to Church of the Living Water, and then through the downtown area, after which he returned home—always energized after watching the city awaken.

This morning as he walked by Faith Church he saw a large sign that said *Rally Against the Food Industry Friday, November 14*. Abigail had handed out a flyer at Bible study, and it looked like the protest involved a lot of the same churches that had come out against Dolly's. The rally was to be at the site of an abandoned paint factory where a new strip mall was going to be built. Activists would advocate for more locally sourced foods as well as healthier food choices for patrons, most of whom would be walking there from the surrounding area. There was talk of occupying the space, like the last strip mall. While it was good to have another brownfield redeveloped, it would house a pizza parlor, ice cream store, and fast food restaurant—all establishments that promoted unhealthy eating and led to obesity.

Evan continued on, past his old home. As it was a weekday, Eddie would likely not be out on the porch. Evan sometimes saw him on Saturday mornings and they chatted. The fact that Evan was now living with Eddie's ex-wife had caused some initial awkwardness, but given that Eddie's children also lived with him, Evan knew it would be best to keep up a cordial relationship with his former neighbor.

Like Faith Church, Church of the Living Water had also hung a big banner outside. Theirs read *Eat Better. Live Better. Love Christ Better.* It was their antiobesity campaign, and Evan had heard from Eddie that it was effective at raising awareness in the congregation.

Evan next walked by a corner grocery store that had three newspaper boxes outside its main entrance. He glanced at the headline of one: *Senator-Elect Amy Peck: Political Outsider Smashes All Newcomer Election Records.* The name sounded familiar, but Evan couldn't remember where he had heard it.

Since the summer, Evan no longer walked just for fitness. He now ventured out to experience something he was too reticent to share with others—the visions he had while walking. He saw things that were not there. Not just a few things, but constant images of a fullness that was not presently evident. Walking the streets of Allentown, Evan claimed back something for the world. He was not really sure what it was, but it had weight and abundance. He thought about sharing his encounters with Anna or Abigail or Joyce or his Trail Tender friend Bill, but he lacked a basic vocabulary to describe it. Even as he interpreted it to himself, he found he used a language that shocked and surprised him so much, he wasn't ready to disclose his experience with others.

He went back to Ezekiel, that weird prophet he had encountered first in his study of the Bible. When he had a vision, Evan said to himself, *I am freakin' Ezekiel. While my people may be in exile, we will be restored. What has been polluted is made clean.*

He walked by an abandoned lot and envisioned rows of tomatoes. Another empty lot, a vineyard. Sometimes he saw rows of carrots and onions. Often there were fruit trees, their branches drooping with a bountiful yield. Waterfalls spouted out of brick walls, and empty parking lots contained mini-creeks. On a chain-link fence he spied green beans, and shiny purple eggplants were in a row next to the mobile phone store.

Now and again rows of corn appeared. Not like the cornfields near Edwardsville, Illinois, or Lemmon, South Dakota—those endless rows of corn where occasionally a kid got lost and the townspeople scoured the field, shouting the kid's name over and over again until there was finally a relieved reunion. Evan's visions included cornfield patches around the city and lovely gardens that